IF YOU LIKE SURPRISES, YOU'LL LOVE
THE NANCY DREW FILES™
COLLECTOR'S EDITION

Check out the coolest mysteries around, as ace teenage detective Nancy Drew takes aim at crime—and takes **you** on a thrill-a-minute ride to the heights of intrigue, romance, and danger!

THE NANCY DREW FILES

They're fun, they're fast,
they're full of excitement. . . .
Because there's a surprise
on every page in every
Nancy Drew mystery.

And the best surprise of all?
One book—three big mysteries!

Books in The Nancy Drew Files™ Series

NANCY DREW® FILES

COLLECTOR'S EDITION

THE WRONG CHEMISTRY
OUT OF BOUNDS
FLIRTING WITH DANGER

CAROLYN KEENE

Aladdin Paperbacks
New York   London   Toronto   Sydney

ALADDIN PAPERBACKS
An imprint of Simon & Schuster Children's Publishing Division
1230 Avenue of the Americas, New York, NY 10020
The Wrong Chemistry copyright © 1989 by Simon and Schuster, Inc.
Out of Bounds copyright © 1990 by Simon and Schuster, Inc.
Flirting with Danger copyright © 1990 by Simon and Schuster, Inc.
Produced by Mega-Books, Inc.
All rights reserved, including the right of reproduction in whole or in part in any form.
NANCY DREW and colophon are registered trademarks of Simon & Schuster, Inc.
THE NANCY DREW FILES and ALADDIN PAPERBACKS
are trademarks of Simon & Schuster, Inc.
Manufactured in the United States of America
First Aladdin Paperbacks edition December 2005
2 4 6 8 10 9 7 5 3
ISBN-13: 978-1-4169-1827-1
ISBN-10: 1-4169-1827-2
These titles were previously published individually.

THE
WRONG
CHEMISTRY

Chapter

One

YOU'RE NANCY DREW—the detective?" Dean William Jarvis blurted out. "I thought you'd be, well, older." The dean, a bear of a man wearing a tweedy brown suit, paused halfway between sitting and standing to stare at the slim young woman in front of him.

Nancy grinned and pushed back a strand of reddish blond hair. "I *am* only eighteen, but it's easier to go undercover as a college student when you look like one." She extended her hand to the dean, and he took it, looking somewhat sheepish.

"I didn't mean to insult you," the dean said quickly.

1

"That's okay," Nancy continued. "I should apologize for wearing jeans to our meeting, but it's a long drive from River Heights to Emerson College. You can't beat jeans for comfort."

The dean's round face reddened, and he gestured for Nancy to sit down. "No apologies, please. Excuse my rudeness. I know you're a top-notch detective, and that's all that matters. Pat Burnett, our basketball coach, told me how great you were at finding the prankster who was harassing his team. I'm just nervous and about at my wit's end."

Nancy settled into an overstuffed chair next to the dean's desk. She purposely kept her tone light and casual. The dean was alarmed. Besides, she'd get more information from him if she acted totally together.

"You mentioned a theft and the need for secrecy on the telephone last night. Can you give me any details?"

The dean leaned forward, touching his fingertips together nervously. He gave her a helpless smile. "That's part of the problem. I can't give you details. This involves the government—and it's all very hush-hush and top secret."

Nancy drew back, startled. "Top secret?"

Dean Jarvis had been very abrupt when he called her the night before and asked her if she

2

could come to Emerson immediately. Nancy had been planning a short vacation with her friends Bess and George but had leapt at a chance to work at the college instead. Nancy's boyfriend, Ned Nickerson, was a student at Emerson, and Nancy hadn't seen him for ages.

Now, looking at the worry lines in the dean's face, Nancy knew she'd have to think of Ned second. Reaching into her brown leather purse, she pulled out a notepad and pen.

"You don't have to tell me government secrets," she assured the dean. "But I'll need to know all the facts that you can tell."

"Are you ready? It's a long story." Dean Jarvis smiled and took a deep breath. "Emerson is host to a visiting professor, Josef Maszak. Maszak is working on a top secret experiment sponsored by the U.S. government. You *do* know what a visiting professor is, don't you?"

"Someone who's on campus for only a semester or two?" Nancy suggested.

"Yes, usually. But this is a little different. Our government is running a special visiting-professor program involving scientists only. Each one is a specialist working on a secret government experiment. It's considered a great honor to have one of these scientists placed at your school."

3

"I'm sure you're proud that Emerson was chosen," Nancy said politely.

"Very," the dean agreed eagerly. "We worked five years to qualify. We had to expand our entire science program. This project is important to me—I won't let it fail."

"No," Nancy said, careful to keep her comments neutral.

"I can't tell you much about what Maszak does," the dean said, "because it's secret and because those parts I can share are far too technical. But twice a month, the government sends him a quantity of a substance called CLT. It's a rare chemical, and the government monitors it closely."

The dean anxiously ran his fingers through his hair. "Twice now, just as Maszak reached a crucial stage of his experiment, someone has broken into his lab and stolen the CLT."

"Is CLT dangerous?" Nancy asked.

"Maszak says no," the dean responded. "He swears there's no known use for CLT, except for his experiment. But it is a rare chemical, so he keeps it under lock and key. I tell you, Ms. Drew, I never dreamed it would be stolen."

"Useless," Nancy repeated thoughtfully. "But someone went to a lot of trouble to steal it." Nancy quickly went on. "Who knows about the thefts?"

"No one." The dean's voice dropped to a whisper. "I haven't reported either of them to the government yet," he admitted. "The first time the CLT was taken, I decided it was some kind of a prank. I thought whoever took it might return it. I admit it, Ms. Drew, I was afraid. Afraid that if I reported the theft, the government would order Maszak to leave. Emerson would be disgraced, our reputation ruined. But after the second theft . . ." His voice trailed off.

Nancy's eyes narrowed. "I'm not sure I like keeping secrets from the government."

The dean looked flustered. "Ms. Drew—Nancy—please help me. Help Emerson. I'm sorry I can't tell you more. If you can't take the case, I'll understand, but I'm asking you to try."

"I *could* use more information," Nancy said, feeling frustrated.

"I'll make a deal with you," the dean said. "Try to find the thief. If you fail, I'll call in the government. But not just yet. Losing Maszak now would be a blow Emerson might never recover from."

Nancy hesitated. "Dean Jarvis," she finally asked, "if I did agree to take the case, could I trust Maszak?"

"Absolutely," the dean swore. "Maszak's an honest man, a truly dedicated scientist . . ." The dean's voice trailed off as he looked directly

5

at Nancy. "At least that's what I used to think," he said slowly. "I guess I don't really know anymore. At this point, I'm not sure whom to believe or whom to trust."

Nancy saw a look of confusion pass over the dean's eyes. "It makes no sense!" he exclaimed. "The lab is constantly locked. The CLT is in an inner lab, sealed by another lock, which also has an alarm. The security guard on that floor gives me the security logs to check each day. Only Professor Maszak and his assistant are even allowed near the CLT, and they all have government clearance."

"And yet," Nancy said thoughtfully, "the CLT has been stolen twice, and the thief knows exactly when to take it. Every sign points to an inside job. But from what you've told me, it *can't* be an inside job."

The dean got up, walked around, and perched on the edge of his desk so he was closer to Nancy. "This sounds impossible, I know, but what we have here is an impossible crime."

Nancy stood up, too. "I'll need as much information as you can get me on Professor Maszak and his assistant," she said briskly.

"I'm sure I can find something in the files." Dean Jarvis sounded hopeful for the first time. "Does this mean you'll take the case?"

Nancy grinned in return. "I may be young, Dean Jarvis, but I am experienced. And the one thing I've learned as a detective is that there *is* no such thing as an impossible crime."

The dean looked pleased. "You do inspire confidence. I can't thank you enough, Nancy."

"Don't thank me until I've solved the case," Nancy said. "Well, I guess we're done for now. I'd like to see Professor Maszak's lab this afternoon, if that can be arranged."

"Professor Maszak already knows about you. I'll tell him you'll be stopping by. As for going undercover, you'll need a story and a place to stay. I've made arrangements for you to take an empty room in one of the dorms. Holland, I believe it is. We'll say you're a transfer student. You're going to work on the school newspaper, and you're writing a story on Professor Maszak. If anyone checks on you, my office will be able to back up your story."

"Good," Nancy said approvingly. "I'll be able to ask as many questions as I need!" She glanced at her watch. "I'll have to start right after lunch."

"Let me take you to your dorm," Dean Jarvis offered.

Nancy colored slightly. "Actually, Dean, I'm late for a lunch date—with my boyfriend."

The dean beamed at her. "Ned Nickerson, right? A star athlete in both football and basketball—a nice young man."

"Yes, he is," Nancy said. Nancy had a vision

of her tall, handsome boyfriend pacing his fraternity living room waiting for her. She hadn't seen him in almost a month. Her heart had raced when she realized that because of this case they would have some time together.

Nancy flipped her notebook closed and slipped it back in her purse. "Can you tell me the quickest way to Omega Chi Epsilon from here?" Omega Chi was Ned's fraternity.

"There's a shortcut no one ever uses," Dean Jarvis said. "Go straight down the main road, and take your second right. I'll send whatever information we have on Maszak and his assistant to the dorm for you."

"Thanks." Nancy scooped up her purse.

Outside the administration building, a chill wind was attempting to dislodge autumn leaves from their branches. It had rained while Nancy was inside, and the ground was slick with wet leaves. Shivering, she zipped up her soft suede jacket and slipped on her sunglasses to protect her eyes from the afternoon sun. She climbed back into her Mustang, flipped on the tape deck, and headed for Ned's fraternity house.

Emerson was a large college with lots of trees and wide-open spaces. The road the dean had recommended was narrow and looked deserted as it wound through the campus arboretum. Nancy enjoyed handling the Mustang around the road's many curves.

As she came around an especially tight turn, Nancy saw a dull green shape lying in the road just ahead. Instantly she stepped on the brakes, her heart thumping. The car screeched to a halt, only inches from the lifeless body of a young man.

Chapter

Two

HER HEART IN HER THROAT, Nancy scanned the accident scene. Her mind, trained by detective work, was already racing. Was the boy the victim of a hit-and-run accident? No. No other cars were in sight. She saw no fresh tire tracks on the road to indicate a skid or sudden stop. Leaping out of her car, Nancy ran to the young man, who was dressed in army camouflage clothes.

"Are you all right?" she asked. "Can you hear me?"

No answer. Nancy crouched down to take the boy's pulse. She just had time to register how strong it was when she heard a voice behind her.

"Don't touch him, and don't make a move."

Nancy whirled around and was now facing another young man in army camouflage. Only he was holding a gun and had it pointed right at her.

Nancy gasped. The newcomer was thin and wore wire-rimmed glasses. Without the gun, he would have looked harmless. But Nancy wasn't making any assumptions, not while the boy had a gun trained on her.

Nancy eyed him uneasily as she slowly got to her feet, her hands up. More people emerged from between the trees.

"Hey, Peter, cut the kidding," a female voice called. A girl with long blond hair jogged easily toward them.

Sheepishly, the boy lowered his gun, giving Nancy an embarrassed smile. "It's not real," he muttered. He walked over to the body on the ground and nudged it gently with his foot. "You better get up, Bob. Here comes Karen."

The blond girl, Karen, reached them just then, glaring at both boys. She was tiny, Nancy realized—she barely came up to Nancy's chin.

"Hi," she said in a breathless voice. She gave Nancy a warm smile. "Sorry—these guys are idiots. Bob, get up!" she ordered furiously, as the "body" jumped to his feet. She turned back

11

to Nancy and offered her the young man's gun. "See, it's a toy, really. A fancy water pistol."

"Water pistol or not," Nancy said in measured tones, "I don't like any gun pointed at my head. And Bob should be more careful," she added. "I could have run into him for real."

Karen flushed and pushed her hair back nervously. Nancy noticed a large, bronze-colored earring shaped like a snake on her right ear.

"Everybody, take a break," she yelled to the small group who had gathered a few yards away, watching them. She turned to Nancy, concern in her clear blue eyes.

"I'm Karen Lewis," she said, "and we're just, um, rehearsing for an event we're staging this week. I think Pete and Bob were trying to see if someone would take them seriously. I'm really sorry. They just got carried away."

Relief and anger coursed through Nancy. "Well," she said, drawing in a long breath, "I guess I've had worse scares."

"Are you a student here?"

"Yes. That is, a new student. I just transferred. My name is Nancy Drew."

Karen groaned. "Oh, no, someone new. Listen, you won't report us, will you?"

"Why would I do that?" Nancy asked. "What exactly is going on here?"

Without replying, Karen turned and searched

the group around her. "Philip!" she called anxiously.

A swarthy man got up from the rock he was sitting on and sauntered toward them. Unlike the others, he wasn't wearing camouflage clothes. Instead, he had on jeans, a black leather jacket, black sneakers, and a white scarf wrapped a little too casually around his neck. A shock of white hair stood out in the wavy black hair that tumbled over his head. He was too old to be a student, but he looked more like a model than a college professor, Nancy thought.

"A problem, Karen?" he asked in a low voice. He wasn't particularly large or stocky, but in the group of students, his presence seemed overwhelming.

"I hope not," she said, eyeing Nancy. "This is Nancy Drew, she's a transfer student."

"Nice to meet you, Nancy. I'm Philip Bangs." Turning his black eyes toward Nancy, he held out his hand, grasping hers with confidence. "Is there some trouble?"

"Suppose you tell me," Nancy said, trying to hide the curiosity in her voice. This was more than a group of overgrown kids playing with water pistols, or Karen wouldn't be so nervous.

Karen turned to Bangs and lowered her voice. "Well . . ." She hesitated. "I never got a permit to use the arboretum. If complaint charges are filed, the dean might kick us off campus."

Nancy cut in, a little irritated with the way Karen acted as if she weren't there. "I'm sure Dean Jarvis has more important things to worry about than permits. Who are you, anyway, some kind of officers-in-training group?"

Philip Bangs gave her a wide, startling smile. "Officers in training!" he exclaimed, as if it were an extremely clever joke. He clapped Karen on the shoulder, and the girl seemed to relax.

"No, we're not part of any army," Bangs said, chuckling lightly. "But we are part of a group. Members of POE—Protect Our Environment. Maybe you've heard of us? You might be interested in joining our group. I have some flyers here. We were merely preparing for Senator Claiborne's visit." Bangs began to dig through his jacket pockets.

"Maybe later, thanks," Nancy said firmly. "I'm late for an appointment. And you don't have to worry about me—I'm not going to file any charges against anyone. It's not my style." Flashing what she hoped was a convincing smile, Nancy climbed back into her car.

The last thing she needed was to get involved with an organized group, no matter how noble their cause. Not when she had a mystery to solve.

As Nancy pulled up in front of Omega Chi Epsilon she spotted Ned instantly. He was sitting on the wide porch, his long, jean-clad legs stretched out in front of him. She was really late, she realized, looking at her watch. Ned jumped lightly to his feet and headed toward her.

"Hey, gorgeous!" he said, waiting for her to climb out so he could enfold her in his arms. "Welcome back to Emerson!"

"Ned!" Nancy hugged him tightly with her eyes closed, breathing in his warm, familiar smell. "I missed you."

"Mmm," he murmured, "I missed you, too." He tilted her head up, his dark eyes dancing. "Give me a kiss."

Nancy leaned back against the car, letting her body relax next to Ned's. This was the kind of welcome she liked!

After a moment Nancy broke away, laughing. "Ned, don't you think we should go inside?"

"And get more comfortable?" he teased, keeping an arm around her waist. Nancy slipped her arm around him, her head fitting perfectly in the hollow of his shoulder, as they strolled toward the frat house.

A crackling fire greeted Nancy as she entered the living room, which was comfortably furnished with overstuffed chairs and sofas. Ned guided her to a sofa in front of the fire.

"Nan, you remember Jan and Mike."

Jan Teller, a small brunette, bounced up and embraced Nancy quickly. "It's great to see you again," she said warmly.

"Ditto for me," Mike O'Shea said. "Don't mind if I don't get up." Mike gestured to the cane lying next to him on the floor. "Jan and I just had a walk. I made it all the way to the gym and back. I'm going to claim invalid's privileges and make *you* come to *me.*"

Grinning, Nancy leaned over and gave Mike a peck on the cheek. He grabbed her hand. "Thanks again for everything you did last time you were here. I know it was pretty rough on you, but you brought me to my senses."

Nancy had met Mike and Jan when she came to Emerson to try to find a practical joker who was ruining Emerson's chance at a basketball championship. Mike had been Nancy's number-one suspect.

Nancy shuddered, remembering the case. Mike *had* been involved, but when Nancy had confronted him, he'd realized his mistakes and tried to put an end to his part in it. Eventually, Nancy did find the real criminal, but not before he'd pushed Mike off a six-story building.

Ned squeezed Nancy's shoulder, drawing her closer to him. She could tell he was thinking about that case, too. Ned had been so upset by what happened to Mike that he and Nancy had broken up for a while. But they solved their

16

problems, Nancy thought thankfully, and they were together again, stronger than ever.

"How are you doing?" Nancy asked Mike.

"Okay." He shrugged. "My back injuries weren't as bad as the doctors first thought, and my leg is healing. I can even walk short distances now without the cane."

"I'm going to rummage around for some chips or something. Anyone want anything?" Jan headed for the kitchen.

"Yeah, bring everything you can carry," Ned called. "I'm starving!"

"Ned, I'm sorry," Nancy said in dismay. "You should have gone to lunch without me."

"And missed my number-one girl? No way! But we will have dinner tonight—at a very romantic little place I know," Ned said. "But what did happen? Did Dean Jarvis keep you talking? I know he loves to talk."

"Partly, but then I ran into some people," Nancy said wryly. "Literally. Do you know about POE?"

Ned groaned. "Not them. Did they try to recruit you?"

"Sort of." Nancy explained what happened in the arboretum.

"Water guns? They're nuts!" Ned exclaimed. "They might mean well, but their methods—" He shuddered.

"Ned's right," Mike agreed. "I'm all for pro-

17

tecting the environment, but I think there are better ways to do it. POE's tactics are weird."

"What exactly do they do?" Nancy asked.

"They go out in the woods where they live off the land and go rock climbing and stuff. And they're always talking about stopping any technology that threatens the environment," Ned said in a steely voice.

Nancy frowned. "Well, those all sound like good causes."

"They *are* good causes," Jan said lightly, coming back in the room. "Ned's exaggerating. Right now they're all fired up about a visit from Senator Claiborne."

"I read about that," Nancy exclaimed. "He's the one who thinks we should sell our national parklands to developers. Most people think he's a genuine nut. If POE is against him, I'll have to be for them."

Jan and Mike exchanged uneasy looks. Nancy noticed Ned's jaw clench and anger wash over his face.

"Did I say something wrong?" she asked warily. She started to put her hand on Ned's shoulder, but he backed away. Nancy felt her heart sink.

"Maybe we should stop all this talking and eat," Nancy said, trying to change the subject. "It's not too late for this snack, is it?"

Ned glanced at his watch. "I'm afraid it is,"

he said curtly. "Anyway, I don't have much appetite now, and we're going to be late for class. Come on, Mike, Jan. We've got to hurry."

Jan helped Mike to his feet. Giving Nancy apologetic looks, they headed for the front door.

"Ned, what's wrong?" Nancy grabbed Ned's arm as he started to follow Jan and Mike out of the room. "A minute ago you were so happy to see me. What happened? What did I do?"

Ned pulled away. At the front door he stopped, his face set in a hard mask. Nancy stared, completely baffled by the change in him.

"If you think POE is such a great group, fine. But just do me a favor, okay? Don't ever mention them in front of me again!"

Chapter
Three

NANCY WAS STUNNED. She'd been so thrilled to see Ned, and now this. It was so unlike him to overreact. Whatever she did, Nancy vowed, she wouldn't mention POE.

She watched as Ned walked off with Jan and Mike. As soon as he had calmed down, she'd find out why her sticking up for the group had upset him so much. But there wasn't anything she could do about it now, so she decided to find her dorm and unpack.

Nancy didn't have to share her room, and it had a private bath. With a sigh, she dumped her bags, plopped onto the bed, and kicked off her shoes. Then she remembered she had promised to let her father, Carson Drew, know when she had arrived.

Rolling onto her stomach, Nancy grabbed the phone and dialed. Her father's voice came over the wire.

"Carson Drew," he answered pleasantly.

"Hi, Dad. Just called to let you know I'm safe and sound."

"I knew you would be, but it's always nice to hear your voice. Have you learned anything more about the case yet?"

Carson Drew was a celebrated lawyer, and he was always interested in Nancy's cases. The famous father had passed his curiosity on to his daughter, and it was one of the things that made her such a good detective.

"It's pretty fascinating," Nancy began. She stopped, having heard a noise in the hall. "Hold on, Dad. Someone's at the door. The dean promised to send over some information, and this is probably it."

Nancy tucked the telephone under her chin and went to the door, dragging the long cord behind her. Before she could open the door, an envelope was slid under it.

Stooping, Nancy quickly grabbed the envelope and opened the door just in time to see the back of the person who had obviously delivered it.

21

"Hey, thanks," she called.

Whoever it was gave a casual wave but didn't turn around or slow down to look back.

"Oh, well," Nancy said to her father, explaining what had just happened. "So much for the natives being friendly." The envelope was much smaller than Nancy had expected. Puzzled, she weighed it in her hand. Judging from the envelope's lightness, there wasn't much information on Professor Maszak at all.

Shrugging, she slit open the flap and gave her father a brief account of her conversation with the dean. She described how secretive Professor Maszak's experiment was, and how difficult it would make her investigation.

"That *is* a problem," Carson said sympathetically. "But maybe this new information will help you out."

"Maybe," Nancy agreed. She pulled a piece of paper out of the envelope and scanned it quickly.

"Nan?" her father asked after a long silence. "Are you still there?"

"Uh—sorry, Dad." Nancy shook herself. "It's—well, there isn't much information here after all."

"Looks like you have your work cut out for you," Nancy heard her father say. "But that's nothing new."

"I guess not," Nancy answered, smiling wryly. "Look, Dad, I've got to go. It looks like this case is going to be harder than I thought."

Hanging up, Nancy stared at the piece of paper in her hand. She hadn't wanted to worry her father, but the envelope wasn't from Dean Jarvis.

Instead, it was a warning, hastily scrawled in bold red ink. "Go home, Nancy Drew. CLT is *not* in your future."

Nancy quickly ran back into the hall, but there was no sign of the messenger who'd delivered the threat. Making her way down to the lounge, she tried to remember what the person had looked like.

She questioned the girl at the front desk, but she hadn't seen anyone who matched the sketchy description Nancy gave either enter or leave the building. In fact, the look the girl gave Nancy as she questioned her made her blush.

"Listen, if you remember anything, let me know. You can leave a note at the desk," Nancy said.

"Sure," the girl said, rolling her eyes.

It wasn't the best start to an investigation. Already, just minutes into the case, Nancy had missed an important clue by not paying attention to what was happening around her. It wouldn't happen again.

She had to admit that part of her mind was still on Ned. Why had he been so angry with her

23

earlier? Well, if she couldn't figure Ned out, at least she could track down the missing CLT.

Squaring her shoulders, she set off for the science labs a quarter mile away toward the center of the campus. A steady stream of students poured from the building entrance, jostling and shouting, obviously in high spirits at the end of the day. Nancy waded through them to the big glass double doors.

An unattended desk stood on one side of the almost deserted lobby. Pausing at the elevator banks, Nancy checked the directory. Professor Maszak's lab was on the third floor.

When the elevator doors opened on the third floor, Nancy found herself face-to-face with a security guard seated behind a desk.

"Signature and ID," he said automatically, without looking up from his magazine. "But classes are over for the day."

"I'm not here for class," she replied to the brim of his cap. "And I don't have an ID. I'm here to see Professor Josef Maszak."

The guard glanced up sharply. "What did you say your name was?"

He reached for the sheet she had just signed. "Nancy Drew. Wait a minute." The guard checked another piece of paper. "Right— you've got clearance." Then he went back to reading. "Last door on your right," he mumbled.

Nancy raised her eyebrows. Some security! The guard hadn't even tried to verify who she was. It obviously wasn't very difficult for anyone to get into the building. She hoped the lab itself was better protected.

Nancy found the door easily and knocked.

"It's open," someone called.

Great security, Nancy thought again as she entered a large, bright room dominated by huge picture windows. Long lab desks, each with a sink and gas outlets, faced the chalkboard in the front of the room. Three or four students were still there, bent over the tables.

"Excuse me," Nancy ventured. "Is Professor Maszak here?"

A freckle-faced boy gestured to a door on his left. A large combination lock was mounted on the wall next to it, but the door was slightly ajar.

"Right there, in his office," the boy said.

Nancy pushed into a much smaller room strewn with lab equipment. Professor Maszak sat on a high stool behind a counter busily doing paperwork. His bush of salt-and-pepper hair obscured his face.

"You're late," he barked.

"I didn't know I was expected," Nancy said pleasantly.

The professor started. He raised his head, his light brown eyes widening in alarm. Color rushed into his face.

25

"Who do you think you are, sneaking up on me like that? How did you get in here?"

"It wasn't very hard," Nancy said pointedly. "Dean Jarvis said this room was always under lock and key."

Maszak had the grace to look embarrassed. "I left it open only for a minute," he said, defending himself. "I was expecting my assistant, Sara," he muttered. "I thought you were she."

"I'm Nancy Drew."

"Oh, now I remember. I *was* expecting you," the fiftyish Maszak said gruffly.

He got up, wiping his hands on a dirty lab coat, and closed the door. "Jarvis told me he'd called you in to investigate." He eyed Nancy closely. "You don't look much like a famous detective."

Nancy ignored the remark and surveyed the room. A ten-foot fish tank ran along the right wall and several open-wire cages covered the left. An industrial-size freezer filled the back of the room. Maszak motioned Nancy over to the fish tank.

"This," he announced proudly, "is my experiment."

The tank held carp of all sizes, but one very large fish swam along the bottom of the tank. Nancy bent closer. The fish was enormous.

Professor Maszak's eyes followed hers. "My

pride and joy," he said. "How old do you think he is?"

Nancy had no idea how to judge the age of a fish. "A year?" she guessed.

Maszak snorted. "Six months," he said proudly. "Can you believe it?"

Smiling slightly, Nancy went to examine the cages. Each one held several mice, which ranged from normal size to several exceptionally large ones.

"I take it CLT is some kind of growth drug," she remarked.

"You're very quick," the professor said. "That's precisely what it is."

Nancy stared at him. What kind of "top secret" experiment was this? First, there was hardly any security around the lab, and then the professor practically boasted about his so-called secret experiment.

"I don't understand," Nancy told him. "I thought this was all restricted information. It can't be as simple as a chemical to grow bigger fish and mice."

Maszak laughed. "Some people get a little carried away with the cloak-and-dagger stuff," he said, returning to his papers and shuffling them. "CLT is a rare, extremely expensive chemical. There are others that give much the same results."

"And it isn't dangerous?" Nancy asked, feeling more and more confused.

The professor snorted. "If you drink it, it'll give you a stomachache. But if you mean, is it potentially lethal, the answer is no."

"The dean told me that both times the CLT was stolen, it was taken at a very crucial time during your experiment."

"Well, yes," Maszak said, "but not during the experiment, *before* it. I treat the CLT in a special way that only I have the formula for. It's a lengthy process. After it's treated, I put the finished product in the freezer. That was when the CLT was stolen."

Maszak threw open the freezer door. On the lower shelf, Nancy saw a large metal cylinder that nearly filled the freezer.

Nancy whistled in surprise. "It's huge! I guess I thought they'd be smaller."

"The amounts are very small," Maszak explained. "The CLT itself is sealed in small plastic tubes. The container helps keep it at the right temperature. I got a canister in this delivery," he continued. "My first delivery was two canisters, and one of them was stolen. My second delivery was only one canister and it was stolen. But I did do work with the one canister that wasn't stolen."

"And now you're about to complete the third treatment?" Nancy asked.

Maszak eyed her with grudging admiration. "As you guessed," he said, gesturing to a mass of test tubes set up at the other counter from where he had been doing his paperwork, "I'm in the final stages of treatment now."

Nancy examined the tubes and beakers on the central counter. They meant nothing to her. Maszak could be telling the truth, or giving her the runaround to hide his real purpose. Without some hard facts about the experiment, there was no way for her to know for sure.

A noise came from the outer lab. Frowning, Maszak hurried to the door. Nancy followed him.

The students she'd seen before had left the lab, but in their place was a girl with brown hair who was standing at a lab table near the windows. She was holding a beaker up to the light. Her scarf and bag had been thrown over a nearby chair, but she still had her coat on.

"You're late again, Sara!" Maszak exclaimed. "Nancy, this is my assistant, Sara Hughes."

As the girl whirled around, a look of fear flashed across her plump face.

"I—I know I'm late," she stuttered, "but I can finish this up in a minute."

Maszak nodded curtly. "Nancy is here to interview me for the paper. She may want to ask you some questions, too."

The girl looked guardedly at Nancy. "Well, I

29

have to get this done right away. I don't have time for questions."

Sara turned back to the setup on the table and gently scooped some dull gray powder into a small measuring spoon.

"At least take off your coat," Maszak said.

Still balancing the spoon in her right hand, Sara began to unbutton her coat with her left hand. She shrugged her shoulders vigorously, trying to slip the coat off.

"Sara, watch yourself," Maszak cautioned. "Remember what you've got in your hands!"

Nancy had an impulse to help, but as she came up behind Sara, the girl suddenly twisted sharply, then stumbled. As she reached to steady herself, the spoon fell from her hand. The gray powder landed in the beaker with a small fizz.

"Watch out!" Maszak cried.

The beaker exploded, sending splinters of glass flying everywhere!

Chapter

Four

CLOSING HER EYES, Nancy threw up her hands to cover her face. She heard Professor Maszak yell to Sara to protect herself as pieces of glass clattered to the floor. Sara gave a little cry, and Nancy heard her footsteps as she rushed out of the room.

When Nancy opened her eyes, the professor was staring after Sara with a rueful expression. He bent to pick up the larger fragments from the floor.

Nancy bent down to help him. "What *was* that?" she asked.

Maszak sighed. "Nothing. A stupid mistake."

Nancy arched an eyebrow.

31

"Sara is supervising two class experiments at once. She wasn't paying attention, and she dropped part of one into part of the other. They didn't agree with each other."

"To put it mildly," Nancy murmured. "Shouldn't she take better precautions with explosives?"

"Neither is explosive by itself. The powder is zinc," the professor said. "And there was hydrochloric acid in the beaker." The professor was silent for a moment, studying the glass fragments nestled in his palm. "But you're right. They shouldn't have been near each other. I'm afraid Sara has been a little distracted lately. I'll have to speak to her about it." He didn't seem to be looking forward to their conversation.

"I have to get ready for a dinner date," Nancy told him, hoping Ned was still speaking to her. "But if I need to ask any more questions, where can I reach you?"

"Here or at home. I live in Adams Cottage, near the main gate. But I'm usually here."

Nancy thanked the professor and left the lab. She decided to head back to the dorm to see if Dean Jarvis had sent the information he'd promised or to check if Ned called. Nothing. She'd have to check with both of them later.

Nancy flopped on her bed and tried to concentrate on the case, but her thoughts kept coming back to Ned. She hated it when they fought, especially when there wasn't any real reason for it. She decided then and there to do whatever it took to make up with Ned.

After a quick shower, Nancy slipped on her blue silk dress—Ned's favorite. In that dress she could smooth out their problems. The soft fabric flowed smoothly over her hips. She brushed back her thick hair, which looked more gold than red in the artificial light, and was just running some clear gloss over her lips when the telephone rang. Nancy's heart leapt.

"Nancy, this is Mike O'Shea. I hope I didn't disturb you."

"No, not at all." Nancy swallowed her disappointment. She'd have to call Ned as soon as Mike hung up. "What's up?"

"Well," Mike said, hesitating, "it's Ned. He ran out of here an hour ago, on his way to the dining hall. He said it was an emergency and asked me to let you know where he was if he wasn't back by now."

So much for the dress! Nancy thought. "Thanks, Mike," she said into the phone. "I'll look for him in the dining hall right away."

What kind of emergency? Nancy wondered as she found her way to the campus dining hall. A steady stream of students walked in and out of the modern glass-and-chrome building. Inside the cafeteria, each student shouted to be heard over rock music blaring through loudspeakers.

Nancy spotted Ned sitting at a table in the corner, his face bent close to a thin, dark-haired girl next to him. One tray of mostly eaten food sat between them. Nancy was happy to see Ned was wearing a coat and tie. Maybe she could salvage their dinner plans after all.

Ned looked startled as Nancy reached their table. Undaunted, she slipped into a chair and put her hand on his arm.

"Nan, I didn't really mean for you to come over here. But . . ." Ned gave her a brief, although distracted, smile and turned back to the other girl.

"Angela Morrow, this is Nancy Drew."

Angela's face was pale against her jet black hair. As she swung her head to greet Nancy a single bronze earring in the shape of a snake slapped gently against her neck. It was the same kind of earring Karen Lewis had been wearing, Nancy noted.

Angela was nervously twisting a piece of paper.

"Excuse me, Angela," Nancy said, "but that earring—are you a member of . . ." Her voice trailed away as Ned shot her a warning look.

"Nancy met some members of POE today," Ned told Angela softly. "She ran into them in the arboretum behind my frat house." Ned

34

turned to Nancy. "Angela's going to be initiated into the group tonight. I'm trying to talk her out of it."

"Ned!" Angela's voice was surprisingly soft. "I've told you, POE is a wonderful organization, a community of people working together to protect our planet. Why is that so hard for you to understand?"

"Angela, look." Ned's voice matched the exasperation in Angela's, and Nancy sensed they had had this conversation before. "I don't trust POE, no matter what you say. Some students in the group are moving off campus to live together in a commune. They've stopped going to classes. They spend all their time in private meetings at POE headquarters, and there's something secretive and nasty about the whole thing."

Angela appealed to Nancy. "We do a lot of good," she insisted. "We have great speakers come to campus—reputable people. And we have a tremendous recruiting effort."

"My point exactly! If it's such a great group, why do you have to work so hard to recruit new members?"

Nancy looked at Ned in surprise. She realized he was genuinely worried about Angela's safety, but he was making her feel very awkward—as if he cared more about Angela than about Nancy herself. Embarrassed by her jealousy, she tried to be more reasonable. There was nothing wrong with Ned having Angela for a friend.

"Ned," she began uncomfortably, "I know you feel strongly about this, but Angela has a right to do what she wants."

Ned glared at her angrily. "I have nothing against free speech, or the right to peaceful protest," he snapped.

Nancy felt helpless. "Have you been to many of their meetings?" she asked.

"Never!" Angela fumed. "He hasn't been to a single one, but he thinks he knows what it's all about!"

"The meetings are useless," Ned argued. "You can only find out what's really going on if you're initiated."

Nancy shrugged helplessly. "Then Angela *should* be initiated. If there's anything wrong with the group, she can find out before getting more involved."

Ned's eyes narrowed. "Right. But what if, once you're initiated, you don't like what you find out?" His voice dropped. "I've never heard of anyone quitting," he warned.

Angela rolled her eyes impatiently. Nancy squirmed self-consciously in her seat. She picked up a book of matches from the glass ashtray. On the cover was an ad for Reiko's, the Japanese restaurant she was hoping Ned would take her to. It didn't seem likely now. Sighing, she slipped the matches into her purse.

"I give up," Angela exclaimed. "Try talking to someone else. Like Philip Bangs. He came to speak to us today. He's a world-famous environmentalist. You'd believe him, wouldn't you?"

Philip Bangs—the man in black in the woods. Nancy felt Angela staring at her curiously.

"I—I met Mr. Bangs today," she explained. "He was quite impressive."

Angela beamed in triumph. "There! Nancy believes me. Bangs is terrific. He studied to be a doctor and is also a computer specialist. He has the medical and scientific training to know what technology is dangerous. He's really inspiring."

Ned growled in disgust, but Angela nodded eagerly at Nancy. "He traveled all over the world and finally settled in South America. But he felt a great need to help people, so he came back to America."

"Angela," Nancy interrupted, "when I met Bangs today he was with a group in the arboretum, playing some kind of game with water guns. He said it had to do with Senator Claiborne coming. Do you know what that was all about?"

Angela lowered her eyes, and for the first time she looked slightly uncomfortable. "POE is going to protest Claiborne's views on national parklands."

"With water pistols?" Ned snorted. "Are you planning to drown him?"

Nancy hid a smile.

"Are you a student here?" Angela asked abruptly.

Nancy didn't blame Angela for trying to change the subject. She'd never seen Ned acting so unreasonably.

"Yes, I recently transferred here," she began, but Ned cut her off.

"Angela," he pleaded, "I'm sorry if I'm acting crazy. I'm worried. Can't we talk about this some more?" He smiled. "I even promise to listen with an open mind."

Angela pushed her chair back and got up. "There's nothing more to talk about," she said lightly, giving Ned a quick peck on the cheek. Then she turned to Nancy. "Nice meeting you. If you want to know any more about POE, just give me a call."

"Angela, wait," Ned said, standing up. "Let me walk you back to your dorm." He turned to Nancy. "Nan? Do you mind? About dinner, I mean."

"No, I guess not," Nancy said.

Relief flooded Ned's face. "I'll call you later. We can have dessert or something," he promised vaguely.

Disappointed and upset, Nancy watched them go. It certainly wasn't the evening she'd had in mind. What was Ned's problem with POE anyway? Why was he getting so upset about a simple college group? There had to be something he wasn't telling her, and Nancy resolved that she was going to find out what it was.

Leaving the cafeteria, Nancy impulsively turned toward the lab. The streetlights cast friendly circles of light in the cold darkness that turned Nancy's breath into puffs of white fog. She turned up her collar to give her ears some protection and dug into her pockets for her leather gloves.

Usually, she thought ruefully, something ruined her time with Ned when she was on a case, but usually it was her fault, not his.

Nancy made out the silhouette of the science building against the sky. Counting the stories, she realized there was a light shining on the third floor. As she watched, someone passed in front of the lab's huge windows. Even from a distance, she thought she recognized the figure. Sara Hughes?

Quickening her pace, Nancy hurried to the lab. If Sara was alone, now was the perfect opportunity to ask the skittish lab assistant some pointed questions about Maszak, his experiments, and CLT.

As she approached the front steps of the building, Nancy heard the distinctive sound of a twig breaking behind her.

From the corner of her eye, she saw a low branch of a nearby tree swaying gently. Probably an owl or raccoon, Nancy thought, not fully convinced. Before she took another full step a hand came down heavily on her shoulder, and before she could turn around, something crashed over her head. Everything went black.

Chapter

Five

"CAN YOU HEAR ME, NAN? Are you okay?"

Nancy opened her eyes to find herself lying in bed in a room flooded with morning light. Ned's face was close to hers, his soft brown eyes full of concern. Her head ached terribly.

"I—I think so," Nancy said weakly. She put a hand to her throbbing forehead. "Except for this headache. Where am I?"

"In the infirmary. What happened to you?"

"Can I tell you as soon as my head clears and I see less than three of you?" Nancy asked.

Ned nodded and took her hand gently. "I'm glad you're awake."

Seeing the warmth in Ned's eyes, Nancy was overcome with relief. She pulled herself up, threw her arms around his neck, and held him tight. Wordlessly, he brushed his lips against her forehead.

"Oh, Ned," she whispered. "What's going on with us? I thought you hated me."

"Hated you? Never! I was so worried about Angela that I got carried away. It's all my fault."

"I'm sorry—" Nancy began.

"Shhh." Ned placed his fingers gently over Nancy's lips. "You rest. I'll do the talking." He eased his chair up close to the side of the bed.

"I acted like a jerk before, and I know it now," he admitted. "When I saw you hurt . . ." His face colored with embarrassment. "I remembered just how much you mean to me. I shouldn't have yelled at you about POE. It was wrong."

Nancy felt tears spring to her eyes. "Oh, Ned—" she began.

"But you don't know what I do about POE, Nan. I know they're in favor of good, sound environmental causes, but there's something wrong with that group. Don't ask me to prove it, because I can't. All I know is, Angela is a very impressionable and trusting girl. Too trusting— she's very easily led. A lot of POE's members are like that. You've got to believe me on this, Nan."

Nancy nodded, impressed by Ned's sincerity. He hesitated. "I know you're on some kind of secret mission here," he said. "And I know you're working hard on the case, whatever it is. But I'd like you to help me with this, too. Do you think you can?"

It only took Nancy a second to make up her mind. "If it's important to you, I'll help," she promised.

Ned leaned over for another hug.

"Ahem," someone cleared his throat behind them. Ned jumped back.

"How's the patient?" A good-looking man in a security uniform stepped into the room. He swept off his cap and settled into the other chair near Nancy's bed. "You look better now than you did lying facedown in the dirt, Ms. Drew."

Nancy eyed him curiously. "I take it you found me?"

"Ned and I found you," he replied, "out cold in the bushes."

"That's right," Ned added. "My conversation with Angela wasn't going anywhere, so I decided to catch up with you. You weren't at the dorm, so I guessed you might go to the science building since you said your investigation would begin there."

"On my security round I saw Ned, and we stumbled on you," the guard confirmed. "You were all alone. The guy who decked you was long gone."

"By the way, Nancy, this is Craig Bergin," Ned said as the guard stuck his hand out to Nancy. "Craig used to work at the gym, checking people's IDs."

Craig's hazel eyes twinkled. "And I got to know Ned really well—he always forgot his ID."

Nancy felt herself smiling at Craig's sunny personality. "Well, thanks for taking care of me." Nancy winced as a sharp pain shot through her head. She closed her eyes.

"Can you tell me what happened?" Craig asked. "Did somebody try to snatch your purse or something?"

Nancy looked questioningly at Ned, who nodded slightly. "Craig's a good guy," he told her.

Nancy smiled at Craig. "I don't think robbery was the motive."

"If you think of anything that might help me catch him, just let me know," Craig offered.

"I will," Nancy promised.

"I've got to go finish my report on you now. You can always find me at Campus Police headquarters."

"I've got to go, too, Nan," Ned said after Craig left. "My coach called a morning basketball practice."

"Basketball? But this is football season," Nancy said, surprised.

"We're playing one exhibition game this fall for charity. It's for a good cause, and I'll come back to see you before lunch."

"Whoa," Nancy objected. "I'm not hanging around the infirmary all day. There's someone out there who's pretty anxious to get rid of me. Besides, I've got work to do."

Ned frowned. "You can't go running around with that headache."

"There's nothing wrong with me that a few more aspirin won't cure. What do you want me to do? Sit here?"

Ned sighed and shook his head. "Why do I even try to argue? Look, let's compromise. Come with me to practice. That way I'll be able to keep an eye on you and make sure you're okay."

"Just sit there?" Nancy said doubtfully.

Ned grinned. "Well, you might chat with someone who knows a lot about Josef Maszak."

"Ned!" Nancy pretended to throw her pillow at him. "You're teasing. Who knows Professor Maszak?"

"Well, it's just a thought," Ned cautioned, "but I have seen Maszak with Coach Burnett. It's worth a try."

After collecting her things, Nancy followed Ned to the Emerson gym. There, Ned left

45

Nancy in the office with Coach Burnett, a tall, silver-haired man in his late fifties. Nancy was seated across from him in a red armchair, the only comfortable chair in the room. The coach leaned back and swung his feet onto his desk.

"I should have known you were here to investigate a mystery. Why don't you ever come up just to see us?" He broke into a smile that reached up to his gray eyes. "Or is Nickerson not as much of a hunk as all the cheerleaders think he is?"

Nancy blushed hotly. "Coach!"

The man laughed. "I'm sorry, Nancy, I shouldn't tease you. After all, I owe you a lot."

"Do you think we could get back to Professor Maszak?" Nancy asked.

"Sure. But I'm not sure how much I can tell you about him."

Nancy tried to hide her disappointment. "Ned said he'd seen you together."

"Well, we've had dinner a few times," Coach Burnett admitted. "But we don't talk about school or chemistry. I know very little personal background."

"At this point, anything would help," Nancy assured him.

Coach Burnett nodded thoughtfully. "Well, he's from Hungary, if you hadn't already guessed. His wife, Linda, is American, though, a

46

linguist, I think. They met when she was teaching in Hungary. Stop me if this isn't the kind of thing you want."

"No, this is great," Nancy assured him.

The coach nodded. "Well, Linda's very sick. I'm not sure what's wrong, but I guess they decided she could get better medical treatment here. That's why they came to the States."

"That explains a lot," Nancy said. "I thought it was strange that a scientist from a communist country could come over here and do research for our government."

"Well, apparently it *was* a problem. Right now Maszak has only a working visa. He's waiting for permanent residency."

"Does he like it here?"

"Oh, yes," Coach Burnett said. "His first love is teaching. He loves his classes and his students love him."

"But he doesn't seem like a happy person," Nancy commented.

"Well, he's got a lot on his mind, with Linda and all. And I guess his work takes a lot out of him." The coach made a face. "All that fooling with biological mutations."

Nancy laughed. "Different people have different interests, I guess." She got up. "Thanks for everything, Coach."

"My pleasure, Nancy."

47

Nancy told Coach Burnett to tell Ned that he could find her in the science library. She headed straight there.

In the biology section she ran her fingers lightly over the bindings, working her way to the end of the aisle. Choosing a few books, she plopped down on the floor in the aisle and began paging through them. She didn't really know what she was looking for. Most of the information on biological mutations showed pictures of just that, mutations.

According to the books, Nancy found there were a few things you could do to an animal to make it grow larger and faster than usual. But the most common way to induce rapid growth was to give the animal a growth hormone. Nancy thought she remembered Maszak bragging about how young the huge carp actually was.

The books all said that the same hormone wouldn't affect different animals the same way, but Nancy was pretty sure that Maszak was using CLT on both the mice and the fish.

Maybe that was the big secret? CLT worked the same on all animals. Nancy frowned. She was no scientist, and her answers seemed all too easy. Nothing there for Dean Jarvis to get excited about. And nothing to involve the government.

Switching her attention to recent scientific

magazines, Nancy spent another hour poring through articles, many of which she didn't completely understand. Just as she was about to give up, she spotted an article describing the futile attempts to give different animals the same growth hormone. It was impossible that any growth hormone would work the same on all of them, the article said. Yet that seemed to be exactly what she had seen in Maszak's lab. Nancy's pulse quickened.

No one thought it could be done, yet she had seen it. A chill went up her spine. Forcing herself to remain calm, Nancy reread the article carefully. No doubt about it. There was only one growth hormone that could possibly achieve this result, the article said, and no one had access to that. It was very rare and unusual. And it could only come from a human!

Chapter

Six

"**N**ANCY! I'VE BEEN LOOKING all over this place for you."

Startled, Nancy dropped her magazine. She looked up to see Ned towering over her.

Nancy gasped. "Ned," she cried, "you look terrible. Something's happened. What is it? What's wrong?"

Ned's face was grim. "It's Angela," he said. "She's gone."

"What are you talking about?" Nancy leapt to her feet, magazines slipping to the floor. "What do you mean she's gone?"

"Angela came to the frat house late last night

and talked to Mike. He said she was pretty upset. When he asked what was going on, she gave him a message for me. She said, 'Tell Ned I'm doing the right thing. Don't worry.' And today, when I went back there, this note was waiting for me."

Ned held up a piece of typing paper. "She says her belief in POE is destroying our friendship and she can't argue with me about it anymore. So she's left school. She's going to give all her time to them."

"Let me see that." Nancy took the paper from Ned and read it quickly. There was something about it—

"Wait a second, Ned, does Angela always type her letters?"

"As a matter of fact, she's taking a typing course right now. She's been typing everything all semester."

"Still"—Nancy shook her head—"she sounds very emotional. I wouldn't sit down and type a letter like this, would you?" She handed the letter back to Ned. "Why don't we pay this group a little visit?"

Ned grinned slyly. "I thought you'd never ask."

Ned helped Nancy shove the books and magazines back on the shelf. Then they made their way across campus as fast as possible.

The headquarters for POE were across a road

from the Emerson campus, in an abandoned business complex. Ned and Nancy followed a driveway that wound through the wooded grounds and ended in front of a large double-story building. Five smaller buildings were scattered among the trees along the road.

The gravelly driveway crunched under Nancy's feet as they approached the main building. No one came out to greet them. In fact, the place seemed deserted.

Ned glanced at Nancy. "Weird, huh?" he asked in a low voice.

Nancy nodded, slipping her hand securely into his. "You said they went on survival camp-outs on weekends. Maybe they left early."

The door to the main building was half open. It swung in noiselessly when Nancy pushed it. They stepped in.

Nancy and Ned found themselves in one large room, in what looked like a warehouse. There was a small, makeshift podium off to one side, with a stack of straw mats piled near it on the bare concrete floor. A delicate iron stairway was built in against the opposite wall, seeming to lead underground. The air inside was cold and smelled of forest dampness.

Twenty feet up on the walls, a catwalk circled the inside of the warehouse. A spiral staircase dropped to the main floor. Beyond the catwalk at one end, Nancy could see small rooms leading off from it. The center of the main room was open to the roof. As Nancy and Ned surveyed the area, a small figure appeared on the catwalk.

"Can I help you with something?" Nancy recognized Karen Lewis, the girl she had met in the arboretum.

"We came to see Angela Morrow." Ned's voice sounded hollow in the large space. "Can you tell us where to find her?"

As Karen headed down the spiral stairs, Nancy thought she saw a shadow lengthen along the wall of the room the girl had emerged from, but no one came out. As she approached, Karen looked at Nancy quizzically.

"Don't I know you?" she asked Nancy. "You look very familiar."

"I ran into your 'rehearsal' in the woods yesterday," Nancy reminded her.

"Oh, right." Karen flushed. "Nancy Drew. And now you're here about Angela?"

Nancy nodded, but Karen kept staring at her, as if she were waiting for her to talk about something else.

Ned shifted impatiently. "Yes," he prompted, "Angela Morrow. Can we see her?"

Karen turned her attention to him. "Right. Angela," she said, repeating his question. "She's not here, I'm afraid. I can leave a note for her if you'd like."

53

Nancy couldn't help thinking that Karen seemed distracted and a bit confused.

Ned locked eyes with Karen. "Angela left me a note saying she was coming to live here."

His words seemed to pull Karen out of her thoughts. She folded her arms across her chest. "As a matter of fact, she will be joining us here. But when students move off campus, they need parental consent. Angela went home to discuss it with her mom and dad."

Before Ned could reply, Nancy laid a hand on his arm to silence him.

"When people come here, where exactly do they stay?" she cut in, smoothly changing the subject. "I don't see any signs of people living here."

"This is just our meeting hall. There are a few offices up there on the catwalk, but no one lives here. We house people in the surrounding buildings. Right now, we have thirty full-time members," Karen boasted. "And we're still growing."

"Karen?" a deep voice boomed from the mezzanine.

They all turned toward the man who appeared on the catwalk.

"That's Philip Bangs," Nancy told Ned in a low voice. "The environmentalist. Angela talked about him the other night, remember?"

Philip Bangs swaggered down the stairs toward them. "Thanks, Karen, for letting me use your phone," he said. "I finally got ahold of the people at Saint Marks University and my speech *is* on for tomorrow. I appreciate your letting me stay but I have to leave for California now." Bangs turned to Nancy.

"It's Nancy Drew, right?" he said. Nancy was again struck by the force of his personality. She nodded.

"And I'm Ned Nickerson," Ned said, maneuvering himself between Bangs and Nancy. "Nice to meet you. We're looking for one of your members. Angela Morrow. Maybe you know her?"

Bangs laughed. "*My* members? I'd love to take the credit, but this is Karen's group. She founded POE. Actually, I've never seen or heard of another group like it. I'm just here because my lecture ran over yesterday and I missed my plane. She's got a great group of kids here," he said generously, clapping Karen on the shoulder warmly. "Earnest, committed—a wonderful group!"

Nancy watched Bangs curiously. For all his smooth manner, he didn't strike her as sincere.

Karen blushed at Bangs's compliment. "Philip, you remember Angela. The thin girl with the short black hair? You saw her off today when she went home."

Bangs furrowed his brow slowly. "Oh, yes!

55

Great kid. Very knowledgeable about politics, too."

"You saw her off?" Nancy interrupted. "You don't remember if she said anything, well, unusual, do you? Or if she left a message for anyone?"

"No, nothing unusual," Bangs replied. "She just jumped into her car and said she'd be back tomorrow."

Karen squared her shoulders and turned to Bangs. "Philip, before you go, I want to schedule another lecture sometime in the spring." The blond girl turned back to Nancy and Ned, dismissing them. "I'm sorry Angela isn't here, but we do expect her back tomorrow. I'll tell her you came by."

Nancy could see that Ned was about ready to burst. She led him outside quickly.

"Angela's father died when she was six years old!" Ned said furiously. "How could she be getting his permission? I don't believe a word they say. What if they're holding her against her will?"

Nancy hesitated. "Angela seemed ready to join them last night. Besides, what would they have to gain by holding her? Does her mother have a lot of money?"

Ned shook his head. "Not that I know of."

"Look, Ned, I hate to say it," Nancy pointed out quietly, "but it might mean nothing. Why

56

would Karen know if Angela's father was alive or not?"

"It doesn't fit," Ned insisted.

Nancy nodded. "You're right. I don't like this, either, but we won't know more until we talk to Angela."

"I could call her at home."

Nancy took Ned's arm. "Ned, you talked your heart out last night and it didn't work. I don't think you'll change her mind now. Let's wait and see what happens when she gets back."

Nancy walked Ned to his history class. He still seemed moody and distracted. Stopping to let the boisterous crowd of students pass them, she gave him a quick kiss and made him promise not to worry. As Nancy watched Ned disappear into the gray stone building, she couldn't help thinking something *was* wrong with POE. She ached to help him find out what it was, but she was here at Emerson to solve a different mystery and she'd better get started.

Heading for the science building, Nancy spied Professor Maszak shouting into a pay phone. Seeing her, he lowered his voice and turned his back on her.

Nancy drifted into one of the phone booths a few feet away, lifted the receiver and pretended to dial. She strained to hear what Maszak was saying but his words were too soft. Then, just as she prepared to give up, he raised his voice.

"I'm doing it," she heard him growl. "I've been doing it all along, and they haven't done anything with it! *They* are the ones wasting time waiting for the processing. You'll get your money. I'll go back to them and see what I can do. You can count on me."

There was a short silence, then Maszak exploded again. "Don't tell me this is important. It's more important to me than it is to you. To me, this is a matter of life or death!"

Chapter

Seven

Before Nancy could react, Professor Maszak slammed down the receiver and stalked away. She filed the conversation away. What was a matter of life or death? If Maszak was hiding important information from her, she wanted to know what and why.

Nancy placed the receiver in its cradle slowly. As a good detective, she knew never to rule out any suspect, no matter how innocent he or she might seem. In fact, it was often the people who seemed most innocent who were most guilty. Maszak could be involved in the thefts himself.

As Nancy hurried after the rumpled professor, she thought about the explosion in the lab. When the beaker blew up, Maszak had been surprisingly understanding about Sara's clumsy mistake. Was he *too* understanding?

Tossing her head back with determination, Nancy resolved to find out as much as she could. If Maszak was lying, he was very good at it. Nancy decided she'd have better luck with Sara.

Turning, Nancy picked up the telephone again and called student information. In no time she'd found Sara's dorm and her room number.

Slipping through the busy lobby, Nancy quietly made her way down the long dorm hallway. Without pausing, she knocked on Sara's door. There was no answer. "Bad luck," Nancy murmured to herself. Now she'd have to waste time tracking Sara down. She knocked once more to make sure, and to her surprise the door pushed open.

Nancy hesitated. Sara wasn't a suspect in the thefts, but she could be. And she might learn something from a quick search of Sara's room.

Inside, the late-afternoon sun bounced off the large mirror over the dresser on one wall. Opposite it, a standard-issue Formica desk was surrounded by posters of animals in the wild. Sara's bed was neatly made.

Moving swiftly, Nancy checked the desk drawers. Finding nothing unusual, she flipped through the looseleaf binders lying in neat stacks on the desk. Sara's notes were written in small, careful script. There was no chemistry notebook, Nancy noted. Sara might have that one with her. None of the other notebooks mentioned Maszak's experiments or CLT.

The bright sunshine playing off the dresser caught Nancy's attention. Among bottles of perfume and makeup samples was a familiar object. Nancy picked it up. A bronze-colored snake earring—the same as the ones worn by Karen Lewis and Angela Morrow.

Nancy felt suddenly chilled. Sara was a POE member, too. That was one coincidence she hadn't expected. Was the group somehow connected to Professor Maszak's research? Even to the theft of the CLT? Had they learned of Maszak's animal experiments? And were they trying to stop them?

Nancy stepped up her search, pulling open drawers, looking for anything that might link the CLT thefts to the environmental group. She heard a noise at the door and saw the doorknob turning. She barely had time to shove the drawer shut and whirl around before the door opened. Sara Hughes's chunky body was framed in the doorway.

Sara stared at Nancy in confusion. "What are you doing here?" she demanded.

"Looking for you," Nancy answered. Her voice sounded surprisingly calm. "I have some questions I'd like to ask you."

"About that story you're writing, right?" Sara eyed Nancy suspiciously. "Shouldn't you have called first?"

Nancy pretended to be a hard-nosed reporter without manners. "Your door was open," she said, shrugging. "I decided to wait here."

"Oh. Well, I guess that's okay." Sara waved her hand at the desk chair and Nancy sat down.

"This is a very important story, Sara," Nancy said. "I need to know exactly what you do for Professor Maszak. For instance," she said casually, "what were you doing last night in the chemistry lab?"

Sara's face went white. Then, without warning, she burst into tears.

"I didn't do anything wrong," she wailed. "I was only trying to catch up on all my work. I've fallen so far behind, and—I don't know what to do!"

Surprised at this outburst, Nancy shifted awkwardly in her seat waiting for Sara's sobbing to subside. "Sara," she asked gently, "do you want to tell me about it?"

Sara took a deep breath. "I'm just so scared,"

she confessed, her voice trembling. "My father lost his job this summer and hasn't been able to find a new one. He's been doing part-time work, but I don't know whether he'll be able to send me back to school next semester."

"What does that have to do with the lab?" Nancy asked.

"Everything!" Sara cried. "I've applied for every scholarship there is, but so far I haven't heard. I'm so upset I can't concentrate on anything. The more I worry, the more I seem to mess up. Professor Maszak already warned me —if I don't shape up, I'll lose my job in the lab."

The anguish on Sara's face was genuine. Her eyes brimmed with tears. "I've been so nervous," she went on. "Between the mistakes I'm making and the thef— I mean, well, I may not have my job for long."

"Thefts," Nancy repeated. "You were going to say thefts."

Sara looked at Nancy with alarm. "No one knows about the thefts—only me and the professor." She drew away suddenly. "Who are you, anyway? I don't believe you're a student reporter at all."

Nancy took a deep breath. "I'll be straight with you, Sara, since you've already guessed the truth. You have to promise me, though, that this is strictly between you and me. If not, the professor could be hurt. Emerson could be hurt."

Sara paled. "I swear, I won't tell anyone. I'd never do that."

Nancy believed her. She had a strong feeling that Sara was no thief. "I'm here to investigate the thefts of the CLT. I'm helping Dean Jarvis."

"Are you from the government?" Sara's eyes widened.

"No way," Nancy assured her. "I'm a private detective. I care about Emerson College, and I don't want to see the school suffer because of the thefts."

Sara reddened and went to her desk, drawing a tissue from a drawer. "So that's what you were really doing in my room. You thought I stole the CLT."

"I don't now," Nancy said honestly. "Sara— will you help me?"

"I doubt if I can." Sara's voice was flat. "All I know is, the CLT was stolen each time right before we were about to begin the experiment."

"Is there something particularly important about that time?"

"No," Sara said helplessly. "It's just another stage in the process. The professor gets the stuff, he treats it, and then we start the experiment."

"Do you help with the treatment?" Nancy asked.

"No one does," Sara said. "He's very secretive about the whole process. I just try to stay out of his way."

Nancy nodded. "Who else knows when Maszak has finished the treatment?"

"The professor, me, and Dean Jarvis."

"No one else? No students?"

"No. But the professor keeps a daily log of the experiment on his computer. I've never seen his entries."

Nancy felt a faint twinge of excitement. "But someone could get into the program and find out that way," she suggested.

Sara frowned. "I doubt it. There's a secret password. No one but the professor knows what it is."

"It doesn't sound good for the professor," Nancy muttered.

"I know," Sara cried. "Ever since the CLT was first taken, I've tried to figure out who did it." She paused and looked at Nancy pleadingly. "But I know one thing—there's no reason for Professor Maszak to take it."

"You're probably right," Nancy admitted. "Maszak has the most to lose if this gets out. And if he needed the CLT for unauthorized experiments, he could have found a better way to get it."

Unless, she thought to herself, he got too greedy. Nancy remembered the telephone conversation she had overheard. CLT was rare and valuable—Maszak said so himself. He also had a sick wife whose treatment was very expensive. Nancy didn't want to alarm Sara, but Maszak had a very good reason to steal the CLT: so he could sell it and pocket the money.

With Sara eliminated, Maszak became Nancy's number-one suspect. But that didn't explain the connection to POE.

Casually, Nancy rose and picked up the earring from Sara's dresser.

"This is a great earring," she said, holding the bronze snake to her ear and modeling it in the mirror. "I've never seen one quite like it."

Sara sighed distractedly. "Oh, that's not mine. I found it in the lab this morning. It must belong to a POE member. I asked around in morning and afternoon science classes and I even put a note on the bulletin board, but no one's claimed it yet, so I brought it back here."

"Oh?" Nancy was intrigued. She turned to look at Sara. "Are there many POE members in your classes?"

"Oh, yes! Well, I mean, there are a couple hundred students in the lab each day. Freshman biology, advanced chemistry courses, there are tons of students in and out. Emerson requires everyone to complete two semesters of a lab science to graduate. The classes are extra popular this year because of Professor Maszak's reputation."

Nancy dangled the earring between her fingers. "Do you mind if I keep this until it's claimed?"

"No. I'll call you if I need it back. Maybe tomorrow—" Sara stopped suddenly.

"Is something wrong?" Nancy asked, concerned.

"Tomorrow." Sara turned her face toward Nancy's. "The professor got his new CLT two days ago. He'll be finished treating it tomorrow. That means—"

"If the thief is going to strike again, it will happen tomorrow," Nancy finished for her. She placed a hand on Sara's shoulder. "Don't worry. This time, we'll stop the person, whoever it is."

As Nancy headed back to her dorm, she wished she was as sure of herself as she had tried to make Sara believe. She had only one day to stop the thief. She was going to have to come up with some answers, and fast.

After a quick dinner, Nancy returned to her room where she collapsed in a chair. It was late, and her head was beginning to ache where she'd been hit. She decided to take a shower and go to bed. Ned had a late practice, so they wouldn't be seeing each other until the next day.

As she went to the closet to grab her robe, Nancy noticed the doorknob on the closet door was smeared with a brownish film. She hadn't seen it that morning when she left.

Uneasily, she wondered what it could be. She checked the rest of the room quickly, but nothing had been disturbed. It was probably nothing, but then again, she wasn't about to take any chances.

Looking around, Nancy spotted a pencil on her bedside table. She picked it up. Going back to the closet, she paused. Gingerly, holding the pencil away from her body, she bent the tip to scrape off a dab of the film. That way, she could examine it.

Nancy gingerly touched the pencil point to the doorknob. But the instant the tip touched the brown film, there was a huge flash. Then, with a thunderous boom, the door exploded off its hinges and came crashing—right at Nancy.

Chapter

Eight

WHO WOULD HAVE DONE such a thing? Do
you have any enemies at Emerson?" Paul Osborne, the chief security guard, bent over a pad
as he made notes on the condition of the ruined
closet door. His scalp was shiny with perspira-
tion.

Nancy perched on the end of her bed as
Osborne and another security guard checked
the damage. The dorm counselor who had
sounded the alarm hovered anxiously in the
doorway.

"I don't have any enemies here," Nancy
replied innocently, with one eye on the counselor.

Osborne lowered himself into a chair, leaving the second guard to finish the job.

"You're lucky you didn't touch the knob with your hands," he said. "That glop doesn't look like much, but it sure packs a wallop."

"Exactly what is it?" Nancy asked. "And where would someone at Emerson get it?"

"Anyone can get it," Osborne said grimly. "You could buy the ingredients at any pharmacy. Two common, safe household items, but put them together and paint it on something and once it's dry—well, you saw the results."

Nancy looked at the ruined closet and shuddered. The door was charred and burned, hanging limply on its hinges. The blow had knocked her to her feet, and she had gotten a bad fright from the shock of the explosion. The fingers on her right hand were burned slightly, but other than that, she was unhurt.

"Then this explosive could be made by anyone who knows a little chemistry," she mused. "But how did you know what it was? Have you seen it before?"

Osborne patted his forehead with a handkerchief. "Actually," he said slowly, "we've seen it three other times. Always on doorknobs. The other times, no one got hurt because they blew when no one was around. It's probably some nut who likes to make explosions. Too bad you

70

didn't come back earlier—you might have caught him in the act. I'd sure like to know who it is."

"We'll have to ask you to check the room to make sure nothing is missing, Ms. Drew," the younger guard called from inside the closet. His round face appeared around the ruined door frame. "Was there anything valuable in your closet?"

"No," Nancy said. "The door to my room wasn't even locked."

"Uh-huh," Osborne nodded knowingly. "Nothing was taken the other times, either. See what I mean? Must have been done by a crank, someone who discovered the mixture and thinks it's a big joke. You're sure you don't have any enemies here?"

Nancy hesitated but then shook her head. If Dean Jarvis had wanted campus security to know, he would have told them about the thefts in the chemistry lab.

Osborne got ready to go. "Well, I'm just glad you weren't hurt. We'll keep investigating, and I may call you later to ask you more questions. If you think of anything that could help us, just give me a call."

"You should call the police," the counselor said angrily.

"Oh, no, wouldn't want to do that," Osborne

warned. "The college likes to keep this kind of thing as quiet as possible." He straightened his shoulders. "Besides, we can handle our own 'police work.'"

"Wait, please," Nancy said. "Can you tell me which other doors were tampered with?"

Osborne looked at her with surprise. "Does it matter? Well, if you must know, the first was the main door to the library. The librarian got there and found a big hole where the knob had been. Then the computer room blew."

"No, the library wasn't first," the other guard contradicted. "The cafeteria was."

"Oh, that's right." Osborne chuckled. "The main cafeteria door was blown wide open. Now, why would anyone want to break in and steal *that* food?" He laughed heartily at his own joke.

"Was anything stolen?" Nancy persisted. Osborne shook his head. "That seems very strange. Why blow up a door if you don't want to get inside? The three must have something in common—the same area, maybe?"

"You certainly ask a lot of questions." Osborne frowned. "But, no, they're spread out all over campus. I wouldn't worry about those other explosions. The more I think about it, the more I've decided yours isn't related. They were set to damage buildings. This one seems to have been set against you."

Nancy sighed in frustration. If there was a connection, she couldn't see it. If she *was* close to catching the thief, she didn't even know it. Well, she was going to get even closer, Nancy resolved, explosion or no explosion!

Nancy spent the next morning investigating everyone who had anything to do with the lab. She spoke to the security guards who were on duty the nights of the thefts. Both men swore they were alert and awake the whole time, and that they had seen no one.

Nancy tried to get through to Dean Jarvis during the day, but he was in meetings until four. She called again at four, only to be told that the dean was on a long-distance call and couldn't be disturbed. She tried to keep her frustration under control.

"This is Nancy Drew speaking. I've been trying to reach Dean Jarvis since this morning. It's very important. I'd really appreciate it if I could hold while you let him know I'm on the line."

Nancy waited. A minute or so later someone else picked up the phone, and Nancy found herself explaining her situation all over again, only to be put back on hold. In the next few minutes she spoke with five different secretaries and told each of them it was an emergency.

Well, Nancy thought, forgiving herself for her white lie, if she didn't get ahold of the dean soon, it could very well become an emergency.

Just as she was losing her patience altogether, Nancy heard a couple of clicks as if the dean had picked up, and then another.

"Nancy?" It was the dean's voice. Quickly, she filled him in on her suspicions.

"Are you *sure* the thief will strike again tonight?" the dean asked worriedly. "I could assign all my guards to the building, but you'd have to be sure."

"No, if he sees any of them we'll never catch him," Nancy objected. "With Ned and me and a couple of security guards on duty, I don't think he can get away."

"I don't know, Nancy. I'm responsible for your safety. I'd feel a lot better if you had some backup."

Nancy promised to be careful. "We don't need help. Ned will be out near the elevators with the guard. If you assign one extra man to watch the outer doors, we ought to have plenty of warning when an intruder enters. I'll hide in Maszak's lab. That should make the lab pretty burglarproof."

"Wait," the dean said, "you'll need to know the combination to get into the interior lab. Did you get it from Josef?"

"Actually, I haven't said anything to Profes-

sor Maszak about tonight," Nancy said carefully. "It has to be absolutely secret. The fewer
people who know about it, the better."

Nancy heard a click on the line. "Dean
Jarvis?" she asked. "Are you still there?"

"Yes, why?"

"I thought I heard you hang up the telephone."

"That happens all the time—these huge telephone networks. Don't worry about it. About
tonight, though, I'll alert the campus police to
keep their eyes open and their radios on. In fact,
I want you and Ned to stop by their headquarters and pick up two walkie-talkies so you can
call for help."

After giving Nancy the combination to the
lock, the dean hung up.

At dusk Nancy and Ned met at the lab. Ned
had agreed to go along with her plan even
though Nancy couldn't explain all the details.
She had promised Dean Jarvis, after all, and
somehow didn't feel right about letting Ned in
on what was top secret work. Luckily he understood. Meanwhile, Dean Jarvis had arranged
for Craig Bergin to be the guard on duty.

"Someone got me reassigned," he told them
happily. "Just in time. It's a little too cold to
have to patrol the campus at night. I've been
asked to keep my eye on the lab."

Nancy and Ned exchanged quick looks.

"Great!" Nancy said. "I'll be working in the lab all night tonight. Um, it's a special arrangement, for that story I'm writing."

"Yes, and I'll be just outside with this, just to make sure things go smoothly," Ned said, patting the walkie-talkie.

Craig shrugged. "Suits me. I'll be glad to have someone to talk to."

Nancy worked the combination to Maszak's office effortlessly. After checking with Ned on the walkie-talkie, she promised to check back in an hour. She set the walkie-talkie down on the long counter and perched on Maszak's stool. There were papers strewn all over the top as well as two big stacks of notebooks. A quick glance told Nancy they were Maszak's students' experiments.

Nancy shuffled through the notebooks. The experiments seemed fairly standard. She checked idly through the advanced biology and chemistry classes, keeping an eye out for any names she might recognize. There were none.

Sighing, she picked up another pile of papers —Maszak's advanced biochemistry students, proposing their final projects. She went through them, noting names and grades and reading Maszak's comments. The experiments were incredible! Some of them were straight out of sci-fi films. One paper in particular caught

Nancy's attention. Maszak had slashed a purple felt-tip pen across the first page and scrawled notes in the top margin.

Looking more closely, Nancy's heart began to pound. The subject of the paper was human growth hormones.

Chapter

Nine

WITH A GROWING SENSE of excitement, Nancy read on. The paper suggested some of the same things she had read in the startling article in the library. The student planned an experiment to see if one kind of animal could accept a growth hormone from another kind of animal. Then, at the very end of the paper, she suggested someday trying a human growth hormone. Maszak's comments were angry and critical, impatiently explaining why the experiment was doomed to fail. He gave the student an incomplete and suggested she pick another topic.

Nancy frowned. If her hunch was correct, the

student wasn't wrong at all—she had simply come dangerously close to copying Maszak's own experiment. With an eerie feeling, Nancy stared at the fish and mice in the lab. Had Maszak already made a major breakthrough? Had he been using a human growth hormone on animals? Was CLT a human growth hormone?

The floorboards in the hall creaked loudly. Quickly Nancy scattered the papers across the counter again. She ducked into a closet and held her breath.

The lab door opened. She could hear someone moving around. At the same instant, she realized her walkie-talkie wasn't with her. She had left it on Maszak's counter. What an amateurish thing to do! She could kick herself.

Concentrating, Nancy pictured the counter in her mind, trying to remember where she had left the walkie-talkie before taking refuge in the closet. Hopefully, it was buried under the stacks of papers. If it wasn't hidden, the thief might realize someone was there. Even worse, Nancy realized as her stomach took a sickening plunge, there was no way now for her to contact Ned.

Pressing the light on her watch, Nancy saw it was nine o'clock. An hour had passed since she last checked in. Ned might come down to see if she was all right. Together, the two of them might be able to overpower the thief—if it *was* the thief out there.

Whoever it was, he was taking his time in the lab. Nancy heard footsteps pacing. Then there was a grunt and something fell to the floor near the closet door. Nancy froze. Pressing her ear against the door, she could hear faint scratching sounds. The seconds passed like minutes. Finally she heard the lab door open and close. Fine, she told herself. I'll just let another minute pass to make sure it's safe to come out.

But before the minute went by, a faint smell of smoke wafted through the bottom of the closet. Nancy put her hand against the closet door. It was warm to the touch. The closet door was on fire!

Nancy yelled for Ned as she snatched some lab coats off the hangers around her. Wrapping one of them around her head to protect her face from the smoke, she grabbed another pile of coats to smother the flames. Taking a deep breath, she leaned against the door. It resisted her efforts. The smoke was getting thicker now. Choking, she leaned against the door, even harder. It gave way and she stumbled into the source of the smoke.

Outside the door, the student notebooks had been piled high and set on fire. The flames licked at Nancy's ankles. She was dimly aware of a smoke alarm sending its piercing warning through the halls as she threw the lab coats down in front of her, trying to smother the burning barricade. She leapt over the note-books, landing on the floor with a thud. Groan-ing, she rolled away from the fire.

Half crawling, she made her way to the freezer unit against the far wall. With her last ounce of strength, she pried the door open. The CLT was gone.

"Nan, Nan, where are you?"

Ned and Craig burst into the room. Craig grabbed the fire extinguisher on the wall and began spraying the fire as Ned rushed to help Nancy.

"I-I'm fine." Coughing and choking from the smoke, Nancy clung gratefully to Ned. He swept her into his arms and stumbled into the hall-way.

"We'll get you to the infirmary, Nan. Just hang on." Ned's voice was choked, from the smoke or his own emotion, she couldn't tell. "You're going to be okay."

Nancy sat up in bed late the next afternoon. "The infirmary nurse says I'm just fine now," she assured Ned. "Look, I didn't even get burned, and I've slept all day."

She held up her hands, and Ned grabbed them in his and kissed them.

"The invincible Nancy Drew." He grinned.

"Goes through fire without blinking an eye. I'm beginning to wonder why I ever worry about you." Ned sank into the chair next to her bed and closed his eyes wearily.

Nancy's eyes clouded with sympathy. "I'm sorry, Ned," she said softly, "I didn't mean to drag you into this case."

Ned leaned close, grinning ruefully. "I guess it proves I'd go through raging fires for you."

How did she get such a wonderful guy? Nancy thought as she burrowed her head into Ned's shoulder. "I don't know what I would have done," she admitted. Her throat closed as she realized how close she'd come to real danger. "If you hadn't been there . . ."

"Shhh," Ned whispered. "What I don't understand is how the thief got past both me and Craig in the hall. It doesn't seem possible."

"It can happen. Don't blame yourself— please. The thief was determined," Nancy said.

Drawing Nancy close, Ned rocked her gently, landing a soft kiss on her hair. "You smell like smoke," he said, laughing.

"Ned, I'm sorry I couldn't tell you what this was about," Nancy began.

"I understand," he told her.

Nancy decided then it was time to take Ned into her confidence. Clearly, she hadn't learned the thief's identity in time to stop the next CLT theft. She was willing to admit she needed help. Quickly, she explained everything to Ned.

"Excuse me, I was told you could have visitors." Nancy and Ned looked up as Dean Jarvis stuck his head into the room. "Am I interrupting something?"

"Dean Jarvis, is there anything new?" Nancy saw him glance at Ned. "It's okay. I told Ned everything. I had to."

The dean hesitated, then nodded abruptly. "Good. Well, then, I checked with security," the dean reported. "As soon as Ned sounded the alarm, they shut all the gates and set up checkpoints at all the campus entrances. As far as we know, no one left campus with the CLT. It's in a pretty big container, after all. There's a good chance it's still on campus."

"I hope so," Nancy said fervently. "I'd hate to think that I sat in the closet while the thief got away."

"It couldn't be helped, Nancy," the dean assured her.

Nancy shrugged. "Did anyone figure out how the thief got in?"

Dean Jarvis shook his head. "No. But don't worry about it. It's not your problem anymore. I'm taking you off the case."

"What?" Nancy gasped.

"It's too dangerous," the dean said firmly.

"This person means business. I can't take the chance that you'll get hurt."

"But, Dean Jarvis, I'm really close now," Nancy objected. "I didn't really get hurt. I'm okay now. Please—I know I can wrap up the case. I just need a little more time."

The dean was unmoved. He didn't say a word, only shook his head again.

"Please, sir? It would save you a lot of trouble. And besides," Nancy added recklessly, "how will it look if you call in the government now? They'll want to know why you didn't report the thefts immediately. If I solve the case and recover the CLT, they can't say a thing."

"Well, when you put it like that . . ." Dean Jarvis began. He paused. "No, I still can't."

"I can solve this case for you," Nancy insisted. "I'm very close already."

"I don't know." The dean wavered.

Nancy smiled. "Think of Emerson. Your science program."

"All right!" The dean threw up his hands. "But only if you promise to come to me at the first sign of trouble."

Ned waited silently until Dean Jarvis had gone.

"Are you really that close, Nan?" he burst out as soon as the dean's footsteps had faded away.

"Almost." Eagerly, Nancy swung her legs off the bed. "And I will solve it soon. Right now, we'd better get over to the lab and find out how the thief got in."

"There's no use in my trying to stop you, is there?" Nancy shook her head. Sighing, Ned went out to wait in the hall while Nancy got dressed.

By the time Nancy and Ned got back to the lab, the mess from the fire had been cleaned up. She could tell from the fine white dust in the room that the campus police had checked for fingerprints.

The room still reeked of smoke. On the desk Nancy found the walkie-talkie hidden under some papers. The thief hadn't bothered to take it.

"Nothing new here," Nancy said. "Let's check with your friend Craig."

Nancy explained to Craig that Dean Jarvis had allowed them to follow up on what had happened. "The story's getting more involved than I thought," she added when he gave them a confused look.

Craig shrugged and looked as baffled as Nancy. "I checked with all the guards myself," he told her. "I even had someone watching the fire escape. The elevators, which weren't in service, were locked for the night. I have no idea how he got in."

"Well, you don't mind if we check around a bit, do you?" Ned asked.

"Not at all. Here." Craig threw his key ring to Ned. "These keys will open everything in the building. Yell if you find anything."

Out in the main hall, Nancy and Ned tried to decide where to go next. Ned leaned back against a closet door, thinking.

"It's a waste of time to check the rooms on this floor," he said. "Security's already checked them all."

Nancy's eyes lit up and a grin spread across her face. "Maybe not all," she said slowly. "Ned—take a step toward me."

"Huh?" Baffled, Ned approached, not sure if Nancy was joking or not.

"That's fine." Grinning, Nancy ducked behind him. "This closet," she said. "We've been looking so hard for big clues, we didn't try the little ones."

The closet was locked. Pulling out Craig's key ring, Nancy tried each key. None of them opened the door.

"Oh, don't worry about that door," Craig said, coming into the hall. "There's nothing behind it."

"You mean the closet is empty?" Nancy asked.

"It's not a closet," Craig said. "It's an old elevator shaft. There was a freight elevator there. You know the kind that works with a key? It hasn't been used in years."

Nancy's pulse quickened. "Is the elevator still there? Does it work?"

"I don't see how it could. They shut it down years ago because it was unsafe. No one in his right mind would get into the thing, even if he could."

Nancy was examining the door, inch by inch. "Ned, Craig—look at this," she suddenly called. "There."

Nancy pointed to a thin crack. It ran around the perimeter of the door. "Someone used this elevator recently," she insisted. "When the door opened, it cracked through these old layers of paint."

Ned and Craig exchanged a look. "You're right," Ned said. "Good work, Nan."

Nancy found a piece of wire and went to work on the lock. She twisted it until she felt something give. With a triumphant smile, she opened the door.

The elevator shaft fell off in front of her. Grabbing Ned's hand to anchor herself, she leaned in and peered down. "How do we call the elevator?"

Craig gestured to another lock on the wall just outside the door. "I guess you can pick this lock. You used to need a key to call the elevator."

Nancy set about trying to open the old lock. Finally it clicked, and she heard the old elevator car creaking up the shaft.

"Sounds like it's been used recently," she murmured. "The thief must have put it in working order."

As they watched, a black cage rose out of the gloom and glided to a halt. Nancy grabbed the handle and pulled the iron accordion door to one side. "Anyone coming with me?" she invited.

Craig and Ned looked at each other uneasily. "It's pretty old—do you think it will carry three of us?" Craig asked.

Nancy's eyes twinkled. "There's only one way to find out."

Chapter

Ten

NANCY TRIED the old elevator lever. It moved easily. Hurriedly, Ned and Craig hopped on, too. She pushed the lever to the right and the cage began to rise. Through the grate, they could see the rough cement walls of the shaft. They passed the fourth- and fifth-floor doors. The elevator stopped on the top floor. The door to the roof level was locked.

"If our thief went to the roof, he'd have to climb down without being seen," Nancy said. "Not very likely. Let's see what happens when we go down."

She threw the switch to the left. Seven

89

floors went by. The elevator settled at the bottom.

"This must be the lobby," Craig commented as he reached for the door.

Nancy shook her head. "No, the building only has six floors. I counted seven. This has to be the basement."

Craig looked at her in surprise. "There *is* no basement," he said.

Ignoring Craig for the moment, Nancy pushed against the outside door. It swung open noiselessly. Stepping out, they found themselves in a small, damp gray room. A light next to the elevator door cast dark shadows around them.

Craig whistled softly. "Well, I'll be—" he exclaimed.

"I'll bet this is the thief's escape route," Nancy whispered excitedly.

The space was empty except for a cobweb-covered fuse box on one wall. A black hole in the wall directly opposite the elevator led to a passageway. There was another passageway on their right. At the end of each, Nancy saw a thin glow of light.

"These are tunnels!" Nancy said, amazed. "It looks like they connect the basements of the buildings."

"That's right," Craig said excitedly. "I've

heard the old maintenance guys talking about using the tunnels in the old days to get from building to building. I thought they'd all been sealed up."

"They're unsealed now," Nancy said grimly. She took a step toward one.

"Nan, hold on." Grasping her elbow, Ned pulled her back. "It's late and it's dark in there. Whoever stole the CLT left almost twenty-four hours ago. Wouldn't it be better to come back tomorrow—with a good flashlight?"

Ned was right, Nancy realized. "Okay," she said reluctantly. "Let's go back to the dorm and plan our next move."

They left Craig at the lab and headed over to Holland. Nancy and Ned had barely entered the lounge when Jan and Mike burst into the room with a girl Nancy had never met. She was wearing a bulky white sweater and green wool pants, and she had curly dark red hair that swung halfway down her back.

Breathlessly, Jan introduced them. "Nancy, this is Amber Thomas. She's Angela Morrow's roommate," Jan explained. "And she's got bad news."

Nancy and Ned exchanged startled glances.

"We'd better sit down," Nancy said.

"Nancy, this isn't like Angela at all," Amber cried. "She was supposed to come back today.

91

She didn't, so I called her house." Amber took a deep breath. "Her mom hadn't seen her. Angela never went home."

"That does it," Ned declared angrily. "I'm going to find her."

Nancy knew better than to try to talk Ned out of it. "At this point," she said slowly, "I think that's the best thing for you to do. But, Ned," she added, "you should wait until morning, too."

Ned smiled. "It's a deal. I'd better get to bed so I can get an early start. Good night, Nan. And don't you guys worry—I'll call as soon as I find out anything."

After a night of troubled sleep, Nancy was hurrying to the science building. As she passed the infirmary, a commotion in the doorway caught her attention. A girl with a shower of long blond hair was pleading with the nurse at the front door. It was Karen Lewis. A brown bundle lay at her feet. Looking closer, Nancy saw it was an injured dog. Curious, Nancy walked over to see what was going on.

Karen was very distraught. She had found the dog by the side of the road and was begging the nurse to take a look at it.

"But I'm not a veterinarian," the nurse kept repeating. "I treat *people*. I don't know the first thing about dogs."

"There must be something you can do," Karen insisted wildly. "If you don't, the poor thing's going to die."

Nancy was right behind them now. "Excuse me," she cut in. Karen whirled around at the sound of her voice. "Maybe there *is* something you could do," she suggested. "Could you describe the dog's condition to a vet? There must be one in Emersonville we could call."

"Well, I guess so," the nurse said uncertainly.

"I'll pay for the call," Karen burst out. The nurse nodded and went inside.

Karen stood silently next to Nancy, avoiding her eyes.

"Is it your dog?" Nancy asked lightly, trying not to put Karen off.

Karen shook her head. "I found it. I was hiking all morning, and when I returned I saw it beside the highway on the edge of the campus."

"And you carried it here?" Nancy was surprised.

"Does everyone think I'm crazy to help this dog?" Karen challenged. "If it was your dog, you'd be happy."

"Sorry," Nancy offered. "You did the right thing."

The nurse returned, smiling happily. "I reached a vet, and he said he was going out and would stop by here." She bent down and put her hands on the dog's side. "He said to check his

93

THE NANCY DREW FILES

gums to make sure they aren't too white or too red, take his pulse, and keep him warm."

As Karen bent to stroke the injured animal, Nancy backed away. Karen was certainly sincere in her love for animals. She was even softhearted about animals that didn't belong to her. Perhaps Nancy was wrong to distrust POE and its members. Ned might be confusing his concern for Angela with his feelings about the group.

There was too much going on, Nancy told herself with a sigh. First the CLT mystery, now the trouble with Angela and POE. At least she felt closer to solving *one* mystery now.

Nancy decided against tackling the tunnels under Emerson without more information. She went to the library and buried herself in a pile of books about the architecture of Emerson. After two books, she found what she was looking for—a series of drawings showing the extensive tunnel system. It spread to every one of the original buildings on campus. The map also confirmed that none of the tunnels went beyond the campus. The thief had to be holding the stolen CLT somewhere on the grounds, Nancy decided.

She was eager to begin her search of the tunnels, but an uneasy feeling nagged at her. She had to check a little further. On a hunch, she went to the section where microfilms of the local newspapers were kept. In the *Emersonian,* the school's paper, she found a feature article on Josef Maszak. It mentioned that he had come from Jamison College, another midwestern school, where he had taught for three years. The Jamison students had given him the Beller Award for excellence in teaching three years in a row.

Nancy remembered the loyalty both Sara and Angela had shown toward Maszak. He really did inspire his students, she realized. Jamison College was in the same sports league as Emerson, and the library kept a record of its rival's papers. Nancy searched that microfilm, too, stopping at the issues that came out when Maszak was at Jamison.

A headline caught her eye: BACTERIA DE-STROYED IN LAB. She felt a tingle of excitement as she read.

One of the school's most important ex-periments involving five different kinds of bacteria had to be destroyed yesterday in the science lab. A sample of rheumatic fever, a disease caused by bacteria, had begun growing out of control. Professor Aaron Miller, who was in charge of the project, was quoted as saying, "We have no idea what happened. The bacteria grew so quickly that we had to take extreme measures to destroy it. Unfortunately, by destroying the bacteria, we also destroyed the cause of its abnormal growth. Now we'll never know what brought this about." No damage or injuries were reported.

There was no mention of Josef Maszak, but he had been at Jamison at this time. Nancy flipped through the rest of the film. Toward the end of the reel, an ad caught her eye. It announced a lecture series on Third World countries. Dr. Pranav Mohammed would discuss famine relief that Tuesday, and consumer advocate Philip Bangs would lecture on the evils of chemical weapons. The lecture series was sponsored by POE.

Nancy froze. Environmentalist groups were probably common at schools, but she was sure Philip Bangs had said Karen Lewis had created POE at Emerson. He had even said there were no other POE groups! He had been lying.

With a start, Nancy remembered the earring Sara had found in the lab. No one had ever claimed it. Was it because its owner couldn't admit to having been in the lab?

This was more than a coincidence, Nancy thought with certainty. The same secret group, the same speaker, and the same professor—they had to be connected, but how?

Chapter

Eleven

NANCY NEARLY FLEW across campus. She held her purse steady, glad she had taken the time to make a copy of the tunnel map.

On the map, she noticed the tunnels led to a dorm only fifty feet from Adams Cottage, where Professor Maszak lived. Nancy intended to take that route herself. If it was unblocked, Maszak would have both a motive and an opportunity for stealing the CLT himself. He'd have a lot of explaining to do, Nancy thought grimly. Philip Bangs might very well be part of his explanation.

After heading straight for the science building, Nancy picked the lock on the freight elevator and stepped inside. The elevator creaked down to the basement. Nancy slid the door open and stepped out cautiously, waiting for her eyes to adjust to the weak light. She pulled out her map and held it under the bare yellow bulb mounted on the cement wall.

According to the drawing, the tunnel in front of her led back toward the center of campus, winding under the gym, toward the administration building. The tunnel opposite went to the dorm next to the professor's house. Nancy pulled out the flashlight she had brought along and played it along the uneven ground. The light was just bright enough to show her the way.

Moving to the mouth of the tunnel, she bounced the small circle of light along the walls. Stepping carefully, her pumps slipped a little on the rocky foundation. From somewhere she heard a dripping noise. A broken pipe? she wondered. She touched the wall gingerly. It was dry.

There was an odd rustling in the corridor. Nancy swung the flashlight around her but saw nothing. The sound didn't repeat itself. Cautiously, she continued. There was a faint light ahead and she could tell that she was approaching another building.

The tunnel opened up and Nancy stepped

into another basement area, lit by a makeshift light, which was no more than a bare bulb attached to a long orange extension cord. The ground was sandier here. Bending down, she made out scuff marks in the dirt. So someone had been here before her! Nancy examined her map. She should be standing directly under the English building.

Could the scuff marks mean someone had come down from *this* building? The basement was empty, without even a fuse box to bring a maintenance worker there on legitimate business. Nancy tried the door. It was sealed shut.

The English building was the last exit before the long, dead-end corridor toward Adams Cottage. She tried to look down the tunnel, but the beam from the flashlight didn't penetrate very far into the darkness. The weak basement light illuminated only the first few feet of the tunnel, but she saw that the footprints led into it. Her muscles tensed.

As silently as possible, Nancy crept down the corridor. She doubted there was anyone down there with her, but she remembered the rustling she had heard. She wasn't going to take any chances. Gingerly, she stepped over the small rocks in the foundation floor.

It was getting harder to see, Nancy realized

suddenly. The light from the flashlight had dimmed considerably. She shook the flashlight but nothing happened. The batteries were fading. Looking behind her, she could no longer see the bulb from under the English building. She decided to forge ahead, anyway.

Shining the light ahead of her, she could see only two or three feet at the most. The tunnel unrolled before her in endless blackness.

The flashlight dimmed even more, and after she had gone only a few more feet, it flickered twice and died. With a sense of dread, Nancy fished out the penlight she always kept in her purse. Its thin beam barely pierced the blackness around her. She stood absolutely still, trying to picture the map in her mind. She couldn't be too far away from the dorm, she reasoned. It would be best to save the penlight for an emergency use and grope her way down the rest of the tunnel.

In the darkness the rustling sounded again behind her. Nancy's pulse pounded in her neck. Was there someone following her? The rustling stopped, but to her horror, Nancy heard a squeaking sound. It could only mean one thing: There had to be mice—or rats, even—in the tunnel with her.

She stopped and reached for the penlight, at the same time telling herself to stay calm. The rats weren't going to attack her, especially if she kept moving. She shone the thin beam ahead of her down the corridor.

Almost running now, she stumbled along the corridor. Her shoes made so much noise against the rough stones she couldn't tell if the rats were running with her. Stay calm, she told herself. You've been in worse situations. It wasn't a very comforting thought.

A rough stone caught the toe of one shoe. Before she could throw out a hand to stop herself, Nancy tripped and sprawled out, face forward, on the damp tunnel floor. The penlight flew from her hand and skidded over the stones. The faint light wavered and died as the tunnel was plunged into total darkness.

Nancy scrambled to her feet. With a sinking heart, she realized she had to keep moving. Unless . . . Trying to squelch her rising panic, she felt in her purse. She took out the map and folded it in half over and over until she had formed a little column of paper. Then she began to twist, until she had made a sort of paper candle. She dipped into her purse for the matchbook she had picked up when she and Ned and Angela were talking in the cafeteria. There were only two matches.

Cautiously, Nancy struck the first match. She heard a hiss and smelled sulfur, but nothing happened. She tried it again. Still the match wouldn't light. Blindly, she touched the match with her fingertip and felt the cardboard stem. She must have knocked the tip off when she struck it.

She had only one match now. She tore it out of the book and struck it on the flint strip. A tiny flame sprang up in front of her face. With great care, she touched it to the folded map and a glow grew into a light just big enough to see by. Holding up her hand to shield the makeshift candle from a draft, she scrambled through the corridor as quickly as she could.

The paper burned quickly. Soon there were only a few inches left. Then Nancy felt the ground even out under her feet. Something glinted dully off to her left. Breathlessly, she ran toward it. Just as she reached the source of light, the flame hit her fingers. She dropped the burning paper, and it fizzled on the cement. The darkness fell around her like a curtain, but it didn't matter now. She knew she was in the dorm basement.

Groping toward the dim reflection, Nancy found the door to the basement elevator. She tried the handle, but it didn't turn. This door hadn't been used lately; the elevator shaft was still sealed.

Nancy realized there might not be a way to get into the dorm from the tunnel. If not, she would have to retrace her steps back the way she had come, with no light this time, taking her chances with the rats. It wasn't something she looked forward to.

Nancy closed her eyes, trying to calm herself. Now she *was* panicking, she thought. From the ceiling to her left she spotted a very faint crack of light. Feeling her way in its direction, she banged her leg badly on something cold and hard. Cursing herself, she rubbed the sore leg, then explored whatever it was she'd bumped into.

Iron stairs! Leading up out of the tunnel. Relief flooded through her as she clambered up them. The glimmer of light she had noticed before formed the outline of a box now—a hatchway cover, Nancy realized. Holding her hands above her head, she fumbled for the latch. Her fingers scraped along the ceiling but finally she found it. She threw it to one side and pushed.

Light flooded the stairway. Squinting against the sudden shock of it, Nancy scrambled out and threw the trapdoor shut.

She was on a quiet lawn, outside the dorm. Resting for a moment, Nancy tried to quiet her pounding heart. Only a few yards from her was the tall, wrought iron fence that surrounded Emerson. Through the fence she could see the thick line of trees that separated the POE headquarters from the college.

As she rounded the corner of the dorm,

Nancy was more determined than ever to speak to Josef Maszak. The tunnel was the thief's most logical escape route, it had obviously been used recently, and it led almost to Maszak's door. One of those facts could be a coincidence —but all three? Nancy didn't think so.

Emerson's main entrance lay about one hundred yards away. And halfway between it and Nancy was Professor Maszak's house.

She marched up Maszak's steps and knocked briskly on the door. A face peered out through the curtains. Nancy lifted up her hand to knock again when the door swung open.

Maszak stared at Nancy. "Yes, Ms. Drew?"

"Professor Maszak," Nancy began boldly, "I have some questions, and I think you're the only one with the answers."

Maszak stepped back. "Please come in."

Nancy walked into a dim living room and sat in the chair he indicated. Maszak made no move to sit. Instead, he stood between her and the door.

"Well?"

Nancy took a deep breath. "Suppose we start with Jamison College," she said. "And the mysterious growth of that bacteria."

At Nancy's question, Maszak's face turned a deathly shade of white. Then he lunged for her, his hands outstretched. Maszak was going to strangle Nancy!

104

Chapter
Twelve

NANCY PUT HER HANDS UP to protect herself.
Maszak must have realized what he was about
to do, because he pulled back, then threw himself into a chair facing her. He stared at Nancy
in stunned surprise.

"The Jamison experiment—how did you find
out?"

"I *am* a detective," Nancy said wryly.

As Nancy watched, Maszak's expression had
changed from defiant anger to helpless defeat.
He slumped deeper in his chair, and all his
usual bluster faded. The professor looked
drawn, even sickly.

"It was a brilliant discovery. And I couldn't pass up experiments with CLT. Yes, some of the CLT had come in contact with the bacteria and produced the abnormal growth. I've been terrified someone here would find out. Then you walked into my office, and I knew you were going to be trouble. I knew you'd uncover the theft."

"That's what I came here for," Nancy said.

Maszak shook his head impatiently. "No, not *this* theft. I mean the theft at Jamison."

The theft at Jamison? Nancy hid her confusion. "Well, the Jamison newspapers put two and two together for me," she bluffed.

"Ah, yes. Of course," the professor said sadly.

"Maybe you'd better start at the beginning," Nancy suggested, trying to sound as if she knew what Maszak was talking about.

Maszak nodded. "I came to America because of my wife's illness," he began. "It was very difficult to get all the necessary permission to teach here. Finally, because of my specialty, we were approved.

"We spent two and a half happy years at Jamison. Linda, my wife, was being treated successfully at the hospital. And I loved teaching."

"That wasn't the first time you began working with growth hormones, was it?" Nancy guessed.

"No, I worked with them in Hungary. It was

the first time I'd had such success, however. And then, just as things were ready to take off, someone stole the CLT."

"But no one ever knew what happened at Jamison," Nancy said, frowning. "Not even Dean Jarvis here at Emerson."

"No, he knew nothing." Maszak sighed. "It was terrible. I walked into my lab at Jamison one morning and the place was a shambles. Whoever broke in had torn the lab apart. The department head wanted to keep it quiet, though he requested a thorough list of everything that was stolen. Of course, I omitted the loss of the CLT."

"But if you didn't take it, why would you cover up the theft?" Nancy asked. "You might have stopped the thief then."

"I thought I would lose my job," the professor said miserably. "I was afraid because of my mistake with the bacteria that people would think I was extremely careless to have the CLT stolen, too. I couldn't afford to take the risk."

"No one would have blamed you for something beyond your control," Nancy assured him.

"Maybe, maybe not." Maszak shrugged. "I'm not used to your freedom here. I couldn't take the chance." He fell silent.

Nancy waited for him to continue. "Is that why you left Jamison?" she prompted.

"Yes. When Emerson applied for a visiting scientist, I asked to come here. But the thefts followed me."

Nancy was almost convinced that Maszak was telling the truth. Why would he risk his whole career and livelihood by stealing the CLT? Still, there was one thing that nagged at her. Nancy hesitated. "Professor, can you explain the argument I overheard you having yesterday on the pay phone?"

The professor reddened. "I was talking to the accountant at the hospital. Emerson hasn't sent the papers for us to be reimbursed by our health insurance yet. I owe a lot of money to the hospital still, but I don't think I should have to pay it with my money when my insurance covers it. The hospital will be paid eventually, but they want their money now. It's a mess."

Maszak could be accused of poor judgment, Nancy thought, but he didn't have to steal the CLT for money. He had insurance.

Nancy looked at Maszak, rumpled and slumped in his chair. She needed more information. Something still didn't make sense.

"Tell me, professor, how did you get involved with Bangs's group?" she asked innocently.

"Bangs's group? What group?" The professor looked genuinely blank.

"I mean POE," Nancy said slowly. "Philip Bangs was at Jamison at the same time the bacteria was discovered growing abnormally and the CLT was stolen. I don't think it's coincidence that he's here now, at the same time as the Emerson thefts."

Professor Maszak gave Nancy a startled look. "What do you mean?"

"I mean," Nancy replied patiently, "that Bangs is known for fighting technology that threatens the environment. He might feel the CLT threatens the future safety of animals. He might be after you to try to prevent you from continuing your experiments."

Maszak stared at her, and then a smile began to spread across his face. He was actually laughing!

"Ms. Drew," he said when he had gotten ahold of himself, "CLT doesn't harm the animals. It is only used to stimulate growth in cells. That's all."

Nancy was determined. "Professor, someone has tried very hard to get rid of me. There must be more to CLT than even you are aware of. Would you come with me to the lab? Maybe you'll see something I've missed."

Maszak gladly accompanied Nancy to the science building. Together, they combed the lab, though neither Maszak nor Nancy was sure what to look for.

"Look for anything that seems out of place," Nancy advised the professor as she stood in the walk-in freezer. "Or anything you've never seen before."

She scanned the third shelf from the bottom, where the CLT containers had been kept. She spotted a short, curly black hair frozen onto a shelf. Carefully, she chipped it off.

"I might take this to the police to be analyzed," she murmured. "Though it could belong to anyone—a student, a janitor, someone who had never even entered the lab."

"It is good to be thorough," the professor agreed.

"Do you have an envelope?" Nancy asked.

"An envelope? I must have an envelope somewhere." The professor looked around him helplessly. "I never realized I had so many papers."

"Here, let me look," Nancy offered. She began rummaging through his drawers.

They were crammed with test papers, lab books, copies of scientific articles. Nancy smiled to herself.

As she opened another drawer, Nancy noticed a piece of Maszak's stationery lying right on the top where it couldn't be missed. She picked it up by one corner. She was positive it hadn't been there before. In the center of the page, an address in Caracas, Venezuela, and three numbers had been neatly typed.

"Professor Maszak," Nancy asked, looking up, "what's this?"

Maszak looked at the paper in her hand. "I don't know," he answered. "I'm sure I've never seen it before."

Nancy looked at him questioningly. A man as messy as the professor couldn't really be trusted to remember which papers were his.

"No, I'm sure I've never seen it," Maszak said. He stared at the paper. "That is a date," he went on, "written European style, day first, month second." He frowned. "It's tomorrow's date. Why would someone put that in my drawer?"

Nancy looked at him thoughtfully. "It's my guess, professor, that the paper was planted by the thief."

"But why?" Maszak looked thoroughly puzzled.

"We don't know that yet," Nancy told him. "But if something were to happen tomorrow, maybe something dangerous or illegal, and this paper was found in your desk, it might be enough evidence to incriminate you."

Maszak shook his head impatiently. "I don't understand what you're saying."

Nancy grinned. "You can't frame someone with false information," she explained. "We have to assume this address has some real meaning. Now all we have to do is find out what that is—before tomorrow."

Maszak rubbed a hand over his forehead. "I'll be ruined. No one will ever hire me again."

Nancy placed a reassuring hand on Maszak's shoulder. "I don't know exactly how yet," she said, "but I'm convinced I can solve this whole puzzle."

She checked her watch. It was already midafternoon. "I've got to hurry, but don't worry," she told him. "I won't let anyone ruin your career."

Nancy left Maszak in his lab and hurried back to her dorm to pick up her car. Then she sped to Omega Chi to find Ned. Mike, Jan, and Amber Thomas were in the living room.

Jan and Amber sprang up as soon as they saw Nancy. "Thank goodness," Jan cried. "Ned called, and we didn't know how to reach you."

Mike struggled to stand up with his cane. "He said he was going to go over there," Mike said excitedly. "To POE headquarters. He thinks he's going to find Angela and bring her back."

"Is he there now?" Nancy asked.

"I'm not sure," Mike admitted. "He could be there, or he might still be at basketball practice. . . ." His voice trailed off. "Do you think I should go over there to see what's up?" he asked Nancy.

Nancy made a quick decision. "I have something to do first," she said, trying to soothe him. "If Ned already went to see Angela, he would have come right back. And besides, we don't know if he went there yet."

"I could find him," Mike suggested.

Walking with his cane, Nancy thought, Mike would be more of a problem than a help.

Her thoughts must have showed, for Mike suddenly looked embarrassed. "Just say the word, Nancy, and I'll do anything. If my best friend's in trouble, I'll help any way I can."

"You can help right now. I need directions to the police station in town," Nancy said.

Amber jumped up. "I know where it is. I have a friend who works there. Why don't Jan and I go with you?"

"Great," Nancy said enthusiastically. "And Mike, you wait here for Ned."

The three girls piled into the car and headed for town. Nancy was forcing herself not to worry about Ned. The information she needed now was crucial. Oh, Ned, she thought sadly, why couldn't you have waited until tomorrow to go to POE headquarters?

If Nancy's instincts were right, POE could be very dangerous. Even fatal.

Chapter
Thirteen

As THEY SPED TOWARD TOWN, Nancy tried to focus on the task ahead. The key to the mystery could be that address in Caracas. When she found out what it meant she would have the last answer to her questions. And the police had a computer that could give her that information.

The police station was a sprawling stone building in the center of Emersonville. Nancy parked and the three girls climbed the long low steps and hurried into the bustling receiving room.

Nancy racked her brain for some way to get access to the computer without giving away the case. At that moment, a handsome young sergeant with black hair strolled through the area.

"Joe!" Amber gave him a quick hug before turning to Nancy and Jan.

"This is Joe Ross," she said. "He'll help you, Nancy."

Joe flashed them a dazzling smile and ushered them down the hall. He was *very* handsome, Nancy decided. She glanced at Amber and saw the soft look in her lovely eyes. Clearly, Joe Ross was more than just a friend.

Joe held the computer room door open for them. "Jan says you need information about a foreign address," he said to Nancy. "But I don't see why you need the police."

Jan knew Nancy was a detective, but she didn't know Nancy was working on a case. With a quick glance at Amber and Joe, Nancy decided she had to break her cover to get the information she needed. Quickly she admitted she was really at Emerson to investigate a theft, leaving out details of Maszak's top secret experiment.

"I'm sorry I can't tell you more about the case," Nancy said sincerely, "but believe me, it's a matter of life or death. You can call the River Heights police to verify what I'm saying."

Joe looked abashed. "I'll have to," he admitted, "or I'll catch it."

He left the room to make the call. In a few

minutes he was back. "Okay," he said, turning to Nancy. "I'll help. What do you need?"

Nancy handed him a piece of paper. "I need to know who or what is at this address."

"Hmm." Joe frowned, running a hand absently through his glossy black hair. "The computer doesn't have a lot of information on foreign addresses, but let's see what it comes up with."

Joe sat down at one of the terminals and entered the address. "Here comes the information now."

Nancy read the computer screen. "The Shiranti Corporation. But who are they and what do they do? Can you find out for me?"

Joe looked apologetic. "I'll do my best," he declared. "But it'll take time. You'll have to wait."

"We don't have time," Nancy said, frowning. "Could you call me instead?"

After giving him phone numbers where she could be reached, Nancy thanked Joe, and the girls headed back to the car.

"Amber, you were a great help," Nancy said admiringly. "Thanks a lot."

"I enjoyed it," Amber said. "Being a detective is exciting."

"Especially when you get to see your boyfriend," Jan teased.

Nancy smiled distractedly as they got back in

the car and drove toward Emerson. Caracas, she mulled. Why was Caracas sending warning bells off in her mind? Then, in a flash, it hit her. South America. Angela said that Philip Bangs had settled in South America before coming back to the United States. She felt a tingle of excitement. All her hunches were playing out. Naturally Bangs, who headed antitechnology groups, would want to destroy the CLT if it harmed animals. He might even destroy it as part of the demonstration Angela had said POE was planning against Senator Claiborne.

"Amber." Nancy glanced at her excitedly. "The minute we get back to Emerson, would you call Joe and see what he learned about the Shiranti Corporation?"

At Amber's confused look, Nancy explained her suspicions about POE. Both girls continued to look dumbfounded but promised to help any way they could.

As soon as they got back to Emerson, Amber disappeared to call Joe. "Here goes," she said when she returned. "Joe found out the Shiranti Corporation is owned by a Caracas family by the name of Rojas. Shiranti is a pharmaceutical company. Does that help?"

Nancy frowned. "Pharmaceuticals," she repeated. "Drugs and medicines."

"Right," Amber said. "They supply drugs to Third World countries to fight disease."

117

A thrill shot down Nancy's spine. Leaping to her feet, she grabbed Amber in a hug.

"That's it!" she exclaimed. "Amber, you just cracked the case. I've got to call Dean Jarvis right away."

Since it was late Nancy had to call the dean at home. She arranged to meet him in his office in five minutes. Leaving Jan and Amber to wait in the dorm for any word from Ned, she hurried to the administration building. She was waiting on the front stairs in the early twilight when Dean Jarvis arrived. Nancy followed him past the night watchman in the lobby and waited while he unlocked his office and closed the door behind them.

"Dean Jarvis," she began, "you told me you get copies of Maszak's experiment logs every day. I need to see where you keep them."

The dean looked distressed. "Why, I keep everything in a locked file." He showed Nancy the filing cabinet.

"No one can get into it," he insisted. "Plus, my office door is locked. And the guard outside is on duty every night at six P.M."

"What about during school hours when you *are* here?" Nancy pressed patiently.

"Well, uh," the dean hedged. "No one is going to slip into my office unnoticed, if that's what you mean."

"Yes, that is what I mean," Nancy said. "Our

culprit needs constant access to those files to know when the professor has finished treating the CLT. What about your secretary?"

"She's been with me for fifteen years," the dean said hotly. "If she was going to steal secrets, she could certainly have started long before this."

Nancy kept her voice cool and neutral, trying not to alarm the dean more than he already was.

"But it could have been someone else who works here, someone dropping things off, delivering messages or packages. You told me yourself, this place is full of people during the day. You couldn't possibly keep your eye on all of them."

The dean dropped his head into his hands and groaned. "You're right," he said. "And I keep everything in that file—everything our thief would need. The schedule of CLT shipments, the codes for the combination locks, notes on the experiment, everything!"

"If someone who works here is working with the thief, it would certainly explain how they knew when I was in the lab closet," Nancy continued. "I told you on the telephone exactly where all of us would be that night. He could have listened in."

The dean looked devastated. "I put your life in danger," he said softly. "I'm terribly sorry." He rummaged through his desk and drew out a list of names. "Here. This is everyone who works here."

Nancy scanned the list. She stopped at the *L*'s. She had found what she was looking for.

Karen Lewis.

"Karen Lewis works in this office?"

The dean nodded. "Yes, for the past five semesters." He shook his head in confusion. "She's a terrific worker, a great kid. I can't believe she'd be mixed up in something illegal."

Nancy nodded. "I know," she said, remembering how concerned Karen had been over the injured dog at the infirmary. "It is hard to believe."

Promising the dean she would explain more later, Nancy ran back to Ned's fraternity house. She burst in to find Mike O'Shea pacing the floor.

"Nancy!" he cried out as she walked in the door. "I heard from Ned, but it doesn't sound good."

Nancy's heart contracted in fear. "What do you mean?"

Mike rubbed his face in agitation. "One of our frat brothers took a phone message from Ned. It was for you, but he left a number, so I called it."

"What did Ned say?"

Distressed, Mike shook his head. "That's just it—Ned didn't say anything. Someone picked up, but then there was silence on the other end. When I said hello, the phone went dead."

"Mike, give me the number," Nancy cried. With trembling fingers, Nancy dialed. The phone rang once, and someone lifted the receiver. There was silence.

Nancy took a deep breath to steady her voice. "This is Nancy Drew speaking," she said.

A distorted voice came over the wire.

"How lovely to hear from you," the voice said. "We have your boyfriend here, Ms. Drew. But if you don't drop your investigation and leave Emerson immediately, you'll never see him again."

Chapter

Fourteen

HER HAND TREMBLING, Nancy put down the receiver. The eerie voice echoed in her ears.

"Was that Ned?" Mike cried. "What's going on?"

Nancy wet her lips, trying to get the words out. "They have Ned," she said in a choked voice. "They threatened me. They said if I don't drop the case now, I'll never see him again."

Mike exploded. "I knew something was wrong," he said. "I should have gone looking for him."

During the conversation Jan and Amber had come in. Jan hurried to Mike's side. "I'm glad you stayed here," she said to console him. "Whoever it is sounds dangerous. Besides, we can help Ned more if we're all together. Right, Nancy?"

They all turned to look at Nancy. She was only dimly aware of them. The disembodied voice was stuck in her head, the warning running over and over again.

"I'm going to call the police," Amber blurted out.

Nancy suddenly sprang back to life. "No," she cried. "Don't. I believe that voice. If we call the police, we may never get Ned out of there."

"Then what are we going to do?" Amber looked as if she might cry, and for a second, Nancy was afraid she might burst into tears herself. With tremendous effort, she forced herself to act stronger than she felt.

"We aren't going to do anything," she said finally. *"I'm* going over there alone to try to get him out."

"You're not leaving me behind," Mike declared. "Not when my best friend's life is in danger!"

"And we won't let you go alone," Jan added. "It's too dangerous."

"Thanks, Jan," Nancy answered, "but the more people there are, the more likely it is that they'll spot us." Nancy didn't want to remind Mike that with his bad leg, he would be less of a help than a hindrance. "I've got to go alone."

"Oh, no, you won't," Jan declared hotly. "You need some kind of backup, and Amber and I are coming. We won't stay behind, so you might as well agree now."

One look at Jan's face told Nancy it was useless to argue.

"Okay," she said. "The two of you come with me. Mike, you can do more good by staying here to sound the alarm if we aren't back soon. Okay?"

Mike looked at her without replying but made no move to follow them out the door.

The girls got into Nancy's car. Without speaking, they drove to POE's headquarters. There were a number of cars parked along the driveway near the entrance. Nancy pulled up behind them.

"I'll have to park on the curb," she said. "We don't want anyone blocking us in."

Getting out of the car, Nancy took a deep breath. She was more shaken than she wanted to admit. The strain of worrying about Ned was making it hard for her to concentrate. And right then she needed to concentrate, more than ever.

The sun had finished setting and the moon was almost full. Its light bathed the trees around them and exposed the buildings clearly.

"What do we do?" Amber asked quietly.

As clearly as she could, Nancy explained the layout of the place, trying to remember as much as possible from her brief visit there.

"If they're holding Ned here, he's probably in one of the smaller buildings they use for sleeping," Nancy explained in a whisper. "I'm going into the large warehouse building," she continued. "If I haven't come out in ten minutes, get out of here—fast. If you find Ned, take him with you and go for help."

"Nancy, it's not safe to leave you alone," Jan protested.

"You'll have to," Nancy said quietly. "I'm not just here to rescue Ned." She had to pause to wet her lips again. "I've got to stop a thief, too."

For a long moment Amber and Jan looked at each other in silence.

"Be careful," Jan finally whispered.

"You, too," Nancy replied.

Nancy had never felt so alone as she did watching Jan and Amber go. Part of her wanted desperately to go with them, to find Ned and forget about CLT and Philip Bangs and the rest of them. But there might be a lot more at stake than just Ned's safety.

She forced herself to wait until Jan and Amber disappeared safely into the first low-lying building. She was about to rise from her crouched position when headlights lit up the drive. A car swung into the driveway, and Nancy ducked behind the tree line.

The car backed off a bit and pulled to the side of the drive. It must be a member, she thought, waiting for someone to emerge from the car, but no one got out. She was going to have to pass right in front of it to get to the doorway.

Lying flat, Nancy began inching her way along the ground. Keeping to the shadows, she made her way toward the main building. It was ablaze with light. The sound of many voices talking drifted outside.

There definitely was a meeting going on, which explained why all the cars were there. Nancy crept around the side of the building and surveyed the path to the front door. Three or four students were hanging out in the entrance. She had to get past them, as well as stand up in front of whoever was waiting in the car on the drive. She'd have to risk it.

Nancy remembered the earring Sara had found in the lab. She still had it in her purse. She slipped it on. Maybe she could pass as a member.

The students around the door barely glanced at her as she walked past them into the room. Breathing a sigh of relief, she crept toward the back of the room and took a seat on a straw mat.

The audience now sat patiently facing an empty podium, waiting expectantly and occasionally murmuring softly to one another. As Nancy watched, a young man got up and stood before the crowd. Nancy recognized him as Bob, the guy she thought was hurt on the road her first day at Emerson.

"Greetings, brothers and sisters," he called. "Now that the preliminaries are out of the way, let's get down to business. It's time to talk about tomorrow's demonstration."

Around Nancy, the crowd burst into loud cheers.

"Tomorrow is a historic occasion for all of us," Bob continued. He paced back and forth in front of them. "Tomorrow, we will capture the attention of the nation. When we stage our protest against Senator Claiborne, the country will know that POE means business. Someone has to protect our environment, and we're the ones to start doing it!"

The students around Nancy jumped to their feet, yelling and waving their arms. Awkwardly, Nancy followed their lead.

She realized they were discussing the plan for their faked gun battle.

"Listen carefully," Bob called when the crowd had quieted. "This event must be carefully orchestrated. You all must do exactly what

127

you're told. Remember, you have a job to do. Now, we need a head count. Everyone who has volunteered as a 'victim,' raise your hand."

As hands went up, Nancy realized she had sat in the middle of a group of victims. To her horror, Karen Lewis got up in front of the meeting to count the hands. Nancy hunched her shoulders and looked down, hoping to escape notice.

"Thank you," Bob called as the count was taken. "The water guns for the attackers are in the closet at the back of the room. All of you who are attackers, pick up a gun and make sure you bring it to the auditorium tomorrow by four-thirty P.M. Don't attract attention by talking together or loitering in the halls."

"Victims" and "attackers," Nancy thought. Exactly what were they planning to do? And what did the demonstration have to do with the CLT?

"Finally," Bob called, "and this is the most important thing—it must look absolutely real. We will warn the senator that unless he puts an end to his reckless plans to destroy our parkland, there will be war in this country. We want him to think this is really happening. I want the people around you screaming in terror. I want them to believe that unless they stop Senator Claiborne and others like him, they'll see a war in this nation and blood on their hands!"

Nancy stared in astonishment. Didn't they realize how dangerous their plan was? If the campus police thought they were using real guns for a real attack, they could begin firing. Most likely, the rest of the audience would panic. It would be absolute chaos. People might be seriously hurt, even killed. Didn't anyone see the danger in that?

Stunned, Nancy looked at the students caught up in their fervor. Obviously, not one of them was thinking clearly.

In the middle of her despair, Nancy noticed Karen Lewis get up and go down the stairs to the basement. Had she recognized Nancy? Getting up quietly, Nancy slipped away from the group and followed Karen.

At the bottom of the stairs, Nancy had to choose between a long hallway that stretched straight ahead and one that veered off to the left. Each hallway had a series of doors along it. At the end of the straight corridor, Nancy saw a thin line of light under a door.

Nancy crept toward the light, flattening herself along the wall and peering into the windows in each door. Through one window, Nancy recognized lab equipment on a counter. Her heart began to pound.

But the room was empty. Nancy continued searching for Karen. Anxiously, she quickened her pace. There was only one door left, at the very end of the hall. She heard nothing from inside.

Taking a deep breath, she slowly pushed the door with her foot. It swung open immediately. The sound of her pounding heart seemed to fill the corridor. When no one reacted to the open door, Nancy gathered her courage and burst inside. Her eyes widened.

On the floor in the corner, their hands tied and their mouths gagged, were Angela and Ned. And they weren't moving!

Chapter

Fifteen

Nancy crashed through the door.

Quickly she rushed to untie them. Not only were they gagged and their hands tied behind their backs but their feet were lashed together as well. Someone was making sure they couldn't even *try* to escape.

Nancy pulled Ned's gag off first.

"Ned," she whispered desperately. "Ned, can you talk? It's me, Nancy."

Ned groaned faintly but made no attempt to speak. They were drugged, Nancy realized. She turned to work on Angela's gag. Gently, she slapped Angela's face. No response. Without

131

their help, she'd never get them out. They were much too heavy to carry.

Amber and Jan would be peeking in the meeting room any minute, but they'd never know to look for Nancy in the basement. And if she went upstairs to get them, something could happen to Ned and Angela while she was gone. Karen Lewis might already be rounding up people to stop her.

As Nancy untied Ned's hands and propped him up against the wall her mind was racing. She'd intended to search for the CLT, but now that she'd found Ned and Angela she could hardly abandon them—and she certainly didn't want to.

Ned's handsome face was slack and a dark bruise swelled on his right cheekbone.

"Ned, oh, Ned, please wake up," she pleaded softly. His eyelids fluttered briefly. "That's it, Ned," she encouraged him. "You've got to help me."

She had bent to loosen the ropes around his feet when she heard the sound of footsteps in the corridor outside. Nancy whirled, searching out a hiding place. Just in time, she ducked behind a stack of cartons.

Karen Lewis stood in the doorway.

"What is this? Ned, Angela?" Karen cried in disbelief. "Oh, no—what happened to you?" From the tone in her voice, Karen seemed genuinely distressed. Nancy peered behind the boxes to see Karen rush to Ned's side, her hand over her mouth.

"Ned," Karen whispered, bending over him. "Can you hear me? Who did this to you?"

Relief flooded through Nancy. Karen had no part in tying up Angela or Ned. She stood up.

"Karen," she whispered desperately. "Don't be alarmed—you've got to help me get them out of here. It's Bangs, he—" The words died in her throat.

Philip Bangs was standing in the doorway. Coolly, he surveyed the room, a wide smile spreading across his face.

"Good evening, Ms. Drew," he drawled. "You caught us at an awkward moment."

Nancy took a step out from behind the cartons. "Don't move," Bangs ordered. Turning to Karen, he said, "Don't panic, Karen. Everything will be all right if you do just as I say. Go wrap up that meeting. Get everyone out of here—before our girl detective tries anything else."

Wordlessly, Karen left the room. At the doorway, she turned, throwing Nancy a look she couldn't decipher.

"You should have left when you had the chance," Bangs said casually. He gestured to the unmoving figures of Ned and Angela. "Now you've put their lives in jeopardy."

"They have nothing to do with this," Nancy exclaimed. "I'm the only one who knows about the CLT."

To her satisfaction, Bangs started at the mention of the chemical. "You have figured it out, then." He grinned and saluted her. "You're more clever than I suspected."

"Let them go, Bangs," Nancy bargained. "I'll help you get away if you do."

Bangs cocked an eyebrow at her. "Will you, now? I'm afraid that's impossible. Your friend Ned here asked a few too many questions about me. So you're lying, Ms. Drew—you're not the only one who knows about CLT." Reaching behind him, Bangs drew a gun from the waistband of his pants.

Inwardly, Nancy groaned. Poor Ned. In trying to help her and Angela, he had put himself —and Nancy—in even greater danger.

"First, come out from behind those cartons where I can see you," Bangs directed. "Sit cross-legged on the floor over there."

Nancy stepped out from the desk and sat beside Ned.

"Not there. Over there," Bangs screamed, taking a step toward her. Quickly, Nancy scooted away.

"That's better. You think he's going to wake up and help you, but you're wrong," Bangs muttered. He walked over to Ned and nudged him roughly with his foot. Ned didn't make a sound.

Nancy cringed. "You're going to pay for this, Bangs," she promised.

Bangs smiled. "Will I? I doubt it. You may be smart, but don't forget I'm smarter. I masterminded this whole thing single-handedly. In fact, POE was created specifically to steal the CLT. Quite clever, I think, when you realize none of the members have any idea what the stuff really is. After all, who would believe that an antitechnology group was stealing an extraordinarily dangerous biological weapon?"

"No one," Nancy said, playing along with the game. She had suspected the true nature of CLT, but Bangs had just confirmed it for her.

Bangs chuckled. "So, you knew what the CLT really was, then. Perhaps you're smarter than I thought."

Nancy pretended to be as cool as Bangs. "Of course," she said. "Once I put the Shiranti Corporation together with the time you were at Jamison, I knew what you were up to. CLT affects bacteria in the same way it affects animals.

"You heard about Maszak's 'accident'—that his growth hormone got mixed up in a rheumatic fever culture and that the disease began growing out of control—and that's why you're so interested in it," Nancy said grimly. "Because a disease that spread so fast could wipe out whole towns at once."

Bangs looked delighted at the thought. "And the best part is, it would be impossible to trace. If you planted CLT in a city water system the relatively harmless bacteria already there would create an immediate plague. No one would know where it came from. Particularly if the hormone itself was shipped in by a well-known pharmaceutical company—along with its regular supply of medicine." Bangs rubbed his hands together gleefully.

Nancy was sickened by Bangs's twisted mind.

"The world is full of dangerous bacteria, Ms. Drew," he said happily. "And CLT would have the same effect on any number of them. We have to thank Maszak for that—his treatment is the key. Somehow, he makes the hormone compatible with the bacteria."

"Yes, something only Maszak knows," Nancy said thoughtfully. "The lab here—you've been using your medical background to try to duplicate Maszak's treatment. But you haven't found it," Nancy stated, realizing the whole truth at once. "If you had, you would have left Emerson a long time ago."

"A nosy girl detective and her macho boyfriend put a little kink in my plans," Bangs said savagely. "But not for long. Karen works in the dean's office. She'll continue to feed me

Maszak's files. Bob is a clever engineering student—he made the tunnels usable for me. I have many people helping, you see. And all in the name of a good cause—saving the world from Maszak's biological weapon."

"You're very clever," Nancy conceded.

Bangs nodded proudly. "You did give me a scare," he said generously. He glanced at Ned and Angela. "I was hoping she would help steal the secret. As a biochem major, she knew the lab, and no one would have suspected her questions. But unfortunately, your friend Ned made her a little suspicious. When Angela learned I was taking the CLT, she tried to warn Maszak. Luckily, I got her away in time."

"But not before she left a clue behind," Nancy said, pulling on the earring she was wearing.

Bangs shrugged. "I almost had her convinced we were taking CLT as a blow against biotechnology everywhere. None of these silly students knows the real reason."

"There are an awful lot of students involved," Nancy said. "You can't keep them in the dark forever."

"I don't need to," Bangs replied. "The little disturbance tomorrow will probably mark the end of POE, anyway. The school will ban them after a stunt like the gun battle they have planned."

"People could be killed," Nancy said coldly.

Bangs shrugged. "If they are, no one will be thinking about my little theft, will they?"

Nancy was revolted. Bangs was a madman, but she had to keep him talking until Ned woke up, or until Amber and Jan brought help.

"So now what?" she asked. "You still don't know the formula. What are you going to do about that?"

"Forget the formula," he said angrily. "I don't need it. I can sell the CLT and cut my losses. I'll still be a billionaire." Bangs waved his gun toward Ned and Angela. "And only the three of you stand in my way."

Nancy licked her lips. "I admire your plan, Bangs," she said, bluffing. "Maybe we could work together."

Bangs frowned. "I always work alone. And I'm wasting time. Say goodbye, Nancy Drew." He aimed the gun at Nancy's head.

Suddenly a figure flew out of the doorway at Bangs, knocking him backward—Karen Lewis. She must have stayed outside the door and listened to the whole conversation.

As Nancy leapt toward Bangs, Karen struggled with him. The gun went off, and Karen sank to the ground, clutching at her left arm. Bangs dropped the gun and fled down the hall.

Nancy knelt by Karen's side. "Karen, are you okay?"

The other girl nodded. "Get Bangs," she gasped. "Don't let him get away."

Nancy hesitated.

"I'm okay," Karen insisted. "Go!"

Karen was right, Nancy knew. If she didn't go now, she was going to lose Bangs. With a last look behind her, Nancy sprinted down the hall. She raced up the stairs, two at a time, and sprang into the meeting room.

The place was in an uproar. The students milled about in confusion, bewildered by the sight of Bangs running out of the building. Nancy desperately pushed her way past them. She burst through in time to see Bangs jump into his car. "Let me through," Nancy cried.

The crowd swelled around her. She couldn't get out!

Chapter

Sixteen

Nancy, what happened?"

Amber and Jan pushed through the crowd toward Nancy.

"Did you find Ned?" Jan asked, panting.

"Or the CLT?" Amber whispered.

"No time to explain," Nancy gasped. "Get me out of here!"

Together, the three girls pushed a clearing through the crowd and made it outside.

Nancy's mind raced. Bangs had left without the CLT. That meant he didn't have it in the building. He must be on his way to get it now.

"Amber, Jan—listen. Ned and Angela are inside. Karen Lewis is there, too. She's been shot. You'll need to get her to a doctor right away."

Amber gasped, but Nancy went on. "Karen is on our side. They're all downstairs, last door on your right. I'm going after Bangs. I don't think anyone else will bother you—but hurry!"

Leaving Amber and Jan gaping after her, Nancy sprinted toward her car.

"Be careful," Amber shouted after her. "Bangs could be dangerous."

She had no idea *how* dangerous, Nancy thought.

Gunning the motor, Nancy drove as fast as she dared, headed for the one place where Bangs could have hidden the CLT.

A glare in her rearview mirror caught her attention. A car's headlights were directly behind her.

Could one of Bangs's henchmen be following her?

It was impossible to see who was behind the wheel. Nancy told herself it was probably just a student leaving the meeting. Bangs hadn't had enough time to instruct anyone to follow her.

Turning onto campus, Nancy swept past the security check post. The guard leapt out when she failed to stop, but she kept on going. The car following her reached the security booth. With a quick glance in the rearview mirror, Nancy saw the other car come to a complete halt. The driver leaned out his window, and he and the guard exchanged words.

It was no one, Nancy thought with relief. Just a student leaving the meeting.

Determined now, she sped toward the cafeteria, the one place on campus where Bangs could have hidden the CLT. After the exploding doorknob incident, the campus police had searched the cafeteria thoroughly. Nothing had been stolen, she remembered, but no one had checked to see if anything had been *left* there.

Pulling into the parking lot at the rear of the building, near the cafeteria kitchen, Nancy braked next to Bangs's red sports car. The cafeteria windows were dark, but the door to the kitchen stood ajar. Holding her breath, Nancy slipped inside. The open door of the walk-in freezer threw a halo of light onto Philip Bangs.

Nancy spotted the light switch and flipped it on. "You won't get away this time," she cried.

Bangs froze, caught in the act of hauling a shiny cylinder of CLT out of the freezer. For a moment he did nothing. Then he bent down abruptly and rolled one of the three huge canisters directly at her.

Just as it was almost on top of her, Nancy

jumped, clearing the canister completely. Bangs actually laughed out loud.

"Very clever," he drawled, advancing upon her.

Nancy drew back and surprised Bangs with a karate kick that sent him spinning. He plowed into a rack of pots and pans, which banged and clattered onto the floor. He recovered quickly and ran toward her again.

Nancy assumed her fighting stance, preparing to fend off a blow. Instead, as he was almost close enough to reach her, Bangs launched himself toward the counter on Nancy's right, reaching for a heavy carving board.

Bangs grabbed the board and slashed it through the air, aiming at Nancy's head. She jumped back but he kept on coming, his arm swinging the block wildly, challenging her.

Bangs advanced and Nancy retreated. He was backing her into a corner, she realized, where she would be trapped. She flung out an arm to ward off his attack and her hand knocked into a box mounted on the wall. A fire alarm, Nancy realized!

If she pulled it, help would come—if she could elude Bangs until then. At the same moment as she moved to pull the lever, Bangs realized what she was doing. He threw himself at the alarm box.

In the same second Nancy spied a frying pan lying a few feet away. She leapt at it even as Bangs was bringing the carving board down onto the glass face of the fire alarm. The glass shattered and the board splintered from the force of the blow.

Sickened as she realized how narrowly she'd escaped that blow herself, Nancy swung the heavy iron pan into the backs of Bangs's legs. His knees buckled and his feet slid out from under him. Bangs fell, crying out in pain and surprise. Her heart pounding, Nancy backed off, waving the pan threateningly above her head.

The kitchen door burst open and two police officers rushed into the room.

"Freeze," one of them shouted, pointing his gun uncertainly, first at Nancy, then at Bangs.

"Not her—him! The one on the floor," a voice from the door directed.

Nancy whirled in surprise. "Mike O'Shea," she gasped breathlessly. "What are you doing here?"

"Well, I couldn't sit around and do nothing," Mike said cheerfully to the crowd.

With Ned's arm securely around her shoulder, Nancy grinned happily from the loveseat. They were in the living room of Ned's frat house, with Amber and Jan sprawled on the sofa, and Karen and Angela perched on pillows by the fireplace.

Sitting in the peaceful room, it was hard to believe that only hours before, they had all been involved in a life-or-death struggle.

"Tell us, Mike," Ned ordered. "How *did* you end up at the kitchen just when Nancy needed you?"

"With two police officers in tow," Nancy added.

Mike grinned bashfully. "It was easy. After Nancy and the girls left, I followed them," Mike explained. "I figured someone better keep an eye on them. I drove after them to POE headquarters and parked along the edge of the road to wait."

"So that was *you* in the car I saw!" Nancy exclaimed in surprise.

"Right," Mike confirmed with a smile. "When Bangs's car peeled out of there, I didn't know what to do. But when I saw you tearing down the driveway, I decided to give you some backup, just in case. I know you're a famous detective and all"—Mike grinned—"but I figured, once in a while, everyone needs a little help from their friends."

"You figured right," Nancy said wryly. She felt Ned's arm tighten around her.

"Anyway," Mike went on, "I stopped at the security gate and told them to call the police."

"And a good thing, too," Ned declared. "But Nancy, how did you guess where Bangs was headed?"

"It was easy, once I realized he didn't have the CLT."

With the mystery solved, Nancy had felt free to fill in the others on all the details.

"I reasoned he didn't have it, because he hadn't been able to get it off campus," she continued. "There aren't too many places you can hide something that big, and frozen, too. Then I remembered the doorknobs."

Angela looked blank. "I don't think I've heard this part."

Nancy smiled at her. "Bangs put an explosive on the doorknob to my closet. He thought he'd scare me away."

"Never!" Ned declared comically.

Grinning, Nancy continued. "I talked to the security men, and they said three other doors on campus had been blown up, too. One of them was the door to the cafeteria. The other two doors, which were to the library and the computer room, were probably hit to disguise the real target."

Jan frowned, looking puzzled. "Then he must have blasted his way in there after he had stolen the CLT."

"Exactly," Nancy agreed. "The tunnels were

the real clue—they connect all the *original* buildings on campus. The cafeteria is a modern building, so there was no way to get in from below. Bangs had to blast his way in there to store the stolen CLT."

Mike whistled. "Pretty clever guy."

"Very clever," Nancy agreed. "My guess is he stored the CLT in the cafeteria for a few days until he could get it safely across the street."

For a moment nobody spoke. Then Karen Lewis let out an anguished moan.

"How could I have been so stupid?" she cried. "I should have known what was going on." She stared down at her hands. Tears began to well up in her eyes.

The others exchanged uncomfortable glances, except for Angela.

"It wasn't your fault," Angela told Karen sympathetically. "He fooled me, too. I thought Bangs wanted to save the world, not destroy it."

Karen nodded and wiped the tears from her eyes. "It's sad, really. In the beginning, we were so full of purpose. I thought POE would do great things. Somehow, helping Philip steal the CLT seemed like the right thing to do. The way he explained it, being chosen for his 'special mission' was a real honor." She spat out the words bitterly. "I never realized what I was getting into."

"That's why I was so worried about Angela," Ned said quietly. "Sometimes, you can get carried away in a group and not even know right from wrong anymore."

"I was in too deep, I guess," Karen said. "Suddenly things were going too fast for me to think clearly. And," she added, looking ashamed, "I guess I wanted to please Philip."

"He's a pretty forceful guy," Nancy put in. "He could have used that power for good, but unfortunately he chose to use it for evil instead."

Karen looked up with fresh tears in her eyes. "But I'm still to blame for a lot of it," she declared. "I helped form the group; I went along with everything he said."

"You didn't know what he was really doing," Ned pointed out.

"No," Karen admitted, "but that doesn't make me feel any better." She gave a weak smile. "I still feel like I got off too easily."

"You got hurt," Amber exclaimed. "That's not 'easily,' if you ask me."

"And you did save us," Angela added, "I mean, in the end."

Karen looked up with a newly determined look on her face. "There is something I can do," she announced. "I can stop the demonstration tomorrow. There won't be any guns in the auditorium, fake or not. And I can turn POE back into the group it should be—a peaceful group, one committed to truly protecting our environment."

Angela turned to Ned, her eyes sparkling. "That's a wonderful idea," she said. "And I'll bet the first one to join your *new* group will be Ned Nickerson."

Nancy gave Ned a special squeeze as everyone laughed.

As Professor Maszak invited Nancy and Ned into his freshly cleaned living room, he was positively jovial.

"Sit down, sit down," he urged. "Can I get you anything?"

"Thanks, but we can stay only a minute," Nancy replied. "I just came to say goodbye."

"I'm so glad you did! I can thank you again for all you've done," the professor said. "I even have a bit of good news. My assistant, Sara— she got her scholarship." Maszak's eyes twinkled. "Now maybe she'll be able to relax and stop blowing things up in the lab."

"I'm sure she will," Nancy said warmly.

"But seriously," he continued, "I want you to know something else. I have realized that nothing can ever justify unleashing my formula on the world again—accidentally *or* on purpose. I destroyed it this morning. I wiped it out of the computer and burned all my notes. And I promise you, I will never create it again."

"But, professor," Nancy asked, "does that ruin your chances of teaching at Emerson?"

"No, no, that's the best part," Maszak said. "Emerson has offered me tenure! My job is now permanent. So what do you think. Ned?" the professor teased. "Maybe next semester, you'll take one of my classes?"

Ned laughed. "No thanks, sir. Your classes are too dangerous for me!"

After saying their goodbyes, Nancy and Ned strolled back to her dorm.

"Well, Nan, I guess you finally have a little free time on your hands." Tenderly, Ned brushed a strand of hair from her eyes.

Nancy smiled. "Did you have anything particular in mind?"

Ned's brown eyes lingered on her face. "I think I owe you one dinner. Why don't you go slip into that silk dress of yours—"

"No way!" Nancy cried. "Every time we split up, something happens. Let's play it safe. We'll order a pizza and eat it in my room—together."

"You mean—alone together, don't you?" Ned teased, taking her hand.

"Alone together," Nancy promised as she tilted her face to meet his kiss.

Out
of Bounds

Chapter
One

YOU CAN DO a lot better than that, Nancy Drew!" said Bess Marvin. She was seated next to Nancy in the first row of the hard bleachers and gave Nancy a playful nudge with her elbow. "Let's use the team's time-out to practice. It's 'BEDFORD! BEDFORD! USE YOUR MIGHT! GET THE BALL AND FIGHT, FIGHT, FIGHT!'" she shouted into the chilly autumn afternoon.

Laughing, Nancy tilted her head and peeked around Bess to give George Fayne a look that said, "She's hopeless." George, who was Bess's cousin and Nancy's other best friend, understood the look perfectly.

1

"She's not easy to please, is she?" George said with a wry grin.

"Okay, Bess," said Nancy. "Is this right?" She took a deep breath. " 'Bedford. Bedford. Use your might. Get the ball and fight, fight, fight!' Any better?" she asked.

Bess pretended to be disgusted by Nancy's lack of enthusiasm and looked straight ahead, out across Bedford High's stadium. She wrinkled her nose and slipped her hands into the pockets of her down jacket.

"Hey! It's hard to root for a team that was your archrival all through high school," Nancy said. "How do you do it, Bess?"

"Bess isn't cheering for Bedford, Nan," George said. "She's cheering for Bill Ellman."

Bess lowered her eyelids and turned to glower at her cousin. She opened her mouth to speak but was interrupted by the team returning to the field. Just in front of the stands the Bedford cheerleaders jumped to their feet to welcome them back.

"Go, Bedford! Hooray, Bill!" Bess cried, standing and waving to the tall, broad-shouldered fullback wearing the Bedford yellow jersey with a royal blue number eleven.

The fullback hardly acknowledged Bess's wave. He simply shot her a tiny nod before donning his helmet and trotting back onto the field to join the huddle. His jaw was set, and a

2

tiny muscle moved in and out just above his jaw bone.

"He's tense," Bess explained. "It can't be easy to lose with college scouts in the crowd."

"Especially since Bradford's been undefeated," George added. Her face reflected genuine concern. Sports were George's major passion, and she must have sensed the tension Bill was feeling.

"There're still four minutes to turn things around," said Nancy, rising to her feet. "GO, BEDFORD!" she shouted, putting her heart into the cheer this time. "BEAT CLIFFSIDE!"

"GO, BEDFORD! BEAT CLIFFSIDE!" The rest of the spectators picked up the cheer and turned it into a slow chant that grew steadily louder and stronger. Spreading out along the edge of the field, the cheerleaders faced the crowd and swayed, first left, then right, with their bright yellow and blue pom-poms held high above their heads.

Cynthia Tyler, captain of the squad and Bess's new friend, stood on the fifty-yard line. Her honey blond curls followed the side-to-side movement. Soon the whole crowd was swaying and singing, supercharged with energy.

"Cynthia's enthusiasm is contagious," Nancy remarked.

George nodded, then smiled. "She isn't just rooting for Bedford, either, you know."

"True enough," Bess agreed. Rob Matthews, Cynthia's boyfriend, was Bedford's quarterback and Bill Ellman's best friend. They had introduced Bess and Cynthia.

"Wave to the camera!" Cynthia called up to the three girls as a local TV cameraman swung by the edge of the field, a hand-held camera on his shoulder.

Bess obliged with great enthusiasm. "To think that Bedford has *three* potential high school All-Americans and a possible state championship!" she said after the cameraman swung past her to pan the rest of the crowd. "What a team!"

"I know about Bill and Rob," George said over the roar of the crowd. "But who's the third player up for All-American?"

"Lonnie Price, number twenty-two!" Bess shouted. "He's the defensive end. Lonnie, Bill, and Rob are best friends. It would be fantastic if they all made All-American *and* won the state championship."

"Here they come!" said Nancy as the team broke out of their huddle and lined up for the next play.

The Bedford fans seemed to hold a collective breath as Rob tossed a pass downfield. Racing to meet it, Bill stretched his arms out, his head up, eyes on the spiraling ball.

Oomph! The air was forced out of him as he

4

was broadsided by a two-hundred-pound line-backer. He did manage to retain possession of the ball, but only by falling on it, though.

"Poor Bill," cried Bess, covering her eyes.

"Don't give up, Bess, Bedford can still win," said George after the whistle blew, signaling the clock to stop.

"You really think so?" Bess asked, worried, her eyes shifting to the scoreboard. Still twelve to seven.

"Sure," Nancy answered, reaching around her friend's shoulders to give her a hug. "One touch-down and they can win."

Bess obviously cared a lot about Bill. When Bess first started dating him, George couldn't help teasing her cousin about seeing a high school boy. But Bess hadn't let the jokes get to her. "Bill's special," she'd said. "Not because he's going to be an NFL star, not because of his superhuman physique and gorgeous aqua eyes, or that glossy chestnut hair of his. He's special because he just happens to be incredibly sweet."

Everything Bess had said about Bill seemed to be true. He had rugged good looks, and despite one or two small mistakes he'd made that day, his athletic talent was impressive.

A sharp whistle brought the girls' attention back to the game. The teams lined up, and the center snapped the ball. As Rob dropped back for another pass, the cheers from the Bedford stands reached new heights. Cynthia's voice was practically hoarse as she urged the fans on.

"They can't lose," Bess murmured worriedly. "They just *can't.*"

"I think Rob's going to run this one himself!" George cried excitedly. Just then the quarterback rolled out, then sprinted down the field. He was racking up a good gain, too, when a Cliffside defender broke free and charged at him.

"Look out!" Nancy yelled as the Cliffside tackle blew through open space and smashed into Rob, knocking him backward. Rob's helmet went flying, its strap broken. With a sickening crack, his bare head hit the ground. The crowd's roar instantly quieted to a nervous murmur.

"He's not moving," Bess said, her eyes glued to the field, where the fallen quarterback lay sprawled. Cynthia stood by the cheerleaders' bench, stunned, her hands to her mouth. The Bedford trainer rushed up to Rob, kneeling at his side.

"Oh, please, please, let him be all right!" Cynthia cried out suddenly, tears rolling down her cheeks.

"Come on," Bess said, leading the way off the bleachers and over to the cheerleaders' bench. Nancy and George followed.

"He'll be okay, Cynthia," Bess told the girl

when they got there. She hugged her new friend's shoulders.

"Look!" George pointed. "He's getting up!"

Nancy turned to see Lonnie Price and Bill Ellman helping Rob to his feet. Slowly they walked him over to the players' bench that was next to the cheerleader squad's. Nancy could tell Rob was still dazed, but at least he was conscious. The worried-looking coach signaled a substitute onto the field, and play resumed with only fifty seconds left in the game.

"Come on, Bedford!" Nancy cried, still at the cheerleaders' bench. Barely audible over the roar of the crowd, Nancy heard Rob and his coach arguing.

"I'm fine!" Rob shouted. "Put me back in!"

"Sit down," the coach ordered, pointing Rob back toward the bench.

Just then a groan went up from the stands. Cliffside had sacked Rob's substitute.

"No! This is our last chance!" Rob said, standing his ground and grabbing the coach by his jacket lapels.

"Fourth down and twenty yards to the goal," George commented sadly. "I guess Bedford is finished."

A huge roar from the crowd drowned out George's voice. Nancy glanced over and saw Rob walking determinedly to the twenty-yard line. He was back in the game!

"Go, Rob!" shrieked Cynthia and Bess.

"He's out of his mind!" George exclaimed.

Rob took the snap and faded back to pass. With linemen coming at him from both sides, Rob couldn't find a free pass receiver, so he tucked the ball under his arm, lowered his head, and blazed through the middle. He broke two tackles and fell into the end zone just as the clock ran out. The new score flashed on the board. Bedford—thirteen; Cliffside—twelve.

"They did it! They did it!" a jubilant Bess shrieked. "State championship, here we come!"

The other Bedford fans had joined them on the field, screaming in triumph and pressing toward the players. The team lifted Rob and Bill to their shoulders and were carrying their heroes up and down the field with fans crushing in on all sides.

Cynthia, knowing she couldn't get close to Rob, ran over to Nancy, Bess, and George. "We're going to Touchdown to celebrate!" she shouted. "Want to come?"

Bess nodded enthusiastically. "You bet."

"Great!" Nancy, Bess, and George followed Cynthia as the girl wove a path through the crowd to the parking lot exit.

They all piled into Nancy's Mustang—George and Bess in back, Nancy and Cynthia up front. "You'll have to give me directions to the restaurant," Nancy said, turning the key to start the engine. "I don't remember Touchdown from the last time I was here for an extended stay."

"I should know the way—I work there," Cynthia said with a laugh. "Just go out Main, then take a right onto Bedford Avenue." She smiled warmly at Nancy. "Did you live in Bedford before?"

"Nancy solved a case at Bedford High once," George answered from the back seat.

"She worked undercover," Bess added proudly. "On a spy case."

"You mean that guy Darryl Gray?" asked Cynthia, putting a hand to her mouth. "You solved that case?"

"George and Bess are my publicity agents," Nancy said, joking.

"Wow," Cynthia said, impressed. "He was delivering secrets to the Russians, wasn't he?"

"That's right," Nancy said, stopping for a red light. "He did help convict the big guys, though. In the end they let him off easy."

They were silent for a few minutes. "I sure hope Rob is really okay," Cynthia murmured finally.

"He will be," Bess said confidently. "They've still got two more games to win. He can't get injured now."

"I don't know." Cynthia fluffed out her hair

with her hands. When Nancy glanced at the girl, she noticed that Cynthia's deep blue eyes seemed sad.

Cynthia pointed the way for Nancy to go, then turned her attention to Bess. "Have you noticed, Bess, when we're out together, the boys are totally absorbed in the team? They act like nothing else matters."

"I have noticed that the past couple of times," Bess said with a nod.

"These guys are on the threshold of big college careers. There's a lot of attention on them," George reminded them.

"There's Touchdown, Nancy," Cynthia said, pointing to a long brick building with a green and white sign. Other kids were pouring into the restaurant, walking under the green and white goalpost that was set up in front of the entrance. Both the *O*'s in *Touchdown* were football shaped.

Nancy managed to find a parking space, and the girls piled out of the car and twisted their way through a crowd milling out front.

"The guys should be here soon," Cynthia remarked, opening the heavy wooden door and looking for a free table. "They have to shower first, though."

"There's a table," said George, spotting a lone empty table in the rear.

After they were seated, Nancy had a chance to look around. Football jerseys, helmets, and insignia hung from all the walls, along with autographed pictures of dozens of football stars. Completing the football theme were two giant TV screens at either end of the restaurant, tuned in to a college game.

The noise in the place was overwhelming. Long lines of thrilled fans stood at the counters, placing orders and excitedly discussing Bedford's victory.

Behind the food counter a tall, thin beanpole of a guy waved to Cynthia and flashed her a goofy grin. He looked silly in his kelly green Touchdown jersey, with its big number 42. Cynthia waved back.

"That's Edgar Chessman," she told the girls. "He's my best friend at this place. Makes a mean block-and-tackle sandwich, too," she added.

Edgar approached them, his grin fading. "A little warning, Cynthia," he whispered. "Pete's on the warpath today. Be cool, okay?"

Cynthia looked puzzled. "That's all right. I'm off today, Edgar," she said.

"Still, I just wanted you to know," he answered, looking over his shoulder at the other side of the restaurant, where two men were obviously having a heated conversation.

"Pete Shepard runs this place for American Theme Restaurant Corporation," Cynthia explained. "That's him over there—the big redheaded guy with the mustache."

"The one who looks like he's yelling?" asked Bess.

"That's Pete," said Cynthia with a knowing sigh.

"Who's the other guy?" asked George, pointing to the guy with dark curly hair that Pete was shouting at.

"Him? Oh, that's Mark Gatwin, the assistant manager," Cynthia said. "He's nice—a lot nicer than Pete, that's for sure."

Almost as if he'd heard her, Pete turned in their direction just then. "There she is!" he bellowed at the top of his lungs, pointing at Cynthia. His small eyes were flashing angrily. Shoving Mark aside, he marched over to the girls' table.

"What's the matter, Pete? What's wrong?" Cynthia asked, her pretty face full of concern.

"Don't play dumb with me, Tyler!" Pete boomed. "You know what's wrong!"

Cynthia cast a worried look at Nancy and Bess before turning back to Pete. "Sorry, Pete, but I don't. Really."

"I'm talking about the fact that you're a thief!" He said loudly enough for most of the onlookers to hear. "You stole money from this restaurant!"

"Th-that's not true," the cheerleader stammered.

"Don't bother to deny it, Cynthia," Pete stated flatly. "I've got proof. Don't show up for work anymore. Got it? *You're fired!*"

Chapter

Two

PETE STARED HARD at Cynthia, who shrank from his powerful gaze. George shot Nancy a questioning look as Bess touched Cynthia's arm supportively.

"I am not a thief!" Cynthia managed to get out.

"Not only are you a thief, you're a liar, too!" Pete shouted. "Get out. Now!"

"Excuse me, excuse me," the accused girl murmured, pushing her way through the crowd to flee from the restaurant. Bess had thrown down her napkin and was running after her, Nancy and George on her heels.

They stepped outside to find Cynthia leaning

14

against the building around the corner from the restaurant entrance. Tears were streaming down her cheeks.

"What a jerk that guy is!" Bess fumed, trying to comfort her friend. "I mean, talk about hostile!"

"It's probably just a mistake, Cynthia," George said. "Maybe the money was misplaced."

Cynthia shook her head. "I don't think so," she said, stopping to catch her breath first. "Edgar told me last week that a lot of money was missing. Then Pete fired Erica Dawson, and we all thought that would be the end of it."

Nancy riveted her attention on the girl. "Wait—Pete already fired someone *else* for stealing?"

"Last week," said Cynthia, nodding sadly. "It's weird, isn't it?"

"I'll say," said Nancy. "Did he press charges against the girl he fired?"

"No. He threatened to, but when her folks hired a lawyer, he dropped everything," Cynthia answered, brushing a stray tear from her eye. "I really need that job, too."

"Cynthia's been saving for college," Bess explained. "Ooh, the nerve of that rat. She's no more guilty than you or me."

"I'd never steal! I couldn't live with myself if I did!" Utterly defeated, Cynthia slumped back against the wall, her head hanging.

15

"There's got to be a way to find out what's really going on," Nancy said, touching the cheerleader's hand comfortingly.

"You think so?" Cynthia asked, raising her head.

"Of course," echoed George.

"That's right," Bess said. "Everyone's innocent until proven guilty."

"But Cynthia can't prove she's innocent," George said. "Unless Pete presses charges, the case will never come to court. It'll remain an ugly rumor and continue to hurt Cynthia's reputation."

"That's true. Erica's been looking all over town for a job," Cynthia said, a sudden catch in her voice. "Nobody will hire someone who's been fired for stealing. Bedford isn't that big, and everyone hears everything eventually."

"Cynthia, do you think Erica really took money from Touchdown?" Nancy asked.

Cynthia's blue eyes focused someplace over Nancy's head as she thought a minute. "When she was fired, I was shocked. I mean, I couldn't believe it, but Pete said he had proof—"

"He might not have had proof, if he didn't press charges," Nancy pointed out.

"I'll bet Nancy's right!" Bess threw in. "Pete was probably lying!"

"And he can't have proof that *I* stole, because I

didn't!" Cynthia insisted through fresh, hot tears.

"There's something very strange going on here," Nancy murmured. "The best thing would be for me to take a job at Touchdown and find out what it is."

Cynthia gulped hard. "Would you? Would you really do that for me?"

Nancy realized the three girls were staring expectantly at her.

"You'd only have to work there until you found out what was going on," Bess said, urging her on.

"Okay," said Nancy. "I'm not a great waitress, but I'd hate to see Pete get away with this."

"Look at this face," Bess said, breaking the heavy mood of the moment by holding Cynthia's face in her hands and turning it from side to side. "Is this the face of a thief? No way!"

Cynthia couldn't help breaking out in a small smile. "Gosh, Nancy. Bess was telling me how terrific you were and all—"

"Hey! There's the girl who stole the money!" Two guys in denim jackets turned the corner of Touchdown and were looking directly at Cynthia. Their faces were plastered with big phony smiles, and they held out their hands, palms up.

"You got some for us?" one of the boys asked, rubbing his fingers against his thumb.

"Come on," said Nancy, taking Cynthia's elbow. "Let's go to my car where we can have some privacy."

Bess, George, Cynthia, and Nancy walked over to the Mustang, trying to ignore Cynthia's tormentors.

"Don't worry, Cynthia," Bess said, opening the door and sliding into the back seat. "Now that Nancy's on the case, it's as good as solved."

"Bess is my biggest fan. Now, tell me everything," Nancy said, facing Cynthia, who was seated beside her in the front. "About Touchdown, Pete, Mark, that guy Edgar—everybody."

"Well," Cynthia began, "when I first got the job, everything was cool. Pete was friendly, Mark was friendly. Everybody got along. Then things started to change."

"When did they start to change?" Nancy probed.

Cynthia thought for a moment. "I guess it was around the beginning of football season," she said finally. "Pete started getting grouchy, then he became kind of paranoid. He started yelling at us whenever we did any little thing wrong."

Cynthia looked as if she was about to start crying again. Without prompting, Bess passed a tissue up to her.

"What else do you know about Pete?" Nancy asked gently.

Cynthia took a deep breath. "Let's see—he's a football nut. I guess that was pretty obvious by

18

the club's decor. He was a star at Bedford seven years ago." Cynthia's blue eyes were fixed, staring out the windshield at nothing.

"He's built like a football player, that's for sure," George observed.

"Did he have a college or pro career?" Nancy asked.

"According to Rob, he had a bad injury his first year of college, and he never played after that."

"You mean Rob knows Pete?" Bess inquired.

"Oh, sure," Cynthia said, turning around to face Bess. "Pete's tight with all the guys on the team. He's like a groupie. Always gives them bags of goodies to take home when they leave Touchdown, that kind of thing."

"What else, Cynthia?" Nancy asked.

Cynthia wound a lock of hair around her finger, corkscrew style, as she thought. "Rob said he tried to be a sports agent after he left college. He still handles a couple of not very successful pro players on the side, but I don't think he really makes any money at it."

At that moment a horn honked close to them, making them all jump. "It's the guys!" Bess blurted out.

Rob and Bill were waving out the open passenger-side windows, and Lonnie was driving. Cynthia quickly checked her reflection in the mirror on Nancy's visor.

"Do I look like I've been crying?" she asked, turning to Nancy.

"Not really," Nancy lied, taking in Cynthia's red-rimmed eyes.

"Hey, there!" Bill shouted as Lonnie steered his car into a space. All three guys seemed to be in great spirits.

"Please," Cynthia said quickly, scanning the girls' faces. "Don't mention all this, okay? Not yet, anyway. I don't want to spoil their good time—not right now."

"Don't worry," Bess told her. "We won't say a word. You can tell them when you have to."

Cynthia flashed them all a quick smile. "Now, come on," Bess urged. "Let's say hi to the guys." With that she opened the car door and got out. Nancy, George, and Cynthia followed her lead.

Cynthia Tyler really was a sweet girl, Nancy thought. She promised herself then and there to help solve the mystery of the missing money and clear Cynthia's name.

"All right!" called the guys as they tumbled out of Lonnie's car. They raised their fists in the air and shouted into the rosy twilight, "We're number one!"

Their breath preceded them in soft white puffs as they sauntered, shoulder to shoulder, up to the girls. Cynthia stood waiting with a big smile on her face. Though her expression was obviously strained, Nancy could tell that Rob was too caught up in his own victory to notice.

"Hey, Bess," Bill said, greeting her with a cozy arm tossed over her shoulder and a quick nuzzle. Bess's face lit up from ear to ear in a dazzling smile.

Rob looked pale, but otherwise he appeared to have recovered from his earlier knockdown. He planted a kiss on Cynthia's lips and gave her an affectionate squeeze.

"Nancy and George," said a grinning Bess, "this is Rob and Lonnie."

"Hi," the guys said, each in turn, taking in Nancy and George.

"Let's go celebrate," Lonnie added, positioning himself next to George. "Your name is George?" he asked, shyly bending his handsome face toward hers.

"It's short for Georgia, but everyone calls me George," she answered, trying to cover her embarrassment with a casual shrug.

"Okay. George. Nice to meet you," Lonnie said, raising his eyebrows and smiling at her. "Are you coming in?"

"I think so," George answered with a quick look at Cynthia.

Cynthia stood still for a moment, obviously trying to decide whether or not to go back in. Her forehead was creased by two tiny vertical lines.

"Come on," said Rob. "I'm starved. Let's get a move on." He took Cynthia's elbow to move her along.

Nancy guessed that Cynthia decided Pete wouldn't say anything to her with three of the Bedford stars as her escorts. He wouldn't want to embarrass these guys.

Sure enough, when Pete saw them, he was cool and distant to Cynthia but polite in front of the boys. "Great game, guys!" he shouted, slapping Rob on the back. "Food is on me, so order whatever you want."

As Cynthia quickly took a seat, Pete shot her a poisonous look, which only Nancy caught.

After Pete returned to the counter, Nancy decided to try to talk to him. "Excuse me," she said to get his attention.

"Yeah?" Pete said, giving her a quick glance.

"My name is Nancy Edwards, and I'm looking for a job. I wondered if—"

"You're Cynthia Tyler's friend, aren't you?" he asked. "Cynthia's not one of my favorite people, you know."

"Well," said Nancy, her response all ready, "I'm actually friends with the other two girls. I only met Cynthia today. When I saw you fire Cynthia, I thought you might need a replacement."

"Have you ever waitressed before?" Pete asked, eyeing her carefully.

22

"Sure, lots of times," Nancy said brightly. She'd only done it once or twice in the course of investigations, but the lie was for a good cause.

"All right, come by tomorrow afternoon, and I'll give you a try," he said with a hint of a smile. "You'll have to work odd shifts for a week or so. After that, if it works out, we can talk about a regular schedule, okay?"

"Great!" chirped Nancy, offering her hand.

Pete didn't take it. "Be on time," he warned her. Then he walked away, leaving her with her hand outstretched.

"I'll be on time, all right," Nancy said under her breath. Lonnie, Rob, and Bill were up at the counter ordering when Nancy got back to the table. While Cynthia listened, Bess seemed to be trying to talk George into something.

"Say yes, George," she pleaded. "Come on. It'll be so much fun!"

"I don't know," George said evasively.

"Don't know what?" asked Nancy, slipping into her chair.

"Lonnie wants me to go out with him tonight," George said. She didn't sound enthusiastic.

"Bill and I are going dancing, and Lonnie wants to take George," Bess explained. "We could double!"

"I don't know," George protested weakly. "I mean, I hardly know the guy!"

Nancy glanced over at Lonnie, who was in line

23

with his friends. He certainly was good-looking, and a talented athlete, too. He and George would seem to have a lot in common. "Sounds like fun to me, George," Nancy put in encouragingly.

"Oh, okay, I guess," said George, blushing a little as the guys returned to the table.

"So? Did you think it over?" Lonnie asked George, flashing her a gorgeous smile of perfect teeth.

"Okay, I'll go," George agreed.

"Great!" said Lonnie. "How about you, Rob? You and Cynthia haven't been dancing in ages."

"You know Cynthia works Saturday nights," Rob said quickly. "She starts in a couple of hours."

"Actually, I'm off tonight," Cynthia volunteered. "But you look tired. I think you should get a good rest tonight, Rob."

"Me? Tired?" Rob raked a hand through his sandy blond hair. "Maybe I am," he admitted with a slow grin.

The order was brought to the table soon, and the hungry group started wolfing down their food. As Bess reached for the ketchup, she rapped Cynthia's glass of water with her knuckles and spilled it all over the table.

"That was so clumsy of me!" she said, embarrassed as she madly tried to sop up the water with her napkin.

"I'll get more napkins," said Rob.

As he stood, Rob suddenly swayed backward. Cynthia reached out to steady him. "Rob? Are you okay?"

"Umm. I'm fine," Rob said slowly. He rubbed the back of his neck. "My head hurts a little, and I got a little dizzy—that's all."

"Let me go for the napkins," Cynthia said, standing up.

"I'm okay. Really." But as Rob took a step away from the table, he suddenly pitched straight forward and collapsed in a heap on the floor!

Chapter
Three

Rob!" CYNTHIA TOOK A STEP and dropped to her knees beside her boyfriend. "Wake up! Oh, no," she moaned, gently rolling him over onto his back.

"He's fainted!"

Nancy knelt on the other side of Rob. Picking up his wrist, she felt for a pulse. "His pulse is weak," she announced. "Somebody call an ambulance!"

"I will." George raced off to find a phone.

"Lonnie, keep everyone back. He needs air," Nancy ordered firmly. Lonnie quickly organized the busboys and waiters in a circle around Rob.

"Rob, Rob!" Cynthia cried. Behind her stood

Bill and Bess, who was biting her lower lip anxiously.

Nancy had placed her ear against Rob's chest to listen to his breathing. It was ragged and shallow.

"He did just faint, didn't he?" Cynthia asked breathlessly.

Nancy looked up and shook her head gently. "If it were just that, his pulse and breathing would be normal," she answered.

Cynthia grasped her boyfriend's hand. "Oh, please, please let him be all right!" she sobbed.

Nancy spotted Bill Ellman beside Bess. "Could you sit her down and get her some water?" she asked.

"Sure thing." Bill nodded, helping Cynthia up. "Come on, Cyn," he murmured.

"He'll be all right, you'll see."

"Here's a napkin. I ran cold water on it," offered one of the busboys.

"*I* don't need it," said Cynthia, taking the cloth and returning to Rob. "I want to be near him." She bent down and pressed two ends of the napkin against her boyfriend's temples.

"Bill, get a jacket and roll it up. Put it under his head," Nancy said, much calmer than she felt. She reached for his pulse again. This time it was so weak, she barely found it. There was no time to waste, so Nancy began to give Rob mouth-to-mouth resuscitation. She blew deeply and repeat-

27

THE NANCY DREW FILES

edly through Rob's mouth, trying to force air into
his lungs.

"Please wake up, Rob," Cynthia moaned.
"Please!"

Nancy sat up to catch her breath, and Bill took
over the mouth-to-mouth for a minute. After
Nancy replaced Bill again, she finally saw Rob's
chest moving. "He's breathing," Nancy whispered softly. Flushed with relief and exhausted
by her efforts, she knelt back on her heels.

"Good work, Nancy—and Bill," said George,
who was standing behind them now. "The ambulance should be here soon."

"Thanks, George." Looking up at her friend,
Nancy's attention was caught by a movement she
saw out of the corner of her eye. Turning quickly,
she was shocked to see the assistant manager,
Mark, rifling through the navy blue gym bag
hanging on the back of Rob's chair! His hands
were deeply imbedded in the bag with Yale
printed on it, and he seemed to be searching for
something at the bottom of it.

Suddenly, as if sensing her eyes on him, Mark
looked up, straight at Nancy. "Here," he said
quickly, yanking a sweatshirt out of the bag. "We
can cover him with this. It'll keep him warm."

"Good idea," Nancy said as Mark tucked the
sweatshirt around Rob. The quarterback was
breathing steadily now. His pulse was regular,
even if it was still weak.

In the distance Nancy heard a siren. Thankfully, the paramedics would soon be there. "Okay, everybody, clear a path for the medics!" Pete bellowed from the front door, where he'd been keeping a lookout for the ambulance.

The paramedics burst in, carrying a stretcher and a medical bag. Gently Bess helped Cynthia to stand up and pulled her back from Rob.

After listening to his pulse and breathing, the medics lifted Rob onto the stretcher and carried him outside to the waiting ambulance.

"Sorry," one of them told Cynthia as she tried to climb in the ambulance. "No one but immediate family rides in the ambulance."

"We'll follow in my car," Nancy said, taking Cynthia's elbow in one hand and grabbing Rob's gym bag in the other. She didn't want to leave it behind for Mark to rifle again. George and Bess picked up their things and trailed Nancy out. Bill and Lonnie said they'd meet them at the hospital.

Opening the door to her Mustang, Nancy threw Rob's gym bag onto the back seat. "Which way is the hospital?" she asked Cynthia as they climbed in.

"Not far. Stay on Bedford to Main," Cynthia told her numbly.

Nancy pulled out into traffic. The ambulance and Lonnie's car were far ahead, though they could hear the siren in the distance.

29

"That hit Rob took today," Bess said. "Do you think that's what made him pass out?"

"Probably," Nancy said, stopping for a red light.

"Oh, I'm so afraid for him," Cynthia murmured softly.

"He's in good hands now," George said comfortingly as Nancy drove on. "There's the hospital up ahead."

"I know it's hard, but try not to worry," Nancy suggested. "It won't do Rob any good."

Nancy quickly parked, and the three girls ushered Cynthia inside the hospital and into the emergency room. Bess stepped up to a nurse seated behind a green counter. Lonnie and Bill were waiting for them there.

"How is he?" she asked the boys.

"He's in with a doctor now," Bill told her.

"If you want to wait, I'll have her give you a status report when she's through examining him," the nurse told them.

"Thanks," said Bess.

"Let's all sit over there," said Nancy, pointing to some orange molded-plastic chairs across from the counter.

"This may take a while. Anybody want anything from the cafeteria?" Bill asked.

"No, thanks," Cynthia answered weakly.

"Why don't the four of you go for something? I'll wait here with Cynthia," said Nancy.

30

Nancy watched the foursome disappear into the hospital elevator. Beside her, Cynthia fidgeted, barely able to control her anxiety. She picked up magazines and tossed them down after flipping through the pages once. She got up, paced, then sat down again.

"Cynthia, what do you know about Mark?" Nancy asked, remembering that she had seen the assistant manager go through Rob's gym bag. "What's he like?"

"Mark?" Cynthia seemed to forget for a moment who Mark was. "Oh, Mark Gatwin! I don't know much about him really, except that he's totally nice to everyone who works at Touchdown. Not like Pete." Cynthia shivered at mentioning his name.

Nancy nodded. "Anything else?" she asked.

"Well, he's about twenty-two, I think. He took a two-year course in restaurant management," Cynthia said, finally settling into one of the orange chairs. "He told me he interviewed for the job as manager, but the corporation picked Pete because he had been a local football hero."

"Did Mark ever say he resents that?" Nancy asked.

"Not in so many words," Cynthia said pensively. "But it's pretty obvious that he does."

"So—Mark wants Pete's job," Nancy said, mulling the idea over. "Do you think he could ever get it?"

31

"I don't know," Cynthia said with a shrug. "Pete must be in trouble with the corporation because of the missing money. I guess Mark would be next in line for the job."

Nancy let out a low whistle. "Interesting," she murmured.

"Nancy," Cynthia asked, her eyes wide, "are you saying you think Mark is the thief? That he took the money to make Pete look bad?"

"I'm not saying anything," Nancy answered tentatively. "It is a possibility, though, isn't it?"

Cynthia let out a big breath. "I guess so, but Mark seems like such a nice guy."

Nancy remembered the intent look on Mark's face as he went through Rob's gym bag. She couldn't help feeling he was doing more than fishing for a sweatshirt.

The two girls sat quietly for a few more minutes. Finally the doctor emerged. She was a tall, well-built woman of about thirty-five, with almond-shaped bluish green eyes. "I'm Dr. Gebel," she said, with a slight foreign accent.

"I'm Cynthia Tyler, Rob's girlfriend. Is Rob okay?" Cynthia asked anxiously.

"We think so," the doctor said slowly. "But he appears to have suffered a moderate concussion."

"From the game!" Cynthia gasped.

"Yes, probably," Dr. Gebel said. "He's resting comfortably now. The X rays looked all right, but we want to do some more tests in the morning, just to be sure."

"Sure of what?" asked Cynthia anxiously. "Do you suspect something else?"

"Well, the preliminary tests showed some unusual results. Not unheard of, but unusual. I just think it's best to be sure."

"Oh?" said Cynthia weakly. "Maybe I should stay for a while," she said softly. "He needs somebody—"

"We've reached his parents," the doctor said. "They're in with him now. Why don't you come back tomorrow morning? We'll know more then, and Rob should be happy for the company by then."

"All right," said Cynthia, swallowing back a lump in her throat. "Thanks, Doctor."

The doctor turned to leave just as Bess, George, Bill, and Lonnie emerged from a nearby elevator.

"Is he okay?" Bess asked nervously as she walked up to her friends.

Cynthia nodded listlessly. "For now," she answered.

"He's got a concussion, and they want to run some tests," Nancy explained. "We might as well leave. Cynthia, I'll drive you home."

Cynthia seemed reluctant to go. Nancy put an arm around her and guided her toward the exit. "I'll pick you up in the morning and bring you right back here for morning visiting hours. That's a promise."

The next day as Nancy drove the twenty minutes from River Heights to the rural outskirts of Bedford where Cynthia lived, she kept replaying the scenes at Touchdown. She couldn't shake the image of Rob lying on the restaurant floor and Cynthia pacing while they waited at the hospital.

When Nancy pulled up to the Tylers' renovated farmhouse, Cynthia was sitting on the porch steps, looking as if she hadn't slept all night.

"Hop in," Nancy called.

Cynthia practically flew into the Mustang. "Thanks for coming, Nancy," she said. "I'm so nervous that I'd be afraid to drive, and I want to see him so much."

Cynthia was really in love with Rob, Nancy thought. Automatically she started thinking about *her* boyfriend, Ned Nickerson. Even though Ned was away at Emerson College most of the year, she thought about him a lot. True love was the greatest, Nancy knew. She only hoped Rob was okay—and that he felt about Cynthia the way she obviously felt about him.

"Where are Bess and George?" Cynthia asked, cutting into Nancy's thoughts. Obviously she had just noticed they weren't there.

"George called and said they'd meet us at the

hospital—to save me a little driving. It's good they're going to do all these tests," Nancy said, returning to the subject of Rob.

Cynthia nodded. "I just hope he's okay. He'll go crazy if he has to sit out the game next week."

The minute Nancy parked in the visitors' lot and turned off the engine, Cynthia was out the door. Nancy trotted to catch up to her. In the Intensive Care corridor, Nancy and Cynthia spotted Dr. Gebel talking to a nurse.

"I'm so glad you've come," the doctor told Cynthia as the two girls approached her. "I would have called but didn't know your last names."

Cynthia's eyes widened in panic. "Why? What's wrong?" she stammered.

"Rob's gone. He left the hospital early this morning," the doctor said simply.

"Gone? You mean, he's been released already?" Cynthia's face was stark white.

"No, I mean he left the hospital—without being released," Dr. Gebel replied tensely.

"You mean—"

The doctor continued in a worried tone, "There could be internal bleeding, or a blood clot—anything could be wrong. Unless he readmits himself, Rob could be in very serious danger!"

Chapter
Four

DO YOU MEAN Rob might *die?"* Cynthia asked, clutching Nancy's arm and staring in wide-eyed panic at the doctor.

"I don't want to scare you," Dr. Gebel said in a kindly but serious tone. "But neither do I want you to underestimate the risk. There have been cases in which athletes who thought they were perfectly fine did die at a later date from internal injuries."

"When exactly did he leave?" Nancy asked anxiously.

"Before dawn. When the nurse came to prep him for his tests, he became very upset and left," the doctor explained, glancing at the medical

36

chart on her clipboard. "He was gone by seven A.M. His parents haven't seen him."

"I can't believe it," Cynthia murmured breathlessly. "That isn't like Rob."

The doctor arched her well-shaped eyebrows and shook her head. "If you find him, tell him that we're here to help him, not hurt him."

"I will," said Cynthia in a determined tone.

Nancy caught sight of Bess and George moving down the corridor toward them. "Hi, everyone!" Bess chirped. "How's Rob doing?"

George must have noticed the grim expression on their faces. "What's wrong?" she asked.

"Rob's gone," Nancy said. "He walked out this morning. He didn't want any tests."

"Why would he do that?" Bess exclaimed.

"Cynthia, I think you should go look for him right away," Nancy said urgently.

"That's an excellent idea," the doctor agreed, lowering her clipboard and giving Cynthia a supportive pat on the arm. "The sooner he seeks medical attention the better."

"Thanks, Dr. Gebel," Cynthia said as the doctor began walking away. "I think I know where to find him," she added to her friends. "But I want to talk to him alone."

"That's probably a good idea," Nancy told her. "Oh, gosh. It's after ten-thirty, and I'm due at Touchdown at eleven. George, can you drive Cynthia?"

"Sure," George volunteered.

"Thanks," Cynthia said softly.

The girls all turned to leave the hospital. "Want to get together after my shift? I'll want to hear about Rob and what happened to him," Nancy said.

"I may not be up for it—I'm pretty worn out," Cynthia said.

"We'll meet you," said George. "At Touchdown at seven?"

"Good," Nancy replied. Then she turned to Cynthia. "I hope Rob will be all right."

"And not *just* for his sake," Bess added. "If he's really injured or sick or something, the Bedford Bears are in real trouble."

"I'll bet that's what Rob's thinking," said Cynthia, a trace of bitterness in her voice. "He wants to win the state championship so much, I don't think he'll let anything stand in his way."

"Not even his health?" George asked gently.

"Not even his own health," Cynthia echoed, her eyes filling with angry tears as she pushed open the wide hospital door. "Sometimes I wish he'd never started playing football in the first place!"

Touchdown wasn't quite as busy that Sunday afternoon as it had been the day before. Gray skies and threatening rain seemed to be keeping the customers away.

"I'm Nancy Edwards," Nancy announced to Mark, who was standing at one of the big-screen TV's, watching a football game. "I'm here to work."

"Oh? I'm Mark Gatwin, the assistant manager," Mark told her.

Nancy smiled. "What should I do first?"

"Go see Pete," Mark answered, looking her over with a pleasant smile. "His office is just past the rest rooms. First left."

Nancy found the narrow corridor behind the rest rooms and knocked on the door. Through a small window in the door, she watched as Pete looked up from a ledger on his cluttered desk.

"Oh, it's you," he said, opening the door for her. "Listen, I don't have time to break you in right now. Just tell Mark to get you a uniform jersey and let you take table service. I'll teach you how to work the registers after lunch." With that he went back to his work, and Nancy went back out to the restaurant.

"All set?" asked Edgar Chessman, his paper serving hat comically askew.

"Not exactly," Nancy admitted. "Pete told me to start out by serving tables. Mark's supposed to give me a Touchdown jersey and set me up."

"He stepped out," Edgar said. "But I can show you what to do. First I'll get you a uniform." He reached into the kitchen, grabbed a jersey, and handed it to Nancy. Then he continued, "The

39

food orders come out over here, see?" He led her over to one end of the counter area. "They stick little footballs with numbers on them. Here comes one now—it's number fourteen. So you take it to table fourteen. See? Nothing to it. Just don't fumble."

"Great. Thanks, Edgar." Nancy had to smile. Edgar was one person who couldn't possibly be guilty of anything worse than telling a bad joke.

Business picked up, but after about an hour it slowed again, and the tables started to empty out. Nancy wondered how much money had been taken in that day so far. With all these crowds, there had to be a lot of cash in the registers. Catching Edgar sitting at a table on a brief break, she decided to chat with him.

"Edgar," she began in a casual tone of voice. "I keep thinking about what Pete said to Cynthia yesterday. Do you think she really took that money?"

"Never!" said Edgar emphatically. "Once a ten-dollar bill fell out of my uniform, and Cynthia came running up to me with it. Would a dishonest person do that? For that matter, I don't think Erica was a thief, either."

"Hmmm. How long have the thefts been going on?" she asked.

Edgar stood up, hooked his thumbs together, stretched his long, gangly arms over his head, and

40

yawned once. "A few weeks. It's really turned Pete into a raving maniac. You saw him yesterday. He flies off the handle about nothing at all. I guess he knows his days are numbered if he doesn't stop the thefts."

"You mean the corporation will fire him if the stealing keeps up?" Nancy asked, following Pete behind the counter.

"Right. Wouldn't you if you were them?" Edgar winked.

"I guess so. Who'd be manager if Pete got fired? Mark?"

"He's Pete's assistant. I guess so," Edgar said with a shrug. "Then this place would really be in trouble."

"How's that?" asked Nancy.

"Mark isn't exactly Mr. Diligent. He lets people come and go as they please. He doesn't even seem to care if people show up for work!"

"That's weird," Nancy commented.

"I guess he figures he's not to blame if things don't work around here—Pete is."

"By the way, Edgar, how much money *has* been taken?" Nancy asked casually.

"Don't know," said Edgar with a shake of his head. "You'd have to ask Mark or Pete that one, but I wouldn't ask, if I were you."

"How come nobody's called the police?" Nancy asked.

41

"So many questions!" said Edgar, holding his hands to his head. "I just work here, remember? You know, you missed your calling, Nancy. You should have been a detective!"

Nancy was startled momentarily. "Maybe I should have," she replied. "Thanks, Edgar. I guess I'd better get back to work."

Later Pete checked on Nancy to see how she was getting along. To Nancy's relief, he seemed in a pretty good mood.

"Ready to learn the registers?" he asked, motioning her behind the counter.

After she learned to use the cash register, Nancy realized that if someone was taking money directly from the registers, the computer would have fingered the culprit by now. Every transaction was recorded for anyone to see.

"You know," Pete admitted a little gruffly, "I'm sorry about what happened with Cynthia. She was a nice enough kid, but I can't keep a thief here."

"Cynthia didn't steal anything from the restaurant," Nancy said, meeting Pete's gaze directly.

Pete returned her stare and was silent for a minute. "I thought you didn't know her that well."

"I know her friends," said Nancy. "I trust their judgment in people."

"Well," said Pete, with a frustrated sigh. "That money was missing from *her* register."

"Why don't you call the police?" Nancy asked as politely as she could.

Pete's face darkened. "Because I know her boyfriend. And I like to keep things in the family, that's why," he growled.

"But what if she is innocent?" Nancy pressed gently. "That could mean the real thief is still here."

"Let me tell you something, kid. Anybody who steals another dime from this place is going to have to deal with me—personally. Now, let's get back to work. Rule number one: don't waste time," he said with a sudden scowl, heading back to his office. "You're on tomorrow from four to ten," he called over his shoulder as he went.

Mark came up to Nancy. "Did the coach lay into you just now?" he asked with a comforting smile.

"I guess so," said Nancy.

"Pete's in big trouble," said Mark, with a gleam in his hazel eyes. "The way I figure it, there must be several thousand missing by now." He seemed to enjoy spreading the information.

"Poor Pete," said Nancy. "It's really driving him crazy, isn't it?"

"I don't feel too sorry for him, though," Mark added. "It's not like it's his only line of work."

Nancy's ears perked up. "Oh?" she said. "What else does he do?"

"Oh, he's got ten percent of—"

"Mark! Get over here!" Pete's voice blasted out. "Are you working today, or what?"

"Excuse me, please," said Mark. With a little bow of his head, he left Nancy to her register.

The rest of Nancy's eight-hour shift was uneventful, except for the dull, throbbing ache in her legs. Stepping outside just after seven o'clock, Nancy was surprised that Bess and George weren't there to meet her. She checked the skies for the rain that had been threatening all day. A huge gray cloud was hovering overhead, so she decided to head on home and call Bess from there.

She was really curious about what could have happened to Rob—and where Bess and George were.

At least she'd learned a bit that day. Pete had a sideline of some kind, some source of extra income. Nancy wondered if it was the ballplayers he managed or something else. She also wondered why he didn't want the police involved with the thefts, even with his job on the line.

Nancy's thoughts turned to Mark. He obviously wouldn't mind having Pete's job himself. There was a lot left for her to find out, Nancy thought as she made her way through the parking lot to her Mustang. She reached in her purse for her keys and wasn't watching where she stepped.

She heard the crunch first. Under her feet small pieces of glass glinted from the parking lot lights. Looking up from her feet, Nancy focused on her car. She couldn't believe it.

The driver's side window had been smashed to bits!

Chapter

Five

NANCY WAS STUNNED, but took only a moment for a deep breath before going to work. She checked out the inside of the car. There was no note or any sort of message. If somebody was trying to scare her off this case, he or she wasn't being very direct about it.

The smashed window could possibly be a simple case of vandalism. It hadn't been a robbery because the car's stereo system was still intact.

"What a colossal drag," Nancy murmured out loud. She'd just spent eight hours on her feet behind a restaurant counter, her legs were aching, her window was smashed, and her best friends had stood her up. To add the final blow the sky opened up just then, and icy cold water rained down on her, drenching her in seconds.

"Oh, great." Letting out a frustrated sigh, Nancy ran back into Touchdown.

"Edgar?" she called out when she saw him at a corner table, eating. "What are you still doing here?"

"I'm working a couple of hours overtime—the other waitress didn't show."

"Any chance of getting a whisk broom, dustpan, plastic garbage bag, and some tape?" Nancy asked, pushing wet strands of hair off her face.

"Sure, but what are you doing? Sweeping out the parking lot in a downpour? You don't have to work *that* hard around here!" A big goofy grin took over Edgar's face.

"Very funny," she said. "Someone just smashed my car window. I have free air conditioning and a new sprinkler system."

"That's really rotten," Edgar said, getting up and collecting the things she'd asked for. "Here, take our resident umbrella, too. We keep it around for moments like this."

"My car's over here," she said, leading the way out of the restaurant and waiting as he opened a worn but colorful golf umbrella.

"Someone really did a number," he said, letting out a low whistle as they walked up to the

Mustang. "Here, you hold the umbrella, and I'll pick up the biggest pieces."

"I'd like to get my hands on whoever did this!" Nancy growled in frustration, holding the dustpan for Edgar as he swept up hundreds of knife-sharp shards from the vinyl seats.

A car pulled into the lot, and the driver honked its horn. Looking up, Nancy recognized George behind the wheel. Beside her, Bess gaped at the sight of Nancy's shattered window.

"Boy, am I glad you guys didn't forget me!" Nancy cried as George pulled into the slot next to hers.

"What happened?" Bess asked, hopping out of George's car and unfurling her umbrella.

"Unbelievable," George echoed, joining her cousin under the umbrella and letting out a low whistle. "Who did it?"

"That's what I'd like to know," Nancy answered, juggling the umbrella as she helped Edgar tape the hole that had been a window. "It wasn't an accident, that much I know. By the way, how come you're late?

"After we dropped Cynthia off, we went out for dinner. And the service was really slow."

"After today I have a lot more sympathy for waiters and waitresses," Nancy said. "I wasn't fast on my feet at the end of the day, either. What about Rob? Did you find him?"

Bess and George nodded. "Finally. Cynthia's going to call to fill you in later tonight. We don't know much, really."

"I know a place not far from here where you can leave the car overnight," said Edgar, patting down the last bit of tape. "It's called Speed-O's, and it's up on Bedford Avenue, across from the library. The guy who runs it is a friend of mine. I know he'll put a new window in for you. In fact, I can call him at home if you want. Just take your car over there and leave it."

"That would be terrific," said Nancy, dumping the glass shards into a nearby waste barrel.

"Just go three blocks down Main, then left for half a block," Edgar said.

"I'll follow you, Nan," said George as she hopped into her car. Bess slipped in, holding the umbrella out the window to twirl the excess water off.

"Okay. And, Edgar—thanks. See you tomorrow—if you're on." After stepping into the Mustang and sitting down, Nancy motioned to George. She stopped before joining traffic and watched in her rearview mirror as Edgar splashed his way from puddle to puddle like a giant umbrella-carrying ostrich.

The rain was coming down in sheets now, and Nancy had to lean close to the windshield to see into the tunnel of light her high beams cut through the rain and fog. Part of the tape came loose, and she was showered with a cold spray all the way to the repair shop.

When Nancy finally did park the car and slip the key into the mail slot of the Speed-O Car Repair, the left side of her head and shoulders were soaked.

"Ah, a nice dry car," Nancy said, hopping into the back seat of George's car. She relaxed against the seat and enjoyed the warm quiet. The steady click of the windshield wipers was comforting, the regular slow beat forcing her heart to quiet to its tempo.

"So, let's hear about Touchdown," Bess said, finally breaking the silence. "Any leads yet on who might be taking the money?"

"Not really. I found out that Pete has a sideline in addition to the couple of pro players he handles. And that Mark wants Pete's job," Nancy said, leaning forward. "Also, there's something very weird about the whole situation."

"What?" George wanted to know.

"There's more going on at Touchdown than just stolen money."

"What makes you think that?" Bess asked.

"The politics of the place. Mark wants Pete's job, but he doesn't really seem to care how the place is run. Pete has these incredible mood swings. One minute he'll be friendly, the next he's like Jack the Ripper."

"How does all this fit in with your smashed car window?" George asked, pulling onto the ramp for the interstate back to River Heights.

"Beats me," Nancy admitted, stifling a yawn. "I haven't the foggiest."

"Sounds like you need a good night's sleep, Drew," Bess advised.

"You're right, Bess. I can hardly think. Working in a restaurant has been a shock to my system," she said. "There's something I'm forgetting—something I'm not considering—but it keeps getting away from me."

"Tomorrow will bring new leads and new angles," George said comfortingly.

"And a new car window—hopefully," Bess added.

The rain had slowed to a fine mist by the time Nancy made her way up the walkway to her house. In the living room Hannah Gruen, the Drews' housekeeper, sat totally absorbed in a book. She didn't hear Nancy enter, so Nancy stood quietly observing her for a minute. A smile formed on her lips. Nancy's mother had died when Nancy was only three, and Hannah was as close to a mother as Nancy had ever known.

"Hi," Nancy called softly, not wanting to scare Hannah. She hung her jacket in the empty closet.

"Oh, hi, yourself," Hannah said, looking up from her reading with a warm smile. "Oh, no. What happened to you? You're soaked."

51

"It's a long and not very interesting story, but a hot bath and bed will fix me right up."

"Your father just called from California to say hello," Hannah said, leaving the room.

"Oh, no, I missed him again!" Nancy moaned. She and her father Carson Drew, a lawyer with an international reputation, were very close. He'd been away on business for over a week, and Nancy missed him.

Hannah returned with a towel for Nancy's hair. "He said he'd call tomorrow. Oh, and you had a phone call from a girl named Cynthia. She said you could call until eleven."

"Thanks, Hannah." Nancy went upstairs, took a hot bath and then dialed Cynthia's number. "You found Rob, I heard," she said when Cynthia came on the line.

"At the video arcade, but I didn't get too far with him," Cynthia said, sounding very discouraged. "He refused to discuss anything with me. He just said I didn't understand and that he knew what he was doing."

Nancy sank onto her bed, shaking her head. "That's incredible! How did he explain to his parents about leaving the hospital?"

"I got the feeling he lied and told them he was discharged, but I'm not really sure," said Cynthia. "Anyway, I was wondering if you'd come to the football practice tomorrow. Rob wants to watch even if he can't practice. I was thinking

52

you could help me talk to him. I can't get through to him, but maybe you can."

"It wouldn't hurt to try," Nancy replied, trying not to sound discouraged. If Rob wouldn't listen to his doctor or his girlfriend, what could she possibly say to convince him to return to the hospital? "What time do you want to meet?"

"About three. Oh, and bring Rob's gym bag, okay? We left it in the back seat of your car, remember?"

Nancy's free hand flew to her forehead and she gritted her teeth in frustration. How could she have been so blind? That's what the thief had taken from her car!

"Nancy? Are you still there?" Cynthia's voice seemed far away as this last bit of news sank in. Nancy considered telling her that Rob's gym bag had been stolen, but she decided the last thing the girl needed was more upsetting news. Tomorrow, she decided, she'd tell both Cynthia and Rob about the bag.

"I'll see you tomorrow," she said simply. "Three."

Hanging up, Nancy remained seated on the bed and tried to stare out the window. But the light room and dark night turned the window into a mirror, reflecting Nancy's image back to herself. Her forehead was furrowed as she concentrated. Why would anyone break into her car to steal Rob's gym bag? Then, in a flash, she remembered seeing Mark rifling through it when Rob had collapsed.

Obviously, something had been in that gym bag—something that Mark wanted pretty badly. Nancy couldn't let Rob Matthews get away without telling her what it was.

By three the next afternoon, Nancy had picked up her car and was walking across the football field at Bedford High toward the bleachers where Rob and Cynthia were sitting, holding hands. As Nancy got closer to the couple, she noticed a familiar-looking navy blue gym bag with *Yale* printed on the side at Rob's feet.

The exact same bag that had been stolen from her car the night before!

Chapter

Six

WHY WOULD ROB HAVE STOLEN his own bag? He could easily have asked for it back. There had to be some other explanation.

"Hi, Nancy," Cynthia called, with a quick smile and wave. "Come on up. We're watching Coach Novak put the team through its paces."

"Hi," said Rob listlessly as Nancy climbed the bleachers. She sat down beside them. Because of Rob's mood, Nancy realized it would be better not to act too suspicious.

Out on the field the team was going through its workout: doing wind sprints, hitting the tackling bags, stretching, and passing the ball.

"I see you found your bag," Nancy said casual-

55

ly, watching Rob's eyes for any kind of guilty look.

"Oh, yeah," Rob said brightly. "Lonnie found it in front of Touchdown. I guess it got left behind in all the excitement."

Rob's response seemed honest, so if he hadn't taken it, who had? Had Lonnie Price broken her car window? If so, why? All he would have had to have done was ask her for it. "That's very strange," she said pensively.

"What do you mean?" asked Rob.

"I saw Nancy pick up that bag and take it with us to the hospital," Cynthia said, understanding what Nancy was getting at. "It was in her car. Right, Nancy?"

"Until someone broke into my car and stole it yesterday," Nancy added, trying to read Rob's face. "Any idea who?"

Rob's eyes screwed up with worry. "No idea at all," he answered, obviously uncomfortable. "But that explains the missing—the missing money."

"There was money in your gym bag? How much?" Nancy wanted to know.

"Quite a bit," Rob said. "About four hundred dollars."

"Do you usually carry so much money in your gym bag?" Nancy asked incredulously.

"Not usually," Rob admitted. "But I was planning on buying something over the weekend."

"So you had four hundred dollars in cash on you?" Nancy asked.

Rob gave her a suspicious look. "What is this, an inquisition?" he asked, not able to keep the annoyance out of his voice. "I wanted to buy a rowing machine for my basement, and they only take cash, okay? Look, the money is gone; let's just drop it."

Nancy let out a low whistle and looked down at the players on the field. "Pardon me," she muttered.

"Rob!" Cynthia broke in. "Nancy practically saved your life yesterday."

"I'm sorry," said Rob, more conciliatory now. "I didn't mean to be rude. I know you're helping Cynthia out by investigating the thefts at Touchdown, and I appreciate what you're doing for her, but this is a whole other thing."

"It's okay," said Nancy, even though it wasn't. Rob looked awfully uncomfortable just then. What did he mean by a "whole other thing"? What was it he wanted her to stay away from?

Biting her lip, Cynthia shot an anxious look at Nancy and nodded toward Rob.

"Rob," Nancy said, remembering her promise to the cheerleader. "When Cynthia and I talked to Dr. Gebel yesterday, she was really concerned—"

"Look!" Rob interrupted angrily as Cynthia turned away in embarrassment. "I know what you're going to say, and I don't want to hear it, okay? Everyone's been on my back about leaving the hospital, and as far as I'm concerned, it's nobody's business but my own."

"It's your life," said Nancy, trying to hide her reaction to the quarterback's outburst. There was obviously no reasoning with Rob.

She lifted her eyebrows and shrugged her shoulders at Cynthia, who hurriedly brushed a tear from her eye and looked down at her feet. There didn't seem to be anything more they could do for Rob.

Nancy stood up. "I guess I'll be taking off," she said.

"See you, Nancy," said Cynthia, swallowing back her tears.

With a wave, Nancy made her way down the bleachers to the field. Then she had a thought. Rob's coach might know something about why Rob left the hospital. If he didn't, he should.

The coach was standing with a stopwatch at the edge of the track, timing his players' speeds in the forty-yard dash. "Faster! Faster, Ellman! Get the lead out!" he shouted as Bill sped down the track in a blur of motion.

Clicking his watch, the coach smiled and called to Bill. "Not bad. Best time yet, in fact—four and six tenths. I've seen pros with slower times. Now give me a hundred push-ups!"

Grimacing, Bill flopped down and began his

push-ups, while Lonnie Price lined up to start his forty-yard dash.

"Coach, could I have a word with you?" Nancy said as the coach turned and gave her a hard stare. "I'm a friend of Rob and Cynthia's.

The muscular white-haired man grunted, "Just a minute." Then, turning to the track where Lonnie Price was crouching, he shouted, "Go!" Lonnie took off like lightning. Only 4.8 seconds later, the dash was over. "One hundred from you, too, Price!" the coach barked. "The rest of you, three laps, on the double!"

He turned back to Nancy. "Okay, what do you want?" he asked curtly. "I'm in the middle of practice."

"Sorry to bother you," said Nancy. "But there's something important I think you ought to know."

"All right," said the coach, pocketing his stop watch. "This had better be good."

"It's about Rob Matthews," Nancy told him, trying not to let Coach Novak intimidate her. "Did you know he collapsed after the game on Saturday? He was taken to the hospital with a concussion, but he left before they could do any tests on him."

The coach was silent for a moment. "Rob's a big boy," he said at last. "I excused him from practice today, so what more do you want me to do?"

"I thought you might advise him to go back for those tests," Nancy said. "He might listen to you."

"Honey," said the coach with an impatient grin, "I've got a team to run here. And this team is two games away from a state championship. Have you ever won a state championship?"

Nancy shook her head.

"Well, neither have I. And neither have most people in this world," he said hotly. "Now, see these kids working their tails off? Most of them are never going to make it to the pros. Winning the state championship will be the biggest moment of their lives. If you think I'm going to bench my star quarterback because he had a dizzy spell, think again!"

"But he may be endangering his health!" Nancy insisted.

"He looks like he's going to be just fine to me," snapped the coach. "As far as I'm concerned, if he says he's healthy, he's healthy—and he plays on Wednesday!"

"Wednesday?" Nancy asked.

"There's a conflict on Saturday, so we have a game on Wednesday at four o'clock. Rob Matthews is my starting quarterback, okay?"

"But that's only two days from now!"

"You got a problem with his playing, get a doctor's note," the coach replied sarcastically.

He abruptly terminated the interview by turning his back on her.

Nancy walked in front of the bleachers toward the parking lot, shaking her head. The sound of a voice raised in anger came out from under the bleachers and made her stop dead.

"I'll kill you, you little turkey!" The voice sounded familiar now. Quickly Nancy ran around the end of the bleachers to get under them. Lonnie was there. He had a skinny blond player pinned against a post, and he was punching him in the stomach.

"Hey!" Nancy shouted as loudly as she could. "Leave him alone!"

When Lonnie faced her, he had murder in his eyes. "Keep out of this!" he growled. The skinny player squirmed and tried to break free of Lonnie's iron grip. His pale gray eyes widened with fear.

"I said, let him go!" Nancy insisted.

Suddenly Lonnie did let go, but instead of walking away, he made a lunge for Nancy. In a flash he had her by the shoulders.

"You keep out of this, you hear?" he hissed through gritted teeth. "I mean it. Stay out of my business, or I'll make you wish you'd never heard of Lonnie Price!"

Chapter

Seven

USING HER ADVANTAGE of surprise, Nancy brought her arms up inside Lonnie's and broke his hold. She immediately took a karate stance, ready for any new attack.

"Calm down, Lonnie," she said in a steady, calm tone, but her effort was wasted. Lonnie refocused his attention on his blond teammate and shoved him hard against the post.

"Coach Novak, help!" Nancy shouted toward the field. "There's a fight! Help!"

Coach Novak's face was blotchy with fury as he strode over to the bleachers. "Price!" he roared. "Are you out of your mind? Lay off him, *now!*"

Novak's voice seemed to get through to Lonnie, who reluctantly released his victim. The blond boy slid down the post and sat in the dirt under the bleachers.

"What are you doing?" asked the coach, grabbing Lonnie by his shirt and forcing him to meet his eye. "Do you want to put your own teammate out of commission before we meet Montvale?"

"I'm—I'm sorry, Coach," Lonnie said breathlessly. "I don't know what came over me." He looked at the other boy as though he were seeing him for the first time. "Are you all right, Dennis?" he asked, genuinely embarrassed. "Sorry, man. I just lost it."

Nancy stood back as the boy named Dennis struggled to his feet. "Holy mackerel," he gasped, rubbing his chest. "All I did was bump into you, you know? It was an accident!"

"I guess I've been on edge lately," Lonnie mumbled. Turning to the coach, he added, "It won't happen again, I promise."

"Then keep your nose clean, Price," he grunted. "Because if you can't take the pressure, you can take a walk, know what I mean?"

Coach Novak's threat panicked Lonnie. "I can take it, Coach. Really I can—don't bench me, please," he begged.

"You sure you're all right, Dennis?" the coach asked.

"Yeah, I'll be okay," the player answered weakly.

"Take the day off," the coach told him. "As for you, Price, don't let me catch you losing your temper again. Is that understood?"

Red-faced, Lonnie looked down at his cleats and ran a hand through his glossy black hair. "Understood."

"Come on, DiVito," the coach said to Dennis. "We'll have a look at those bruises." The two of them walked off toward the locker room together, the coach holding Dennis up.

His dark eyes full of shame, Lonnie turned to Nancy. "Sorry I came at you like that," he said as they walked out from under the bleachers. "I don't know what got into me."

"I don't, either," Nancy said, genuinely confused. For someone who had just been so threatening, Lonnie was acting pretty gentle and kind.

"Listen, please don't say anything about this to your friend George, okay?" he pleaded. "I don't want her to get the wrong idea about me."

The *right* idea, you mean, Nancy thought. "Look, I have to go," she said, pulling her purse up over her shoulder. "I'll be late for work."

With that, Nancy trotted off to the parking lot, relieved to escape Lonnie and his mean temper. As she got into her car, Nancy found herself mulling over Lonnie's outburst. What had made him react so violently? And then made him so sweet afterward? She decided then and there to warn George to be careful. Lonnie Price was unstable, at best.

The car radio announced it was four o'clock. In a panic, Nancy realized she was already late for work! She drove to Touchdown as fast as possible without breaking the law. The last thing she needed was to be fired from Touchdown just when things were heating up.

The minute Nancy stepped through the door of the restaurant, she sensed she was in luck. Pete was nowhere in sight.

"The boss is out," said Mark, playfully checking his watch as Nancy dashed into the restaurant. "You're twenty minutes late, though."

"Sorry," said Nancy, stepping around the counter area and inside to the kitchen where the staff kept their green and white jerseys.

"Doesn't bother me," Mark said with a laugh. "Pete's in charge of employee efficiency, not me. He told the corporation I had nothing to do with it."

"Well, I'll get to work right away," said Nancy, pulling on the Touchdown jersey and hurrying to her position behind the counter. Not a minute later Pete walked into the restaurant.

"That was close," Edgar Chessman whispered as he passed her on his way to the soda dispenser.

Nancy smiled out of sheer relief. "Hi, Pete," she called out as he approached her.

"How are ya?" Pete asked, not waiting for an answer as he walked past her toward his office.

"Hey, Nancy, I need you to do me a favor," Edgar said.

"Sure, Edgar," Nancy said, still glad she hadn't gotten into trouble for being so late. "What is it?"

"Someone needs to restock the ladies' room, and, well, since you're the only girl working right now . . ." Edgar fumbled.

"Say no more." Nancy chuckled. "Just show me where the stuff is."

Edgar pointed out the stockroom and covered for her while she headed for the ladies' room. She finished and was just pulling the door shut when she heard a muffled voice coming from the direction of Pete's office down the hall.

Curious, Nancy gingerly made her way to the end of the corridor. When she reached Pete's office, she shot a quick glance through the small pane of glass in his door. Pete was standing at his desk holding what looked like an unopened envelope, his hand resting on the phone receiver.

He tore the envelope open and pulled out a sheet of paper. A look of pure panic crossed his face as he read it. Then he flopped down in his dark green swivel chair and rubbed his face wearily.

Nancy ducked back as Pete swiveled his chair directly toward her. The last thing she wanted was for Pete to catch her snooping. Inching back to where she could see him, she watched as he dialed his phone. Apparently, there was no answer on the other end. Tapping his fingers on the desk, Pete waited, then finally slammed the receiver back in the cradle.

Who was he trying to reach? Nancy wondered. What could the note possibly say to upset him so much?

Nancy didn't have time to figure it out, however. Pete suddenly stood up and stuffed the letter into his pocket. His jaw clenched, he headed for the door.

Nancy looked around for an escape route, but there was none. A pay phone was just across the corridor. She made a move for it, intending to pick up the receiver and pretend to be talking.

Before she could make her dash, though, Nancy felt a hand grip her arm, slowly tightening its grasp. She turned to meet Pete's icy eyes boring into hers.

When he spoke, Pete's voice was menacing and cold. "I think you've got some explaining to do, Nancy Edwards," he said. "What were you doing spying on me just now?"

Chapter
Eight

S PYING ON YOU?" Nancy managed to say, giggling like a young schoolgirl. "I was just coming back from the ladies' room."

"Oh, really?" Pete grunted. Nancy held her breath and watched him decide whether or not he believed her. Finally he relented. "Well, get back to work," he said gruffly. "And don't let me catch you near my office again."

With that, he strode toward the restaurant. Nancy's heart pounded wildly as she followed him out of the corridor.

As she slid back behind the counter, Nancy overheard Pete talking to Mark by the far register, where Mark was going over receipts.

"I want you to take over for today, Mark," Pete was saying. "I've got to go somewhere."

"You're going?" Mark repeated in amazement. "But you just got here!"

"Just take care of things," Pete snapped, grabbing his coat before barreling out of the restaurant.

Nancy looked out a side window as Pete hurried across the parking lot to his white car with its gold and blue Bedford Bear bumper sticker. If only she could find out where he was going in the middle of a workday, she thought, frustrated. She was sure his leaving had something to do with the note he'd just read, but how could she follow him to prove it? She was just beginning her shift and couldn't walk out. Or could she?

Looking over at Mark, she quickly improvised a plan.

"Um, Mark? Could I talk to you a minute?" Nancy asked anxiously. If she was going to follow Pete, she didn't have a moment to lose.

"Sure, Nancy," Mark said, giving her a wide grin. "What's up?"

"Oh, Mark," Nancy lamented breathlessly. "I know this is terrible, but I just called home, and my dad reminded me that I was supposed to pick up my aunt and uncle at the airport today. I said I'd do it before I got the job here, and they're *really* depending on me." Nancy made sure to emphasize her speech with heavy sighs and guilty, uncomfortable looks.

"Can't your dad pick them up, Nancy?" Mark asked reasonably.

"Well, he would, but he can't drive," Nancy said, thinking fast. "He broke his ankle a couple of weeks ago on a fishing trip."

Through the front windows, Nancy saw Pete's car pull out of the parking lot, then turn left onto Bedford Avenue. Nancy nibbled a finger nervously. "I know I should have told you before, but I completely forgot about it," she added helplessly.

The assistant manager let out a sigh. "Go," he said simply. "But try to be back as soon as possible, okay?"

"Thanks a million, Mark," Nancy said jubilantly. "You're a doll!" Whipping off her jersey and hanging it on its hook, she raced out of the restaurant and made for her car. If only it wasn't too late!

As she pulled out into traffic, she didn't see Pete's car anywhere. She did know the direction he'd gone on Bedford Avenue, so she headed that way. At every intersection, she slowed and searched both side streets. Cars honked behind her, and she waved them past her.

Frustrated that she was wasting precious time, Nancy did keep going on Bedford Avenue, though.

Just as she was about to give up, she spotted

Pete's white Toyota parked in the lot beside a huge old building. The sign outside said McCann's Gym & Bodybuilding Center. Why had Pete left the restaurant to work out so close to the dinner rush? It seemed completely bizarre.

Nancy parked half a block away and pulled a pair of aviator sunglasses and a lilac-printed scarf out of her glove compartment. It wasn't much of a disguise, but it would have to do. At least the scarf would hide her distinctive reddish gold hair.

She hurried to the building and pulled open the old-fashioned door. A red and gray sign pointed to a glass door on the first floor.

McCann's Gym was sleek and modern. A quick glance at the reception area told Nancy the gym was designed primarily for men. Through the glass doors, Nancy could see nothing much but punching bags, tackling blocks, and free weights. Scattered throughout, men were straining to lift heavy weights free-form. Pete's burly form and distinctive red hair were nowhere to be seen. Nancy stepped inside.

A good-looking, dark-haired guy wearing a form-fitting red T-shirt with a McCann's logo stepped up to the maroon and black reception counter.

"Can I help you?" he asked. "Looking for someone?"

"Hi," said Nancy, lifting her sunglasses to the

71

top of her scarf-covered head. "Um, actually, I was thinking of joining McCann's."

The guy behind the counter shot her a grin. "We don't have many female members. In fact, we don't have any."

"Really? Why not?"

"Well, this is what some people call a rockhead gym," he said. "It's not for everybody."

"I'm not sure I understand," said Nancy, confused. She'd never heard the term before. "What's a rockhead?"

The guy behind the counter smiled and explained, "A rockhead is a body fanatic. Somebody who pumps iron for breakfast, lunch, and dinner. We say they're built like rocks with brains to match."

Nancy laughed at the joke. "Are you including yourself in that description?" she asked.

"Me? Oh, no. Actually, I'm the house intellectual," he countered with a grin and a wink.

"Well, could I at least see some literature?" she asked.

"Sure. I know we keep brochures around here somewhere. There's a lounge around this corner, if you want to wait there."

With that, he sauntered off, disappearing behind a door marked Employees Only. Alone, Nancy glanced around again.

As far as she could tell, Pete wasn't in the gym. If he was in the locker room or shower, she'd

have no chance of finding him. Still, the receptionist might know something about Pete. Nancy
decided to wait in the lounge until he came back
with the brochures.

Before Nancy could make her way to the
lounge, though, she heard voices moving toward
her. One of them was Pete's! Perfect.

Backing off, she looked for cover. The only
place she could find was the counter by the
reception area. She crouched down behind it and
listened.

"You've got to help me out, Doc," Pete was
saying in a whisper. "I'm in real trouble this
time."

"Doc," whoever he was, answered Pete in
calm, reassuring tones as he dropped something
metallic—a key? Nancy wondered—on the
counter above her head. "Don't worry, Pete," he
said. "It'll work itself out. Besides, you've handled it up to this point."

Handled what? Nancy wondered. What kind
of trouble was Pete in?

"Yeah, but now it's getting out of hand," Pete
complained. "How long can I keep this up? I'm
telling you, I'm at the end of my rope!"

"You're all upset about nothing. If you have to
spend a little money, well, that's life," Doc
advised.

"What about you? I thought we were in this
together?" Pete said, his anger barely in check.

"Pete," said Doc, an edge of steel creeping into his mellow voice, "I *can't* help you. Think of my reputation."

"But, Doc—" Pete protested.

"You're just going to have to handle this yourself," Doc interrupted coldly. "You'd better not screw up anymore, either, Pete. One person knows already, and as far as I'm concerned, that's one person too many."

"I told you, there was nothing I could do about it," Pete complained.

"And I'm telling *you* that it's your problem," Doc responded, his voice hard as steel now. "You take care of it. Now, if this keeps up, it's all over. And not just for your boys—for you, too, my friend."

Chapter

Nine

I WON'T MESS UP, DOC," Pete promised, sounding like a scared kid.

"I know you won't," Doc told Pete. "That's why we do business together—because I can count on you." The man's voice was no longer cruel and cold, but it had regained its calm warmth. "Look, let's go soak in the whirlpool. You look like you need to relax a little."

Without another word, Pete and Doc walked away from the desk. Peeking out from behind the counter, Nancy caught a brief glance of Doc from the rear: graying, well-groomed hair, big broad shoulders, and upright carriage. He was wearing a gray T-shirt, running shorts, and gray sneakers.

What Nancy wouldn't have given for a look at his face!

Nancy saw them opening the gym's interior door. When she was sure it had closed shut again, she slowly stood up from her hiding place.

"Well, hello, there," came the voice behind her. Nancy straightened all the way up to find the receptionist, brochures in hand, staring at her behind the counter.

"I was leaning over the counter and I dropped a bracelet," said Nancy, covering for herself.

"Did you find it?"

"Luckily, yes," Nancy replied, jiggling her left arm to show her bracelet. "I've got to get the clasp fixed." She came out from behind the counter.

The receptionist raised his eyebrows doubtfully, but obviously he decided to go along with her story. "Well, I found the brochures," he said. "Here's one about McCann's and another on our personal fitness program. And, of course, this one about our specialized bodybuilding courses. What would life be without them, huh?"

"Thanks," said Nancy, smiling as she reached out to take a few.

"Maybe we could talk about it over dinner? I'm off in half an hour," he said, standing close as he handed the papers to her.

"Er, no thanks," Nancy demurred. "I really have to get going. I'm working tonight."

"Maybe some other time? If you give me your phone number—"

"Well, I guess I could take yours," she countered.

"Sure," he said, writing it down on a slip of paper and handing it to her. "Name's Jake, Jake Deaver. And you're?"

"Nancy," she answered quickly, pocketing the paper. "Nice talking to you, Jake." With that, she stepped quickly to the exit. She didn't want Pete coming out of the gym and spotting her there. Besides, she had promised Mark to hurry back.

"He said, 'If this keeps up, it's all over for you.'" It was ten-thirty at night, and Nancy was filling Bess and George in on what she had learned that day.

"Sounds heavy," murmured Bess, who was sprawled in an oversize chair, her brow furrowed.

"What could he mean?" George asked from the sofa, where she sat with her long legs tucked under her. "If what keeps up?"

"That's what I'm trying to figure out," Nancy said softly as she paced the room.

"Maybe he meant the stealing?" Bess suggested.

"What would a doctor have to do with the thefts at Touchdown?" Nancy asked, flopping down next to George and staring up at the ceiling.

"Just a thought," said Bess, tugging on a blond curl.

"I just thought of something," Nancy said, jumping up and pacing again. "Doc said it would be all over for Pete's 'boys,' too. We know Pete's a sports agent on the side, so maybe his 'boys' are his clients."

"Good idea, but how do we find out?" George asked.

"There's something I need to ask you two," Nancy said, resettling herself in an armchair. "Have you heard anything unusual about Lonnie or Bill or Rob—actually, about any of the guys on the team?"

"You already know that Bill's been getting more and more calls from college scouts," said Bess. "Now he's super nervous about the next two games. In fact, that's all he ever talks about anymore."

"How about Lonnie?" Nancy asked George. "Have you seen anything of him?"

"I talked to him late last night," said George. "He said he wants to see me, but I don't know. After what you just told me about the way he acted at football practice—"

"Try to find out what's eating him, but be careful, okay? He seems to have a pretty mean temper," Nancy told George.

"Don't worry. I don't intend to get him mad,"

George said with a smile. "What should I be looking for?"

"I don't know," Nancy said, biting her lip.

"Look, Nancy, I'm not going to spy on Bill," Bess protested. "I mean, it's okay for George, she just met Lonnie—but I really like Bill!"

"Who asked you to spy on Bill?" Nancy asked. "There is something you can do to help, though."

"Oh, brother. What is it?" asked Bess with a friendly smirk.

"How about throwing a party for the Bears after the game on Wednesday? I have a feeling we could learn a lot from them about Pete."

"A party? Sure!" Bess chirped, delighted with the plan. "That sounds great! Just leave it to me."

The next day Nancy made the trip from River Heights to Bedford in record time. She wanted to make a good impression on Mark and show up early for her eleven o'clock shift.

Stopping for a red light not far from the restaurant, she saw a familiar-looking guy walk out of a building across the street from her. She wouldn't even have noticed him, except for his furtive movements. His shoulders hunched, head down, collar up, he was obviously trying to make himself inconspicuous. Why do people act that way when they don't want to be noticed? Nancy asked herself with a chuckle.

She took another look. It was Rob Matthews. Nancy watched as he continued to stride down the street, casting quick glances behind him.

Nancy checked out the sign on the building: West Bedford Medical Clinic—Private. Was Rob having more problems with his health? Intrigued, she pulled into a parking lot and went inside.

The West Bedford Medical Clinic was decorated with pastel watercolor landscapes and wicker furniture. A middle-aged receptionist wearing a white smock and small gold earrings sat behind a desk, typing.

Nancy glanced at a framed declaration of patients' rights that hung on the wall next to the receptionist. The first right listed was that of privacy. Nancy let out a sigh. She realized she wouldn't get any information by coming right out and asking about Rob.

"Excuse me," Nancy asked. "Is my brother still here? Rob? Rob Matthews?"

The receptionist looked up and gave her a surprised look. "He just left," she explained.

"Oh, no," Nancy lamented. "I was supposed to pick him up."

"Well, he didn't say anything about being picked up. Are you sure?"

"I thought I told him I'd get him," Nancy answered, letting her shoulders drop. "I guess we've all been so worried about Rob. How did it go today, anyway?"

The receptionist looked confused for a minute. "He wasn't here for any treatment. He just picked up his test results."

"Yes, I know," Nancy said, putting on a worried frown. "Were they okay?"

"Sorry, we can't give out test results, honey," said the woman with an apologetic smile. She pointed to the sign on the wall. "Not even to the immediate family."

"It's that bad, is it? Poor Rob—" Nancy made the most of her acting talents.

"It's tough," clucked the receptionist. "Believe me, I know what you're going through. I had a nephew once—a wrestler. No matter what we said, he just wouldn't quit. Why do they want to do that to themselves? It's a shame."

Nancy felt goosebumps rising on her arms. "I know what you mean," she said, wishing she did.

"Listen, you're his sister," said the woman, her eyes sympathetic. "Can't you get him to cut it out? His liver can't take it forever, you know. They never think it'll happen to them, but it does. And liver damage can be permanent," she added ominously.

An elderly client stepped into the clinic just then and walked up to the desk. The receptionist turned to him and gave him a form to sign.

"Well, thanks," said Nancy, slowly retreating outside, and into her car.

Liver damage? Nancy tried to figure every

angle. As far as she knew, Rob didn't drink. But the woman in the clinic had said, "Can't you get him to cut it out?"

Full of concern for Rob and his unknown problem, Nancy turned off Bedford Avenue and pulled into Touchdown's parking lot. Through the front window, Nancy saw a red-faced Pete Shepard standing close to Edgar, whom Pete had backed up against the counter.

Nancy rushed into the empty restaurant in time to hear Pete bellowing at Edgar.

"You'd better have a good explanation for this!" the manager was shouting. "Do I have to fire every single employee in this place? How many times am I going to get ripped off, huh? I put you in charge of watching the registers, and what happens? The biggest chunk of change yet is missing, that's what!"

"But P-Pete," Edgar stammered pathetically. "It wasn't me!"

Nancy approached the scene carefully, not wanting to incite Pete's anger by asking any questions.

"Sorry doesn't cut the mustard, Chessman!" Pete screamed. "Stop protecting people. Just spit it out—who stole the money, huh?"

"I—I don't know, P-Pete," Edgar hedged. "Honest, I don't."

In his terror Edgar backed off to one side, knocking over a metal dispenser of straws. The straws scattered as if they were in a giant game of pickup sticks.

"Now look what you've done, you idiot!" yelled Pete, bending over to scoop some of them up. Nancy got to her knees and started helping, and so did Edgar.

"Sorry!" said Nancy as she accidentally bumped into Pete. She turned to look at him and caught sight of something bulky falling out of his pants pocket.

The manager must have felt the package drop to the floor because he reached down in a flash to snatch at it.

But Pete's hand wasn't as fast as Nancy's eyes. Before he could stuff the package back in his pocket, Nancy spied a small, flat silver key at Pete's foot. And clenched in the manager's hand was a fat envelope—stuffed with cash!

Chapter
Ten

NANCY COULDN'T HELP but stare at the envelope as Pete grabbed it off the ground and fumbled for the key. Pete glanced up at Nancy and knew she had seen the contents of the envelope. He shot her a poisonous look and stuffed the money in his jacket pocket. Clutching the key protectively with one hand, he used the other to point at Nancy.

"Mind your own business, Edwards," he snarled. "Or you'll be sorry."

Pete backed out of the restaurant as the others stood in stunned amazement.

"What was in that envelope anyway?" Edgar asked. "Explosives?"

84

Nancy ran a hand through her silky hair and blew out a deep breath. "Beats me," she said softly.

"Are you okay?" Mark asked, putting a comforting hand on Nancy's shoulder.

Thinking quickly, Nancy called upon her acting talent. "Not really," she murmured weakly. "I hate it when people yell at me. It really upsets me." She pressed her fingers to her temples, hoping to squeeze a tear out of her eyes. "Why does Pete hate me like this?" she asked helplessly.

From the corner of her eye, she spied Pete's car screeching out onto Bedford Avenue, turning in the opposite direction from McCann's Gym. Where was he going this time? She'd give anything to find out.

"Oh, I'm sure he doesn't hate you. He's just got a lot on his mind these days," Mark said reassuringly.

She gulped hard and put her hand to her forehead. "Maybe I'm super sensitive today because of this headache. It's killing me. I think I'm coming down with the flu or something," she complained.

"Well, if you're not feeling well, you should take the rest of the day off," Mark said quietly.

Convincing Mark wasn't very hard, Nancy thought. Her plan was working—if she hurried she would be able to follow Pete. "Won't you be shorthanded?" she asked, doing her best to sound sincere.

"It's okay," said Mark. "Pete shouldn't go around upsetting the help, you know."

"Thanks, Mark," said Nancy, brushing away a big crocodile tear.

Nancy walked slowly out of the restaurant. As soon as the door closed behind her, however, she raced to her car.

Traffic was heavy, and Nancy despaired of ever finding Pete's white car. In a few blocks, though, she did catch sight of him, stuck trying to turn left in a line of cars at the intersection of Main and Bedford.

Nancy finally caught up with Pete again when he pulled into the parking lot of the redbrick post office near the municipal building. Slowing down, Nancy watched as he got out of his car and trotted inside, his hand against the bulge in his pocket.

"That must have been a post office box key he was holding," Nancy murmured to herself as she steered into a space directly across the street from the entrance. Was Pete going to put the money in a box?

When Pete came out, the bulge was gone from his pocket, and Nancy assumed she had the answer to her question. She slid down in her seat as he glanced around.

Now Nancy faced a dilemma. She could wait to see if anyone she knew showed up possibly to claim the money, or she could follow Pete to see where he was going now. She had no idea which mailbox Pete might have used, so Nancy decided she had to follow Pete.

She glanced at her watch before starting her car. It was twelve-thirty.

"Stealing from your own restaurant?" Nancy whispered. "Is that where you got the money?"

From a safe distance Nancy followed as Pete drove to a modest neighborhood on the west side of town. He pulled up in front of a small white house that needed a paint job. In front of the house was a mailbox with the name *Shepard* in large gold letters. Pete checked the mailbox and, finding it empty, went inside.

Nancy was frustrated that all she'd found out was where Pete lived. Hardly big news.

Glancing into her rearview mirror before pulling away from the curb, Nancy froze. A battered Chevy puttered down the street and parked several cars in front of her. Sliding down in the seat, Nancy peeked out as a tall, birdlike figure slid out of the car and strode up Pete's front walk.

Nancy squinted against the glare, then blinked to make sure she was seeing correctly.

Edgar Chessman!

Opening Pete's storm door, Edgar dropped an

envelope between it and the main door, then loped back to his car and drove off. The whole sequence had taken maybe twenty seconds.

Nancy knew she shouldn't, but she walked briskly up the walk and slipped the envelope out from between the doors, praying that Pete wouldn't catch her.

The envelope was sealed shut and had no address or any other writing on it. Shoving the envelope into her jacket pocket, Nancy ran back to her car to head back to River Heights.

At home she could steam the envelope open. That way if it needed to be sealed again, no one would be the wiser.

Nancy raced into the kitchen, where she filled the blue enamel kettle with water and turned the fire on under it. Then she went to the phone and dialed Bess's number.

"Bess?" she said when her friend picked up. "Can you and George come over right away?" she asked. "I think I may have found something that's going to help us break this case."

"You're kidding!" Bess said excitedly. "I'll get George, and we'll be there in five minutes."

The water was bubbling inside the kettle. Soon white steam was pouring out of the spout. With Hannah's kitchen tongs, Nancy held the envelope over the stream of hot vapor until the glue came undone.

Inside was a single sheet of plain white paper, folded once. The message on it was composed of glossy letters cut from magazine ads.

"You're still short five thousand," the message said. "Have it at the post office by Friday noon, or kiss your dreams goodbye!"

Chapter

Eleven

Edgar Chessman?" George said after Nancy filled her in on what had happened. "A blackmailer?"

"I know. It's hard to believe, isn't it? But I saw him." With a shake of her head, Nancy laid the blackmail note down on the kitchen table.

"'Kiss your dreams goodbye,'" Bess read, focused on the letter still. "What dreams?"

"I wish I knew," said Nancy, sitting down at the table and leaning back in her chair.

"What's next, Nan?" asked George, pulling up a chair for herself and sitting down next to her friends. "Are you going to put this back in Pete's doorway?"

"Not right away," Nancy answered, lightly fingering the letter. "I have a feeling I can learn more by *not* delivering it. I want to see what Edgar does when Pete doesn't come up with the money."

"But wouldn't it be the perfect trap to return the letter?" Bess urged. "You could call the police—"

"And they could catch Pete in the act of handing over the money!" George finished for her cousin.

"Not so fast, guys," said Nancy, running a hand through her hair. "There's nothing illegal about giving somebody money. Also, we don't know *why* Pete's being blackmailed, or what that guy Doc has to do with this whole thing. There's a lot more we have to find out."

"You're right," murmured George, leaning on an elbow with her cheek on her palm. "This case is weird."

"Let's concentrate on what we *do* know," Nancy suggested. "Sometimes that helps."

"We know Edgar is blackmailing Pete," Bess offered.

"It sure seems like that's the case," said Nancy with a nod. "But, remember, *Pete* doesn't necessarily know who his blackmailer is. This letter is anonymous."

"True," George agreed.

"I think it's rotten of Pete to accuse Cynthia of

stealing when he's the one taking money from his own restaurant to pay a blackmailer!" Bess said in a sudden outburst.

"Hold on, Bess," Nancy replied reasonably. "We don't have any proof that Pete is stealing from Touchdown, though it certainly does look that way."

"Are you going to tell Cynthia what's going on?" George asked.

"Maybe I'd better," Nancy said thoughtfully. "She's been so anxious."

"The news should help her enjoy the party more. I'm really excited about it—assuming Bedford beats Montvale tomorrow."

"Are you coming with us, or do you have to work, Nancy?" George asked.

"I wouldn't miss the game for anything," Nancy said with a smile. "After all, Pete's going to be there. And wherever Pete goes, I go."

"It's all so incredible," said Cynthia, shaking her head in disbelief the next day before the opening kickoff. "I can't believe Pete's stealing the money from Touchdown."

The stadium was packed for the big game, and anticipation was running high. Nancy, Bess, and George had gotten front-row bleacher seats just behind the cheerleaders' bench. Cynthia was looking up at them, her eyebrows drawn together and her mouth open slightly.

"Well, I can't say for sure yet," Nancy went on. Looking down on the field, Nancy saw Rob practicing tosses. "Oh, and Cynthia," she went on, "there's something else—it's about Rob—"

The referee's whistle blew, signaling the teams to enter. A roar went up from the excited crowd.

"It can wait till later," Nancy said. "You'd better start cheering. The team needs you."

"Right. See you later, Nancy. And thanks for all the good work." Cynthia went off to join the other cheerleaders on the fifty-yard line as the players were introduced one by one. When Bill Ellman's name was called, Nancy noticed a puffy white bandage around his finger. "Hey, Bess, what happened to Bill?"

"Oh, didn't I tell you?" Bess said. "He broke his ring finger at practice yesterday."

"He broke a finger?" Nancy said, amazed.

"Yeah, but he won't let it stop him from playing," Bess added.

"That's incredible," Nancy murmured, wondering if her friend was finally starting to tire of going out with a guy so obsessed with football. "How can he play with a broken finger?"

"Beats me," Bess confessed. "You know, I'm beginning to wonder about Bill. He's so completely wrapped up in himself and the team. All I did was ask him if his finger hurt, and he told me it was none of my business."

"Bess," George said with a shake of her head, "maybe it's time to dump this guy."

"I don't want to talk about it," Bess mumbled.

George and Nancy exchanged a knowing look over Bess's head, but they didn't say anything more about Bill.

"Here comes the kickoff!" shouted Bess as the players lined up on the field.

The whistle blew, and the Bedford kicker booted the ball downfield. The Montvale man caught it but was wiped out by Lonnie Price before he could run a yard.

"Boy," said George with a little whistle, "that was some hit."

The game got rougher. On the next play a Montvale player had to be helped off the field, limping badly. After that, Lonnie delivered a late hit to Montvale's quarterback, sending him to the sidelines, too. By the end of the first quarter, the officials were blowing penalty whistles almost every other play. Even though five of the Montvale players had been sidelined, the team had scored two touchdowns because of all the calls against Bedford.

Down at field level, near the team's bench, Nancy spotted Pete, standing up and screaming, "Go get 'em!" Whenever a Bedford player came off the field, Pete would go over and pat him on the back. Bill and Lonnie gave him high fives, but most of the other Bedford Bears either ignored him or pushed him aside.

"How can he enjoy this?" George wondered, observing Pete. "It's just the kind of thing that gives contact sports a bad name."

"He's that kind of guy," Nancy said with a disgusted shrug.

Down on the field a Montvale player took a shot in the head from Bill Ellman and ran off, clutching at his nose.

"This is horrible!" Bess cried, turning away in shock. "Can't the officials do something?"

"They're doing all they can, Bess," George answered. "Bedford is racking up penalties like crazy. They just had a touchdown called back, remember?"

In the end, though, Bedford came out on top. They'd defeated Montvale by a score of seventeen to ten. The jubilant team marched around the field, their faces ghostly from the unnatural glare of the stadium lights, with their coach on their shoulders. A core of their most ardent fans crushed in on them from all sides.

Nancy turned to George and Bess. "Some game, huh?"

Bess seemed a little stunned. "I guess that's what they call 'winning ugly,'" she said ruefully.

"Check it out," George said, pointing to the field, where a Montvale player tried to shake

Lonnie Price's hand. Lonnie gave him a shove instead. The rejected ballplayer shook his head in disbelief.

"I wonder what the college scouts will think of that," Nancy mused as the three girls walked down the two steps to field level. Cynthia was waiting for them, her eyes welling up with tears.

"Oh, Nancy," she said, her breath turning to puffs of white vapor in the cold November evening. "I'm so ashamed. They acted like brutes!"

"Hey, cheer up, Cyn," said one of the other cheerleaders, trotting by and giving Cynthia a pat on the back. "We're one game away from being state champions! Watch out, Carlisle, here comes Bedford!" The happy cheerleader ran off to join the crowd circling the players.

"Even Rob," Cynthia moaned. "That wasn't football, it was— I don't know what it was."

"Cynthia," said Nancy, putting an arm around her. "I need to talk to you privately."

George and Bess had to leave to get ready for the party, so they said goodbye. Nancy led Cynthia off a short distance to where they couldn't be overheard. "Cynthia," Nancy asked gently, "Rob doesn't drink, does he?"

"Rob?" Cynthia's eyes grew huge. "No way. He's too involved in training to mess up like that."

"Are you sure?" Nancy asked.

"Positive!" was Cynthia's reply. "What made you even think that?"

Nancy hesitated and decided not to tell her what she'd learned at the clinic. The girl was upset enough already.

"Nancy, I'm scared. The way the guys are acting, all these other strange things that are happening—I don't know what's going on."

"Don't worry, Cynthia," Nancy said with an assurance she didn't really feel. "We'll get it all figured out."

Bess's house shook with the sound of a hundred or so Bedford High kids dancing, talking, and whooping it up. Everyone seemed to have forgotten or forgiven the disgraceful way the team had played in the flush of victory.

"Bess really knows how to throw a party!" Nancy shouted to George, who walked over to greet her friend.

"Isn't this fun!" Bess called out merrily, bouncing up to them.

Coming from behind her, Bill Ellman slipped an arm around her waist. "Hey, where are you escaping to, Bess? How about a dance?"

"Okay," Bess said, taking his hand and walking over to the dancing area.

As they walked off, Nancy could swear Bill had turned and given her a look of sheer hatred. What was wrong with him? Nancy wondered, startled.

"He certainly seems happy," George remarked. Obviously, George hadn't caught Bill's poisonous look at Nancy.

"We're number one!" Lonnie Price shouted as he entered the party, his clenched fist aimed at the ceiling. A huge cheer erupted from the guests. "Hey, beautiful!" Spotting George, he put his arms around her and gave her a huge hug.

George resisted feebly and finally pulled herself from his grasp. "Well, hello to you, too," she joked.

"Let's dance, George!" Lonnie shouted, grabbing her by the wrist and pulling her off.

Nancy spied Rob and Cynthia in a corner of the dining room. Rob was pale, and Cynthia was frowning.

Walking up to them with a smile, Nancy said, "Hi, guys. How come you're not dancing?"

"Don't feel like it," Rob mumbled in an unfriendly tone. Cynthia looked over at Nancy and shrugged her shoulders helplessly.

"Rob's been feeling dizzy," she explained anxiously.

Rob stared hard at his girlfriend. "I said, don't tell anybody," he fumed.

"But Nancy's my friend, Rob—" Cynthia protested softly.

"I said, don't tell *anybody,*" Rob reiterated, his

voice filled with frustration. "What are you, dense?"

"You don't have to get nasty about it," Cynthia said, shrinking back against the wall. "Sorry, Nancy."

"Listen, I'll see you guys later, okay?" Nancy said, backing off. What's eating him tonight? she thought to herself as she turned away.

Nancy watched Lonnie and George on the dance floor for a while, then circulated, chatting with the other guests and sampling the great food Bess and George had whipped up.

About an hour into the party Nancy noticed Rob moving furtively toward the kitchen. He was up to something, Nancy decided. But what?

She followed him. Off the kitchen was a pantry with stairs that led to the basement. Poking her head inside, Nancy noticed the door to the basement was half-open. She heard guys talking on the steps.

Standing at the basement door, Nancy pressed her ear to the wooden barrier and listened to the muffled conversation.

"Are you sure?" It was Rob's voice, and it wasn't hard for Nancy to make out who the other two guys were—Lonnie Price and Bill Ellman.

"Definitely," Lonnie replied. "Hogan said he knew her when she was working on that Jake

Webb case. You know, that guy Darryl who was spying for the Russians."

Fear shot through Nancy. Her cover was blown.

"Maybe she doesn't know anything," Bill suggested anxiously. "She's really friends with Bess and George, you know."

"Don't be an idiot, Ellman," Lonnie snapped. "She's onto us, all right."

"Look, you guys," Rob said, sounding scared. "Maybe we should just cool it, huh?"

"What's gotten into you lately, Matthews?" Lonnie demanded. "We've got one more game. You can't back out now."

"But the doctor said—"

"Forget the doctor, Matthews!" Lonnie demanded. "Do you know how many scouts are coming to see us next week? You know what they can do for you? A scholarship at a major university. Maybe a future shot at the NFL."

"But—"

"Rob," Lonnie went on, his voice more soothing, "my doctor said the same thing. But it's going to have to wait one more week."

Nancy remained rooted to the spot and held her breath, hoping they'd reveal their secret.

"What about Nancy Drew, guys?" Bill Ellman asked nervously. "What if she already knows?"

"We'll have to shut her up, that's all," snarled Lonnie.

"What does that mean? How are you going to shut her up?" Rob asked, fear sounding in his voice.

Nancy's spine stiffened as she heard Lonnie's menacing retort. "Never mind," he snarled. "You just let me handle Nancy Drew myself."

Chapter
Twelve

Nancy backed out of the pantry, her heart pounding. Lonnie's promise to "shut her up" sounded real enough. Wincing, she remembered the way Lonnie had pummeled his blond teammate under the bleachers.

"Come on," Bill said, his voice getting louder as he started up the steps. "Let's get back to the party."

Stepping lightly, Nancy dashed through the kitchen and back into the living room. She spotted Bess and George, who were standing alone, talking together.

"What's wrong, Nancy?" George asked the

moment she saw her friend. "You look like you just saw a ghost."

Rob, Bill, and Lonnie had just come into the dining room. Nancy could feel their eyes on her.

"I need some air," Nancy told her friends, guiding them each by an elbow. "Let's grab our coats and go outside."

"Nancy, I'm worried. What's the matter?" Bess asked anxiously when they had closed the front door behind them.

Nancy leaned against the railing on Bess's front porch and told them about the conversation she'd just overheard, leaving out Lonnie's threat. There was no point in worrying her friends needlessly.

"So now your cover is blown," Bess concluded, shaking her blond curls.

George let out a low whistle. "Bad break," she murmured.

"This could be a real problem," Nancy added, shaking her head. "If they tell Pete, there could be real trouble."

"Nancy, what do you think Rob meant about his doctor telling him to stop?" Bess asked nervously. "Do you think he's got some sort of disease?"

"I doubt it," George put in. "He wouldn't be in good enough shape to play football if he did."

"Good point," said Nancy. "I'm not sure what's going on, but I can tell you one thing. If we don't figure it out by the last game, we might never do it."

"Nancy," said George, her dark eyes alive with concentration, "this couldn't have anything to do with Pete, could it? Maybe when Rob and Bill talked about their doctor, they meant that man named Doc?"

"The guys are friends with Pete," said Nancy. "And they've all been acting nervous and hostile lately. Something is definitely up. When Doc referred to 'the boys,' maybe he did mean—"

"Hi, girls. Good to see you, Nancy." Lonnie Price's sarcasm cut into the chilly night. "Getting a little air?"

Nancy and her friends spun around to face Lonnie and Bill. Bill's eyes bored into Nancy's.

"I was just saying good night," Nancy fibbed, trying to sound casual as she stepped down off the porch. "I could use a good night's sleep. Do you want a lift, George?"

"I'll take you home, George," Lonnie offered, turning on his most charming smile.

"Actually, Lonnie, I'm kind of tired. I think I will go with Nancy," George announced with a smile as she stepped down the porch steps. "See you tomorrow, Bess. And good night, guys!"

By ten-thirty the next morning Nancy was back at the West Bedford Medical Clinic. This time she hoped she'd be able to get in to see Rob's doctor.

"Hello, there, honey," said the receptionist with a warm smile of recognition. "How's your brother doing?"

"Not too well," said Nancy with a frown. "He won't talk to us, and I'm afraid he's still—you know."

"Mmmm." The receptionist nodded, her brows furrowing.

"I know you won't discuss the test results with me, but if I could just talk to the doctor—maybe he could give me some help on how to reach Rob." Or maybe, she thought, I can get a solid clue about what's really going on.

"I'll see what I can do for you. Just wait right here." The receptionist went off to speak to the doctor. A few minutes later she returned, saying, "It may be a wait, but Dr. Treschel will see you."

Nancy flipped through magazines for the better part of an hour until the receptionist finally signaled her to come to the desk.

"Dr. Treschel can see you briefly," she said. "First door on the right."

The doctor's office was painted dark green and decorated with oil paintings of wilderness scenes. From behind a mahogany desk, Dr. Treschel, a dark-haired man of about forty, looked up.

"Ms. Matthews?" he asked, meeting her eyes with a steady gaze. "How may I help you?"

105

"Doctor," Nancy began, taking a seat by his desk. "We're so worried about Rob. We don't really understand what's going on, and he won't talk about it. Could you—"

Holding up a palm, the doctor frowned. "We often get concerned family members in here. But you must understand, our patients have a right to privacy."

Nancy let out a disappointed sigh and looked down at the dark green carpeting. "Can't you break your rule, just this once?" she pleaded.

"I'm sorry," Dr. Treschel said, a look of genuine concern in his eyes. "Please tell your parents, though, that Rob is seriously jeopardizing his health."

"You mean—?" Nancy murmured helplessly, feeling tantalizingly close to learning the truth.

"I mean exactly what I told him. He's got to stop. Right away." The doctor added a meaningful stare. He ran a hand through his glossy hair and smiled sadly. "See if you can talk to him. If you'll excuse me—"

With a frustrated sigh Nancy stood up and walked out. Once more her attempt to find out what was happening to Rob had led nowhere.

Nancy left the clinic, planning her next move. At a nearby phone booth, she fished the brochure from McCann's Gym out of her purse and punched in the number. Jake Deaver understood a lot about the mental and physical makeup of athletes. Maybe he could give her some insight into the kind of danger Rob was in.

"McCann's," came Jake's familiar voice.

"Jake? It's Nancy. Nancy Edwards. Remember me? I came in the other day to look the place over, and you said—"

"Of course I remember you," came the smooth reply. "Have you decided to take me up on my offer for dinner?"

"As a matter of fact, I have," she answered. "How about lunch?" she asked, glancing at her watch. It was eleven-fifty—she'd have just enough time to get to McCann's by noon.

"Lunch is fine," he said. Nancy could almost feel the smile in his voice.

"I'll see you in ten minutes, then, at the gym." She hung up and, walking with new determination, got into her car and headed for McCann's.

"Hello, there," said Jake, looking up with a warm smile when Nancy walked into the reception area of the gym.

"Hi," Nancy replied. "Thanks for meeting me."

"Thanks for inviting me," he said, lifting a gray jacket off the coatrack near the file cabinet and slinging it over his shoulder. "There's a quiet little place near here called Le Corner Bistro. I thought we could go there."

"Sounds great," Nancy said, smiling at the name of the restaurant.

They walked out of the building and rounded the corner past a group of stores to the restaurant.

"After you," said Jake, gallantly holding the door open for her.

Nancy walked in and spotted a booth near the back of the place. "How's this?" she asked Jake.

"Fine with me," he answered, slipping into the booth and signaling a waitress whose dark hair was knotted on top of her head.

Nancy and Jake ordered two mineral waters while they looked over the menu. "The quiche is excellent," he told her.

"I think that's what I'll order. With a green salad," Nancy told him.

The waitress returned and set two glasses and two bottles of water in front of them.

"Two quiches with salads," Jake told her.

As soon as the waitress was out of earshot, Nancy met Jake's gaze and sighed. "Jake, I'm hoping you can help me," she said.

"Anything," he promised. "Just ask."

"It's about my girlfriend's boyfriend. He's a real jock, you know? He's been acting kind of weird lately. He won't talk to me about it, but he's been having dizzy spells, and he's always acting hyper and angry. He even passed out. His pulse was uneven, and his breathing was off, too."

"I see a lot of that at the gym," Jake said with a knowing nod.

"You do?" Nancy asked, surprised. "Tell me about it."

"Oh, we've got guys passing out there all the time. I told you they're crazy, remember?"

"I don't get it, though," Nancy said. "People pass out just from sheer exertion?"

"Well, yeah, they do sometimes, but that's not what we're talking about here, is it?"

Nancy leaned in toward him.

"I sympathize," he said, taking a sip of his water. "See, I was into that garbage myself once. Really bad mood swings, headaches, always getting dizzy. I wound up in the hospital, finally, and it was a good thing, too. My liver would have been shot if I'd gone on much longer."

"Your liver!" Nancy gasped.

"Yup," he replied with a regretful shake of his head. "Fortunately, I quit."

"I don't understand," Nancy prodded. "Quit what?"

Jake paused and gave Nancy a long look, obviously wondering if he should tell her. Finally he spoke up. "Steroids, Nancy. It sounds to me like your friend is on steroids."

Chapter

Thirteen

S TEROIDS?" Nancy said the word slowly, carefully. Finally. Now she had the missing piece of the puzzle, the one that had eluded her for so long.

"Yeah, steroids," Jake murmured, shaking his head. "They're real bad news and terrible for your health, but a lot of guys take them anyway. The kind you see most is the one that's worst for your liver—dynazol."

"Dynazol!" Nancy remembered running across it once before, on a case she'd solved with the Hardy brothers. "Steroids do cause mood swings, hostility, and dizziness, too. Don't they?" Nancy asked breathlessly.

"All of the above," Jake said with a nod. "Like I said—steroids are bad news. And dynazol is one of the worst."

"Whew." Nancy sighed, and then took a sip of her mineral water. "Everything you're saying makes perfect sense."

"Everyone thinks they can get away with it," Jake said, his face suddenly sad. "But after a while—and when someone's already blacking out, that time isn't too far away—their health just falls apart. At that point it's a short downhill ride."

A chill slowly made its way over Nancy. Rob had obviously begun his "downhill ride." No wonder he looked terrible and seemed so fragile. His body was being ravaged by one of the most potent drugs around. "Why do people do it to themselves?"

"Lots of reasons," Jake explained as their lunches arrived. After the waitress left, he continued. "You said your friend's a jock, right? Well, if he's hot stuff, then he's probably under a lot of pressure to succeed. Steroids build muscles, stamina, and physical strength. Unfortunately, they do a lot more harm than good. See, the harm's invisible for a long while, sometimes long after it's too late. In the end steroids destroy a lot more careers than they create."

"And it goes on a lot, huh?" Nancy asked.

"You wouldn't believe how widespread the use

of the stuff is. You don't even have to be a big-time jock to take it. Some guys use the stuff just to impress the girls. They want bulging muscles to show how strong they are. Trouble is, when you're sick, nobody looks good."

"Jake, how do people get their hands on the stuff?" she asked.

Jake looked at her sharply. "You mean, how is your friend getting them, right?"

Nancy's eyes met his evenly. "That's exactly what I mean."

"There are a few ways. Doctors can prescribe the drugs, but no ethical doctor will. Most people get it from underground contacts."

"Such as?" she wanted to know.

"Coaches, mostly. A lot of coaches'll do anything to have winners. They don't care about their athletes' long-term health."

Nancy thought of Coach Novak. He certainly seemed to be the type to want to win, even at the expense of his players' health.

"Jake, this has been a very educational lunch. I really appreciate your talking to me," Nancy said after they finished eating. She reached into her purse, wanting to pay for lunch and get to Bedford High right away. The time had come to confront the Bears' coach.

"Wait a minute!" Jake protested. "You're not going? We haven't had a chance to talk about you. Let's get together again, okay?"

"Jake, I like you a lot," Nancy explained softly, "but the truth is, I already have a boyfriend. You know how it is—we're in love."

"How come all the good ones are taken?" Jake said. "He's a lucky guy, Nancy."

"Thanks," Nancy said with a little laugh. "And, of course, I want to pay for lunch."

"Forget it, will you?" he said, grabbing the check from her. "One of these days you'll buy me lunch. Good luck with your friend, Nancy. If he wants to talk to someone who's been there, have him give me a call."

"Thanks," Nancy said, touching his shoulder lightly and smiling at him before she turned to leave. "You've been terrific, Jake."

Excited and energized by her new information, Nancy flew to her car and hopped inside. As she drove to Bedford High, Nancy knew there was no reason Coach Novak would talk to her, especially if he was the one providing his players with steroids.

But, Nancy reasoned, if the coach didn't know anything about his players taking steroids, he would talk. Either way, the coach was her best bet right then.

Within fifteen minutes Nancy was sitting in the coach's tiny office. As gently as she could, and carefully observing his reaction, Nancy told him her suspicions.

"You want to repeat that?" said Coach Novak,

the anger in his voice barely suppressed. He leaned across his desk and shot Nancy a disdainful look. "I'm not sure I heard you right."

"I said, I have reason to believe some of your players are using steroids. Dynazol, to be exact."

"Uh-huh." The coach folded his arms on his chest and leaned back again. "And who exactly do you think you are to be accusing my players, Miss Nancy Edwards?"

"Drew. Nancy Drew. I'm a detective, sir. I solved a case once before here at Bedford High. It involved Jack Webb's murder."

"Oh, yeah? I don't remember you being involved in that," the coach said dubiously.

"Mr. Parton can verify it, if you ask him." Talking to the school principal would surely convince the coach that she was telling the truth.

"Mr. Parton retired," the coach shot back. "He moved to Florida. There's a new principal here at Bedford."

"Oh." Nancy let out a breath and tried to decide what tack to take next. Getting through to the coach was proving to be hard work. She decided to try the direct approach. "Are you supplying the team with steroids?" she asked, watching his face for any signs of guilt.

"Don't make me sick," growled the coach, staring back at her hatefully. "I want to win. Not cheat."

Something in the way he said it convinced

Nancy that he was telling the truth. Still, if he wasn't providing the drugs, somebody was. But who?

"I'm sorry, Coach. I know how disappointed you must be. Believe me, I wouldn't be here if I didn't have a good reason to suspect steroids," Nancy explained.

The coach shook his head again. "I don't believe this," he said. "I'm on the verge of winning my first state championship in twenty-seven years of coaching, and you come in here and tell me it's all the result of steroids!"

"I'm not saying that, Coach Novak," Nancy objected. "I'm just saying you should find out if it's true!"

"Wait a minute—did the coach at Carlisle put you up to this?" he asked, his nostrils flaring. "I wouldn't put it past him. He wants the state championship as much as I do. This is just the sort of thing I'd expect him to pull."

"I don't know who or what you're talking about, Coach Novak," Nancy said, losing her patience. "What I *do* know is that somebody is feeding steroids to at least three of your star players, maybe more—and the drugs are seriously endangering their health. Now, if you won't look into it, I'll have to go to the principal and ask him to—"

"Go ahead!" steamed the coach. "But I don't think you'll get very far. The new principal and I

115

are very close. I know for a fact that he wants to see us win the state championship as much as I do. He wouldn't tamper with the team's morale and do something crazy a week before the championship game."

Nancy gritted her teeth and sighed. The coach was probably right. She didn't have any evidence for her theory.

"I'll tell you what," the coach said at last. "After the game, if you want to pursue this, I'll discuss it with you again. Meanwhile, why don't you just go back to wherever you came from and leave us alone?"

Nancy said nothing. Coach Novak obviously didn't want to rock the boat right now before the championship game, and there was no use trying to convince him to change his mind. As if to emphasize his point, the coach got up and walked over to open the door for Nancy.

"Goodbye, Ms. Drew," the coach said with a slight grin. "Thanks for your help, but I can manage my own team, thanks."

"Okay, I tried," Nancy murmured, getting up and leaving the office.

As she walked down the hall toward the parking lot exit, Nancy tried to plan her next move. Behind her, she heard the click of a door closing. Then a shuffling sound. Was it her imagination, or was someone following her?

She turned but saw nothing. Don't be ridiculous, she told herself. There was no place safer than a high school during the daytime. Still, the feeling of someone following her persisted. With a sigh of relief she reached out to pull the metal bar on the exit.

But an arm across her neck stopped her. Gasping for breath, Nancy felt another strong arm reach around her waist and squeeze with a vise-like grip.

Fighting panic, Nancy clawed desperately at the iron arms that had her pinned tight. It was no use. Her strength was no match for her attacker's. Nancy fought desperately for breath, then remained just on the edge of blacking out.

"This is a warning," said a gravelly voice in her ear. "Don't mess with success, Nancy Drew—or you might wind up dead!"

Chapter
Fourteen

WITH ONE FINAL SQUEEZE around her neck that made Nancy see stars, the iron arms shoved her up against the exit door. As she fell against the steel bar, it gave and the door flew open, making Nancy fall headlong out of the building.

"So long, sweetheart," her attacker whispered as she fell to the pavement. The door was pulled shut. After Nancy caught her breath, she staggered to her feet, hoping to get a look at her attacker. It was too late.

The door had no handle on the outside. Nancy pulled on it, but it didn't budge. Her anonymous attacker was safely inside, making his getaway.

Rubbing her neck and leaning against the door

while she recovered her composure, Nancy tried to place the voice. Coach Novak? Nancy didn't think so.

Breathing hard, Nancy touched the tender skin on her neck lightly. As her hand came away, she noticed a small strand of jet black hair in her fingers.

In a flash, she realized the iron arms and gravelly voice had to belong to Lonnie Price. So he had kept his promise to "shut her up."

Well, Nancy decided, she had a promise of her own to keep, and Lonnie's intimidation tactics weren't going to stop her.

It was almost time for her shift at Touchdown, so Nancy headed for work.

Driving along the tree-lined streets of Bedford, Nancy's mind was churning with thoughts and images: Cynthia's being fired by Pete; Doc's threatening tone at the health club; Edgar's dropping the blackmail letter at Pete's; Mark's indulgence with the staff.

Then there was the situation at Bedford High, an entire team being torn apart by wild mood swings and all the other effects of steroid use.

What did it all add up to? Nancy was working on two cases at once, and they were tearing her concentration apart. What had started as the simple impulse to help a new friend had turned into two tough, dangerous situations.

"Hi, everyone," Nancy called as soon as she

got inside the kitchen at Touchdown. Touchdown was relatively empty. The lunch rush was over, and it wasn't time for the dinner crowd yet. For now the place was quiet.

"Hello, Nancy. How ya doin'?" It wasn't much of a greeting, but for the first time since Nancy had met Pete, his smile seemed to be genuine.

"Nancy!" Edgar Chessman approached her the second she took up her position behind the register. "There's something you've got to hear."

Nancy finished opening the register, took out a stack of bills, and turned to him eagerly. "Yes?"

"See, there was this bullfrog who wanted to get to California, and he met a turtle—"

Nancy listened to the long rambling joke as she counted up the cash from the lunch crowd.

Just as the punchline was coming, Pete's voice came from behind them. "Quit clowning around, Chessman," Pete growled. "I've got to talk to Nancy right away. Meet me in my office, pronto."

"Okay," Nancy said apprehensively, putting the money back into the register and closing the drawer.

Nancy followed him to his office, her heart pounding. If Lonnie had told him that she was a detective, Nancy's career at Touchdown was over right now.

She needn't have worried, though, because when Pete sat down at his desk and glanced at her from under his thick eyebrows, his expression was almost apologetic.

"Mark said you were upset 'cause I yelled at you," Pete said from behind his desk.

"Oh. Well, I guess I was," Nancy replied.

"Sometimes I shoot first and look later," Pete confessed, looking downcast. "Sorry."

"Do you still think I stole the money?" she asked, looking him in the eye.

"No," he murmured ruefully. "I don't know who's taking it, but the accountant tells me another five thousand is gone."

You're stealing it, you big phony! Nancy thought. But she played along, not wanting him to know what she suspected.

"Nancy, I am happy with your work here at Touchdown," Pete said. "You've been working out well. I'd like to give you a regular schedule and up your salary fifty cents an hour."

Nancy did her best to look happy. "Great!" she said, forcing a smile.

"That's all," Pete told her, leaning back in his chair. "You can go back to work now."

"Sure," Nancy said with relief. So Pete *didn't* know she was a detective after all. That would give her a little time, at least, to find the evidence she needed to prove he was stealing from Touchdown.

An hour or so later customers were beginning

to stream into the restaurant. Soon the dinner rush was in full swing.

"Hey! How's the food in this joint?" said a familiar voice. Nancy looked up and saw Bess Marvin's smiling face staring into hers.

"Hi, Nan!" Bess said. Behind her were George, Lonnie, Rob, and Bill. Nancy sneaked a brief glance at Lonnie, but his attention was focused on the corner of the dining room.

"Hi, Pete!" he called out. "How ya doin', buddy?"

"Hey, guys!" Pete called out cheerfully, coming up behind Nancy and leaning over to shake the guys' hands. "Great game the other day." Turning to Nancy, he added, "I'll take this order myself."

Nancy stepped out of the way as Pete filled up the to-go bags with food and drinks.

"I put some little goodies in there for you," Pete said to the players with a wink.

Nancy noticed a dark look cross Lonnie's and Bill's faces when they heard what Pete said. Rob looked scared. Motioning for Pete to follow him, Lonnie walked down to the end of the counter area as Nancy took the money for the order. Bill followed the other two guys, taking the bags with him.

Glancing sideways, Nancy watched Lonnie whisper in Pete's ear. He looked back at her from time to time. Pete's face took on an expression of amazement and alarm, and he glared at Nancy.

So much for her cover—Nancy sensed it was being blown at that very second. Her career at Touchdown had come to an abrupt end.

At the same a time a light bulb was going off in Nancy's brain. Pete's reference to "goodies" in the bags was too tantalizing to let pass. If Pete was providing the players with steroids, the bags would be the perfect way to pass them to his favorite football stars!

Making sure the guys didn't see her, Nancy quickly put two burgers and a soda into another bag.

"George," Nancy whispered to her friend, handing her the new bag, "see if you can switch this bag for one of the others without the guys seeing you. Hide the original, and be sure to call me later—at home. Okay?"

"Gotcha." George nodded, slipping the bag into her tennis bag. "What's up, Nan?" she asked.

"Tell you later," Nancy replied. "What are you doing going out with Lonnie?" Nancy asked.

"I'm not—not really. Bess and I were coming in here for supper to go, and we ran into them in the parking lot. I've got a tennis tournament tonight at Millbrook, and Bess mentioned it. They all want to come watch. What could I say—no?" George asked.

"You all set?" Lonnie asked George, ignoring Nancy completely. "Let's go."

After they had left, Nancy looked around for Pete but didn't see him. Wherever he was, though, it hardly mattered. If Nancy's hunch was right, Pete had just blown it royally. And if George could make the switch, Nancy was sure she'd have her first hard evidence—steroids in a bag from Touchdown.

A few minutes later Nancy watched as Lonnie stormed back into the restaurant, holding a bag in his hand. Looking annoyed and upset, he walked into the hallway leading to Pete's office.

"Uh-oh," Nancy said under her breath. "Here it comes."

In less than a minute Lonnie was out of the restaurant again, followed by Pete, who called to her from the hallway. "Nancy!" he called out. "Come over here!"

Nancy walked bravely up to him. "Yes, Pete?" she said, much cooler than she felt.

"You're fired!" he said, spitting each word out. "Get out of here!"

Nancy didn't ask why, and she didn't argue. Pulling off her Touchdown jersey, she folded it neatly and put it on the countertop.

"Goodbye, Edgar," she said, giving him a wave of her hand. "It's been nice working with you." And I'll be seeing you tomorrow at the post office, she added to herself on her way to the door.

That night Nancy's phone rang at nine-thirty. "Nancy," said George excitedly. "That little scene in Touchdown was incredible."

"You made the switch, didn't you." It was a statement, not a question. Nancy knew from Lonnie's second visit to Touchdown that George had been successful.

"I sure did," said George. "Have I ever let you down?"

"Never," Nancy agreed. "Did you look inside the bag?"

"I wasn't going to, but Bess was curious, so—"

"And?" Nancy asked eagerly.

"We found a packet of pills," George replied grimly. "Is that what you were looking for?"

"That's what I was looking for," Nancy confirmed. A rush of pride shot through her. "Good work, George."

"I don't get it," said George. "What are they? Drugs or something?"

"They're steroids, George," Nancy said. "And you know what else they are?"

"What?"

"They're *evidence,* that's what. Evidence that proves Pete Shepard has been illegally handing out drugs to high school football players!"

125

Chapter
Fifteen

At 11:45 THE NEXT DAY Nancy was parked on the street across from the Bedford post office, in Hannah Gruen's car.

"Just in case someone recognizes my Mustang," Nancy had explained to George and Bess, who were waiting with her.

George leaned back in the front seat and finished off the tea she'd picked up at a nearby doughnut shop. "Didn't the note say the money had to be there by noon? Edgar should be here by now," she said, crushing the cup and putting it back in the bag it had come in.

"Right," said Nancy, peering farther down the

126

street through a pair of black binoculars. "So far nothing."

"What a nightmare," Bess murmured from the back seat. "Don't those guys know what they're doing to themselves by using steroids?"

"Let me tell you something, Bess," said George, fluffing up her short dark hair with both hands. "When you're an athlete and you're really good, wanting to be the best can take over. You'll do anything to make yourself stronger or faster."

"I still can't believe what a jerk Bill turned out to be," Bess said with a sigh.

"Don't worry," Nancy said with a smile. "There'll be other guys."

"You always say that, Nancy," said Bess.

"And she's always right," George pointed out.

"Oh, be quiet, both of you. Can't you see I'm devastated?" Despite her words, it wasn't too hard to tell that Bess would have no problem getting over her crush on Bill. "What a waste of talent," she moaned.

"You can say that again," George agreed. "When this situation gets blown open, he's bound to be thrown off the team and lose any chance of a college scholarship."

"I hate to see it happen," Nancy said, keeping an eye on the post office for Edgar's approach. "They played with fire and they're going to get burned. Hopefully, the guys will be able to put this all behind them. Pete, on the other hand—"

"I don't understand, Nan," Bess said. "What does he get out of all this? Money?"

Nancy didn't know how much money Pete stood to make by selling steroids, but she didn't think it could be all that much. "I have a feeling there's more to Pete's involvement than that," she speculated.

"Like what?" George asked.

"Remember, Pete's a players' agent," Nancy reminded them. "Maybe he has some kind of secret agreement with the guys. Say, if they make it in the pros, he'll get a piece of their money in exchange for steroids now."

"It sure would explain Doc's remark to Pete about 'you and your boys,'" Bess put in.

Nancy kept her eyes fixed on the entrance to the post office. "It's just a theory, remember," she told her friends. "But I think we can assume that Pete's getting the steroids from that guy Doc. Doctors would have access to the stuff, after all. The trouble is we have no proof of anything—yet."

"We've got proof of one thing," Bess corrected her. "We know Edgar Chessman's blackmailing Pete."

"We know only that he delivered a blackmail note, for sure," said Nancy. "Though it is a little weird that he'd drop off a note one place and pick up the money at another," she said, almost to herself. "Where is he, anyway?" Nancy murmured, tapping her fingers impatiently on the steering wheel.

"It's after noon," Bess said, checking her watch. "You'd think he'd have been here by now."

"You'd think he'd be in more of a hurry to claim five thousand dollars," George said with a wry smile.

Nancy's eyes were fixed on a figure in her rearview mirror. "Wait a minute! Here comes someone from Touchdown now. But it's not Edgar—it's Mark."

"I don't get it," Bess said, pursing her lips as Mark disappeared inside. "You saw Edgar delivering the blackmail note. It can't be Mark!"

"This case is complicated, isn't it?" Nancy murmured.

At least it was one case now, not two, and Nancy could sense a breakthrough coming.

"Here he comes again," said George, letting out a slow whistle. "He looks irritated."

"No fooling," said Bess. "Duck, everybody! He's looking this way."

The three girls crouched down in their seats to avoid being seen. When they came back up for a peek, Mark was gone.

"Okay," Bess said to Nancy. "What now?"

Nancy was busy thinking, a plan forming in her mind. One sure way to get the confessions she needed was to lay a trap. "I think we've got to be aggressive in this case," she said. "I want to arrange a little meeting of all the people involved and invite the police to listen in."

"Good idea," said George excitedly. "How do we do that?"

"Do you guys know where Bill's, Lonnie's and Rob's lockers are at school?" she asked.

"Cynthia will know," Bess said eagerly. "I can probably find her during her study period. It's at one o'clock."

"Great," Nancy said with a jubilant smile as she started her engine. "Now let's find a stationery store and a magazine stand. We need to put together some notes for you to take to Bedford High."

Within a few minutes the girls had everything they needed.

"Now," said Nancy. "Where can we work?"

"How about that coffee shop?" George suggested, pointing to a small railroad car diner across the street from the magazine stand.

"Perfect," said Nancy, marching across the street.

"May I help you?" asked the elderly waitress after Nancy and her friends settled into a cracked vinyl booth.

"Anybody hungry?" Nancy asked as she spread the magazines out on the Formica table.

Bess shook her head, and George shrugged.

"Just three teas, I guess," George told the waitress, who went off to get them.

"Look for *field, football, payment,* and *Doc,*" Nancy told Bess and George, shoving a stack of magazines toward them.

Half an hour later the written messages for Lonnie, Bill, and Rob were finished.

Meet at the football field, tonight at 8. Be on time—it's urgent. P.

Another note was composed of words cut from magazines.

Shepard—Come to the football field 8:00 tonight, with final payment of $5,000, or else. By the way, I know about your pal Doc. Bring him with you. I want you both there, on time.

"Let's hurry," Nancy told her friends, putting enough money on the table to cover their bill and a generous tip. "I'll give you a lift to Bedford High, do a couple of errands, pick you up, and we'll drive back to River Heights."

Nancy drove over to Bedford High, and while Bess and George were inside delivering their messages, she went to a corner phone booth and dialed the local police.

"Hello," she told the officer who answered. "I'd like to speak to Chief Boyle. It's Nancy Drew."

Only a minute passed before the chief got on the line. "Nancy Drew!" he said cheerfully. "It's been a long time. Good to hear your voice again. Got a problem over there in River Heights?"

"Actually, Chief Boyle, the problem's here in Bedford." She proceeded to tell him everything that had happened, feeding coins into the phone whenever her time ran out.

"So you want us to show up there? Catch them in the act of exchanging the steroids?" the chief offered after he heard what Nancy had to say.

"I think you should be there," Nancy suggested.

"I'd hate to see you girls in danger," the chief murmured. "Maybe you should stay home."

"I want to be in on the end—if I can, Chief," Nancy said.

"All right," the chief said with a reluctant sigh. "Where will we meet you?"

"Under the bleachers," Nancy told him. "Near the fifty-yard line."

The chief sighed. "If you're right about this, Nancy, it's going to be a big scandal. Town pride may never recover."

"It'll recover, Chief," Nancy assured him. "You know what they say—the truth makes you free."

Before heading back to pick up Bess and George, Nancy had one more thing to do. She got in her car and drove over to Pete's house to deliver her little note.

On the way she went over her plan again. She hoped the guys would arrive first, wondering what was going on. Then Pete and Doc would show up and deny inviting them. He'd probably tell them about the blackmail, and then they'd decide to wait for the blackmailer to show up.

Nancy's face tightened. She had one more note to write. Since she didn't know whether the blackmailer was Edgar or Mark, though, she'd have to write notes to both.

As Nancy turned the corner to Pete's block, her mind was filled with thoughts about the upcoming evening. Slowing down in front of Pete's house, Nancy's attention was drawn to a figure walking up to Pete's mailbox.

Nancy would have recognized that goofy gait anywhere. It was Edgar Chessman.

Once in front of the house, Edgar turned, climbed the front steps, and slipped an envelope inside Pete's storm door. Then he turned and went back down the steps.

In a desperate attempt to avoid being seen, Nancy ducked down in the front seat as Edgar walked directly toward her.

Had he seen her, or had she gotten down in time? Nancy held her breath.

After a few seconds she felt safe enough to peek in the rearview mirror. The street was empty.

Turning to look out her window, Nancy gasped when she came face-to-face with Edgar's bulging eyes.

"Hiding from someone?" he asked.

Chapter

Sixteen

NANCY FELT HERSELF FLUSH RED. "Edgar, I—I—" she stammered.

What happened next took Nancy completely by surprise. Edgar gave her a friendly pat on the shoulder. "It's good to see you," he said cheerfully.

"Good to see you, too," she replied, not sure of what to say.

"Did you come to ask Pete for your job back?" Edgar asked.

"No, I didn't," she answered tentatively. "Actually, I was just driving by. What are *you* doing here?"

Edgar pointed in the direction of Pete's house. "Just leaving a note for Pete," he said.

Nancy's eyes widened. "What's in it?" she asked, trying to sound casual.

"I haven't the foggiest idea," Edgar quipped, putting on a funny face. "Mark asked me to bring it by."

Mark! A light bulb went on. "Edgar, has Mark asked you to deliver any other letters to Pete's?" she asked.

"Oh, yeah." He nodded casually. "I must have been here half a dozen times this month. They're staff schedules. Sometimes Mark forgets to give them to Pete at work."

"I see," Nancy said slowly. So that was how it worked. Looking at Edgar's open, innocent face, Nancy was certain that he wasn't a blackmailer, but only an unwitting tool of a clever criminal.

"Do me a favor, Edgar," Nancy asked. "Go get that note and bring it over here."

"Okay." Edgar trotted back to get the note, then came back to the car. "What now?"

"Open it, and read it out loud."

"Staff schedules are super boring, Nancy," Edgar said. "They're just charts with—"

"This one may not be so boring," Nancy said pointedly. "Go ahead and open it."

"Okay," Edgar said with a shrug. He opened the envelope, unfolded the note and read: "'You'll be sorry you didn't deliver. One more

chance—five grand, tomorrow at ten A.M.'"
Edgar lowered the note slowly, his eyes round
with amazement. "What is this? Blackmail?"

Nancy tapped her fingers on the steering wheel.
"You got it, Edgar."

"But I don't get it. Why is he blackmailing
Pete?" Edgar asked, scratching his head.

"I'll tell you about it later. But first I need you
to help me out," Nancy replied.

Edgar narrowed his eyes, and a grin opened up
his face. "Okay, Sherlock," he answered. "What
do I have to do?"

"You can start by putting this in Pete's doorway," she said, giving him the note she'd written
for Pete.

After Edgar returned with his comical loping
stride, he asked, "What now?"

"I'd like you to leave this in Mark's bag when
you get to Touchdown, okay?" Nancy handed
him the note addressed to Mark.

"I feel like the merry mailman," Edgar joked.
Then he read the note Nancy handed him. "'I'll
have your money tonight, eight-oh-five at the
football field. Be on time.'"

A sly smile lit up his face. "You're too much,
Nancy," he said. "Like I said before, you should
consider becoming a detective."

"I already am one, Edgar," Nancy said with a
small laugh. "My real name is Nancy Drew."

Edgar's jaw dropped. "You're *Nancy Drew?*"

he exclaimed. "And all this time I was working right next to you, not even knowing!"

Nancy shrugged modestly. "Can you meet me at the football field at seven-thirty? There'll be a few other people there, too."

"I wouldn't miss it for the world," said Edgar. "Nancy Drew, huh? I can't believe it!"

The phone was ringing when Nancy got home. "Nancy, I heard you were fired," came the worried voice on the other end of the line.

"Yes, but it's all right, Cynthia," Nancy told her. "I've solved the case. We're going to spring a trap tonight. Do you want to be there?"

"And how!" said Cynthia excitedly. "Who are we talking about?"

"That's something I have to tell you about— first." Nancy told her about Rob's drug involvement and asked if she still wanted to go.

"I do because Rob needs help."

"Meet me at the football field at seven-thirty."

It was already very dark when Nancy, Bess, George, Cynthia, and Edgar assembled at the fifty-yard line. Nancy looked around at all their faces. Everyone was serious and determined.

"Okay," Nancy told them. "Here's the plan. First, we all hide under the bleachers."

"All in one place?" Bess wanted to know.

"No," Nancy answered quickly. "I'll be in the

middle, at the fifty-yard line. You guys space yourselves out every ten yards or so. That way, no matter what gets said, somebody's sure to hear it. Also, try to stay in eye contact with one another."

"What exactly are we supposed to listen for?" Edgar asked.

"Anything. A good witness remembers everything. Some of what you hear may be pretty shocking, but no matter what happens, don't move or make a sound until I signal you. Understand?"

"Got it, Nan," said George, shooting her friend a special smile. George had helped Nancy many times before, and Nancy knew she could trust her totally.

"It's a quarter to eight," Nancy announced, glancing at her watch. "Let's go."

From her position behind the bleachers, Nancy was pretty sure she'd be able to hear and see everything on the field when the others showed up. She was right. At about eight, two hulking figures came walking toward them from the parking lot.

"I could kill the guy," Lonnie Price muttered as he and Bill Ellman strode across the field to the fifty-yard line. "I mean, who does he think he is, backing out at a time like this?"

Standing nervously next to him, Bill asked, "Do you think he'll rat on us to the coach?"

"He'd better not," Lonnie growled in reply. "What time is it?"

"Just about eight," Bill answered. "There's Pete's car. He's parking."

A few minutes later Nancy saw Pete and Doc appearing at the edge of the field. A smile crossed her face as she watched them approach. So Doc had risen to the bait. But where was Rob? It was past eight now, and he still wasn't there.

"Hi, guys," said Pete warily. "What are you doing here at this time of night?"

"What do you mean, 'What are we doing here?'" Lonnie asked, challenging him. "*You* told us to show up here at eight!"

"I did not!" Pete said, astonished.

"Yeah, right," Bill snorted in disbelief. "If you didn't, who did? Your friend here?"

"Oh, this is Doc, by the way."

"Doc what?" asked Lonnie.

"Just Doc to you," said Doc, in a condescending tone of voice. "I'm the source of your success, if you get my meaning."

Nancy shot a quick glance over at Cynthia, who had her hand to her mouth in shock.

"Be nice to Doc," Pete told the boys. "You wouldn't want to be left high and dry before the Carlisle game, would you? Where's Rob, by the way?"

"He punked out," Bill explained.

Doc spoke out. "Should we be worried about him?" he asked.

"I don't know," said Lonnie. "But listen, if you didn't write those notes to us, who did?"

Pete shuffled around a bit. "I haven't the vaguest idea. Probably the same person who told me to be here."

"And just who is that?" Lonnie asked.

"I really don't know," Pete admitted. "See, boys, somebody's been onto us for the past few weeks, and, well, I've had to pay him off."

"Blackmail?" asked Bill.

"That's right," said Doc. "He knows about the steroids, and he's holding it over us."

"Does he know about our contracts with you, Pete?" Lonnie asked.

"No, and he's not going to find out, either. When you boys are big, and I'm getting ten percent of each of you, the money he's getting now won't look like much. If he knew about our contractual agreements, he'd be asking for a lot more money than he is now."

"He should be here any minute," Doc added. "He thinks he's going to collect his final payment." Nancy heard the man laugh in a menacing tone. "He is, in a way."

"Maybe Bill and I shouldn't be here," Lonnie hedged.

"You stay right where you are, and be quiet,"

Doc commanded him. "You two are in this up to your necks, and you're not backing out now."

The four men came over and sat on the bleachers less than two feet from Nancy, waiting for the blackmailer to show up. She held her breath as the boards creaked over her head. Stealing glances to her left and right, she saw the looks of surprise on the faces of her friends. They all had their eyes on her, waiting for her to give the signal.

"Hello, over there!" called a voice from across the field. The four sitting figures in front of Nancy rose to their feet as one.

"Mark!" Pete gasped. "I should have known it was you. You rotten snake, I ought to—"

"Hello, Pete," said Mark cheerfully as he approached the fifty-yard line. "And Doc, too. What a pleasant surprise. You don't know me, but I know you. Hello, boys," he greeted the players. "Fancy meeting you here."

"You crumb," Pete snarled, stepping down from the bleachers to meet Mark head on. "You've got a lot of nerve, you know that?"

"I wouldn't talk if I were you," said Mark. "Providing steroids to minors isn't exactly in the Boy Scout manual, Pete. Neither is stealing from your own restaurant. The corporation wouldn't take kindly to that, you know."

"You tell them, and I'll kill you!" Pete raged, grabbing Mark's lapels.

"Let go of me, you ape," Mark said with a gasp. "Doc, call off your dog. He can't seem to see his own self-interest, even when it stares him in the face."

Pete loosened his grip. "What does he mean, Doc?" he asked, still looking at Mark.

"He means," Doc said, "that we must all hang together, or we shall all hang separately."

"Exactly," said Mark, smoothing his shirt after Pete let him go. "Now, you should have a payment for me, right? Five thousand dollars, wasn't it?"

"I couldn't get it on so little notice," Pete snarled. "Why did you tell these guys to show up, anyway?" he added, pointing to Lonnie and Bill.

"What are you talking about?" Mark snapped. "I never told them to show up. Besides, I left you a note days ago and told you to put the payment in the P.O. box. When it wasn't there, I sent that idiot Edgar over to your house with the other note, about tomorrow. Then you wrote me that you'd have the money tonight. Make up your mind, Pete."

"I never wrote you any note," Pete said incredulously.

Mark looked at him briefly, a look of anxiety

143

spreading over his face. "Wait a minute," he said slowly. "If you didn't write me a note, who did?"

Nancy looked left and right again, wondering where the police were. They were late. Everyone was ready, so Nancy decided to proceed. Raising her hand, she gave a signal for the others to sit tight. Then, taking a deep breath, she straightened up and walked out from under the bleachers.

"*I* wrote the note," said Nancy, calmly facing the startled group. "By the way, I heard everything you said just now," she announced, looking at them one by one.

"You!" Pete gasped.

"That's right," she repeated coolly. Nancy listened for any sign of the police arriving. So far, nothing. Hurry, Chief, she prayed.

"Let me at her," Lonnie spat, his fists clenched rock hard. "I'll kill her if I have to!"

"Stay away from her!" cried Edgar, suddenly jumping out from behind the bleachers and tackling Lonnie.

"Edgar, no!" Nancy cried out. Forced to keep her attention on the other three, Nancy was unable to come to Edgar's aid as Lonnie grabbed Edgar by the neck.

"Hurting Edgar isn't going to do a thing for you!" Nancy yelled at Lonnie. "Face it. The game is over and you lost."

"No, young lady," Doc contradicted her in a menacing tone. "I'm afraid you've got it all wrong. The game's not over till it's over."

With that, Doc reached into his inside jacket pocket. Nancy stared in horror as the man pulled out a small silver pistol and aimed it right at Edgar!

Chapter

Seventeen

BEFORE NANCY COULD REACT, George flew out from under the bleachers, knocking Doc's arm away from Edgar's head. As the gun hurtled through the air, it discharged, leaving an acrid smell as it landed somewhere on the dark field.

"George!" Nancy said gratefully.

George was hanging on Doc's back. She and Edgar were both wrestling him to the ground. Bess and Cynthia also emerged from the bleachers, rushing to help.

Nancy's eyes shot to Pete, who was just about to move in to help Doc.

"Bess!" Nancy shouted. "Get him!"

146

Instantly Nancy and Bess ran at Pete, tackling him in perfect football fashion.

Red-faced and dogged, Bess struggled to hold on to Pete's ankles, taking a few kicks in the process, as Nancy tried to pin his arms. Just then the sweet music of police sirens sounded in the distance.

"You're not going anywhere," Nancy told the squirming Pete as she bent his arm behind his back and held it there.

"Nancy, look! Lonnie, Bill, and Mark— they're running away!" Bess shouted in distress.

Nancy looked up to see Bill making for the parking lot and Lonnie about to escape under the bleachers. Mark was racing for the far goalpost.

But the glare of sudden spotlights around the field and the words "Freeze! Police!" made all three stop in their tracks.

"Looks like we got here a little late, Nancy," said Chief Boyle. "You wouldn't believe the traffic in this town."

"Oh, I wouldn't say you were late, Chief," Nancy said with a big smile. "I'd say you got here just in time."

There was a huge party at Touchdown Saturday night. Mobs of crazed, triumphant Bedford fans were celebrating the victory of the Bears over Carlisle in the state championship game that day, despite the absence of the team's three

147

stars. Nancy and her friends were celebrating the successful ending to a difficult case.

"Here's to the new manager of Touchdown!" said Nancy, raising her soda glass high in the air. "Thanks for everything, Edgar. It couldn't have happened to a nicer guy."

"Gee, thanks, Nancy," said a bashful Edgar. In addition to his manager's badge, he was sporting a big black eye. Still, Edgar was ecstatic. "Imagine, me, on the front page of the Bedford *Herald* —and managing Touchdown for American Theme Restaurants, too! Pretty good for a guy who's got to be the world's worst football player."

Everybody laughed heartily at that one. The very thought of Edgar Chessman on a football field was hysterically funny.

"Can you sit down and join us?" asked Bess, making room for Edgar next to her.

"Just for a few minutes," he said, looking around warily as if he expected the boss to fire him for laziness. "It's a busy night. We're going to need you back at work, Cynthia."

"Thanks, Edgar," said Cynthia, sitting on Bess's other side, holding hands with Rob.

Rob had been at the game, cheering louder than anyone for the guys on the team. Dennis DiVito had replaced him at quarterback. He had performed heroically, winning the game with a scrambling run in the last seconds.

Lonnie and Bill hadn't even bothered to show up. All three stars had been thrown off the team and put on probation for the rest of the year.

Still, Rob seemed happier than he had in a long time. "It's a real relief, now that it's all over," he said, giving Cynthia's hand a squeeze. The two of them looked as if they were the lovingest couple in town.

"Nancy, I'm going to pay you back for the damage to your car, I promise," he said shame-facedly. "I was the one who told Lonnie to smash your window. I was terrified you'd find the pills and that Cynthia would figure everything out."

"From now on we're not hiding anything from each other," Cynthia said, looking into Rob's eyes.

"From now on I'm never going to do anything I have to hide," Rob promised her.

"Rob," Nancy asked, "how did it happen? How did you get into steroids in the first place?"

"Well, one thing led to another, I guess," Rob said, the painful memory showing on his handsome face. "Pete was always hanging around, telling us how great we were, how big we were going to be. When he told us he wanted to be our agent, we were flattered. I don't think any of us realized what we were signing on for when we agreed to have him as our agent if we ever went pro."

"Thank goodness those contracts will be declared null and void!" Bess said.

"My dad showed them to a lawyer," Cynthia explained, "and he said they'd never hold up in court."

"Go on, Rob," George prodded him. "You were saying?"

"Anyway," Rob continued, "when Pete gave us the steroids, I was kind of scared, but he told us they were okay, that he knew lots of pros and college players who used them. He said they'd make us play at the top of our ability. And he was right about that. The games definitely felt more intense."

"Intense isn't the word for it," George murmured. "The Bedford-Montvale game was more like a street brawl than football."

"I know," Rob said regretfully. "We were pretty pathetic. I just wasn't thinking right. I felt weird and dizzy all the time, but I also felt like I couldn't stop taking them. There were all those scouts and the interviews and the flattery—it really gets to you. Like I said, I'm just glad it's over."

Just then Coach Novak made his way over to their table. "Mind if I bust in for a second?" he said, all smiles.

"Hi, Coach," Nancy greeted him.

"I just wanted to thank you, Nancy, and tell you I'm sorry I ever mistrusted you."

"It's okay, Coach," Nancy said with a grin. "I understand how you felt. Congratulations, by the way. The second string really came through, didn't they? That kid Dennis DiVito was like greased lightning."

"Ha!" crowed the coach. "Goes to show you, there's a lot to be said for emotion in this game. And you," the coach continued, buttonholing Rob. "Stay off that stuff from now on, you hear me? You have a great future ahead of you."

"I'm going to make you proud of me, Coach," said Rob, his voice choking up. "You wait and see."

"Everybody makes mistakes. As long as you learn by them, that's what counts," said the coach. "Well, I've got to get back to my public. Take care, all."

"I'd better get going, too," said Edgar, standing up. "I want to show the corporation good profits this month."

"See you later," Nancy told him, turning to her friends. "By the way, guys, did I tell you I'm going to visit Ned next week?"

"Next week? When?" Bess asked excitedly.

"Right after we give our testimony. We're going to his family's place in the country. It sure will be nice to get away from football for a while."

A roar went up in the front of the restaurant.

"What's that?" George asked.

The answer was apparent when Edgar nailed up a banner that read "Bedford Bears, State Champs."

"We may be the state champs," Cynthia said, turning to Nancy with a wide grin, "but you're the world champ of detectives!"

FLIRTING
WITH DANGER

Chapter

One

"THIS IS THE LIFE," Nancy Drew whispered to Ned Nickerson as he took a breakfast croissant from the tray held out by the uniformed maid.

Ned grinned and shrugged as he took a cheese danish from the same tray. "What can I say?" he whispered back. "I know how to pick my friends."

Nancy and Ned had arrived at the Beverly Hills home of Josh Kline, Ned's friend and college classmate, the night before. Josh, who was majoring in filmmaking at Emerson College, had landed a summer internship at a

1

famous Hollywood movie studio and had moved back home for the summer. He'd invited Nancy and Ned to visit, and they were both looking forward to an exciting vacation in Southern California.

"I can't believe you're ready to graduate from high school, Rachel," Karen Kline, Josh's mother, remarked from the end of the table. There was a rueful expression on her pretty, tan face. "It seems like yesterday that we brought you home from the hospital. Doesn't it, Allen?" she asked her husband, a lean, gray-haired man seated at her right.

Nancy looked on as Allen Kline beamed at his daughter. "We're really proud of you, Rachel."

Rachel Kline brushed a long lock of sun-streaked blond hair away from her face and gazed straight at her father. "I know," she said. "You've only mentioned it about fifteen times in the past week."

There was irritation in the girl's voice, Nancy thought. Karen Kline sighed, and Allen Kline reached out for his wife's hand. Nancy exchanged a look with Ned, who gave a slight shrug. There was a short silence as Rachel stared out through the French doors of the dining room at the aquamarine waters of the

2

swimming pool with a distracted expression in her pretty brown eyes.

"I know I'm looking forward to going to your graduation," Nancy put in, trying to ease the tension.

"Me, too," Ned said. "After everything Josh has told me about Ocean Highlands High, I can't wait to see the place."

"It is pretty amazing," Josh said, glancing at his sister.

Rachel didn't meet his eye. Instead, she got up from the table. "If it's okay with you, I'm going to change."

Allen Kline cleared his throat and pushed back his chair. "That's fine, Rachel. I have to get going, too."

After Rachel and her parents had gone upstairs, Nancy and Ned lingered at the breakfast table, talking to Josh and making plans for the next few days.

"I can't wait to see the studio," Nancy told Josh excitedly.

"What else should we do?" Ned asked his friend.

"Let's see." Josh counted his fingers. "There's Malibu, and the tour of the stars' homes. Grauman's Chinese Theater. And you really should go up into the hills. You get a great view of L.A. from there, especially at night. It's totally romantic."

Ned gave Nancy a wry grin. "Now, there's an idea," he said.

Nancy felt herself blushing but was secretly glad. Since Ned was away at school, they didn't get to spend too much time alone.

"We'll have to check it out," she said, giving him a light kiss on the cheek. "But right now, I think I have a couple of things to do."

She excused herself to go upstairs. After she left the spacious dining room for the entryway, Nancy glanced up at the huge crystal chandelier overhead. Like the rest of the house, it was spectacular.

Passing a mirror as she started up the elegant, curving staircase, Nancy smiled at her reflection. Her blue eyes were bright, and she'd pulled her shoulder-length, reddish blond hair back into a French braid. In a few days, she hoped, she would have a golden tan to take back to River Heights as a souvenir.

She just wished she could show this place to her best friends, Bess Marvin and George Fayne. It was as good as any of the sets on the TV soap operas.

Reaching the top of the stairs, Nancy turned left, heading toward her room. It was really more a suite than a room, with its own whirlpool bath and a view of the tennis court and swimming pool. Her sandaled feet sank into the thick blue carpeting.

She paused outside Rachel's room to say hello because the girl's door was open.

"Dennis, I can't do that!" came Rachel's voice, her tone hushed and serious. "You don't know how my parents are counting on this. I can't let them down!"

Just then Rachel turned and saw Nancy standing in the hallway, peering into her room. Her brown eyes widened with alarm, but in a flash she recovered and managed a shaky smile.

"Listen, I've got to go. I'll talk to you later," she said. Without another word she hung up the phone and turned to Nancy with a perfect smile. "One of my friends is a little nervous about the ceremony," she explained lightly. "He has to make a speech."

It occurred to Nancy that Rachel might be hiding something. She seemed too quick to explain away her conversation. Maybe it was nothing, but Nancy didn't think she had mistaken the troubled look in the girl's eyes.

Rachel went to her closet and took out a beautiful white dress with a pink satin sash. "I'll be wearing this to the graduation party," she said. "What do you think?"

"It's great," Nancy answered. Then she lifted one hand in a wave. "I'll let you go now. I'm sure you have a lot to do."

Rachel nodded. "I've got to go over to the school and pick up my cap and gown, for one thing," she said, sounding rushed and jittery. "And then there's my hair. . . ."

Nancy grinned. She could remember how nervous she'd been for her high school graduation. Maybe it was just edginess that was making Rachel act a little weird. She headed on to her own room, where she chose a turquoise sundress for the afternoon graduation ceremony. Then she flopped down on the bed to write postcards to her dad and George and Bess back home in River Heights. The girls would love to know what it was like to be a guest in a Beverly Hills mansion.

As she wrote Nancy kept pausing to think. She was sure she'd heard a note of desperation and fear in Rachel's voice while she was talking to her friend Dennis on the phone. Just what was it that Rachel couldn't do?

Several hours later the gym at Ocean Highlands High School was crowded with well-dressed, tanned people who all seemed to be talking at once. Nancy, standing beside Ned, craned her neck, trying to find Rachel among the eager seniors. The ceremony was going to begin in a few minutes, and there was no sign of her.

Ned took Nancy's arm and pulled her aside by the doors, which opened onto a breathtaking view of the Pacific Ocean. In the dazzling June sunshine, the sea looked as turquoise as Nancy's dress.

"Okay, Drew," he said, his eyes dancing with amusement, "what's bugging you?"

Nancy didn't even try to sidestep the question. Ned knew her too well for that. "I was looking for Rachel just now because I was worried about her. When I was passing her room this morning, I overheard her talking on the phone. She was really upset, Ned."

Ned frowned. "About what?"

"I don't know," Nancy said. "It was more her tone of voice than what she said. She sounded really scared."

"What did she say?"

"Something like, 'I can't do that—you don't know how much this means to my parents.'" Just then Nancy spotted Mr. and Mrs. Kline in the group of parents, guests, and graduates. They appeared to be anxious and a little worried as they approached Nancy and Ned.

"Have either of you seen Rachel?" Karen Kline asked them.

"No," Ned answered, trying to smile reassuringly. "She's got to be around here somewhere. After all, this is her big day."

"We'll help look, if you like," Nancy volunteered.

Mrs. Kline nodded gratefully. "That would be wonderful, Nancy," she responded. "Thank you."

"You go this way," Nancy told Ned, pointing to her right, "and I'll head over there. By the time we meet at the other end of the gym, we'll have found Rachel."

"Okay," Ned agreed, and he took off after the missing graduate.

Rachel was nowhere. Nancy even checked the girls' bathroom and backstage in the auditorium, where the ceremony would be held.

Nancy was really getting worried by the time she returned to the gym and found Ned. He hadn't had any better luck. Josh was with Ned, but he didn't share everyone else's concern.

"Don't worry about it, Nancy," Josh said. "Rachel likes being center stage too much to miss her own graduation. When her name is called, she'll be there to get her diploma."

Josh seemed pretty confident his sister would show up. "I hope you're right," Nancy said as Ned took her hand and led her into the auditorium after the Klines.

As soon as the crowd was seated the principal of Ocean Highlands High, Mr. Jeffries, greeted them. Then he introduced the valedictorian, who made the first speech. After several more speeches and award presentations, it was time for the graduates to get their diplomas.

The Klines and Ned and Nancy waited eagerly for Rachel's name to be announced.

"Rachel Kline!" Mr. Jeffries finally called out.

None of the students seated in front of the small stage stood up.

"Rachel Kline," the principal repeated, and still there was no response. There was a buzz in the audience, though.

Ned and Nancy exchanged a look. Josh bit his lower lip and glanced over at his father. Karen Kline sat up in her chair, her eyes desperately scanning the group of students in their caps and gowns.

"Rachel Kline!" the principal tried one last time, but the pretty blond girl didn't appear.

"Something terrible has happened, I just know it," Mrs. Kline whispered, her lips trembling. "Rachel's gone!"

9

Chapter

Two

ALLEN KLINE looked at his wife with a confused expression on his face. "There has to be a reasonable explanation, Karen," he whispered. "Maybe she got sick—"

"She probably thought she had time to go for a soda," Josh said, trying to comfort his mother.

"I'm sure she's okay," Nancy said. Inside, though, she wondered. Could this have something to do with the conversation she'd overheard earlier?

Around them, the graduation was continuing. "Come on," Nancy said to Ned. "Let's go out with the Klines."

Ned nodded, and they stood up to follow Allen Kline as he steered his wife out of the auditorium. Josh followed.

Outside in the hall, Karen Kline's face was pale beneath her carefully applied makeup. She reached out for her husband's hand. "I just know something terrible has happened— she'd *never* miss her own graduation!"

Ned spoke up. "Listen, Josh, I think your parents should go home and wait there to see if your sister calls. We can look for her."

"Great idea, Ned," Nancy said. "There's no point in your hanging around here," she told the Klines reassuringly.

Josh gripped his mother's trembling hands in an effort to calm her. "Ned and Nancy are right, Mom. You and Dad should go home. We'll try to find Rachel and catch a ride later."

Allen Kline wrapped his arm around his wife's shoulders. "Josh is right, honey. If Rachel is having a problem, she'll probably try to call us. We're not doing any good here." He turned to Josh, Nancy, and Ned. "We'll be waiting to hear from you," he said, and he led his wife out to the parking lot.

The applause from inside the auditorium

told Nancy the graduation ceremony was about to conclude. In another few minutes the hallway and gymnasium would be crowded with people, and that would make searching for Rachel even harder.

"Let's fan out and check inside the building again," she suggested. "If we don't find her, we'll search the grounds, too."

Ned glanced down at his watch. "Let's meet in the parking lot in half an hour and compare notes."

Nancy nodded thoughtfully. "I'd like to talk to some of Rachel's friends, find out when they last saw her. Do you know any of them?"

"There's Beth Hanford," Josh answered. "She's Rachel's best friend, so she'd know everybody they hang out with."

"Is there a special guy? I heard Rachel talking to someone this morning—I think his name was Dennis." If she could find Dennis, he might know where Rachel was.

Josh shrugged. "I don't think I've heard Rachel mention him, but Beth would know."

"Good—" Nancy began.

The wave of laughing graduates coming through the swinging doors of the auditorium interrupted Nancy. Soon parents and other well-wishers were crowded around them, taking pictures and offering hugs and congratulations.

"We'd better start looking for her," Ned said, nudging Josh.

"Right," his friend said. While the boys went in opposite directions to look for Rachel, Nancy approached one of the graduates and smiled.

"Excuse me," she said to the girl, who was adjusting the tassel on her cap, "but could you tell me where to find Beth Hanford?"

"Sure," the graduate replied, looking around. "That's her over there. The one with the dark hair and big hoop earrings."

Nancy spotted Beth standing between two happy people who were probably her parents. She made her way over through the milling, delighted crowd.

"Beth?" she said, smiling and holding out one hand. "My name is Nancy Drew, and I'm visiting with the Klines. I was wondering if you've seen Rachel today."

Beth's bright smile faded, and she shook Nancy's hand distractedly. "No," she answered slowly. "I thought it was weird that she didn't show up when they called her name."

"Did you speak to her at all today?" Nancy asked.

Beth's pretty face had virtually drained of color. "No. What's wrong? Has something happened?"

Mr. Hanford spoke up then. "Is there anything we can do to help?"

"I don't think so. Rachel seems to be missing, but her brother and my friend are looking for her."

"I hope she's okay," Mrs. Hanford said. "I'm sure her mom and dad are really worried."

Before Nancy could answer, Beth broke in. "I'd like to stay here and help look for Rachel," she said to her parents. "Would that be okay? I mean, is it all right if we celebrate later? I'd feel awful if I didn't try to find her."

Mrs. Hanford smiled gently. "Of course, dear. Your dad and I will be at home. Let us know if we can help."

"Thanks," Beth said to her parents. Then she turned to Nancy, pulling off her graduation cap. "The first thing I want to do is get out of this gown," she said. "It's really hot."

Nancy followed Beth into a room where special clothing racks had been set up and helped her out of the gown. Underneath it she was wearing a bright yellow dress with a high collar.

14

"Beth, do you think Rachel could have run away?" Nancy asked.

Beth appeared to be troubled for a moment. She started to say something, then stopped herself. Finally she murmured, "No. Rachel wouldn't run away."

"You're sure?" Nancy prodded. Was the girl covering for her friend? Beth seemed as if she might be holding something back.

She shook her head resolutely. "I'm sure. Running away is dumb, and Rachel knows that. Besides, things are good for her at home." She stared off for a moment, then met Nancy's eyes again. "I'm ready. Let's go."

Nancy led Beth back into the crowd of graduates milling around in the gymnasium by a table spread with sandwiches and sodas. "Does Rachel know anybody named Dennis?" she asked as the girls scanned the group for any sign of Rachel. "I heard her talking to him this morning, and she sounded pretty upset."

Beth's face paled visibly. "Dennis," she said to herself in a whisper. When she saw Nancy looking at her, though, Beth recovered quickly. "He's just a guy she hangs out with sometimes. No big deal."

"Did he go to school here at Ocean Highlands, too?" Nancy asked, being careful to

15

keep her voice light. She didn't want Beth to get defensive. The girl seemed reluctant enough as it was.

"No," Beth answered as she and Nancy approached a group of kids. "I mean, yes, but he's older. He graduated last year."

"I see," Nancy replied, still trying to put Beth at ease. "Are he and Rachel serious about each other?"

Beth's eyes came quickly back to Nancy's face and widened. "You mean, are they in love?"

Nancy nodded, waiting.

Beth's expression was troubled. "They've been dating for a while, but I don't think they'd elope or anything like that. Rachel's parents would have a fit."

Nancy knew Beth was right. Even if she was in trouble, Rachel didn't seem like the type to just run off and worry her parents unnecessarily. If she had wanted to go off with Dennis, and her parents didn't approve of him, she might not have told them, though. Dennis seemed like the logical link to Rachel's disappearance.

"Did you see Dennis around this morning?" she asked.

Beth shook her head. There was still a scared expression in her eyes. Nancy found herself wondering again what the girl was hiding.

She was about to ask Beth another question when a good-looking guy with wavy brown hair and blue eyes came up to them. He was still dressed in his cap and gown.

"Have you seen Rachel?" he demanded angrily before Beth could say anything.

"No. I was hoping you had," Beth said. "Mike, this is Nancy Drew, a friend of the Klines. Nancy, Mike Rasmussen."

"Hi, Mike," Nancy said.

Nancy saw Mike's eyes take in her turquoise sundress. "Hi," he replied with new interest.

Beth was tapping her foot. "Never mind the flirting, okay, Mike? Nancy and I need to find Rachel. We're really worried about her, and her parents probably are, too. Haven't you seen her at all?"

Mike frowned. "She was here earlier. I saw her when I came to pick up my cap and gown."

"Was she alone?" Nancy asked.

"Yeah," Mike answered. His tone told Nancy he thought it was a stupid question.

"Did she seem to be worried about anything?" Nancy asked, choosing to ignore his attitude.

Mike thought for a moment. "Well, she was a little rushed. Now that I think about it, she didn't take her cap and gown at all. She just hung around for a few minutes, then left."

17

Nancy glanced at her watch. "I've got to meet Josh and Ned in the parking lot," she told Beth. "Maybe they've had better luck than we have."

"I hope so," Beth said, almost in a whisper. "I really hope so."

She and Nancy made their way through the diminishing crowd to the front doors of the high school. It was a big school, clean, well designed, and well built, and Nancy paused for a moment to admire the view of the ocean. She and Beth started toward the parking lot. There were still a lot of cars around, but she didn't spot Ned or Josh.

"Have you and Rachel been best friends for a long time?" Nancy asked.

"Since first grade," Beth confirmed. She stared down at the pavement for a few seconds. "She tells me everything—or I thought she did. You'd think she'd have mentioned it if she planned to skip graduation."

Nancy shaded her eyes from the bright afternoon sunshine and scanned the parking lot for Ned and Josh. Wherever they were, she hoped Rachel was with them, safe and sound. "Maybe something came up," she said. "Are you absolutely sure Rachel wasn't in any kind of trouble?"

Beth hesitated for a long time before answering. "Yes," she said finally. "I'm sure."

"Nancy!" a familiar masculine voice called. "Over here!"

Nancy spotted Ned calling to her. "Come on! I think we've found something," he shouted.

She and Beth sprinted toward the two boys, who were standing beside a silver Camaro in the far corner of the parking lot.

"It's Rachel's car," Ned explained when they caught up.

"There's no way she would have left her car behind," Josh stated. "It's practically like her baby."

Nancy didn't know what Josh had expected to find in the car. Was he hoping that Rachel would be sitting inside, waiting? Nancy knew Rachel's brother had been disappointed, though. It was empty.

Josh looked first at Ned, then at Nancy, his handsome face full of strain. "Are you thinking what I'm thinking?"

"What's that?" Nancy asked, studying his face.

"That my sister's been kidnapped!"

Chapter

Three

KIDNAPPING ISN'T the only possibility, Josh," Nancy said gently, noticing that the keys were still in the ignition. She tried to catch Beth's eye. It appeared more and more likely that Rachel's friend was wrong about the girl not being in some kind of trouble. Rachel must have been in a big hurry if she'd left the keys in the car.

"Let's go back to your place and find out if your parents have heard anything," Ned said, laying a hand on his friend's shoulder. "Maybe Rachel's there, and we're all standing around worrying for nothing."

Josh checked out the silver Camaro again. "She's even left the keys in the ignition," he pointed out with a frown. "I don't like the look of this at all."

"Ned, why don't you and Josh take Rachel's car back to the house? Beth, can you drop me off?" The girl nodded. Nancy wanted another chance to try to find out what Beth wasn't telling her.

Josh nodded distractedly as he and Ned climbed into the Camaro. Beth led the way to a yellow Volkswagen.

Once they were in the car, Beth gave a little sigh and reached up to drape the tassel from her graduation cap over the rearview mirror. "This day isn't turning out at all like I thought it would," she said.

"No, I guess it isn't," Nancy said, feeling sorry for the girl. "Are you sure you've told me everything?" she ventured.

Beth swallowed hard. "I'm sure." Her expression told Nancy that she wasn't going to say anything more. Beth started the car.

"Everything will be okay" was all Nancy could say. She just hoped she was right.

When Nancy and Beth pulled into the Klines' driveway, Ned was waiting for them. Josh had probably gone inside to be with his parents.

21

"Is she here?" Beth asked eagerly.

Ned shook his head. "No. And the Klines were really upset when they found out Rachel had left her car."

Ned and Nancy and Beth found Josh watching his father talk on the telephone when they went inside. Mr. Kline was on the phone with the police, trying to file a missing persons report.

Nancy glanced at Ned. They both knew from experience that the police wouldn't be able to do a thing for twenty-four hours. Until that much time had passed, a person wasn't considered legally missing.

"I'm telling you, her car was found in the school parking lot!" Mr. Kline yelled into the receiver. "The keys were in the ignition! Now, that indicates that there is at least a possibility that our daughter has been kidnapped!"

"Where's your mother?" Nancy asked Josh in a quiet voice.

"Upstairs, in Rachel's room," Josh said. "She's pretty shook up."

Nancy excused herself and went upstairs with Beth close behind.

Karen Kline was sitting on Rachel's bed, crying softly. She looked up hopefully at the noise, but when she saw it was Nancy and Beth her face fell.

Beth sat down on the bed beside Karen Kline and said, "Please don't cry, Mrs. Kline. Rachel's probably going to come walking through the front door at any minute, with a perfectly good explanation."

"Has Rachel ever run away before?" Nancy asked, trying to keep her voice as gentle as possible.

Karen Kline looked shocked. "Oh, no!" she said quickly. "We've never had any trouble with Rachel at all." Her face became pale again. "I'm so afraid she's been kidnapped," she said, as though she was afraid even to speak the words. "Allen and I aren't rich, even though we live very well. All our money is tied up in the house. Someone must have gotten the idea that we could pay a king's ransom—"

Nancy touched Mrs. Kline's shoulder. "There's no reason to jump to conclusions. We have to wait to see if anyone calls or sends a ransom note," she said.

"I don't think she was kidnapped," Beth remarked slowly, staring at Rachel's dresser.

"Why?" Nancy asked.

Beth left her place beside Mrs. Kline to walk over to the bureau. The top was crowded with a jewelry chest, a music box, makeup, perfume, and a framed picture of Rachel with the rest of the cheerleading squad. "Because

23

Rachel's bank is empty," she said, excitement rising in her voice. She pointed at an expensive electronic bank on Rachel's dresser.

Mrs. Kline jumped up to see for herself. "You're right!" she said, holding up the bank. "And I know that she had taken money out of her account and was keeping it here. Now it's gone!"

Karen Kline dashed for the door. "Allen!" she cried out into the hall.

Nancy and Beth followed Mrs. Kline downstairs. While Mrs. Kline talked with her husband, Nancy and Beth joined the boys outside by the pool.

"Rachel must have run away," Beth announced. Then she explained about the missing money.

"But why would she have done that?" Josh wondered. "She seemed a little edgy this morning, but she's not the type of person to run away. She knows Mom and Dad love her."

"I'd like to question a few more of Rachel's friends," Nancy said thoughtfully, watching as sunlight danced in golden patches on the pool's cool blue water. "Somebody must know something."

"There's a party down at the Surf Club later," Beth put in helpfully. "Why don't you all come? That'll give you a chance to find out if anybody knows what's going on."

"Good idea," Nancy said, looking at her watch. "What time does it start?"

"Soon—at six," Beth answered. "But it'll go late. Bring your bathing suits. Everybody's planning on swimming after they've had dinner and danced for a while."

Josh and Ned agreed to attend the party, but they said they probably wouldn't feel like swimming. "I just hope Mr. and Mrs. Kline will be okay," Beth said in a faraway tone. "They don't deserve this."

Beth's words struck Nancy as odd. She was about to ask for an explanation when the girl glanced at her watch. "Well, I guess I'd better get home—my folks would like to see me before I take off. Catch you at the party."

"Right," said Ned.

"I guess I'll go inside and see if I can do anything to help my folks," Josh told them.

Ned pulled up two deck chairs for him and Nancy. "What do you think?" he asked after they were settled.

Nancy was staring at the clear California sky and frowning. "My guess is Rachel probably ran away," she said after a while. "She took her savings. On the other hand, why would she be in such a rush that she had to miss her own graduation? And why didn't she take her car?"

"I can't explain the graduation ceremony. But she doesn't need the car if she's with somebody else," Ned pointed out.

Nancy snapped her fingers. "You know, you're right. Someone like her boyfriend Dennis, for example."

Nancy explained what Beth had told her about Dennis.

"So you think they're together?" Ned asked.

"I don't know about that. But I do know one thing: this party should be very interesting."

"I recognize that look, Nancy," Ned said with a smile.

"What look?" Nancy asked.

"That look that says you're happy to be on a new case."

Promptly at six Nancy, Josh, and Ned left for the party in Rachel's car.

The Surf Club turned out to be a nice restaurant overlooking the beach. Tables were set up on the terrace, complete with colorful umbrellas. A band was playing the latest hits. Just beyond the terrace was a dance floor crowded with graduates and their dates determined to have a good time. Waiters in white coats were bustling around, setting out a buffet dinner on a long table back on the terrace.

While Josh and Ned went to get sodas, Nancy stood observing the crowd. Mike Rasmussen approached her almost immediately, bringing a pretty brown-haired girl with him. Nancy saw Beth coming toward them, too.

"I don't suppose anybody's heard anything from Rachel," Mike said, sounding almost testy.

Nancy supposed he was just concerned, like everybody else. "Nothing yet," she said.

"I'm Jessica Bates," the girl beside him announced. "And if you want my opinion, you're all wasting your time looking for Rachel. It's obvious that she's run off with her punk boyfriend, Dennis Harper," she finished smugly.

Mike glowered at Jessica, but before Nancy could ask her what she meant, Beth was beside her. She looked terrific in a green silk jumpsuit.

"I can't imagine why any of us would want your opinion," she said sweetly. "You don't like Rachel, and everybody knows it."

Jessica drew back, looking insulted. She started to say something, then stopped herself.

"I'm Nancy Drew," Nancy told her, since no one had introduced the two.

Jessica glared at Beth for a moment before lifting her chin and turning a smiling face on Nancy. "Welcome to Beverly Hills," she said. "I'm sure you'll find it's a very exciting place." With that, she turned and walked away, Mike following her to the buffet table.

"Still no news?" Beth asked, watching Nancy's face.

Nancy shook her head. "No news," she confirmed. "Tell me about Dennis Harper," Nancy said firmly as Ned and Josh joined them at one of the umbrella-covered tables.

For a moment fear flickered in Beth's eyes, but then she sighed and answered, "Rachel broke up with Mike about a month ago to date Dennis. He's kind of wild—Dennis, I mean. He graduated from Ocean Highlands last year."

"And?" Nancy prompted.

"Dennis works at a stereo equipment store in West Hollywood," Beth went on. "It's called Sound Performance. Mike works there, too."

Nancy glanced at Mike, who was standing in line at the buffet table next to Jessica. "He's not exactly crazy about Dennis, I take it."

Beth gave a nervous giggle and shook her head. "You've got that right," she agreed.

"Do my parents know about this Dennis

character?" Josh asked. "This is the first I've heard about him since I got back from school."

Beth shrugged. "I don't know what Rachel told your mom and dad," she said.

Ned was looking at the buffet table. "Let's eat," he suggested. "I'm starved."

The four of them got plates, but Ned was the only one who ate much. Nancy was eager to question some other kids to find out more about Rachel and Dennis Harper.

No one was eager to talk, though, and after another hour, Josh wanted to leave. He was understandably worried about his parents, and of course, he wanted to know if there had been any new developments. There was always the hope that Rachel had called or gone home while they were at the party.

"Are you going to start your internship tomorrow?" Ned asked Josh as the three of them headed for the parking lot.

Josh shrugged. "I'm not sure I could concentrate, knowing Rachel might be in trouble."

Nancy had already decided that their best chance of finding Rachel was to find Dennis. She decided to pay a visit to Sound Performance first thing in the morning.

They went to the Camaro and were about to get into the car when they noticed a piece of paper tucked under one of the windshield wipers. Nancy pulled it out and saw that it was a program for the Ocean Highlands High School graduation ceremony.

As her eyes scanned the page Nancy felt a rush of fear.

"Stop looking for Rachel or you may get hurt," someone had written in large black letters. "Love, The Kats."

Chapter

Four

NANCY HANDED THE PROGRAM to Josh. "Read this," she told him, her thoughts racing. Just who were these "Kats," and who was the note intended for? Were they threatening just her, or were Ned and Josh included? Was it just some prank, or could these Kats have something to do with Rachel's disappearance?

As Josh scanned the program Ned read it over his friend's shoulder. He gave a low whistle.

"I don't get it," Josh murmured. "Why are these Kats threatening us?"

Ned's expression was worried. "They obviously don't want us to find Rachel," he concluded, following Nancy's train of thought.

Nancy nodded. "That's what I decided, too," she told Josh. She took the program from him and read it again. "I do get notes like this all the time," she told Josh, to relieve his fears.

"And they haven't stopped you before," Ned pointed out ruefully.

With a smile, Nancy answered him. "You got that right, Nickerson. I'd say we have more reason than ever to find Rachel Kline."

The next morning Josh's parents convinced him to go to the movie studio. They promised they'd call if there was any news about Rachel. Mr. and Mrs. Kline were going to go to the police to convince them to file a missing persons report, then to the bank to find out if Rachel had closed out her savings account.

After dropping Josh off at the studio in Rachel's car, Ned and Nancy consulted a map and set out for Sound Performance.

It was a warm, sunny day with hardly any of the usual L.A. smog. As they drove along with the car windows open the wind felt good in Nancy's hair, and her spirits lifted. Finding out where Dennis worked was the best lead they had.

"I have a feeling that if we find Dennis Harper, we're going to be closer to finding Rachel."

"You think he kidnapped her?" Ned asked, keeping an eye out for their exit.

"I don't know," Nancy answered. "We don't have a ransom note." She thought for a moment. "Maybe they have run away. One thing's sure: Rachel's missing, and I overheard a conversation she had with Dennis that might involve him. Chances are they're together."

They found Sound Performance across the street from a large shopping mall. The building was a little run-down, and two of the neon letters in "Performance" were burned out. Inside, the store was crowded with merchandise, though, and there were a number of customers checking out the VCRs, camcorders, color TVs, and stereo systems.

A young salesman approached them immediately. "Welcome to Sound Performance," he said. "May I help you?"

Nancy hoped to spot Mike Rasmussen. She remembered Beth had told her he worked there, too. "We'd like to talk to the owner."

"You mean Mr. Lindenbaum?"

Nancy nodded. The salesman looked mildly disappointed but turned and pointed out a middle-aged man with a few strands of hair combed over his large bald spot. Mr. Lindenbaum, in pink slacks, an open-necked shirt, and a cardigan sweater that barely closed over his stomach, was busy selling a customer a new TV.

Nancy and Ned waited until he was finished before walking over to him.

"Mr. Lindenbaum?" Nancy held out her hand. "I'm Nancy Drew, and this is Ned Nickerson. We'd like to ask you a few questions."

"Ralph Lindenbaum," he said with a smile. "Happy to be of service. What did you have in mind, a nice young couple like you?" His gaze shifted slightly to take in Ned. "A microwave? A VCR? We have both new and reconditioned appliances—"

"We'd like to talk to Dennis Harper," Nancy broke in politely, glancing around the store. "Is he here today?"

Ralph Lindenbaum looked decidedly less friendly. "What do you want with him?" He almost spat out the question.

"A friend of ours is missing," Ned answered, his hands resting on his hips. "Her name is Rachel Kline, and she and Dennis were dating."

Ralph scratched his head and carefully smoothed his hair back over the bald spot. "I could tell that kid was no good," he said. "Punk haircut and all. I'd heard he'd been in trouble before I hired him, too. Just thought I'd give him a chance." He paused to sigh dramatically. "Harper isn't around here anymore. I fired him day before yesterday, when some speakers turned up missing. It wasn't the first time things were missing when he worked. I made sure it was the last time, though!"

Nancy was worried. What if Dennis had stolen the equipment to have money to run off with Rachel? Or if he was a thief, there was a chance he could be a kidnapper, too. If that was the case, Rachel could be in serious danger.

She forced herself to stop thinking the worst. First they had to find out if Rachel was with him. "Can we have his telephone number, please?" she asked. "It's very important that we find him."

"This way," Ralph grumbled, turning and walking toward the back of the store. He rubbed the back of his neck with one hand as he moved. "Knew that boy was bad news," he muttered.

"Do you know Rachel Kline?" Ned asked.

"Never heard of her," Ralph mumbled, pushing open the door to a cluttered office. The desk was buried in invoices and telephone

35

messages. "The police involved in this?" he asked, flipping through a small metal file box on a battered credenza.

"As of today, yes," Ned said. "Rachel's been missing since yesterday."

"Here it is," Ralph said, pulling a card and handing it to Nancy.

There was no address, just the name Dennis Harper, which was scrawled sloppily, and a phone number. Nancy copied it down in a notebook she always carried with her and handed the card back. "Do you know where Dennis lives?"

Ralph shook his head. "Sorry. Can't help you there."

"Thanks," Nancy said with a note of frustration. At least they had a telephone number. It was a start.

"No problem," Ralph answered. Then, with a shrug, he added, "You're probably going to find out that loser has left the country."

"I hope you're wrong," Nancy said, but she found that she was thinking the same thing. Still, there was no solid reason to suspect Dennis had kidnapped Rachel. "Thank you," she said, snapping her purse closed.

"Thanks," Ned added, holding the door open for Nancy. "Where to from here?" he asked once they were back outside.

"To the nearest telephone. We're going to give Dennis Harper a call."

Ned stopped at a fast-food restaurant and ordered sodas to go while Nancy went to the pay phone.

"No luck?" he asked, holding out a cup to her once she had returned.

Nancy shook her head. "Nobody answered."

Ned shrugged. "Maybe we had the wrong number. You said his handwriting was terrible," he said before taking a sip of his soda. "Maybe we should call directory assistance."

"Good idea." Nancy took another coin from her purse. "Be right back."

Nancy punched in the number for directory assistance and asked for Dennis's number. After a short pause, a recorded voice came on the line.

"I'm sorry. At the request of the subscriber, that number is unlisted."

Nancy hung up the receiver and drummed her fingers against the side of the phone booth. She let out a sigh and headed back to Ned.

"Strike out?" he asked, reading her face.

"Yep. Unlisted. We're back to square one."

"Look, Nancy," Ned said, putting his arms around her. "We'll find him—and her. I know we will. Let's head back to the Klines', have a swim, and put our heads together. A little sun may get us thinking more clearly."

Nancy smiled. Ned was good at reassuring her. "Okay. Maybe Rachel wrote down his address somewhere," she added. "We can check her room."

Nancy and Ned were back at the Klines' house before Mr. and Mrs. Kline. Ned headed upstairs while the maid told Nancy that they wouldn't be back until late that night. They were going to visit some of Rachel's friends' parents, and then there was a private party for some of the graduates and their parents.

"A party?" Nancy echoed, surprised.

"They think they might be able to learn something from Rachel's friends," she explained as she headed back to the kitchen. "You and Ned are invited, too. And I'm sure Josh will be going."

Remembering what little help Mike and Jessica had been the night before, Nancy doubted that Rachel's friends would tell her parents much. Still, there weren't many leads in the case, and they had to start somewhere.

"Nancy?" Ned came up to her in the hallway. "There's no address book. I just looked. I couldn't find a thing in Rachel's room with even Dennis's name on it. She really kept this guy a secret, didn't she?"

"It looks that way, but why?" Nancy asked. Before Ned could answer, the maid came back to tell them she'd set a late lunch by the pool for them.

"Thanks," Nancy said absently. "How about that swim, Nickerson? And how about a party later?"

When Nancy came downstairs that night dressed in a black tank top, roomy white overshirt, and black-and-white-checked mini-skirt, Josh and Ned were standing at the foot of the stairs. Both let out whistles.

Nancy grinned. "You don't look so bad yourselves," she said, taking in Ned's red dress shirt and beige chinos. "Ready?"

The three of them set out for the party, which was being held in an ultramodern house perched on the side of one of the San Gabriel foothills. The place was surrounded by redwood decks, and the views of Los Angeles at dusk were spectacular.

Josh introduced Nancy and Ned to the host and hostess of the party, longtime friends of the Klines, and then he and Ned went off to get cold drinks.

Nancy was standing alone at the railing of the deck, thirty feet above the pool, which was full of shouting, laughing kids. As she watched the setting sun she felt sad, thinking that Rachel should be there, having fun and celebrating with her friends.

She heard someone behind her. "It's about time, Nickerson," she murmured without turning. "I was just thinking about enjoying the view with you."

She started to reach out for Ned. But before her hand moved a couple of inches, two strong hands struck her hard in the back. In the next instant she was sailing headfirst over the deck railing!

Chapter

Five

As she fell through the air Nancy reached out desperately for a handhold. Nothing. She was vaguely aware of the swimmers' screams and panic-stricken faces as she plummeted headfirst into the pool.

The water closed over her. Sinking quickly to the bottom, Nancy almost blacked out when her shoulder struck the concrete floor of the pool. The pain was intense. Gasping but trying not to swallow water, she propelled herself up to the surface.

When she finally bobbed up, she looked

around, and one of the first things she saw was Ned hurrying through the crowd toward her. Josh was close behind.

Nancy lifted her eyes to the terrace high overhead, but she knew it would be useless. The deck was empty. Whoever had pushed her was gone.

"Are you all right?" everyone asked at once, crowding around her.

Nancy nodded, realizing how lucky she'd been to land in the deep end of the pool instead of the shallow one. A bruised shoulder was hardly anything. "I'm fine. Did any of you see who pushed me?"

The swimmers glanced at one another and shook their heads. Until Nancy had actually fallen into the pool, they'd all been having too good a time to notice anything happening on a deck thirty feet above their heads.

Disappointed, Nancy kicked slowly to the side. Her clothes were heavy with water, but Ned was there with a hand extended to help her climb out.

"What happened?" he asked. "Are you hurt?"

"One question at a time," Nancy replied with a shaky smile, drying her face and pushing back her hair with a corner of a towel someone tossed to her. "I was standing up there on the deck, admiring the view, when I heard someone behind me. I thought it was you. The next thing I knew, someone had pushed me, and I was falling into the pool."

Karen and Allen Kline ran up just then with some of the other parents. Again Nancy explained what had happened.

Mrs. Becker, the hostess, offered Nancy a change of clothes. After Nancy had slipped into a pair of dry white shorts and a red T-shirt, she went back to the pool and joined the Klines and Josh and Ned. Allen Kline was in the middle of telling his son what little he and his wife had learned that day.

"So the police took the report, but they said there wasn't much they could do. At least not until there's a ransom note—if there is one." The fear in his voice was evident.

"There hadn't been any other recent withdrawals from her savings account," Karen Kline added in a bleak voice. "I just don't know what to think or even what to hope for."

"Don't worry, Mom," Josh told her. "We'll find her, or she'll probably come back on her own."

"Josh is right, Mrs. Kline," Ned offered. "The police will do what they can, and Nancy and I will do what we can, too."

Karen Kline gave Ned a small, warm smile.

"I'm really grateful for your help." She reached out for her husband's arm. "I'd like to go home now, Allen. If Rachel does call, I'd like one of us to answer instead of the maid."

Allen nodded sadly. "We're not accomplishing anything here," he agreed. "Good night, kids. Thanks for your help, and I'm sorry about your accident, Nancy."

Nancy managed a smile. "Don't worry about me. Please, before you go, could I just ask you a couple of questions about Dennis Harper?"

Mr. and Mrs. Kline seemed to become tense at the mention of Dennis's name. "Do you know him?" Nancy went on. Ned raised a hand ever so slightly, telling her to go easy.

"Not well," Mr. Kline answered after reflecting a moment. "He certainly isn't the kind of boy we'd expect Rachel to like. He's got one of those punk haircuts and a pretty tough attitude to match it."

Nancy explained that she and Ned were concentrating on locating him. "Do you have any idea where he lives?"

"You think Rachel's with him?" Josh asked before his mother could answer.

"Well, of course, we don't know," Ned explained. "Still, it may not be a coincidence that he's not around and Rachel's missing."

Deep furrows showed in Mrs. Kline's forehead. "You'd better tell the police to track him down, Allen."

"I'll do that right away," Mr. Kline agreed. "If she is with him, she could be in trouble. I knew we should never have let her go out with him!" With that, Allen Kline disappeared inside the house to use a telephone. Mrs. Kline and Josh quickly followed him.

Ned and Nancy remained at their poolside table. He turned to her. "Any idea who pushed you?" he asked.

"Not a clue," she said, laughing. "There's a pattern here, though. Whenever we're around Rachel's friends, someone tries to scare us off."

"What do you think it means?" Ned asked.

Before Nancy could answer, Beth, Jessica, and Mike came toward their table, towels slung around their necks. There was another guy with them, someone Nancy didn't recognize.

"This is Peter Henley," Beth said. "I don't think you've met him. Peter, this is Nancy Drew and Ned Nickerson. They're friends of Josh Kline's from school."

"Hi," Peter said with a smile as the four of them pulled up chairs and sat down at the table.

"Ned and I went to Sound Performance today, looking for Dennis," she said to Mike Rasmussen. "Sorry we missed you."

"I'm off a couple of days this week because of graduation," Mike replied.

"Mr. Lindenbaum said he fired Dennis because some stereo equipment turned up missing," Ned put in.

Mike looked at Beth, Jessica, and Peter before meeting Ned's gaze and nodding. "I'm not surprised," he said bitterly.

"What do you mean?" Nancy asked.

"You'd better tell them. It's all right. I know how you feel," Jessica said with a sigh.

For a moment Mike hesitated. Then he shrugged and muttered, "Okay." His eyes met Nancy's. "I was really in love with Rachel. Maybe I still am, a little. When she broke up with me to go out with Dennis, it hurt a lot. Then when I figured Harper was ripping off Sound Performance, I didn't know what to do. I wanted to tell Rachel, but I thought she wouldn't believe me."

"Why did you think he was stealing?" Nancy asked, leaning forward a little in her chair. "Did you see Dennis take something?"

Mike shook his head. "No—if I had, I would have turned him in. There were just coincidences. Also, he seemed to have a lot of

46

money for a guy who worked part-time for minimum wage."

"Dennis is a jerk," Jessica said disdainfully, fiddling with the straw in her glass. "I think he's behind all these robberies."

"What robberies?" Nancy was quick to ask.

Peter joined the conversation. "Somebody's been ripping off houses in Beverly Hills lately," he said. "Expensive stuff like VCRs, video cameras, and equipment have been missing."

Beth was fiddling nervously with her pendant, a gold cat with white opals for eyes, and Nancy noticed she was a little pale. "Dennis always hung out at the Snake Pit," she put in. "It's a kind of crummy place downtown. Maybe that's where to look for him."

"Yeah, I'd see him there a lot when I was working," Peter added.

"You work there?" Ned asked.

"Sometimes. I like the music. The crowd's okay. An under-eighteen place. You know. No drinking, just music, video games, pinball, and fun." Peter slouched in his chair. "I never liked Dennis, though. He's a bit rough for that place."

"Do you think someone there might know where he is?" Nancy asked.

"I can think of a few people to ask," Peter offered.

Now we're getting somewhere, Nancy thought. "How about going now?"

"I'll go find Josh," Ned said with a nod of agreement, pushing back his chair.

Fifteen minutes later Nancy, Ned, and Josh were headed for the Snake Pit, following Mike, Beth, Jessica, and Peter. The club was in one of L.A.'s seedier areas, with a lot of empty warehouses.

"Some artists and musicians live down here," Josh explained. "It used to be dangerous, but now it's mostly trendy."

They met Rachel's friends in the club's parking lot, and Nancy took the lead. Her cases had taken her to worse places than this, she thought as she pushed open the heavy metal door.

The Snake Pit was full of smoke, and there were black leather jackets everywhere. The crowd—girls *and* guys—looked pretty tough.

Up on the stage a band hammered out earsplitting music. Nancy couldn't make out any of the words. Waitresses in vinyl miniskirts squeezed between packed tables, carrying trays of soft drinks.

"Does anybody see Dennis?" Nancy asked, raising her voice to be heard over the noise.

Jessica, Beth, and Mike shook their heads.

Peter was busy saying hello to someone he knew.

"It's early," Josh said, scanning the crowd.

"Is there anybody here you'd recognize as a friend of Dennis's?" Nancy asked.

"We don't hang around with this crowd," Jessica shouted just as the music died.

People at surrounding tables turned to stare at her, and the girl slipped down a little in her chair.

"Did my sister ever tell you she wanted to run off with this guy?" Josh asked Beth. "I mean, seeing this crowd he hung out with, I can't believe she would."

"No," Beth answered quickly, her eyes widening. "Of course not. I didn't even think she was all that serious about him."

"She was serious enough to dump me for the guy," Mike put in sadly.

"I don't know why you don't just forget her and start going out with somebody else," Jessica said coldly. Everyone stared at her in stunned surprise.

"Should we 'just forget' that Rachel is missing, too?" Mike demanded, his tone furious.

"If she's missing, it's her own choice!" Jessica spat out the words. "She and that boyfriend of hers are probably in Mexico somewhere, laughing at all of us!"

"Arguing won't get us anywhere," Ned said, interceding quietly.

Beth was shifting around in her chair, her eyes moving anxiously over the crowd. Once again, she was fingering the little gold cat on her necklace. "I think we should get out of here," she said with a shiver. "This place gives me the creeps."

Just then Mike leapt out of his chair, nearly toppling the sodas off the table.

"What's got into you?" Jessica asked, moving out of his way.

"There's Dennis!" he shouted, pointing past the stage.

Nancy jumped up and looked in the direction Mike was pointing. Before she could catch a glimpse of Dennis, though, the lights went off and the whole club went black.

Chapter

Six

NANCY REACHED UNDER the table for her purse. She rummaged inside, pulled out her penlight, and pointed it in the direction Dennis had taken.

Even in its dim light, though, Nancy could see that the boy had disappeared. Mike was standing by the edge of the stage, and Ned and Josh were next to her.

When the lights came back up again a few seconds later, Mike took off in the direction where Dennis had disappeared. Nancy, Ned, and Josh were right behind him. They pushed their way through the crowd, back by the club's dressing rooms, and outside. Nancy's first instincts were right, though. Dennis appeared to be gone.

In the parking lot Mike shoved a hand through his hair and sighed.

"We've lost him."

"Maybe he doubled back and is inside," Nancy suggested.

"I don't think so. We all saw him take off this way," Ned pointed out. "He's not here."

Nancy didn't like giving up, especially when they'd come so close to finding Dennis.

"We can look around inside," Mike agreed, "but I don't think we're going to find him."

Back inside the club, Nancy and the others looked for any sign of Dennis. Ned went off in one direction while Mike and Josh checked out the dancers and people sitting at tables in another direction.

When they all met back at their table, Beth asked Mike if he'd found anyone who'd seen Dennis.

"Nope. We struck out," Mike said with a frown.

Peter Henley came by just then. Nancy asked him if he'd spotted Dennis around the club.

Peter shook his head. "If he was here, I

didn't see him," he said. With that, he went off to dance with a girl with bleached blond hair and spiked black boots.

"We might as well get out of here," Mike told Jessica and Beth. "We're wasting our time."

"It took you long enough to figure that out," Jessica muttered. She and Beth both seemed relieved as they got to their feet.

"Coming?" Mike asked Nancy, Ned, and Josh.

"I think we'll stick around for a while," Josh said.

Mike shrugged. "Good luck," he replied. He, Jessica, and Beth hurried out of the club after asking Peter if he wanted a ride home. He shook his head no and continued dancing.

"What do you think Dennis was doing here?" Ned asked when the three of them were alone.

"My guess is he came to talk to someone," Nancy offered, her eyes scanning the crowd. "From the way he took off when he saw Mike, it didn't seem like he was here to have a good time."

"Should we start asking around to see if anyone here knows Dennis or Rachel?" Ned wanted to know when the three of them were alone at the table.

"Sounds good to me," Josh answered. "Nancy, you'd better stick with one of us."

Ned's eyes sparkled as he watched Nancy react to Josh's innocent remark.

"I'll be fine on my own," she said pointedly.

Josh looked at her in surprise, then a grin broke out across his face. "Sure. Sorry, Nancy."

She smiled. "No problem. How about if you guys take opposite sides of the room while I cover the middle?"

Ned gave her a salute. "Yes, ma'am," he said.

Nancy drew a deep breath and approached a table where eight people were sitting. She looked as friendly as possible. "Hi, I'm looking for Dennis Harper, and I was wondering if any of you know him."

Eight pairs of eyes turned up to her face. Eight pairs of suspicious eyes. None of them seemed to recognize Dennis's name.

"Why do you ask?" inquired one girl.

"I've got some questions to ask him."

The girl's gaze took in Nancy's shorts and T-shirt with distaste. "You a cop?"

"Don't be an idiot, Marcy," put in one of the guys at the table. "She's too young to be a cop."

"Maybe," said Marcy.

"I'm just a friend," Nancy told them.

Marcy's eyebrows rose. "Of Dennis's?"

"Of Rachel Kline's, actually."

The band launched into a throbbing beat, and most of the kids got up to dance, but Marcy and another guy stayed behind. Marcy appeared very curious. "Is Dennis in any trouble?"

"Maybe," Nancy said, sitting down in an empty chair and ignoring the stare from the guy with Marcy. "Did you know Rachel's missing?"

Marcy wouldn't meet Nancy's eyes. "Rachel Kline." She said the name with a touch of scorn. Nancy was sure that Marcy knew Rachel, whether she'd admit it or not. "Are her parents blaming Dennis?"

Nancy shrugged. "Nobody's blaming anybody. Rachel's family is really worried, of course. We're just trying to find her—and him."

"Dennis was in here earlier," Marcy confessed reluctantly. "But he's gone now."

"Do you know what he was doing here?"

Marcy pulled back at the question. "No," she said. She turned to start talking to the guy at the table.

55

"It could be important," Nancy pressed gently.

At that moment the guy interrupted. "Let's dance," he said to Marcy, wrenching her out of her chair. It was clear he thought she'd said too much as it was.

During the next half hour every person Nancy talked to denied knowing Rachel and claimed not to have seen Dennis that night.

Ned joined her as she left the last table. "No luck," he said, spreading his hands. "I even tried the guys in the band, and Josh talked to the kitchen crew and the waitresses. If anybody here has ever heard of Harper, he's not admitting it."

Nancy nodded. "I came up dry, too. What do you say we get out of here? I'm getting a headache."

"Let's find Josh," he agreed, taking Nancy's hand and pushing a path through the crowd.

As they were leaving Nancy noticed something scrawled on the wall beside the front door and stopped for a closer look. There, among the phone numbers, names, and other graffiti, was a drawing of a cat with white eyes.

It looked familiar, but Nancy didn't know why until they were outside, where it was quieter, and the evening air was pleasantly cool. Beth Hanford came into her mind, and Nancy remembered the necklace she'd been wearing at the party earlier that evening—a gold cat with white opal eyes.

She caught Ned's arm and pulled him back inside. "Look at this," she said, pointing at the cat. "Doesn't it look familiar to you?"

Ned thought for a moment, then nodded. "Beth was wearing a necklace like that," he said.

Nancy frowned as they went back outside to catch up with Josh. "It probably doesn't mean anything," she mused. "Still, it's an odd coincidence."

Nobody said much on the way back to Beverly Hills—each was lost in his or her own thoughts. Where could Rachel be? Was she safe? If Dennis *had* kidnapped her, why hadn't he sent a ransom note? And what had he been doing in the club that night? It seemed like a pretty big risk for him to be seen in public if he had anything to do with Rachel's disappearance.

The house was all lit up when they arrived at the Klines', and there was a police car in the driveway. Nancy's heart started pounding. She hoped the police had brought good news. She hurried into the house behind Josh and Ned.

57

"Mom!" Josh yelled the moment they were through the front door. "Dad! Where is everybody?"

Karen Kline appeared at the top of the grand, curving stairway. "Up here, dear," she said, her voice shaky.

"What's going on?" Josh demanded, racing up the stairs. "Did they find Rachel?"

Slowly Mrs. Kline shook her head. "No," she said. Then, without saying anything more, she walked down the hallway, moving as if she was in a daze.

Josh followed her at top speed, and Nancy and Ned came behind him at a slightly slower pace. It was obvious that something shattering had happened, and they didn't want to intrude.

Ned took Nancy's hand and gave it a slight squeeze. The light was on in Rachel's room, and they could hear Mr. Kline speaking in an angry, agitated voice.

Mrs. Kline explained to Josh as Mr. Kline talked with a police officer. "When we got home, we checked to see if your sister was back. This is what we found."

Pausing at Rachel's doorway just then, Nancy gasped.

Rachel's room had been ransacked!

Chapter

Seven

Every dresser drawer had been emptied onto the floor, and the contents of the closet and bookcase were scattered everywhere. Even the mattress and box spring had been torn from the bed.

Nancy noticed a video camera lying on the floor in the corner. There were tapes scattered all around it.

"Take a look at this," she said, heading for the camera and bending down to get a closer look. In that moment Nancy ruled out burglary—the rest of the house was apparently

59

untouched, and no thief would have left such an expensive camera behind.

Josh nodded. He was acting worried and distracted. "Rachel's interested in filmmaking, too," he said absently.

"I don't think it was a burglary, Mr. Kline," the police officer said as Rachel's father walked him out.

"Nothing's missing?" Nancy wanted to know as she went to stand at Mrs. Kline's side.

"Not as far as I can tell," Karen Kline answered. "Not even my jewelry." Nancy could see that she was on the verge of tears. "And I don't think we surprised whoever it was, either," the woman went on. "I mean, we didn't see anyone leaving the house. It had to have happened while we were still at the party."

"A burglar wouldn't have left without that camera," Ned said, voicing Nancy's conclusion. "Not to mention the rest of the stuff in the house."

"How could anyone get past the housekeeper? She should have heard a noise," Nancy said.

"Mrs. Morgan is a very sound sleeper, and her rooms are at the far end of the house. She also forgot to set the burglar alarm before going to sleep, so the intruder had no problems getting in and back out," Mrs. Kline answered with a slight shrug of her shoulders.

Nancy went back to the videotapes and studied them carefully. All had obviously been labeled by Rachel, with titles like "Day at the Beach," "Girls at the Mall," and "Boys Worth Watching." Nancy smiled sadly and turned back to the others. "Are the police going to dust for fingerprints?" she asked.

"I don't know how much good it will do," Mrs. Kline replied. "Allen and I touched lots of things while we were looking to see if anything was missing. The officer also said it wouldn't help unless whoever broke in had a prior record."

"Still," Nancy said, "fingerprints might offer an important clue. Suppose the culprit *does* have a record?"

Mrs. Kline nodded distractedly. "I'll ask Allen to speak to the police," she said, and she hurried out.

"Let's go talk," Josh said after a long sigh. Nancy nodded, and she and Ned followed him out of Rachel's room.

After Mr. and Mrs. Kline went off to bed, Josh, Ned, and Nancy sat down in the den with glasses of lemonade and a bowl of chips.

"It's been a long day," Josh said, rubbing his eyes. "And a confusing one. I just don't understand what's happening."

"Whoever broke in tonight was looking for something very specific," Nancy offered. Ned nodded his silent agreement. "But what?"

"The only thing we know for certain is that it must be connected to Rachel," Ned said. "And maybe also that it was something that could explain where she is now."

"Maybe." Nancy thought for a moment. "But we wouldn't know what the connection was."

"Here's another question: Who pushed you over the deck tonight, and why?" Josh asked.

Nancy shrugged. "Someone in Rachel's crowd who doesn't want us to find her, that's my guess."

"Could it have been Dennis?" Ned wondered.

"I doubt it," Nancy said firmly. "Judging from the way he ran out of the Snake Pit tonight, I don't think he'd risk being seen at a party."

Josh stood up. "I can't think anymore tonight, that's for sure. If you have time tomorrow, come by the studio and we can talk. My mom and dad are making me go to work every day. They think it's best if we try to stick to our normal routine."

Nancy smiled. "I agree with them."

After Josh went up to bed, Ned reached out to give Nancy a kiss. "Alone at last," he murmured into her hair.

"Don't worry, Nickerson," Nancy told him with a laugh. "You'll have me all to yourself tomorrow."

"Why? What happens tomorrow?" Ned asked curiously.

"Tomorrow we're going to track down Dennis Harper. No matter what."

As soon as Nancy got up the next morning she tried Dennis's phone number for what seemed like the fiftieth time. Still no answer. After quickly dressing in white slacks and a roomy blue cotton shirt, she hurried downstairs.

Josh, Ned, and the Klines were already in the dining room. The doorbell rang almost as soon as Nancy sat down at the table.

"That must be Lieutenant Heller," Mr. Kline said, getting up to answer the door himself. "The police promised to bring a fingerprint expert."

Everyone left the table to follow the two people upstairs to Rachel's room. The fingerprint woman sighed when she saw the mess the intruder had left. Fingerprints would be almost impossible to lift.

"I checked with your neighbors last night," the lieutenant said. "None of them saw or heard anything out of the ordinary while you were out."

"And nothing is missing," Mrs. Kline added. "We double-checked everything."

"Are there any leads on my daughter, Lieutenant?" Mr. Kline asked. "Have you been able to locate her boyfriend, Dennis?"

Lieutenant Heller raised his hands in a helpless gesture. "No leads, I'm afraid, Mr. Kline. But I do have an address for the Harper boy, and we're checking up on him."

Nancy's heart started to race. So the police knew where Dennis Harper lived. "Could you give me his address, Lieutenant?" she asked.

At the lieutenant's quizzical expression, Karen Kline explained that Nancy was an amateur detective and that she was helping them find their daughter.

"Hey, I've heard of you," Heller said with a smile. "I read about you in a paper somewhere. What do you know—Drew's your name, right?"

Nancy blushed, and Ned gave her a little poke in the ribs. "That's right. Could you give me Dennis's address? I'd like to check his place out."

The detective pulled a notebook from his shirt pocket, flipped it open, and read off an address. Nancy made a note of it and thanked the lieutenant.

"You won't be able to get in—unless he's there," he said, closing the notebook and tucking it away again. "And if he is there, he probably won't let you in. I can tell you that we went over that apartment with a fine-tooth comb and came up blank."

Nancy nodded. She still wanted to go out there herself. She'd ask Josh if they could borrow Rachel's car to drive out to Dennis's place.

Josh glanced at his watch. "I'm going to be late for work if I don't leave right now," he said, his tone apologetic. "If you guys want to use the car, you can drive me to work and take it," he said, reading Nancy's mind.

"Go ahead, Josh," Mr. Kline urged. "Try to have a good day."

Nancy lingered for just a moment after Josh and Ned went out, talking with Lieutenant Heller. "I understand there've been a lot of other break-ins in the community lately," she said.

Heller answered her as if she were a colleague. "Yes," he said with a nod. "There have been, and we've been getting nowhere with them."

"Just as you're getting nowhere finding our daughter," Mrs. Kline put in, sounding a little peevish.

The lieutenant's strong but ordinary face showed compassion as he met Karen's gaze. "We're trying, Mrs. Kline," he said quietly. "But the unfortunate truth is, we're swamped with reports of missing teenagers. It's an epidemic."

"Nancy!" Ned's voice called to her good-naturedly, from a distance.

"I'd like to talk to you again soon," Nancy said to the lieutenant.

He nodded and handed her his card. "Take care, Ms. Drew. We may be dealing with some very dangerous people. Please be careful."

Just as Nancy reached the bottom of the stairway the telephone rang. Mrs. Morgan answered it and held out the receiver of the hallway extension. "It's for you, Nancy," she said.

Nancy was surprised. "Hello?"

"Nancy, this is Beth Hanford." Beth sounded scared and anxious. "I need to talk to you. In person."

"I was just going out," Nancy answered,

conscious that Ned and Josh were waiting. She didn't want Josh to be late for his job because of her. "Could we meet later?"

"Twelve o'clock," Beth said. "The pizza place in the Golden Hills Mall?"

"I'll be there," Nancy promised after Beth gave her directions.

Nancy hung up and dashed out to catch up with Josh and Ned. The three of them got into the Camaro and headed for the movie studio.

"I hope they get a break in this case soon," Josh said as he maneuvered the sporty car through the early-morning traffic. "I don't think my folks—or I—can take much more."

Nancy and Ned were silent. There was nothing either of them could say to help.

When they reached the studio gates Josh's mood improved. It was obvious to Nancy that he loved his job after only one day. He gave a cheerful hello to the guard who checked his ID, and he asked for one-day passes for Nancy and Ned. Driving through the lot, they passed people dressed in costumes from every period.

"Visitors can come onto the lot on the other side if they buy a ticket," Josh explained. "They're not supposed to wander into this part, but it does happen sometimes."

Josh passed a lot of expensive cars to park the Camaro among some older, battered models. "Why don't you come over and look around for a couple of hours? A change from the case might do you some good," Josh said.

Nancy and Ned nodded their agreement, and Nancy said, "Just for an hour. We've got lots to do." She was interrupted just then by a screech of tires and a loud crash.

Josh chuckled. "Don't worry, Nancy," he said. "It's just a scene being shot."

They wandered over to the set where Josh was working. An outdoor scene was being blocked, and Nancy and Ned found places to stand and watch where they were out of the way. Josh was already at work helping the assistant director's assistant.

"We'll only stay for a little while because I want to check out the address Lieutenant Heller gave me for Dennis Harper," Nancy explained. Then she filled him in on her appointment with Beth. "All right with you?" she asked.

"You bet." They were silent for a few minutes. "It'll be weird to sit in a theater and watch this," Ned whispered after a couple of minutes. Nancy's mind was mostly on the case she was trying to solve, but she did manage to smile and nod.

Ned appeared to be fascinated watching the hero of the movie—a well-known star—

rehearse. The actor jumped out of one car, leaving the door open behind him, and dragged a man out of another car parked nearby.

Nancy's mind wandered more and more until finally she knew she couldn't stay there another minute.

Josh had wandered off, and Nancy and Ned were looking for him so they could pick up his car keys. They were wandering behind the set when Nancy heard the roar of a car's engine behind them. She turned to look back and gripped Ned's hand.

In the next instant her heart jumped into her throat. A green sports car with tinted windows was bearing down on them at top speed! In another second they'd be run over!

Chapter
Eight

NANCY DIDN'T WASTE TIME talking. She dived to her right, pulling Ned with her. Belly-flopping onto the hard-packed earth, they rolled out of the car's path just as its wheels flew past, sending out sprays of dirt. The right tires missed them by no more than a foot.

"Are you hurt?" Ned asked, helping Nancy up.

"No," she said breathlessly. "Come on!" Her eyes were riveted on the car as it disappeared around a corner.

She and Ned took off after the car at a dead run. They had to get a glimpse of the driver.

When they made it around the corner, they found the car abandoned, with the door on the driver's side hanging open.

Josh and a couple of other crew members wandered toward them from the direction of their set.

"What happened?" Josh asked, seeing how filthy they both were.

Nancy was still checking for any sign of the driver, even though she knew it was probably hopeless. Whoever had tried to run them down was long gone.

"Somebody tried to kill us," Ned explained. "Fortunately Nancy saw them coming, and we rolled out of the way just in time."

"I'll call studio security," a guy in a plaid shirt called out. Another guy went to inspect the car.

"This is getting pretty heavy," Josh said, standing beside Ned and Nancy. "Somebody's playing hardball now."

"Maybe we can get a lead from the license-plate number," Nancy said hopefully.

Josh shook his head. "It's a studio car—we're using it in the movie. Whoever wanted to run you down must have ripped it off when the prop people were busy."

Within a couple of minutes a man and woman in security officers' uniforms arrived.

"What happened?" the woman asked.

Nancy explained that she and Ned had been walking along when someone tried to run them down, and the man in the jeans and plaid shirt told how the vehicle had been stolen from the property lot a few minutes earlier. Unfortunately, no one had seen anything.

"I think we should let Lieutenant Heller know about this," Josh said. He was pale under his suntan. "You two could have been killed."

Ned put an arm around Nancy and gave her a quick squeeze as he tried to reassure his friend. "We're okay," he said quietly.

The security people left, telling them there wasn't much they could do without a description. Nancy kicked herself for not having gotten a better look at the driver.

Finally a man in a baseball cap called out, "All right, everybody! Back to work. We've got a picture to shoot!"

Josh was reluctant to leave Nancy and Ned. "I'd better go," he said. "Maybe you two should get out of here before something else happens."

Nancy glanced at her watch. "Could we take your car now, Josh?" she asked. "We'll pick you up later."

"Sure," he answered, tossing the keys to

Ned. Then, with a slight wave, he turned and followed the others back to the movie set.

"I think we'd better go change," Ned said, looking down at his dusty clothes. Nancy's were even worse, since she had put on white slacks that morning.

"Me, too," she said.

"You're sure you're okay?" Ned asked as they walked through the lot to where Josh's car was parked.

Nancy gave him a squeeze. "I'm fine, Nickerson. How about you? You hit the ground just as hard as I did."

Ned grinned. "I'll live. Though it has occurred to me that hanging around with you might not be the best way to have a long and happy life."

Nancy chuckled, but then her expression turned serious. "Any idea who it was?"

Ned's grin had faded into an angry frown. "Don't know. Maybe the same person who shoved you off the deck at the party," he answered.

They'd reached Josh's car, and Ned opened the passenger door for Nancy. "One thing's sure—we had to have been followed from the Klines'," Nancy pointed out as she slipped into the car.

"You're right," Ned agreed, starting the

ignition. He turned to face her. "Nancy, maybe we should think about dropping this. The police are on the case. Whoever this person is, he or she is dead serious."

"You know I don't walk away from a case until it's solved," Nancy pointed out. "And it wasn't necessarily the same person who pushed me. There could be several people involved."

"If you had been hurt—"

"But I wasn't, Ned. And neither were you. Look, we're not stopping until we find Rachel and figure out what's going on."

"I just hope we survive that long," Ned said, pulling out of the parking lot.

When the two of them arrived back at the house less than a half hour later, Mrs. Kline greeted them at the door.

"My goodness," she exclaimed, taking in their clothes. "What happened?"

Nancy didn't want to alarm the woman, but she couldn't tell a lie, either. "There was an accident at the studio," she said. "But no one was hurt."

Mrs. Kline's eyes were wide with worry. "What kind of accident?"

Nancy glanced at Ned before reluctantly replying, "We were almost run down by a car."

Josh's mother gasped. "What?"

"Apparently somebody wants us to stop asking questions," Ned said quietly.

"Which means we might be getting close," Nancy added. "Mrs. Kline, have you heard anything from the police about the fingerprints?"

Even before Karen answered, Nancy could tell by her expression that the news was disappointing. "They did find a set of strange prints," she said. "But whoever broke in has no criminal record, so nobody can be identified."

Nancy sighed. "I'm sorry," she said. "I take it there hasn't been any other news?"

Mrs. Kline shook her head, and her eyes moved over Nancy's and Ned's clothes again. "Maybe you should just let the police handle this. Allen and I would never forgive ourselves if something happened—"

"We've had experience with situations like this," Nancy broke in gently, squeezing Mrs. Kline's hand. "And I promise we'll be careful."

With that, Nancy and Ned excused themselves and went upstairs. Once in her room, Nancy washed and changed into a pair of blue cotton shorts and a matching top. Downstairs,

Nancy found Ned waiting to go to the Golden Hills Mall to meet Beth. Dennis's apartment would have to wait until later.

Once they were in the car and headed toward the mall, Ned glanced over at Nancy quickly as he steered the car onto the highway.

"What do you think Beth wants to see you about?" he asked.

"Something about Dennis's relationship with Rachel, I hope," Nancy replied. The two were silent until Ned parked the car and the two of them headed to the cool, glass-topped shopping plaza.

After consulting a directory, Nancy and Ned found the colorful sign over the door of the pizza place.

"Do you want to talk to her alone?" Ned asked. He thought Beth would probably feel uncomfortable opening up with him there.

Nancy shook her head. "She sounded pretty anxious on the telephone this morning. Whatever it is, she's having a lot of trouble holding it in."

They entered the restaurant, and Nancy spotted Beth in a corner of the room. Jessica was standing beside the table, her hands thrust into the pockets of her jean jacket. She didn't look friendly.

Nancy and Ned approached as quietly as they could.

"You'd just better not spill the beans, Hanford," Jessica was warning an ashen-faced Beth in acid tones. "Because if you do, you'll pay for it!"

Chapter

Nine

WHEN SHE TURNED AROUND and faced Nancy and Ned, Jessica's cheeks were glowing with color. The girl took one hand out of her jacket pocket to push her hair back, and a piece of paper slipped to the floor.

"Spill what beans?" Nancy challenged Jessica. It was obvious to Nancy that she had overheard something important. She wasn't going to let Jessica off.

Jessica and Beth were both caught off guard. Beth's face was white, but Jessica had recovered quickly. "You know, Nancy," Jessica said tartly, "I'm getting a little tired of all your questions. It just so happens that what Beth and I were talking about is none of your business."

Beth bit down hard on her lower lip, then bolted out of her seat. "I can't talk to you now, Nancy," she said hurriedly. "Sorry!"

Before Nancy could think of a way to stop her, Beth raced out of the restaurant without a backward glance.

Nancy folded her arms and turned to Jessica, who raised her chin a degree and stared defiantly into Nancy's face. Nancy wouldn't let Jessica get away.

"I'll get some sodas," Ned said, and he went over to the counter.

"Sit down, Jessica," Nancy said. She could tell the girl was hiding something, and she was determined to find out what.

Jessica shook her head. She pushed back her brown hair again and gave Nancy a steely stare from her icy blue eyes. "Why should I?" she asked with a smirk.

"Whatever you said really scared Beth," Nancy began.

Jessica shrugged. "Beth is a wimp," she said.

Nancy thought about the fall she'd taken from the Beckers' deck and the near miss on the studio lot that day. She wondered if Jessica could have been behind one or both attacks.

The girl seemed to be good at threatening people, and it was only one step further to actually endangering a life. She confronted the girl.

"You know, Jessica," she said, "whatever it is you're hiding, I'm going to find out. And if you're involved with Rachel's disappearance, the charges might be very serious."

A shocked expression passed over Jessica's face, but she quickly composed herself. When she spoke, her words were harsh and bitter. "Rachel deserves whatever she gets," she said. With that, she stormed toward the door, almost knocking down Ned, who was carrying three sodas on a tray.

Jessica *is* hiding something, Nancy thought. She didn't even try to defend herself. Quickly Nancy went over and retrieved the piece of paper that had fallen from Jessica's pocket. She hadn't wanted Jessica to see her pick it up.

"What happened?" Ned asked, setting down the tray and glancing over Nancy's shoulder as her eyes scanned the note.

On the front of the paper was a sketch of the cat she and Ned had seen on Beth's necklace and on the wall at the Snake Pit. "'Special party at Kat Club Headquarters,'" she read out loud. "'Four twenty-two Beach Drive. Seven P.M.'"

"When is it?" Ned asked.

"It's tomorrow night." She tapped the cat drawing with her fingernail. "I have a feeling we're about to make a major breakthrough."

Ned pushed one of the sodas toward Nancy and sat down opposite her. "Did you find out anything from Miss Personality?"

Nancy sighed. "No. And there's probably no use in trying to talk with Beth, either. Jessica really intimidated her. After we leave here, let's go to Dennis Harper's apartment."

Ned narrowed his eyes. "I don't think that's such a good idea, Nan. After everything that's happened, I think we should let the police handle Harper."

"But—"

"Look, he could be the one who's been trying to scare you away. Maybe he knows you're on to him. He could be laying a trap for you right now."

Nancy had to admit that Ned had a point. Dennis Harper could be dangerous. "How about if we go later with Josh?" she asked. "With three of us, we should be safe."

"You don't let up, do you?" Ned said in mock exasperation. Nancy shook her head. "But now I think an afternoon in the sun beside the Klines' pool won't hurt, either," Ned suggested.

Breaking out in a wide grin, Nancy offered her hand for a shake. "It's a deal," she said.

When they arrived at the Klines', Allen Kline wasn't at home. He had forced himself to go to his office for the afternoon. Mrs. Kline was speaking to the police on the telephone. She shook her head, indicating that there were no new developments, so Nancy and Ned went upstairs to change.

Fifteen minutes later they were sitting with their feet dangling in the Klines' pool. "Not one word about the case," Ned said, laying a finger to Nancy's lips just as she was about to open her mouth.

She slipped into the water and swam out to the middle. Ned took a plunge off the diving board. While they were swimming, Nancy forced herself not to think about the case once. By the time they were drying off, her mind was clearer.

"I guess we'd better get Josh," Ned said, touching Nancy's cheek briefly with one finger. "You know, Nan, I wish we could be together like this more often."

Nancy nodded and studied her handsome boyfriend. What other guy could make her laugh and would help her out on cases the way he did? Nancy reached up and threw her arms around his neck as Ned wrapped his arms around her waist. She looked up into his warm brown eyes and was drawn closer to him. Before she knew it, they were caught in a breathtaking kiss that seemed to last forever.

"Wow," Ned murmured when it was over. "I love you, Nancy."

"I love you, too, Ned," Nancy said into Ned's ear. Reluctantly she pulled away and met his eye. "We'd better get going. I think Josh would resent having to walk all the way home."

As they headed to the studio ten minutes later traffic was especially heavy. Nancy and Ned were a few minutes late to pick Josh up at the studio gates. He appeared to be tired and discouraged.

"Any word?" he asked as they drove away.

Ned was still at the wheel. "Sorry, buddy," he said sympathetically. "As far as we know, there haven't been any new developments."

"We did find out about something called the Kat Club," Nancy told him. "They're having a party tomorrow night, and Ned and I are planning to crash it. Want to come along?"

Josh was frowning. "The Kat Club?"

Nancy reminded him about the threatening note they'd gotten the night of the party at the

Surf Club. "These Kats, whoever they are, don't want us around. Crashing their party is the best way to find out just who they are."

When they arrived back at the Kline house, Mrs. Morgan told them Mr. and Mrs. Kline were having dinner in their room. No one needed to say how difficult the last few days had been for them.

"I hope they'll let us know if there's anything we can do to help," Nancy said. "Josh, I want to ask you a favor—"

Just then the phone rang, and Nancy and Ned paused while Josh answered it. As he was hanging up he gave them a weary smile. "That was the studio. I have to go back to work for a few hours."

After Josh left, Ned said, "You're disappointed we can't go to Harper's place, aren't you?"

Nancy nodded. "But I guess it can wait. First thing tomorrow, though, right?"

"Right. Now how about—"

Mrs. Morgan came to find them. "Dinner is ready," she told them. "If you don't mind, I've set the table in the kitchen."

"Thanks, Mrs. Morgan," Nancy said.

"I'm starved," Ned said.

"What else is new?" Nancy replied, giving him a friendly punch in the side.

In the kitchen crisp seafood salads and warm rolls waited for them. Ned took a couple of sodas from the refrigerator and filled both their glasses.

Nancy sat down and picked up her fork. Through the kitchen windows she could see the swimming pool sparkling turquoise in the early-evening summer sun. She let her mind wander, chewing thoughtfully. "I think I'll call Beth later," she said after a while. "Maybe she's ready to talk now."

"I wouldn't bet on it," Ned answered, breaking a roll apart and buttering it generously. "It looked to me like Jessica scared her but good," he said.

"About what, that's the question," Nancy said. "What if she knows where Rachel is, and Jessica was warning her not to tell?"

"That doesn't make any sense," Ned said, pushing back his plate. "Why would Jessica not want us to find Rachel?"

"I don't know," Nancy admitted. "It is a little confusing. If Beth is really Rachel's friend, she'd find some way to let us know where she is."

"I'd say so," Ned agreed. "We still don't know how this Harper guy is involved," he pointed out.

"Jessica seems to think they've run off together," Nancy said. "Still, if that were the case, I think Rachel would have called her parents by now to let them know she was safe."

"What do you say we try to watch a movie on the VCR?" Ned suggested.

Reluctantly Nancy agreed. There was nothing more for her to do that night. Nancy and Ned rinsed their plates and cups and set them in the dishwasher. Then Ned took two cans of soda from the refrigerator, and they headed to the den.

Nancy looked at the tapes lying beside the VCR. She smiled when she saw *Casablanca,* one of her favorite old movies. "Can you stand it again?" she asked Ned. He smiled and then switched on the big-screen TV after slipping the tape into the VCR.

Ned settled himself on the couch next to Nancy, head back, arms folded across his chest. They waited, but nothing came on the screen. Frowning, Nancy got up and took the tape out. "Somebody must have erased it or something," she said. She put the tape aside and picked out another one.

She popped it into the machine. Almost immediately a famous mystery movie lit up the screen. Nancy settled down beside Ned again, and his arm came to rest comfortably around her shoulders.

Midway through the movie, the telephone rang. Knowing Mrs. Morgan was off for the night, Nancy answered it after only two rings.

"Kline residence," she said. From the other end Nancy could hear a low, rhythmic roar that sounded like the ocean.

"This is Rachel Kline," the caller said in a soft voice that Nancy recognized. "Could I please speak to my mom and dad?"

Chapter

Ten

Don't hang up, Rachel!" Nancy cried out. She signaled Ned, who bounded off the couch and out of the room at the sound of the girl's name. "We'll put your parents on right away."

"Okay," Rachel answered in a small voice. "But please hurry. I don't have much time."

"Where are you?" Nancy asked softly. "Are you all right?"

"I can't answer your questions," Rachel replied. She sounded as though she was about to burst into tears. "I'm just calling because I know my mom and dad must be awfully worried."

"We can help you," Nancy continued persuasively. "But first we need to know where you are."

"Rachel!" Karen Kline's frantic voice came on the line. "Rachel, honey—"

Feeling awkward about intruding, Nancy quietly hung up the receiver. Ned came rushing back into the room while she was rewinding the movie they'd been watching and putting it back into its case.

"Did she tell you anything?" he asked expectantly.

Nancy turned and shook her head as she met his eyes. "No, but she sounded really scared, and she said she didn't have much time."

Ned put his arms around Nancy. "At least we know she's okay," he said.

Nancy was about to give Ned a hug when Karen Kline came running into the room in her robe, followed by her husband.

"She hung up!" Rachel's mother cried, hugging her arms around her chest. "I was so close to finding out where she was when the line went dead!"

Allen Kline tried to comfort his wife. "At least we know she's alive."

"Did you hear anything in the background before she hung up?" Nancy prodded. "Any other voices?"

"No voices." Karen Kline paused, thinking. "There was a low murmuring—"

"The ocean," Nancy said. "I recognized it as soon as I picked up the phone," she explained.

Allen Kline's expression brightened. "Rachel must be somewhere close to the water."

"But where?" Mrs. Kline asked. Her voice sounded weary and desperate again.

"Don't worry, Mrs. Kline," Ned told her. "We'll find her. We've got one good lead: We know she's somewhere by the beach." He met Nancy's eyes. They both knew that in Southern California that really didn't mean much.

"I'm calling the police," Mr. Kline said. "They should know about this right away."

"I could use a glass of iced tea," Karen Kline said. "Anyone else?"

"I'll help," Nancy offered, following Mrs. Kline out.

"We should call Mike," Karen Kline said as she took a pitcher down from the cabinet.

"Mike Rasmussen?" Nancy asked, surprised. She took four glasses down from the cupboard and set them on the breakfast bar.

"I like Mike," Mrs. Kline said. "I trust him. Not like this Dennis." She sighed and looked as though she was about to cry again. "I can't help thinking none of this would have happened if Rachel hadn't taken up with him in the first place."

Josh came in through the back door just then. He perked up at the sight of Nancy and Mrs. Kline. "What's going on?"

Mrs. Kline put her arm around her son while Nancy finished making the iced tea. "We heard from Rachel just now. She hung up before we could find out where she was, but we know she's all right."

Josh let out a relieved sigh. "That's great, Mom. She's okay."

"We do know one thing, though," Nancy told him. "I distinctly heard the sound of the ocean in the background. Your sister is somewhere by the water."

Josh looked puzzled for a moment. "That could be anywhere, though. Did it sound like she was calling long distance?" he asked.

Nancy shook her head. On a hunch, she recited the address Lieutenant Heller had given her for Dennis Harper. "Is that near the water?" she asked.

Josh thought for a long moment, then nodded. "Yeah. I think it is."

"It's possible she was calling from there," Nancy said thoughtfully.

"The police checked his place out and didn't see any sign of Rachel. Or Dennis," Josh said.

"True," Nancy agreed. "It may be a long shot, but it's worth a try. Ned and I will go there tomorrow. There's got to be a clue of some kind," she said emphatically. She hoped so, anyway.

Mrs. Kline picked up the tray. "I think you should get Mike to go with you, Nancy," she said as they headed back into the den. "You and Ned shouldn't go alone. I'm going to call him first thing in the morning. I just want this to be over."

"Don't worry, Mrs. Kline," Nancy said reassuringly. "I have a feeling she's okay." Secretly, though, Nancy wondered. What made Rachel Kline hang up so fast? If she really was safe, why couldn't she talk or come home? Nancy knew they'd better find her. And soon.

Everyone was gathered in the dining room for an early breakfast the next morning when Mike Rasmussen showed up. Mr. Kline invited him to join them.

"Thanks," Mike said cheerfully, sitting down. "I've already eaten, but I could use some tea."

Mrs. Morgan poured him a cup from the pot on the side table and set it in front of him.

Mike's face had an eager expression as he looked at Mrs. Kline. "So you heard from

Rachel," he said. "What did she say? Is she okay?"

"She's alive," Mr. Kline replied. "I'm afraid that's about all we know." He touched a napkin to his mouth and set it aside. "We're hoping you can tell us something, Mike. Any little detail we might have overlooked. Are you absolutely sure that Rachel didn't confide in you before she disappeared?"

Mike lowered his eyes for a moment, and his broad shoulders sagged a little. "Rachel stopped talking to me after she gave me back my class ring," he said. He met Mr. Kline's gaze again. "I wish I could help you, I really do, but I don't know any more than you do."

Nancy jumped in. "Ned and I are going to Dennis Harper's place today," she told Mike. "I was hoping you'd come with us. You might notice some sign that Rachel had been there that we'd miss."

"We think Rachel might have been calling from there last night," Josh put in.

"Why?" Mike asked. He hadn't touched his tea.

"We heard the surf in the background," Mr. Kline answered, his face pinched and tired-looking. "I called the police, but Heller was off duty last night," he said with irritation.

"Allen," Mrs. Kline said softly. "They're doing the best they can."

"Well, their best isn't good enough!" snapped Mr. Kline. He was dressed for the office, and he stood and excused himself from the table. "I'll call Lieutenant Heller from my study," he said in quieter tones. Josh left the room with him, since his father was giving him a ride to the studio. Nancy and Ned were going to use Rachel's car.

"Ready?" Nancy asked, turning to Ned.

He nodded, pushing back his chair.

"We'll let you know the second we find anything," Nancy told Karen Kline before they left the dining room. The woman nodded silently, obviously afraid to hope for too much. She had had too many disappointments so far.

Ned, Nancy, and Mike set out for Dennis Harper's apartment a few minutes later, with Mike giving directions.

"Did you and Rachel get along pretty well?" Nancy asked cautiously, turning to look at Mike in the backseat as they sped along the freeway. "Before the breakup, I mean?"

Mike stared out through the side window, and Nancy saw a muscle tighten in his jaw, then relax again. "Most of the time," he answered, without turning his head.

Since Mike seemed to hang out with Jessica so much, Nancy decided to feel him out about the girl. She was especially curious about why Jessica had intimidated Beth in the pizza place the day before. "Are Jessica and Beth good friends?" she asked.

"No way," Mike blurted out. Then, after a long time, he added, "Jessica is nobody's friend."

"Then why does she hang around with your crowd?"

Mike shrugged. "Something to do, I guess."

"What makes her so nasty?" Nancy persisted. "Yesterday she was pretty hard on Beth."

"I don't know," Mike said noncommittally. "I know for a fact that she dislikes Rachel—intensely. That's mainly because she's jealous. Rachel has always been more popular and done better in school." He pointed toward a green and white sign on the edge of the freeway. "Take this exit and turn right," he said.

Ned followed Mike's instructions. "What do you think Beth could know that she's too scared to tell us?" he asked.

"I don't know," Mike said with a shrug of his shoulders.

Nancy shrugged, too, and then concentrated on the road.

Dennis's apartment was in a large, run-down complex within a hundred yards of the beach. After getting out of the car, Nancy checked the mailboxes in the hall and found out that Dennis lived in number seventeen. They found it on the side of the building facing the water, on the ground floor.

Nancy rang the doorbell. "Dennis!" she called out when there was no answer. Nothing came back but the sound of children laughing somewhere nearby and the soothing rush of the waves on the beach. "Try the knob," Ned said.

Nancy reached for it, and it turned. The door of the apartment opened with a little push.

"Dennis?" Nancy called again, stepping slowly over the threshold. The sight of the living room made her draw in her breath sharply. The chairs and sofa were overturned, and the screen on the small TV set had been smashed, scattering shards of glass all over the cheap carpet.

"Be careful," Ned warned, stepping in behind Nancy. "There might still be someone here."

Nancy moved on to the kitchen. All the dishes had been pulled from the cupboards and broken on the floor. Houseplants had been dumped from their pots and ground into the mess of shattered glass, and the cotton curtains had been pulled off the wall, along with the rods that held them.

Mike whistled under his breath. "Somebody is really mad at this guy," he said.

"Or looking for something," Nancy said, remembering the scene in Rachel's room. She went on through the apartment, finding the bedroom and bathroom much the same. There was no sign of either Rachel or Dennis, though.

"Freeze. Police!" ordered a man's voice as Nancy stepped back into the demolished living room.

Lieutenant Heller lowered his gun at the sight of Nancy. "What are you doing here?"

"Looking for Dennis and Rachel," Nancy answered. "The door was open, and we were worried."

The detective returned his revolver to the holster beneath his suit jacket and slowly took in the mess. "I hope you haven't touched anything," he said.

Ned and Mike were standing just behind Nancy, one on either side. "We haven't," Ned said. "We just got here."

"I take it this happened since you were here last time?" Nancy asked, stepping carefully over a broken vase.

The detective nodded. "Yep. My men came by last night. When Mr. Kline let me know Rachel had called, I thought I'd double-check this place. I didn't expect to find it like this, though."

He went to the telephone, lifted the receiver with a handkerchief, and punched in a number with the end of a pen. "This is Heller," he said, then he barked out the address and asked for a fingerprint person.

Mike's gaze landed on a denim jacket lying on the floor. He walked over and picked it up, his face gray. "This is Rachel's," he said, turning around and holding the garment close to his chest for a moment.

"Let me see," Lieutenant Heller said gently.

When Mike held out the jacket, a piece of paper slipped to the floor. Nancy reached for it.

She found her voice shaking as she read the note out loud: " 'We're in terrible trouble. Find us. Please.' "

Chapter

Eleven

As soon as Nancy finished reading the note, Mike leaned back against the wall, clutching Rachel's jacket to him, his eyes fixed on the floor.

Ned looked on with a worried expression on his face. "Do you think Rachel wrote it?" he asked.

"Let me see that," Lieutenant Heller said, holding out his hand.

Mike glanced at the piece of paper as Nancy gave it to the lieutenant. "That's Rachel's handwriting, all right," he said, his voice shaking.

Nancy looked around the ransacked apartment. "What are you going to do now?" she asked the detective.

"Ask for more manpower," the policeman answered. He went back to the telephone and called the station in the same careful way he had before.

Nancy turned to Rachel's ex-boyfriend. "Are you okay, Mike?"

The boy nodded glumly, but his grip on the jacket was still so tight that his knuckles glowed white. "I—I think I just need some fresh air," he said haltingly. He stumbled toward the open door, and Nancy watched as he went down the hall.

"This is hitting him hard," Ned commented to Nancy.

Nancy nodded thoughtfully. "He must still love her," she replied.

The lieutenant completed his phone call and turned back to Nancy and Ned. "Was he all right?" he asked, cocking a thumb toward the door that Mike had taken out. "He looks as though he's been kicked."

"He's the guy who went with Rachel until about a month ago," Nancy explained. "They broke up when Rachel started dating Dennis Harper. Obviously, Mike still cares about her."

"This can't be easy for him," the lieutenant said. Then he went outside to find Mike. Nancy followed, with Ned close behind.

"You seem pretty shook up," the policeman said to Mike, who was sitting on the front steps. "You must care a lot about this girl."

"I do," Mike agreed. Then, quickly, he corrected himself. "Did."

"Mike, is there anything you can think of that would explain why Rachel might be in danger?" Nancy asked.

"Or what might have made her leave that note?" Ned added.

"I know what you think," Mike snapped, still holding Rachel's jacket across his lap. "You think maybe I'm connected with this somehow, that I wanted to get even with Rachel or something! Well, I wouldn't hurt her. I really loved her!"

"That's not what we're saying, son," the lieutenant said in a gentle voice. "We're just looking for some kind of lead."

Mike lowered his head. "I don't know what to tell you. I'm just as confused as you are. All I want is to find her before something really bad happens."

The lieutenant nodded and rose to his feet. "So do we, son. So do we." He paused for a moment. "I'll need the jacket for evidence," he said, holding out one hand. Mike gave the jacket to him.

Two squad cars pulled up, and three uniformed officers—along with the woman who had come to the Klines' to lift fingerprints—came across the narrow lawn.

At the sight of them, Mike got to his feet and stood staring out toward the ocean.

Mike was lost in thought and seemed unaware that Nancy and Ned were standing next to him. "Those cats can be dangerous," he muttered under his breath with a shake of his head.

Nancy touched his arm. "What did you mean just now?" she asked. "About cats being dangerous?"

Mike almost jumped at the question, but he recovered his composure almost immediately. "I just meant 'those guys,' criminals in general," he said. Nancy thought Mike was acting a bit flustered. "Look," he said suddenly, glancing at his watch and trying to smile, "I've got to get to work pretty soon. Think you could drive me back to the Klines' so I can pick up my car?"

"Sure," Ned answered.

"I'll ask the lieutenant if it's okay for us to leave," Nancy added.

Minutes later they were in the Camaro.

Soon after they arrived back at the Klines', Ned and Nancy watched Mike drive off to work.

"Come on, Nickerson," Nancy said, grabbing his hand and leading him back to Rachel's car.

"What's up?" Ned asked.

"I don't know exactly," Nancy said as Ned started up the car. "But I get the feeling Mike's hiding something. Remember what he said about 'those cats'?"

Ned nodded and pulled out into the street. Mike's car was making a turn at a stop sign up ahead.

"I'll bet you anything it's got to do with those cat symbols we've been seeing." She counted them off on her fingers. "Beth's necklace. The graffiti on the wall at the Snake Pit. And this invitation." She pulled it out of her purse.

"So you think Mike knows who these 'Kats' are?" Ned asked.

"There's only one way to find out. I hope if we follow him, we'll learn more."

Up ahead she spied Mike's blue sports car. Ned kept as much distance between the two vehicles as he could without losing sight of Mike.

Soon the sports car zoomed up a freeway

ramp. At the moment, Nancy knew, they were headed in the general direction of Sound Performance, where Mike had said he was going. Still, she recalled what Mike had said about having a few days off. Was he going to work or not?

"I doubt if Mike is involved in Rachel's disappearance, though," Ned threw in as Mike slowed down for an exit. He dropped back a few car lengths, then took the same ramp. "He seemed honestly shook up back there."

"It could have been an act, though," Nancy said. She was almost disappointed when Mike headed straight for Sound Performance, turned into the parking lot beside the store, and got out of his car. She'd been so sure they were on to something.

Ned cruised past to go around the block. "He might know he's being tailed," Ned said. "In which case, he's leading us on a wild-goose chase."

"Or he's really going to work," Nancy said.

Ned pulled into the parking lot of the car wash across the street. The sign overhead pictured a big pink elephant, outlined in neon, spraying water out of its trunk. "Maybe. Let's just sit here and watch for a while.

"You know what?" Ned said after a few

minutes. "Why didn't Rachel tell you where she was last night on the phone?"

"There could be an easy explanation," Nancy answered, keeping her eyes on Mike's car. "Maybe she was afraid of being caught talking on the phone."

Just then Mike came strolling out of the front door of Sound Performance. He walked straight toward the parking lot and got into his car.

"Pretty short workday, huh?" Ned said, starting the car.

"I'll say," Nancy agreed.

Mike's sports car made a U-turn, and he drove past them without glancing in their direction. Ned waited a few beats and then pulled out behind him. There were three cars between the Camaro and Mike's sports car.

After driving on the freeway for a while, Mike took an exit leading back to the general vicinity of Dennis's apartment. Nancy sat up a little straighter in her seat, intrigued.

Mike took several unexpected turns, but Ned managed to keep up. Eventually, they were on a street called Beach Drive—the ocean within sight.

The name of the street seemed familiar to Nancy, and she took the Kat Club invitation out of her purse. Sure enough, the party scheduled for that night was being held on Beach Drive. She had the growing feeling that their chase had been worthwhile.

A few minutes later Mike stopped in front of a small two-story beach house. There were cars parked everywhere, and Nancy and Ned kept their distance.

"This is it," Nancy whispered, seeing the cat logo painted above the front door.

"You mean—" Ned began.

Nancy nodded. "Yep. I'll bet you anything this is the Kat Club."

"That means that for all his denying it at Dennis's apartment, Mike does know these Kats! Or is one!"

The words were barely out of Ned's mouth when Nancy saw two people she knew come out of the Kat Club and greet Mike—Beth and Jessica. In her mind she saw Beth playing with the cat necklace around her neck.

Nancy's words caught in her throat. "They're Kats, too!"

Chapter
Twelve

Tʜᴇʏ'ᴠᴇ ʙᴇᴇɴ ʟʏɪɴɢ to us all along!" Nancy said.

Ned grabbed her arm. "Wait a minute. We don't know that they're Kats. We don't have proof that any of them are behind the note we got."

"But they know Kats," Nancy pointed out. "That much is obvious. And they probably know who left that note. Ned, we've got to get in there and find out what's going on."

Ned shook his head. "Not now. There's too much chance of being seen."

"You're right," Nancy agreed reluctantly. "I

guess we'll have to come back tonight as we planned. But, Ned"—Nancy stopped short —"I just had a terrible thought. Suppose they're holding Rachel in there? Her note did say she was in terrible trouble. We know one of the Kats doesn't want us looking for her. What if they're the ones hiding her?"

Ned backed the Camaro around a corner. "Her own friends? Why would they do that?"

Nancy ran a hand through her hair distractedly. "I know it doesn't make sense. Think about it, though—Mike was lying to us about the Kats. He might be lying about not knowing where Rachel is. Beth obviously knows more than she's telling, too."

"It might all be perfectly innocent," Ned pointed out. "Although I doubt it. All I know is, it wouldn't be smart to go in there in broad daylight. Not with so many people around."

Nancy hated leaving when they could be so close to finding Rachel. She knew Ned was right, though. They'd be no help to Rachel if they were caught.

"Next question," Ned said, when they were on the freeway again, headed toward Beverly Hills. "Do we call in the police?"

Nancy considered carefully. "No," she finally answered. "Let's keep this to ourselves until we know what's going on. As you said, we don't have any proof."

"And the Klines?"

"I don't think we should get their hopes up," Nancy said. "We don't even know if she's in there."

Back at the Kline house, the afternoon passed slowly. Mrs. Kline stationed herself by the telephone, hoping for another call from Rachel; Josh and Mr. Kline were both at work.

Nancy felt guilty about not saying anything to her about the Kat Club, but she didn't know what she'd say. They really didn't know who the Kats were or if they were holding Rachel. She still didn't know if Dennis was a Kat, or if he was responsible for Rachel's disappearance. She'd just have to sit and wait until dark and sneak into the Kat Club.

Before dinner that night Nancy changed into black jeans, black sneakers, and a dark sweatshirt. Breaking-and-entering clothes, she thought with a rueful smile, pulling her hair back into a ponytail.

Downstairs she found Ned, who grinned at her and winked.

When Allen Kline came home from work, they all had a quiet dinner beside the pool.

Both the Klines were lost in thought and said very little during the meal.

"Lieutenant Heller told me about Dennis's apartment being ransacked," Mrs. Kline said at one point. "He thinks Rachel might have called us from there. Fingerprints were found that matched some of those in her room. Her jacket was there, too." The woman's composure crumbled, and she began to cry. "And there was that awful note!"

Nancy's thoughts raced. So the person who'd been looking for something in Rachel's room had also tried to find it in Dennis's apartment. But what was that person looking for? Evidence? Proof? Of what? Were the Kats behind the break-ins, too?

After saying good night to the Klines, Nancy and Ned hurried to the nearest freeway entrance. Since there was still a lot of light, they took their time getting to the beach house.

When they got to the Kat Club, the place was all lit up, and even more cars were parked around it than before. Loud music filled the air.

"Okay, Drew, this is it," Ned said, stopping the car well out of sight, around the corner from the Kat Club. "What's the plan?"

"A little romantic stroll along the beach, I think," Nancy said with a smile.

"Then, maybe, we sneak in the back way?"

"You got it."

"Let's agree to stick together as much as possible."

Nancy nodded, and they got out of the car. Circling the club, they made their way around the back to the beach. Nancy could see there was a barbecue on the back deck of the club.

They sneaked up on the beach house, moving through the shadows cast by the other buildings along the shore, and then slipped under the deck. Above them, people were laughing and chattering as loud music continued to blare out. Nancy was grateful for the cover the sound gave them as they knelt down in the sand.

She spotted a basement window and pointed it out to Ned. He nodded, and within a few seconds he had it pried open.

Ned crawled through first, helping Nancy in after him, and they stopped to get their bearings. The place was dark, but after a few moments their eyes adjusted, and they could see a lot of boxes stacked all around them.

Nancy took a penlight from the pocket of her jeans and switched it on. Lifting the lid of one box, she looked inside.

"Ned," she whispered, "there's a VCR in here."

111

Ned nodded, and they began to check out the other boxes. They found camcorders, stereo components, and more VCRs. Nancy's mind was racing. Why was the basement of the Kat Club full of such valuable items?

Nancy was just about to open her mouth to speak when, at the top of the steps, a door opened, letting in a shaft of light. Ned put a finger to his lips and pulled Nancy behind some boxes. They held their breath as they heard someone move down the stairs and rummage around the basement before heading back upstairs again.

"That was close," Nancy whispered to Ned when they heard the door click closed at the top of the stairs.

"I think the room right up there is full of people," Ned whispered. "Let's look around and see if we can find another way upstairs."

They explored the whole basement, but all they found were more stereos, camcorders, and VCRs.

"Are you wondering what I'm wondering?" Ned asked.

"What's the connection between the Kats and all this equipment?" Nancy whispered back. "You bet I am." She reminded Ned of what Jessica had mentioned about the robberies in Beverly Hills.

"You don't think that was the Kats?" he asked, shaking his head.

"Could be," Nancy said, her excitement rising. "Except if this stuff is stolen, what's it doing in boxes?" she wondered out loud.

"I say we keep exploring a bit more to see what else we can find," Ned said.

"But I think we really have to check out the first floor. We'll have to go up that way eventually," Nancy said, pointing to the stairs.

The door opened just then, and Nancy and Ned barely had time to duck into the shadows again. They stood side by side behind a stack of boxes, their backs to the concrete wall.

"You're getting paranoid, Hanford," came a voice Nancy recognized as Jessica's. "There's nobody down there," she said derisively.

Nancy closed her eyes tightly for a moment and automatically held her breath. After the door closed again, she exhaled.

"I need to hear what they're saying up there," Nancy told Ned.

He squeezed her hand. "Okay. I'm right behind you."

They climbed the stairs with painstaking slowness. Ned feared that someone would open the door to reveal them in a splash of light. They were almost to the top when the knob turned and Jessica's voice said, "Come on, Hanford, we'll go down there right now, and I'll prove to you that you're imagining things."

Ned and Nancy pressed against the wall along the stairs as the door opened a crack and a head peered through.

"I guess you're right," Beth said. "I am being paranoid. But I could have sworn somebody was there when I went down to the freezer to get more steaks for the barbecue."

The door closed again, but not quite all the way. It was open a crack, and Nancy hoped they wouldn't be seen.

Keeping her movements as quiet as she could, Nancy took a quick peek through the opening in the door and saw Beth and Jessica sitting at a kitchen table, drinking sodas. Mike came into the room just then, and Nancy almost gasped out loud when she saw the man behind him.

It was Ralph Lindenbaum, the owner of Sound Performance! What was *he* doing at the Kat Club?

Nancy glanced down at Ned, not daring even to whisper. She put her eye to the keyhole. Jessica was scowling, while Beth looked absolutely terrified. Nancy straightened up and placed her ear against the door to listen to their conversation.

"I'm telling you, Ralph," Mike was saying, "you've got to let me take care of things my way. Nancy Drew and that friend of hers are on to us."

"I'm still running this show, kid," Ralph said furiously. "Besides, Peter Henley's idea is more my style!"

"You promised nobody would get hurt!" Beth cried.

"Oh, shut up," Jessica told her disdainfully. "You're in this as deep as the rest of us, Hanford, and you'd better not get cold feet and blow the whistle on us."

"Nobody is going to turn us in," Ralph insisted.

"Hanford might," Jessica said, her words dripping acid. "She's been acting like a scared rabbit from the first."

Nancy peered through the opening again. Ralph was bending over the girl's chair, his hands on her shaking shoulders, his voice steely. "Don't forget, kid, if we get caught, so do you."

Beth began to sob. "I wish I'd never heard of the Kat Club!" she wailed.

Ned gripped Nancy's sweatshirt and gave a little pull. He didn't need to say anything to let her know they had more than enough information to give the police. It was time to get out.

115

As he stepped down, though, his step creaked. Desperate to know if the others had heard, Nancy looked directly into the kitchen.

Ralph appeared to be oblivious to the noise, as were Jessica and Mike. Then Nancy glanced at Beth, who was sitting in her direct line of sight.

The girl was staring into Nancy's eyes. Nancy and Ned were caught!

Chapter
Thirteen

NANCY DIDN'T ALLOW HERSELF to panic. As she planned her escape she slowly turned her head from side to side, silently begging Beth not to give her away. For one heart-stopping moment Beth looked uncertain, but then she shifted her gaze.

"What is it now?" Nancy heard Jessica demand sourly.

Beth jumped up and ran out of the room. Nancy let out her breath.

She wanted to stay to check out the rest of the house, but she knew that would be too dangerous. Beth could change her mind at any time and tell Ralph what she'd seen.

Ned caught Nancy by the back of the shirt again and pulled. His message was clear—things were getting too hot, and it was time to leave.

She nodded toward the window where they'd crept in, and then they made their way carefully down the stairs.

Ned gave Nancy a boost up through the window. He was right behind her, and they lay down quietly listening to the party above them on the deck.

Sticking to the shadows, Nancy and Ned fled from the Kat Club as fast as they could.

"We just barely made it out of there," Nancy said breathlessly, once they were both inside the Camaro and Ned was starting up the engine. "Beth looked right at me."

"But she didn't say anything," Ned mused out loud, frowning as he pulled away from the curb.

"No. I think she knows she's in way over her head." Nancy rattled off what they knew. "The Kat Club has to be up to no good. All that stuff in the basement has to be stolen. They know we're on to them, and they're afraid of the police. Ralph Lindenbaum is obviously their ringleader, and maybe Peter Henley."

"So what do we do now?" Ned asked.

"Go back to the Klines' and call Lieutenant Heller," Nancy said with a nod. "He should know about this right away. And so should Rachel's parents."

"But we still don't know where Rachel is, or how deeply involved she and Dennis are," Ned said.

Nancy touched his arm. "Maybe we did find her. She and Dennis might have been at the club. The police can check it out. Let's go."

They made their way through the light freeway traffic back to the Klines'.

"Do you think Rachel could have anything to do with the burglaries in the Hills?" Nancy asked.

"I hope not," Ned answered.

Nancy settled back in her seat and folded her arms. "The Klines probably won't thank us if we find out that Rachel is up to her eyeballs in this whole mess."

"We have to do what's right," Ned reminded her.

Josh was just getting out of a late-model pickup truck as they pulled up. He said a tired goodbye to whoever had given him a lift home and waited in the driveway for Ned to bring the Camaro to a stop.

"I see I'm not the only one who's had a

long day," Josh said. "What have you two been up to?"

Ned sighed. "I think we'd better talk about that inside," he answered. The three of them walked around to the back of the house and entered the kitchen through the rear door.

"I'm starved," Josh confided, opening the refrigerator and peering inside. "We had a dinner break, but that was hours ago. How about you two? Hungry?"

Nancy shook her head. She headed straight for the phone and dialed the police precinct.

"We definitely found the Kat Club tonight," Ned told his friend.

"Please ask Lieutenant Heller to call Nancy Drew at the Kline residence," Nancy said to the officer answering her call, then she hung up. "Ned's getting a little ahead of himself," she said, joining the guys at the breakfast counter. She quickly told Josh about finding Dennis's apartment ransacked and the note Rachel had left.

Ned went on to explain about sneaking into the Kat Club and finding what they assumed was stolen stereo equipment.

Josh sank onto a kitchen stool, his sandwich forgotten. "Do you think Rachel's involved somehow?" he asked quietly.

"We think there's a chance," Nancy said

simply. "They could be holding her some-place. Maybe even there. We really don't know anything about Rachel's part in any of this. I have a call in to Lieutenant Heller."

Josh shoved a hand through his hair. "If they are holding Rachel, they might panic if they see the police coming. They might hurt her."

Nancy had considered that but knew Heller would be careful. "I'm going to talk to Beth Hanford," she said. "Right now. She was really upset at the club, and I think she might have gone straight home. Maybe I can make her see that she's Rachel's only chance—"

Ned touched her shoulder to interrupt her. Nancy looked at Josh. He was staring right through her and appeared to be in shock.

Confused, Nancy gazed up into Ned's grin-ning face. "If you'd stop talking for a minute," he said, "you might stumble over a major clue."

Nancy turned. "What?"

A blond-haired girl was standing in the kitchen doorway. She was tired and rumpled-looking in worn jeans and a flannel shirt. Sobbing, she flung herself into Josh's arms.

Rachel Kline was home.

Chapter

Fourteen

OH, JOSH," RACHEL SAID, gasping through her tears. "I'm sorry—I'm so sorry."

"Take it easy, Rachel," Josh murmured into his sister's hair. "It's okay. You're home now. Everything's going to be okay."

Slowly the girl's sobbing stopped. Her shoulders only moved gently up and down. "Why don't you tell us what happened?" Nancy asked. "It'll make it easier if you talk about it."

Rachel swallowed and shuddered one last time before beginning to talk. "Dennis and I were in hiding at his sister's house," she explained softly. "Last night we went by his apartment to pick up some things he needed. Peter Henley and a couple of the other guys caught us there. I told them I had to go to the bathroom. I wrote a note and put it in my jacket and hoped you'd find it. Then they dragged us to the Kat Club." A haunted look reappeared in Rachel's eyes. "They locked us up in the attic." Her eyes brimmed with fresh tears. "Dennis is still there."

"He's still there? How did you get away?" Nancy asked.

"Jessica untied me so I could use the bathroom," Rachel answered. "There was some kind of scuffle downstairs. When she went to see what it was, I grabbed her from behind. I put my hand over her mouth and pushed her into a closet." She paused, paling as she relived the experience. "She was kicking and yelling, but the music was so loud, nobody could hear her. I put a chair under the knob so she couldn't get out."

Nancy nodded. "And Dennis? Where's he?"

Rachel looked miserable. "Someone was coming up the attic stairs, so I took off. I decided it would be better to go for help than get caught again. I climbed out a window and down a tree." She dried her eyes with the back of one hand. "I'm so afraid of what Peter and the others will do to Dennis when they find out I'm missing."

"I'll call Mom and Dad," Josh said gently. "They've been crazy. We'll get the police to help Dennis."

Rachel reached out and grabbed his arm when he started to walk away. "No. Please. I can't face Mom and Dad until I've done everything I can to make this right, Josh. That's why I left in the first place."

Ned did walk over and dial the police. He left instructions for Heller with the address of the Kat Club.

"Rachel," Nancy began. "Why did you and Dennis take off? What is it you have to make right?" she asked gently.

The girl was silent. She looked uncertainly from Nancy to Ned to Josh. "I can't explain," she said finally. "We have to get back there as soon as possible."

"First I'm letting Mom and Dad know you're back," Josh said firmly. "And where we're going." He headed for the door.

"No! Please, Josh!" Rachel started to cry again.

Nancy stepped in. "Hold it a second, Josh." She turned to the girl. "Rachel," she said gently, "why are you so afraid to tell them you're back?"

"Because then I'll have to explain why I left. And I can't do that until I make everything right," she repeated.

"Why did you leave?" Nancy prodded.

"And why on graduation day?" Ned asked. "Was something going to happen?"

Ned's question set the wheels turning in Nancy's mind. "Were the Kats about to frame you and Dennis?" she asked.

The look of surprise and fear that passed over Rachel's face told Nancy she was right. "Tell us about it," she prodded.

"Beth told me Peter was going to plant stolen equipment in Dennis's car," Rachel explained in a rush. "Stuff from Sound Performance. Ralph had already fired him to set it up."

"Why would Peter do that?" Nancy asked.

Rachel bit down hard on her lower lip. "I think he knew Dennis and I were . . ." The girl's voice started shaking, and she had a hard time going on. Rachel's predicament was obviously tearing her apart.

"Did Peter think you were going to rat on the Kats?" Ned asked.

"About what?" Josh asked. "I'm still confused about what's going on here," he said, raking a hand through his hair in frustration.

Nancy explained, going on her hunches and what the girl had said so far. "Rachel and Dennis were going to tell the police that the Kats were behind the robberies in Beverly Hills. They knew because they had taken part in them. Am I right?" she asked Rachel.

The girl lay down her head on the breakfast counter. A slow nod was her only answer.

Josh was obviously shocked. Instinctively, he reached over to stroke his sister's hair. "It's okay, Rach. Don't cry. It'll be okay."

"Rachel," Nancy began, "I know this isn't easy, but you've got to tell us everything. How did you get involved in the first place?"

Josh continued, "Nancy's right. You made a big mistake, but you've got to tell us the whole story."

"I can't," Rachel moaned softly.

"It's the only way out," Ned said. "Tell us who put you up to it. Was it Ralph?"

Rachel's head shot up. "Ralph! How do you know about Ralph?"

"You just said he fired Dennis to help set up Peter's frame," Nancy pointed out. "We saw him tonight at the Kat Club. Just how is he involved?" she asked.

Rachel paused for a moment and looked at

the three of them. "He sold the stuff we took," she admitted finally.

It all made sense. Ralph fenced stolen equipment from his store, selling it as new. He must have erased the serial numbers, replaced them with phony ones, and used his connections to get empty boxes to put the equipment in. His customers never knew they were getting used equipment. The warranties were probably forged, too. "And it was his idea for you to steal it in the first place?" Nancy asked.

"We didn't have any choice," Rachel said in a whisper.

"I don't understand," her brother said, confused.

Rachel's words echoed in Nancy's ears. They didn't have any choice. "Did Ralph have something on you?" she asked on a hunch.

"Yes, he did," Rachel admitted quietly.

"What was it?" Ned asked, sensing they were about to get to the bottom of Rachel's trouble.

"I guess I'll have to show you," she said in a resigned voice. "You know everything else."

With that, she led the way out of the kitchen and into the den, where Nancy and Ned had watched a movie. She went to the shelf of neatly filed movies and ran her finger over the backs of the cases until she found what she wanted. Rachel pulled out the *Casablanca* tape. When Nancy had tried to play it, she had thought it was blank.

Rachel put the tape into the VCR and turned on the machine and the TV. There was nothing but snow on the screen until Rachel pressed Fast Forward, stopping about halfway through the tape. She pressed Stop and Play, and a shadowy scene took shape.

Nancy watched closely, unable at first to figure out what was going on.

Then she recognized the inside of Sound Performance, the stereo equipment store. There were five shadowy figures moving around, picking up different items and carefully carrying them to the back of the store.

Nancy took a step closer to the screen. One by one, Nancy identified the people—Jessica, Beth, Mike, Peter, Rachel, and another, whom she assumed to be Dennis.

She realized that what they were watching was the store security tape—showing the members of the Kat Club stealing from Sound Performance!

Chapter
Fifteen

WHEN THE TAPE went blank again, Josh reached out and punched off the VCR. Nancy could tell that Ned's friend was in shock. Rachel covered her face with both hands. "I—I don't know what to say, Josh," she whispered. "I never meant for any of this to happen."

Nancy put a hand on Rachel's shoulder. "What exactly did happen? Why did you rob the store?"

Rachel gazed at Nancy with miserable, red-rimmed eyes. "I didn't want to do this, and neither did Beth. But the guys—Mike and Peter—kept pressuring us. They said it was a practical joke they wanted to play on Ralph—Mr. Lindenbaum."

"You didn't think you'd be caught?" Ned asked in a surprised voice.

"Beth and I figured nobody would get in trouble if it was only a joke. Besides, the guys told us that since we knew about it, we were already involved." She paused and tossed her long hair back over one shoulder. "I know it was stupid, but we went along," she added, her voice shaking.

"Tell us about the rest of it in the car on the way back to the club," Nancy gently suggested.

"We carried the things outside to a truck parked in back," Rachel continued in the back seat. "Mike said we were going to give everything back after Mr. Lindenbaum stewed for a bit. Since he worked there, I guess he suspected Ralph was already selling stolen stuff. He didn't think Ralph would have the guts to report our robbery to the police. We didn't take much—only enough to worry him."

"What made Mike want to do it in the first place?" Josh asked.

"He's into dares," Rachel explained. "At least he was, before this. When Peter suggested it to him, they thought it would be kind of fun. Shake Ralph up a bit."

"That didn't happen, though, did it?" Nancy asked, turning to look at Josh and Rachel.

Rachel choked back her tears. Josh reached out and drew his sister to him for the first time since he'd seen the tape. "Go on, Rachel," he said calmly.

"No, it didn't," Rachel said, with her brother's arm securely wrapped around her. "Ralph called each of us and told us we'd better be at his store that night at closing time or we'd end up in jail."

"So you went?" Ned prompted gently.

Rachel nodded. "We were scared not to. When we got there, we found out we were in big trouble."

"So he put you up to robbing houses?" Josh asked, his anger evident.

"He showed us the tape," Rachel explained. "We hadn't thought about it."

"How did you get the tape?" Ned wanted to know.

"Dennis stole it the night before we went into hiding," Rachel explained.

"So Ralph used the tape to blackmail you into burglarizing houses," Nancy concluded.

Rachel nodded again glumly. "Yes."

"You were perfect for the job: You all came from this area, except for Dennis, so you knew which houses had alarms and how to beat some of them," Nancy went on.

"Why would this Lindenbaum character want a bunch of kids to steal for him?" Josh demanded.

"He knew how to doctor the serial numbers," Nancy explained, "so he could sell any stolen stuff in his store. Since he had something on them, the Kats were useful to him. Am I right?" she asked Rachel.

"Yes," the girl confessed quietly.

"That still doesn't explain why you ran away," Josh said to his sister.

"I think she wanted to get out of the ring, Josh," Ned said from the driver's seat. "Along with Dennis."

"When Beth told me Dennis was going to be framed," Rachel explained, "we got scared. We decided to run away until we had proof against Ralph and Peter."

"Why didn't you just come to us?" Josh asked. "Mom and Dad would have helped."

"Sometimes people don't think rationally when they're scared," Nancy said, glancing at the clock on the dashboard. "Speed it up just a bit, Ned. We should get to Dennis quickly."

Rachel's eyes took on a haunted look. "I

don't know if they'll hurt him. When they found us, they couldn't decide what to do with us. But now when they find out I'm gone . . ."

"I hope Lieutenant Heller is there already," Nancy said. "You did tell him to meet us, Ned, didn't you?"

Ned nodded. "I didn't talk directly to him. I only left a message," he added.

"What about all those other kids who were at the party tonight?" Nancy asked Rachel. "Were they blackmailed into stealing, too?"

Rachel swallowed hard. "Some of them were into it—like Jessica. They thought it was a kick. You know how it is." At that, she lowered her eyes for a moment, finding it difficult to face Nancy. "My mom and dad are just going to die when they find out what I did."

Nancy reached out and took Rachel's hand for a moment. She told her about how her room had been broken into. "Do you think one of them was looking for the tape that showed you robbing the store?" she asked.

After a long time Rachel nodded. "Probably. It could have been Peter. He turned Dennis's apartment upside down trying to find it while we were there. We told him Dennis didn't have it."

"He must have known you needed it to take

to the police," Ned pointed out. "To prove that Ralph was blackmailing you."

"I guess," Rachel said, nodding.

Ned took the Beach Drive exit and brought the car to a stop in the same place where he and Nancy had parked earlier. All but three cars were gone from the front of the club. The music had been turned off, but lights were still on inside the beach house.

Rachel scanned the cars. "Mike and Ralph and Peter are still here," she said.

"We'll have to be really careful," Nancy said. "By now they must know you're gone. They'll be looking for us. I wonder where Lieutenant Heller is. Why wouldn't the police be here by now?"

After a short conference the four decided the basement window would be the best way to get in. Ned crawled through first, then Nancy, then Josh, and finally Rachel.

"Come on," Nancy said, heading toward the stairs. Ned was right behind her, with Rachel close behind him.

Josh stopped Rachel. "Let Nancy and Ned go first," he said in a low voice. "They've had experience at this stuff."

Reluctantly Rachel agreed. Nancy started up the steps, her heart pounding. There was a chance their break-in could fail. If they were caught, it would be a matter of stalling for time until the police showed up. Where were they? she wondered again.

The kitchen light was out, and the door squeaked a little as Nancy pushed it open.

She waited to see if anyone had heard the sound. When no one came, she pushed the door a little farther. It glided open, nearly crashing against the wall. Moving silently, Nancy crept into the kitchen and looked both ways.

There was a pantry on the right, but it was empty. To the left was a lighted hallway.

When Ned, Josh, and Rachel had all joined her in the kitchen, she turned to face them. "We'll search the first floor," she whispered. "Everybody, be careful!"

The first room off the kitchen was cluttered and had a view of the ocean. There was a computer set up on a desk in front of the window. Nancy stole closer and saw a pile of disks. One was clearly labeled Inventory.

Very efficient, she thought. Ralph Lindenbaum was keeping a record of all stolen merchandise.

Nancy picked up the small plastic disk and tucked it into the pocket of her jeans. Lieutenant Heller would find it fascinating reading.

Another room opened off that one, and two

more after that. The entire floor appeared to be empty.

Reaching the foot of the stairs leading to the second floor, Nancy braced herself. Quietly she stole up the stairs, stopping when she heard voices behind a door at the far end of the dark hallway. A slice of golden light shone out from under the door. Just to her left were stairs that Nancy knew must lead to the attic.

Signaling the others to remain hidden, Nancy sneaked forward until she had reached the door with the light shining around its edges. Drawing a deep breath and letting it out slowly, Nancy crouched and peered through the keyhole. She couldn't see much, just the back of someone's T-shirt.

"I say we get rid of him tonight," she heard Peter saying. "Rachel got away, and she's probably spilled the whole thing by now. I don't know about you two, but I'm taking my share of the money and getting out of here!"

Nancy's heart hammered against her rib cage as she heard footsteps in the room moving toward her. At the last second they stopped.

"I'm going to Mexico," Mike said dismally. "There are probably warrants out for our arrest right now."

"Don't be so sure she's talked," said Ralph.

"She knows we've still got Dennis. I bet she hasn't said a word. She really cares about that guy."

"Don't remind me," Mike snapped.

"If she doesn't talk," Peter put in, "Beth will. She's been on the verge of breaking for days."

Nancy got up from her crouched position and eased backward along the hallway, keeping her eye on the door the whole time.

Just then, the door opened.

Nancy darted up onto the attic steps. Rachel was already there. They could only guess where Ned and Josh were. It was too dark to see, and they didn't dare move.

"I'm not going to stick around here waiting for the cops to show up," Peter said.

Nancy prayed they wouldn't decide to check on Dennis right then. If they did, they'd run right into her and Rachel. Rachel's rapid breathing sounded so loud to Nancy that she was sure it would give them away. She just hoped the three men wouldn't hear it. They were standing so close that Nancy could have reached out and touched them.

Ralph was shaking his finger in Peter's face. One glance to the left, and he'd be looking straight at them. "The trouble with you, kid," he lectured, "is that you're too hotheaded. You act first and think later. That leads to mistakes."

Nancy's heart was beating so hard she thought it was going to burst at any moment. She ran her tongue over her lips and waited. Where were Ned and Josh?

"Like pushing Nancy Drew off the deck at the Beckers' party," Mike said with contempt. "And trying to run her and her boyfriend down with a car!"

"Shut up, Rasmussen," Peter warned.

So it was Peter who had tried to scare her off that night at the party. And Peter who had nearly run her and Ned over!

Lindenbaum slapped both boys on the back and said, "Now, now, no arguing. Let's go downstairs and figure out a good, solid plan. We're okay as long as we don't lose our heads."

If Ned and Josh had hidden on the stairs, they were about to get caught. Nancy held her breath. Luckily Ralph and the boys went past them and down the stairs without incident.

"Ned!" Nancy whispered into the darkness, afraid to use her flashlight. "Where are you?"

A nearby door opened soundlessly, and Ned and Josh appeared. Rachel didn't waste any time in leading the way up the attic steps. Pushing the door at the top open, the girl ran into the lighted attic.

138

Dennis, a good-looking guy with spiky brown hair and wearing jeans and a white T-shirt, was sitting in a chair, his hands and feet tied. When he saw them, his eyes lit up.

Nancy immediately began untying him while Rachel bent to put her arms around his neck. "You didn't think I wouldn't come back, did you?" she said.

"You should have stayed away," Dennis replied, a worried tone in his voice. "You know how dangerous those guys are."

"I couldn't leave you here," Rachel insisted.

Nancy finished untying Dennis's ankles. She looked over to where Ned was keeping watch at the top of the attic steps. There wasn't any time to waste. They had to get out fast.

"Who are these people?" Dennis asked, standing and trying to get the circulation going in his legs.

"It's okay," Rachel said, reassuring him. "This is my brother Josh, and his friend Ned Nickerson is over there. This is Nancy Drew."

Dennis nodded slowly. "You told them, didn't you?" he whispered to Rachel.

"I had to," she answered. "It's all over, Dennis."

"We have to get out of here fast," Nancy said firmly. "Can you make it out that window and down the tree?" she asked Dennis.

He shook his head, indicating his legs were still too shaky.

Nancy grabbed Ned's hand and led the way carefully back downstairs. She kept her eyes wide open for any sign of Mike, Peter, or Ralph.

They made it safely down to the first floor. Nancy could barely hear Ralph's booming voice. It sounded as though it was coming from the deck outside. With a wave of relief she realized that if they were really careful, they could head back out through the basement.

Nancy led the way into the kitchen, Rachel and Dennis right behind her, Josh and Ned bringing up the rear.

Just as she was opening the door to the basement Nancy heard a voice behind her.

"Welcome to the Kat Club."

She turned to see Ralph, Peter, and Mike standing in the doorway leading to the deck. Ralph's hands held a drawn gun as he smiled at his uninvited guests.

She looked over at her friends' shocked faces. They were caught.

Chapter
Sixteen

THESE TWO," Ralph went on, smiling sardonically at Dennis and Rachel, "aren't going anywhere. They know too much." His gaze took in Nancy, Ned, and Josh. "Now, of course, you do, too."

Nancy swallowed. Whatever happened, she couldn't lose her cool. "It's too late, Mr. Lindenbaum. You can't get away with this."

Ralph ignored her. His smile had faded, and he was glaring at Dennis. "You know, you should have been in jail already."

"Why?" Nancy put in. "Because you tried to

frame him for stealing equipment from your store?"

Ralph gave Nancy a shocked look. "We're on to you," Ned told him. "We know what you've been up to."

Dennis put his arm around Rachel, but his eyes never left Ralph's gun. "You're a creep, you know that, Lindenbaum," he sneered. "And that frame was the lowest. I knew you'd guessed that Rachel was about to break down and tell her folks what was going on, so you decided to pin the blame for everything on me."

Nancy glanced at Rachel, then at Ned and Josh. She made a sign that told him he should be prepared to jump Ralph and Dennis and Peter. Ned gave her an almost imperceptible nod.

"I want the security tape, Rachel," Ralph said. "The one that shows you kids robbing Sound Performance."

Rachel shook her head. "It's over, Ralph," she said steadily. "Give up."

Lindenbaum held his gun steady on Rachel. "The other Kats are willing to pretend the whole thing never happened!" he said furiously. "Why couldn't you cooperate?"

He reached out and grabbed Rachel by the arm, shoving the gun into her rib cage. "Now

I'll tell you what you're going to do, little lady," he crooned into her ear. "You're going to tell me where that tape is, and do you know why? Because your boyfriend Dennis and all your friends here are going to be in real danger until I give the word to let them go, that's why!"

"Let her go," Dennis said, his eyes flashing.

Ralph laughed. "Let's take them upstairs and tie them up," he said as Peter drew a gun of his own and held it on them.

"Let's go!" Peter barked, his eyes glinting. "Everybody up to the attic!"

"Anybody tries anything," Ralph warned, "and the girl gets shot."

There was nothing to do but put their hands up and do as Ralph said. Even if Ned and Nancy could have gotten the jump on Peter, Ralph was still holding his gun on Rachel at very close range.

As they climbed the attic stairs, though, Nancy was already devising a plan. They'd have to act fast, before their hands and feet were tied.

"Wait a minute!" Mike rasped, hovering in the doorway once they were all in the attic. "I'm not going along with anything like this! Let Rachel go, Ralph. You're hurting her!"

Peter turned on him. "As if you cared. Get

the rope, Rasmussen!" he snarled. "And I'm not going to tell you twice!"

In that moment Nancy's eyes met Mike's. She asked him a silent question: Who will it be, Mike—them or us?

She drew a deep breath and signaled to Ned. Her eyes turned toward Peter. She silently counted to three, then threw herself at Peter's knees.

The boy's gun flew out of his hand and fell to the floor, out of reach. With Ned's help Nancy wrestled him to the floor.

Rachel began screaming at the top of her lungs. The result was ear-shattering. Then she stomped down hard on Ralph's instep, and he howled in pain and rage and dropped his gun. Nancy scooped it up in one quick motion.

Josh caught Mike by the back of the collar before he could escape down the stairs. He threw him roughly to the attic floor.

Mike just sat there with his hands away from his sides to show he didn't want any part of the fight.

Dennis went to Rachel and took her in his arms. The girl burst into tears. "It's over," she murmured into his shoulder. "I can't believe it's finally over."

Nancy and Ned tied Ralph and Peter to the poles that supported the attic ceiling while

Josh pushed a scowling Mike into the chair where Dennis had been held and bound his hands behind his back.

"Come on, Ned," she said, "let's go downstairs and wait for the police."

Rachel was drying her eyes. "Come on, Dennis," she said sadly. "Let's go with them. I don't want to be in the same room with these guys."

"You'll never prove anything!" Ralph spat out, glaring at Nancy.

"Oh, no?" she asked. "This basement is full of stolen goods. I bet the lease on this place is in your name. We've also got a roomful of people who are willing to testify that you blackmailed them into stealing for you." She paused, pulled the computer disk from her pocket, and held it up. "Your inventory. This should be proof enough, I think."

"I'll keep an eye on them while you go downstairs and wait for the police," Josh said to Nancy and Ned. "Look out for Rachel, will you? She's pretty upset."

Ned slapped his friend on the back. "Don't worry, buddy. Everything's okay now."

Downstairs Rachel was sitting at the kitchen table with Dennis. She looked up as Nancy sat down at the table next to her. "What's going to happen to us?" she asked.

145

"I'm not sure," Nancy replied. "Burglary is a felony, but the judge might be lenient because Ralph coerced you."

"My mom and dad are going to be so upset!"

"I'm sure they'll deal with it. The most important thing to them is your safety."

"What about Peter?" Rachel asked. "And Mike?"

Nancy sighed. "My guess is that the courts will be pretty hard on Peter, considering what he did."

"His parents are going to be really angry," Rachel said.

"I honestly don't know about Mike, but he's obviously in pretty deep," Nancy said.

Rachel nodded sadly. "Where's Josh?"

"Upstairs, standing guard," Ned replied, laying a hand on Rachel's shoulder.

At that moment three uniformed officers came into the kitchen, their guns drawn. Lieutenant Heller was close behind.

He looked as if he'd dressed hurriedly, and he was surprised when he saw Nancy. "Sorry for the delay. They didn't call me right away. They thought Ned's call was a prank. Someone who knew about the case saw the note, and then we got into high gear. So tell me what's happening."

"We got Rachel back and solved the Beverly

Hills robberies. The ringleader is Ralph Lindenbaum—he's upstairs, in the attic, with his right-hand man, Peter Henley, and Mike Rasmussen," Nancy replied.

The lieutenant's gaze fell on Rachel. "Hello there, young lady," he said kindly. "We've been looking for you."

"Rachel and Dennis have a few things they want to tell you," Nancy said quietly.

The detective got out his notebook and sat down at the table. The uniformed officers, in the meantime, were going up to bring down Ralph, Mike, and Peter.

"Read them their rights, then take them downtown and book them," Heller said without looking away from Rachel and Dennis. "Now let's hear it, kids—right from the start."

Slowly, haltingly at first, Rachel explained how she and Beth and Jessica had joined in the robbery at Sound Performance, thinking it was a practical joke. Then she went on to say that Ralph had used the security tape, which had been running that night, to blackmail them into committing further burglaries.

"What about you, Dennis?" the lieutenant asked quietly when Rachel had finished speaking. "How did you get involved?"

Dennis lowered his eyes for a moment, then met the lieutenant's gaze squarely. "I'm guilty," he said. "I guess I pretty much knew what was going on when Rasmussen and Henley planned the rip-off at Sound Performance. I should have stopped them from getting the girls to join in, but I didn't."

"I'm going to have to take you and Rachel down to the station for questioning," the detective said. "And I have to be honest with you—there's every chance that you'll be charged, Dennis."

Dennis swallowed visibly, and his arm tightened around Rachel's shoulders. "What about Rachel?"

"I don't know. One thing I do know, though—I need the names of all the other kids who were involved."

Rachel lifted her eyes to Josh's face, and her brother nodded solemnly. "Beth Hanford," she began in a small, shaky voice. "Jessica Bates . . ."

It was late when Mr. Kline brought an ashen-faced Rachel home from the police station. His face was grim as he greeted his anxious wife. "Charges have been filed against all the kids," he said. When Mrs. Kline gasped, he added, "Our attorney thinks Rachel will probably get a long probationary period and some public service, since she was essentially coerced into the crime. Dennis may get off lightly, too, since he was prepared to go to the police when he and Rachel took off."

"What about Ralph and Peter?" Nancy asked.

"Lindenbaum is being charged with grand theft, kidnapping, and conspiracy," Mr. Kline explained. "Henley, too, only he's got assault and attempted murder added on for good measure."

Mrs. Kline put her arms around Rachel. "You're exhausted, dear. You have to get some sleep. And so should you," she said, turning to her son.

Josh shook his head. "I'm due at the studio in an hour," he said. "I'll just take a shower and grab some breakfast."

Nancy was exhausted, but she knew she was probably too wound up to sleep. "What about Jessica and Mike?" she asked. "What's going to happen to them?"

Rachel looked sad. "They'll probably have to go to jail for a while."

"And Beth?"

"She wanted to tell from the first," Rachel said. "And you said she didn't give you away when she saw you peeking out of the cellar door."

"There's one last thing," Nancy said, remembering how Dennis had disappeared from the Snake Pit that night. "What was Dennis doing at the club if you two were laying low?"

"He wanted to reason with Peter," Rachel said. "I told him it was useless, but he wouldn't listen to me. Then, when he saw Mike and everyone else there, he was afraid he'd be caught. That's why he took off."

"What I don't understand is why you let this go on so long," Karen Kline said to her daughter in a sad voice. "Why didn't you call us sooner? You knew we'd have helped."

Rachel sighed. Nancy could tell it was the one thing the girl couldn't really explain. "I thought Dennis and I could take care of it ourselves. We'd gotten into the mess, and somehow we had to get out of it."

"Don't ever think that way again," Allen Kline told his daughter. "You know we're here for you, no matter what you do."

"It wasn't easy for you, was it, Rachel?" Nancy asked, genuinely concerned.

The girl swallowed hard and looked at her family. "No. I'm just glad it's all over."

"Me, too," Josh said, and he turned to Ned and Nancy. "Now maybe you two can have that vacation you planned."

Karen Kline smiled at her son's effort to

cheer them all up. Allen put an arm around his daughter.

Nancy hooked her arm through Ned's. "That sounds great. I have to admit I'm ready for a little relaxation."

Ned grinned at her. "Me, too. For a while there it was beginning to look like we'd have to go back to River Heights to get it!"

"What would you say to a nice romantic walk on the beach?" Nancy suggested playfully.

"No spying on anyone?" Ned asked with a gleam in his eye.

"No spying," Nancy assured him. "This time it'll be the real thing."